JAKE LYNCH

THE LOST SAINT

BOOK 1

ISBN 979-8-9893828-3-5 (paperback)
ISBN 979-8-9893828-7-3 (hardcover)
ISBN 979-8-9893828-9-7 (ebook)

Printed in the United States of America

*To all those who are struggling
and trying to find purpose.*

FOREWORD

This story is a work of fiction. While it entails a unique character and religious elements, the events and stories are entirely fictional.

While the stories and characters may be fictional, the message is still very real. And remember, as this is a novel, some of the elements have been tweaked to add a certain level of entertainment. However, they have not been changed to completely remove the core of what they represent. So please, take some things with a grain of salt, and don't take everything you read completely literally. While some of the messages are more direct than others, I urge you to think deeply about some of the values that this book portrays throughout the story.

Since I am a fallible human being, there are some religious elements that I may not be able to describe perfectly, but I still strive to paint at least a well-enough picture. I hope I did a good job.

Now, after getting all that out of the way, I hope you enjoy the story.

Prologue

Production Studio

10:00 hrs, 17/8/2280[1] (22 A.F.)

The camera shuffled as the crew secured it into place. An open seat waited in front of the camera. A middle-aged woman with long blonde hair, stepped into the lighting and sat down in the open chair. Her eyes glanced around, checking all the faces, taking in her surroundings. The director saw the lack of confusion on the woman's face. This was a woman who knew what she was doing and wasn't afraid of any discomfort.

"Well, shall we get started?" she asked. The director gulped and took a deep breath.

"Yes, that's a great idea." He gestured to the cameraman and the red light blinked on. The director turned to the woman, observing her cream-colored pants and white shirt. She was very good-looking but had a gaze that alerted everyone that she knew what she was doing. Most of the guests he interviewed were worrisome people who weren't used to being in front of a camera, especially with there being so few of them these days. The woman waited, her crisp blue eyes shining in the lighting.

---

1. World Time (day/month/year)

"So . . . how are you feeling?" he asked.

The woman nodded politely. "Fine."

The director relaxed. At least she was a courteous woman and not some kinzka from down south.

"I just wanted to ask a couple of questions to get the discussion rolling if that's fine with you."

The woman nodded again. "Fine."

"So, tell us your full name."

The woman said, "Hello, my name is Carmen Fisher."

"And where are you from, Ms. Fisher?"

"I am from Aquila."

"And how old were you when you met Marcus?"

Carmen pondered for a long moment, reviewing all the memories she had of Marcus. Both the good and bad. It took her a while to come up with a suitable answer.

She laid her hands properly on her lap. "The first time I met Marcus was when I was about six years old."

"And how old was Marcus when you first met him?"

Carmen didn't take as long to answer this time but she still put some thought into it. "He was about six."

"And what was he like when you first met him?"

Carmen pondered for a moment. "Quiet." She took her eyes off the director and then returned her gaze to him. "He was quiet most of the time." Carmen made a circular gesture around her face. "He always seemed to be somewhere else, even when he was here."

"And I take it Marcus was not your biological brother?"

Carmen shook her head. "No. He was my adopted brother."

"Were you close?"

Carmen nodded slightly. "Very."

"And how did you react to his death?"

For once, Carmen looked lost. She looked down to find a proper response as if assessing whether she knew the right answer or not. She raised her head and said, "I didn't expect it, and I did expect it."

"How so?"

"Given the manner of it, I don't think any of us could have expected that to happen. Let alone Marcus dying."

"There are some who argue he's still alive."

Carmen's tone grew cold. "He's dead. Whether you believe it or not, he's not coming back." She tilted her head and added, "For good reason."

The director looked confused. "Do you mean to say that you're glad he's gone?"

Carmen's coldness shattered and her weakness came forth. "No, I . . ." She fought the welling tears. She inhaled a sharp breath, holding herself together. "I'm just glad that his suffering is over." She took another breath. "That's why I want his story to be told."

The director nodded in understanding. "Which is why we're here, to record Marcus's story and get it out there to the world."

Carmen whispered, "I'm aware," and nodded. "I'm aware . . ."

The director asked, "Could you take us through what happened to him right after The Fall? And please explain what The Fall is."

Carmen nodded, regaining her strength and poise. "The year was 2258. Humanity had undergone a series of conflicts called the Great Wars. Throughout these wars hundreds of millions had died, but as the wars escalated, the worst occurred. Nuclear fallout resulted in the destruction of the major world powers of the time, killing over a billion people in the process. But surprisingly, a majority of the world remained untouched as mostly the major world powers were destroyed.

"With most of the world powers gone though, the remainder of the world recovered and saw new opportunity. With no one to challenge them, new powers arose from the ashes. And intertwined in them all, was the story of the Saint . . ."

CHAPTER ONE

THE STORM WITHIN

"A man without purpose is nothing."

—ANONYMOUS

Location Unknown

02:13 hrs, 15/04/2258 (10 days after The Fall)

The rain tore through the trees, drenching the world in mud as Marcus dragged himself through the storm. The wound in his left side of his chest had opened up again. He gritted his teeth and pushed forward, the pain exceeding his daily threshold. His wound felt warm as the red blood soaked through the white bandages. He limped forward, out of breath, and then fell to his knees. The rain poured down his head like makeshift tears.

The storm was growing worse, but it wasn't the gale that was tearing at him. It was the battle inside his mind that wore him down. The storm surrounding him was nothing compared to the storm within. His heart and mind were in turmoil. His thoughts and soul raged, unable to comprehend what just happened.

"I have no home," he whispered. "I've lost my country, my family, my friends."

Marcus realized for the first time what kind of situation he was in and just how serious things were. He finally whispered the horrible reality he found himself in. "I have no reason to fight anymore." Before, he'd had a purpose, but now he had no objective. No reason to keep going.

He tried to catch his breath, his knees drenched by the mud and rain, trying not to fall over. Because if he did, he would die.

He raised his eyes back to the muddy road, pushing off the tree, knowing he had to find shelter or at least a place that would keep him warm. He didn't care too much about the rain drenching his body or the lack of feeling in his fingers. He had been through all that before and more. This time was no different. On his back he carried a black sword dangling in its sheath over his right shoulder and SR75k rifle slung over his left. He also carried a large kukri blade stowed safely behind his lower back. On his left thigh was a .44 magnum revolver with a six shot cartridge, and on his belt he carried multiple throwing knives. He wore a large black leather jacket matching his black cargo pants. His left hand wore a glove covering all fingers except his index finger so he could fire his rifle without issue, but it didn't give him any protection from the cold. He had to get away. He had to keep going.

He pushed off the tree and continued walking through the mud. His breathing slowly became irregular and his vision blurred. He was beginning to lose consciousness. In the distance, he spotted a nearby village, one that wasn't ravaged by the constant years of war in this part of the world. If he could get to that village maybe they would help him. But it was still about a kilometer away. He managed to get a little closer before he found a nearby trunk and collapsed against it.

⟨⟨— —⟩⟩

Marcus awoke to an open sky and a sore neck. He raised his head and realized he had fallen asleep with his head hanging over a large tree root. His neck was going to be stiff all day. He rubbed it with his left hand and looked around, taking in his surroundings. The forest was a surprising beautiful bloom of green, yellow, and orange flowers. The morning rain had soaked the roads, filling the fertile soil beneath with rich and satisfying water. Marcus enjoyed seeing life all around. He wasn't used to so much life at once.

The sky was finally clear as the massive ash clouds from The Fall had finally dissipated after ten whole days of looming in the distance. It had become a grim sight but now things were beginning to settle again.

He leaned back against the tree, finding a brief calm after the storm and allowing the morning sunlight to gleam over his chiseled face. He had a crisp black beard and a square chin. The years of constant fighting wore on his body, making him look a few years older than he really was. But his age didn't matter. He was still alive and that's all that counted.

He exhaled, finding he was feeling no less exhausted now than he was last night. His right hand rested on his chest wound, finding fresh blood seeping from beneath the bandages. He had slept sideways on the injury and that caused an uproar of pain to shoot through his already shot-through chest and shoulder wound. His left shoulder was damaged but it was not out of the fight. He could still use it to a moderate extent so long as he didn't reignite the bleeding. "Lucky shot," he groaned. Lucky, meaning he was lucky that it hadn't killed him. But Marcus understood that luck had nothing to do with it. He sighed, feeling the warm sun on his face, piercing through the shaded leaves. And then, the voices came.

"MARCUS! HELP ME! HELP ME!"

Marcus fought to keep his thoughts focused on the current situation, but the demons were fighting hard to come to the surface. He tucked his thoughts away and looked around, hoping to find something to eat and a place to rest. He may be sitting now, but he was losing blood. He needed to get to a doctor or at least find some materials that he could treat himself with. He had treated wounds before. After all those years of war, treating the wounded was child's play, but that didn't make it any fun. What he needed was more materials and some medicine, or else infection would settle in, and he wasn't in the mood to lose an arm.

"Maybe they already killed me," he whispered, pushing harder on his wound.

"This too shall pass."

Marcus sighed in relief. "Maybe not." He groaned as he stood himself up, the pain in his left shoulder shooting up from a seven to a ten. He could feel his face was becoming discolored.

Marcus marched as best he could toward the town. The morning light helped as he couldn't see the road well last night. The roads were still a nightmare, but he had been through a nightmare and back so he was used to it. He was so out of breath it grew difficult to keep track of the time but that didn't matter; he had to get to the village. After what felt like six hours, he made it.

It was a small community of roughly fifty people and a few houses. He saw children running about and stopped. His shaking grew worse as his mind retreated to old memories. *Why am I thinking of this now?* He fought to keep himself present and continued moving forward.

Marcus came up to a wooden house with a straw roof, reminding him of a medieval town with a lack of technology. He knocked with what little strength he had on the pale wooden door. A man with a bald head and grim face opened it to look at him.

The man did a quick once-over, said, "We don't accept your kind here," and slammed the door. Marcus didn't have the energy to react and moved on to the next building. He was greeted with the same result, this time from a woman who appeared friendly but wasn't. Marcus tried again, crossing the center of town, avoiding the children as best he could. He knocked on the remaining doors in the village, but every household took one glance at him and refused to help.

Marcus was nearing passing out. His vision became blurry as he headed back into the forest. Maybe he'd find something more useful out there than with these people. He avoided the children playing, keeping a good thirty feet away from them. If they approached him, he didn't know what he would do. He'd probably shoot them. Marcus shook his head. *No. I . . . I can't shoot them. That would be wrong.* But he remembered all the times when he'd had to. The lives he'd had to save.

Marcus drifted back into the forest until he was well out of view of the village. It wasn't long until he heard some rustling and turned to find three men and one woman surrounding him with spears. Although he could hardly call them "spears," as they were more a mishmash of whatever these thugs could find and taped together to try and give them the advantage in a fight.

"Nice gun you have there," one thug with a round face croaked. He had an eyepatch over his left eye and was missing a couple of teeth. "You look like you're prime picking. Allow us to end your suffering."

Marcus took his hand off his wound, letting the blood seep. His eyes scanned the number of hostiles, assessing their strengths and weaknesses, feeling the adrenaline course through his body.

Four hostiles, armed with spears, three men, one woman, stances improper, no firearms, no bows, thin bodies. Good.

Marcus let his pack slide off and kicked it forward. He made the mistake of dropping it with his wounded shoulder, causing the pain to shoot through his body like hot lightning. A thug with frizzled black hair and the female wearing a black bandana glanced down at the pack. That was a mistake. Marcus lunged forward, grabbing the spear of the black-haired thug and wrenching it from his grip in an instant. Marcus twirled the spear around his body and swiped the bladed end into the man's neck. He used the opposite end to smack the woman hard in the left temple, leaving her dazed on the ground.

Two down.

Without hesitating, he sidestepped, using the weapon to block the incoming spear thrust at him. Marcus backed off, gaining distance, and threw the spear at the nearest thug, missing the one with the eyepatch but nailing the other thug in the throat, impaling the man into the nearby tree.

"Why you!" The eye-patched thug lunged forward, yelling.

Marcus saw his incoming thrust and predicted it, pivoting as the man missed Marcus entirely and plunged his spear into a tree. This man had clearly never faced an adversary with training before. Marcus quickly punched the thief in the face and he stumbled back dazed. Despite his pain, Marcus drew the sword from the sheath over his right shoulder, pulling the dark blade free. It gleamed in the sun, eager for blood, as Marcus sliced the man with his sword three times, creating a star of gore across his whole body. The movements were so fast it was hard to keep up. The thug dropped to the ground, unable to comprehend the speed of the man in front of him. He was dead before he hit the dirt.

Marcus turned to find the woman coming to, but he quickly used his left arm to grab the woman's jacket and pull her within range.

The woman begged as she tried to reach for a knife, "NO NO NO!" Marcus plunged the blade callously into her neck, splicing through her spine and esophagus. She died instantly. Marcus pulled the sword from her body and used the woman's jacket to clean off the blood.

Hostiles eliminated.

Marcus did one final check to make sure there was no counterattack. But no one was around. No one cared. One of his legs gave out and he knelt, taking in the sight of the four hacked bodies around him. Blood pooled in four puddles as if in a perfect ritual, mixing with the fallen leaves of the forest, creating a tapestry of beauty and blood. Marcus sighed and closed his eyes, lowering his head in shame. Not for himself, but for these people he'd just killed.

Another four lost, he thought. He didn't feel regret for taking their lives. He felt regret for how they ended. Children who had grown up only to die in some forest trying to steal from a stranger. He glanced down at the bodies covered in blood, then began field stripping them for anything useful. He found tin flasks filled with water, some crackers, and even a long scarf, which he used to bandage his wound. It wouldn't stop an infection, but he had some time with that.

He checked the full canteen and understood that there must be an abundance of water nearby. Marcus left the bodies, not because he didn't want to spend another moment with them, but to wash his wounds and clean himself up from all the blood splattered on him. Slicing those thugs caused his black jacket to stain red. He didn't care, just as long as he got it cleaned soon.

Would have gone better if you had used the bullets.

But it would be a waste to use bullets on them.

Marcus flexed his injured shoulder, the SR75k rifle still slung over it. It was rare for people to have weapons other than a bow and sword these days. Roughly one in ten people owned a gun, and even then, they didn't have much ammunition. After the Fall, society had retreated into medieval times with a slight mixture of modern technology involved. Marcus had plenty of ammunition, at least for now, but in time he knew it would go fast.

Marcus came upon a small lake and saw an electric mill nearby. Not many things surprised him but the sight of the ingenuity was rare these days. Some nearby village must be using the water to power their town. It was clever thinking in a world with little electricity. That's why hydro dams became so important, and the oil left in the world had been quickly fought over. Marcus's mood turned grim at the thought. *Oil. What a waste.*

After scouting the lake for an hour, Marcus deemed it safe. He removed his magnum from his left thigh, his throwing knives from his belt, as well as his rucksack, then his jacket. Despite removing most of his clothes, he kept his secondary blade, a long kukri, on him at all times. He'd had to use it more than once and it was dangerous when combined with his sword. The kukri specialized in cutting and slicing movements, with its slightly angled blade making it ideal for cutting down targets quickly. It wasn't the best when it came to thrusting and stabbing but it was still an ideal weapon for unarmored opponents and quick attacks. His black sword was also ideal for cutting with its slight curve on the blade, but it also had a sharper point, making it strong for thrusting. It had a sixty-one centimeter[2] long blade and a thirteen centimeter[3] long hilt with a guard crafted into it. It was an ideal one-handed sword for combat.

He knelt in the small lake, feeling the coolness of the water on his ankles. Marcus's eyes continued to scan the area, never feeling completely safe, even when he let his guard down. But if something happened, it

----

2. 24 inches

3. 5 inches

happened. Nothing he could do about it, and worrying wasn't going to change that. It never did.

Marcus wiped his face clean of the blood, cleaning his short black beard and hair, rubbing down his rough skin until it was clean. He made sure to keep his shoulder out of the water to prevent infection, but he did clean the majority of his body. He would boil some water later and use it to clean his wound. Marcus filled the extra canteen he'd picked up from the thug as well as his own. Bubbles left the metal containers as they were filled with water.

Later, Marcus boiled the water and soaked a flap of cloth taken from the dead thugs in it to drape over his shoulder. Even things taken off your enemy could still be useful. Marcus wiped his wound with clean water, observing the bullet hole that had gone through his left shoulder and exited out his chest. But somehow, his bones and were intact, meaning it wasn't a major injury; in fact, it was amazing Marcus was still able to use his left arm at all.

Not smart, Marcus. Luckily, he had found some Prozac in one of the thug's pockets. Medicine was hard to find these days, so some random thug having it was surprising, but Marcus was tired of surprise.

After he had cleaned his wounds, he returned to the corpses he had left behind and checked them for identification, anything that would help him understand who these people were or if they had any relatives. But he found nothing and part of him was relieved. He didn't want to know whose lives he just took and inside himself he knew he didn't care, but he wanted to. He wanted to care again, but it had been so long that he had forgotten. At least he was trying.

Marcus dug rudimentary graves for the four corpses and used his kukri to carve makeshift crosses using bark he stripped from a tree. He laid the crosses in front of each grave and observed the sight.

He knew the woman's begging would haunt him, at least until he heard the next voice, and the next voice, and the next, and on and on it would go. Marcus stared passively for a little longer, then moved on.

《——》

The day was ending and the world was turning dark. Marcus knew it wasn't a good idea to sleep outside at night alone, especially since he had just encountered thugs, so he made his way toward the village again, hoping they wouldn't attack him. The ground squished beneath his black boots, the grass and soft soil lush with nutrients from the rain and forest surrounding him. It was a nice sight, so good someone should make a painting of it.

Marcus felt better now that he had the Prozac in his system to prevent infection. He knew he would run out of Prozac eventually, so he would do some foraging tomorrow for herbs with healing properties when the sun was up. It would be dangerous to go searching in the dark. Anything was a danger now that he was alone. It frustrated him. He was used to being with a team, always having someone watch his back, and now he had no one. Just himself. He would make do, he always did, but it helped relax Marcus when he had an ally, or at least someone who wouldn't kill him.

Marcus made his way back to the same village, this time keeping clear of the residents and finding himself a nice small shack away from their homes that contained a donkey and some sheep.

The village was not doing well. The buildings were decrepit and heavily worn down. The wood of most of the homes was splintered and worn. He looked and saw empty stalls in the shack and could tell that times had been tough. Marcus lay his pack and weaponry down on a bale of hay. If the owner came by and found him, he would leave and have no hard feelings. It wasn't his home anyway. Besides, it would do for his . . . problem.

After doing a quick search for weapons and other traps throughout the small shack, Marcus took off his rifle and throwing knives, keeping his magnum, kukri, and sword on him just in case, before he went to sleep, hoping his phantoms wouldn't haunt him again.

‹‹—•—››

"MARCUS! HELP ME!"

Cold sweat permeated Marcus's body. He could hear the scream now as clearly as back then.

"MARCUS! HELP ME!"

Marcus looked over and saw his buddy Matt shouting from atop the mountain. Shouting for help, shouting for him. "MARCUS! HELP ME!"

Marcus's heart was pounding. He was in full combat gear, with his Remington MK 50 in his hands. It was a DMR-style weapon, ideal for long distances, and was half considered a sniper rifle given its semi-automatic tendencies and its fifteen round magazine. He remembered they were fighting off the terrorist group called Laziç, the religious sect that swore to kill anyone who wasn't their own. The Laziçs were swarming the mountain and getting closer. Marcus raised his MK 50 rifle and fired, down one, down two, but for every hostile he took down, two more would show up. Their position was getting overrun and Matt was getting farther and farther away.

Marcus lifted his rifle, staring straight up at a Laziç. Marcus had caught him off guard and fired, but the bullets fell from the barrel like rocks. Marcus saw that the Laziç looked to be only sixteen, but even a sixteen-year-old is extremely dangerous when they have an automatic AK84 rifle in their hands. The teenager raised his rifle straight at Marcus and grinned a wicked smile. Marcus was swapping mags, hoping to reload in time. He swapped the mags and pulled the charging handle, racked a round in the chamber, and fired. But the bullets kept falling.

He could feel the impending doom as the teenager lifted the rifle straight at him and open fired. Marcus could feel every 7.62 FMJ round strike his body, feeling every bullet and every blood vessel tear from the impact. He knew it was a dream, so why wasn't he waking up? He wanted to scream and cry out, but nothing came from his mouth. He tried harder and harder until he woke up screaming as loud as he could.

Marcus searched for his magnum and sword, unsheathing the blade and taking the gun from the holster. He was covered in sweat and could feel his heart thumping at a hundred miles an hour. He was breathing hard, feeling the cold sweat permeate his body through all the layers of his clothing. It took him a couple of minutes to realize he was awake and remember where he was. He looked up at the stars and checked how long he had been asleep. He wasn't surprised when he found that he had only slept ten minutes.

Marcus leaned back on the bale of hay and tried to relax, feeling the yearning for sleep pull at his eyes. But he couldn't go to sleep again, not after that nightmare.

No, not a nightmare. A memory. He remembered his friend Matt, and how he'd loved the way he played guitar. He remembered his friend was dead, even if he'd see him again someday. Marcus wanted to cry but he didn't have any tears in him.

Marcus saw a light flicker from the nearby village. The same bald man from before stepped out of his home with a bow and arrow nocked. He spotted Marcus and fired a shot at the door next to him. Marcus didn't flinch.

The bald man shouted, "GET OUT OF HERE! We don't want your kind!"

He nocked another arrow and fired again, this time closer to Marcus. Again, Marcus didn't flinch as the arrow struck next to his head and planted into the wood frame of the shack. He only sighed and picked himself up.

Marcus grabbed his gear and headed out into the darkness, this time heading north, hoping to find another village somewhere. He made it less than ten feet away from the barn when an arrow struck him in his right shoulder. Normally a person would shriek in pain, but Marcus didn't feel anything. He only turned and looked at the bald man as he shouted, "Don't let us find you out here again or we'll kill you!"

Marcus glanced at the man with a sullen face and broke the arrow. He continued to make his way north, in hopes of finding a place to rest and address his new wound.

CHAPTER TWO

LAYTHIA

"Where does a man like me belong after everything that's
happened? Where do I call home now?"

—THE SAINT

Location Unknown

14:18 hrs, 17/04/2258 (12 days A.F.)[4]

It had been getting harder to find game as he traveled further into the forest and his water supply was getting low. After a couple days of walking, he found he was nearing the end of the forest. He had been able to hunt a couple of deer and even eat some lizards, but what lay ahead of him was a different landscape. Marcus checked his water supply and saw it was empty. He would make do, but that wasn't the problem. The problem was how Marcus felt right now. His mood had dropped even more after that village encounter. He was beginning to feel more depressed, which was not helped by the lack of sleep and constant nightmares.

Marcus tried to flex his right shoulder after pulling the arrow out and treating the wound with some herbs he'd found. He was lucky to find Vistra in the forest, a purple-red plant known for its medicinal purposes. If he hadn't been taught about it in training he would have probably died. Marcus kept some Vistra with him, as he knew he would need it later.

---

4. A.F. (After The Fall)

He came to the edge of the forest where before him stood the sight of a small city. His focus dredged upon the city with its spiked wooden walls and large Main Gate.

Marcus studied the city for a minute, curious there was a city here at all. He didn't remember seeing a city like this one on the maps before The Fall. So where in the world was he?

He didn't want to go into the city, but there was no other water source around that he knew about, so they had to have a well in there.

Marcus approached the gate, joining the flow of people entering. He could see red face paint on the guards as they stood at each corner of the door and on the catwalk above. Some of them had rifles, but they were the Barista FK models that were most useful about a hundred to two hundred years ago. The Baristas were reliable weapons if put in the right hands. Despite their age, they were remarkably accurate and worked with the ammunition of the times. They were bolt action but had been designed that way, making them more like sniper rifles than close-range weapons. Regardless, having a gun or anything else these days qualified as dangerous. Marcus had seen men kill other men with a rock or even their own teeth. Anything could be a weapon if you used it right. And any weapon became more dangerous the more efficient the person wielding it was.

Marcus was unsurprised when the front guard noticed him immediately. This guard had a sharp triangular beard and a mullet haircut. He wore a tunic and brown leather armor but it clearly didn't fit him. It was hard to take a man seriously when he dressed so awkwardly.

The guard put his hand on Marcus's chest. It took every fiber of Marcus's being not to kill him; all his training and instincts argued for it. But he held back, knowing it was stronger to not let his emotions control him than to lash out.

The guard spoke in an accent. "We don't accept your kind here."

Marcus replied evenly, "Where is *here* exactly?"

The guard stifled a laugh, "This is Laythia buddy. Yous never heard of it?"

Marcus ignored the jest and pondered. He hadn't heard of Laythia before. *So this must be a new city.* He thought.

Marcus looked behind him and pointed a thumb at the forest. "What forest is that?"

The guard was starting to be less amused by this stranger. "That's the Arghast Forest dumbo. Everybody knows that."

It was then Marcus finally realized where he was; surprised at how far he had traveled.

Then, it struck Marcus like a sledgehammer that all of his previous knowledge of the world is outdated. And that the maps would have to be redrawn because of The Fall. Everything he once knew was now different. It was a whole new world.

Marcus asked another question, "Do you have a well here?"

The guard raised his chin. "That we do. Whatzit to yous?"

"I would like to use it, please." Marcus spoke calmly, trying his best to keep himself together. After getting little sleep for nearly ten days, he was definitely short on patience.

"Water's expensive, sonny."

Marcus glared at the man. "I'll pay."

The guard smirked at him. "Give me the rifle and I'll let yous in, and then yous go pay for some water."

Marcus stared at the man, tired of this. He whispered, "Please."

The guard stepped forward, getting up in Marcus's space. "Nah, nah. Yous see, we have a—"

Marcus struck the guard three times around his abdomen. The guard's eyes puffed out of their sockets. Marcus had hit him so quickly and efficiently that the man could not breathe despite still being standing. Marcus slid a pair of gloves from his pack into the hand of the guard as his payment and walked into the city.

Lovely town, he thought.

Marcus followed the crowd, but he stuck to the sides of the road leading up the hill. He knew there would be a Townsquare somewhere, so he only had to follow the people to it. But Marcus found he was shaking being around so many people. He hated feeling contained. It went against all his instincts to be trapped, surrounded by so many possible hostiles. He gritted his teeth and kept going, trying to find the water.

He approached the Townsquare set up near the top of the hill. The whole city was built into the slant of a mountain with the largest building at the top, probably a dining hall or the house of the wealthiest person around. Marcus's eyes dropped to see the well in the center of town. The soldiers surrounding it had some Viper 6 model weapons. They weighed 2.54 kilograms[5] and fired 9x19mm Parabellum ammunition at a rate of 800 rounds/min at a velocity of 400 m/s[6] with an effective range of 200 meters.[7] They were highly reliable submachine guns that had come out recently, just before the Great Wars ended. Whoever was running this town had access to some resources.

Marcus saw a line waiting to use the well. It was perfectly understandable. In these times, water was rarer than weaponry, and finding it was very difficult. Marcus had made sure to remember that last lake he'd found, knowing it would come in handy later.

Reluctantly, Marcus got in line, waiting as the next fifty people went to draw water from the well. The crowd increased in size and Marcus found himself with a person in front and behind him. He hated the prospect of a stranger on both sides. They could attack him at any time.

He looked up at the cloudy sky. *Lord, please protect me.* He remembered a verse he had memorized. *"Don't be afraid, for I am with you. Don't be discouraged, for I am your God."* Marcus repeated the verse in his mind and relaxed. Quoting Scripture always helped calm him.

"*NO NO NO!*" He could hear the woman from a few days ago, screaming

---

5. 5.6lbs

6. 1,312ft/s

7. 656ft

as he plunged the blade into her throat. He could feel the heat on the hilt of the blade as the friction rubbed on his hand.

"Hey," a woman said as she pushed him from behind, and Marcus snapped out of his memory and reacted on impulse. He punched the woman in the face, knocking her back into the crowd of people.

Marcus found he was shaking, feeling anxiety course through his whole body. His eyes quickly searched the crowd for potential hostiles. The four men in front of him proved pretty hostile, as he had just punched the leader's wife.

Marcus gestured with his hands in a calming defensive move, but the lead man didn't heed the warning. "I am sorry," Marcus said. "Please forgive me. I didn't mean to harm your wife. You see—"

"The only thing that I saw was yous punch my missus," the man said.

Marcus tried to steady himself. "It won't happen again. I promise."

The man shook his head. "Yeah, I don't care!"

The man threw a punch and the rest of the group joined in. Marcus could have easily killed them all, but he knew he was under guard here in the city, so he refrained from using his weapons. Marcus tried to raise his arms, but a bullet through one shoulder and an arrow in the other caused him tremendous pain when he used either of them. The first man threw a punch, but Marcus swiped the man away and let him tumble. The other three did the same and Marcus made a fool out of all of them.

Marcus glanced at the well. All he wanted was some water. After a couple of minutes of dodging every blow the four men threw at him, all of them were exhausted, except for Marcus. All four ended up on the ground, with the wife coming back to consciousness and chanting to tear Marcus apart.

Marcus tilted his head at the four men with their hands on their knees. "Are you finished?" he asked, but they were all too tired to answer.

The husband raised a finger at Marcus. "Yous . . . yous . . ." he started to say, but he couldn't get the words out.

Marcus noticed the guards were watching the chaos with glee, hoisting their weapons up like they were hot stuff. *They don't even care. They just find it entertaining.* Marcus stepped back in line and waited his turn.

At the end of a line was a table distributing water and trading goods in return for it. Marcus approached the table and a young man behind it didn't look up at him as he wrote something down. "That's twenty geld, please," he said.

Marcus said, "I don't have geld."

The young man kept writing. "Do you have any other items of value?"

Marcus pulled out a lighter he'd taken from the thugs a couple of days ago and placed it on the table.

The young man didn't even look at the lighter before saying, "No."

Marcus took out a spare set of gloves and socks. The young man finally looked at him, resting his hands atop one another like some monk. He smiled at Marcus, but it was an arrogant smile, one that said, *"I dictate how much you pay and how much you'll get."*

Marcus pulled out a magazine from his rucksack and propped the five SR75k bullets on the table. He might as well have given the man gold teeth. The young man stared wide at the bullets and then smirked at Marcus. "That will get you only a quarter full." Marcus reluctantly took out his canteen and placed it on the table. The young man pointed with his pen. "And your sword, too."

Marcus glared at him, too tired to be haggled with. He leaned over and whispered, "Don't push it, kid."

The young man grinned at him and shouted to one of the guards, "Get this man his water, but give him only a few drops just to spite him!"

Marcus stared at the guards, knowing they would follow this little twerp's every command. Marcus wasn't in the mood to get in a fight with the authorities so he stood by and watched as the guards poured only a few drops into the canteen. He shifted his thoughts elsewhere.

"And this same God who takes care of me will supply all your needs from his glorious riches, which have been given to us in Christ Jesus."

Marcus closed his eyes and waited for them to complete the process.

A guard handed him the nearly empty canteen. Marcus glared at the young man again and walked away, trying not to feel cheated. He left the city, avoiding the guard holding his ribs at the Main Gate, and went to make camp outside, hoping to find something to eat.

《——》

Marcus used his kukri to slice a chunk of meat off a squirrel he caught. It had been a tough throw, but he was able to hit it with one of his throwing knives, which were pretty reliable at close range and quick to throw. Marcus had had to use them a time or two, and they proved very useful in quick circumstances.

He sat perched against a tree, the forest surrounding him as the fire burned before him with a squirrel cooking above it. Marcus wasn't eating; he stared into the calming fire trying to lose himself, yet also trying to come to grips with what had happened after he left the military. He put his hand to his head. The fire crackled and flickered.

Marcus knew he couldn't keep it all in. He could feel the grief hit him like a shadowed wave. He didn't cry, but he lowered his head in submission at the realization of what had happened. He could feel the effects of it slowly hitting him. The reality sinking in. The loss.

He realized how quiet it was. How calm the world was. Marcus wanted to feel surprised, but nothing surprised him anymore. He was having a hard time feeling much of anything these days. He shrugged his right shoulder, the one pierced by that man's arrow, but he didn't feel any pain.

Marcus reached over and sliced a piece of meat off the squirrel. He accidentally sliced the blade too hard and the kukri cut his forearm slightly. Marcus watched the blood seep out with blank curiosity, but he didn't feel any pain. It should have terrified him but it didn't. He looked at the wound unphased. He didn't know why but he cut his forearm again and watched as blood seeped out from the new wound. Again, nothing.

"I don't even feel it," he said. He knew it was a reflection of the state of his heart. Now that things were calm and the world finally had some peace, the demons from Marcus's past were beginning to come forward. He tried to think of it all, all the wars he'd been through, all the lives he'd lost while serving with great men. He tried to contemplate it all but was quickly lost.

He came back to the present with the question, *What now?* He paused when he found he had no answer. He stared into the fire, trying to enjoy the peace of the world for once, to enjoy a world without war. But all it did was make him feel empty inside. In war, he had a purpose, a set of talents and skills that he put to good use. Now, he was fending off cheap thugs and getting swindled by rich kids for a few drops of water.

It was strange; in a way, he missed war and how he'd felt useful to the world. He did not miss the casualties of war. All the men he'd lost both because of him and not. But it was all he knew, and he'd never imagined himself doing anything else. Marcus tried to picture himself sitting in some city working at some administrative desk job, but he knew that would be utter hell for him.

He exhaled and looked up to the heavens, the open blue night sky sparkling with small stars. "Lord, what do you want me to do? I gave everything up to do the right thing. Now what?" He was met with the usual silence. Marcus lowered his head and sighed. "Thy will be done."

It didn't make him feel any better, knowing his God had a plan for him, when he didn't know what God had in store. The lack of an answer, the lack of a direction, drove him insane. Marcus needed an objective. Something to work towards. A goal to complete. An enemy to fight. But now there was no enemy. Only the demons within and all the time in the world, trapping Marcus in the prison of his own mind.

《———》

He could see the young guard from the gate laughing at him. All of the townspeople were laughing at him as well, pointing their fingers in mockery.

Marcus could feel anger flare up inside as he stared at the crowd, trying to ignore their comments. He knew they didn't hate him; they hated the one he represented. But even a man as tough as him could still feel the daggers of their malice. They hated him, even when they'd never met him before. Flames erupted behind the crowd but they didn't notice. The fire grew hotter and hotter as Marcus called out to warn them.

"Look out! Fire!" Marcus shouted, but they ignored him as the flames grew. Marcus tried yelling again, "Fire! Turn away or you'll die!" They merely shook their heads as the flames engulfed them. Their laughter turned into cries for help, but it was too late. They were all burning to death.

Marcus watched in accepted horror as an arrow struck him in the shoulder, seeing the bald man there behind him. "We don't want your kind here!" the man said as he fired again, and again, and again at Marcus, who was unable to dodge the arrows striking his body. But Marcus didn't feel any pain from his injuries.

Only the pain of their hatred towards him.

Marcus lowered his head. "I'm sorry."

He awoke to find the fire still lively in front of him. He had slept for only a couple of minutes. Marcus sat up a little, feeling the silence around him, the lack of urgency in the air. It was peaceful in the forest, but that peace dredged up the demons inside him.

For a while, Marcus stared at the fire trying not to think of anything. He had nothing but time to think, however. Staring at the fire at least gave him something to look at. With his mind clear for the first time in months, a question appeared.

Have you ever considered what you would do after the wars?

The question gave Marcus pause. Men long forgotten would ask Marcus what he would do after the wars, but he never had an answer. Most of the men he'd served with had dreams of what they would do when they went back to their civilian lives, but not Marcus. He hadn't thought much about the question because there wasn't much to think about. He simply hadn't believed he would live this long. It was one of the things that alienated

Marcus from his own men in the military. Oh, how he missed them, yet he also remembered that he'd never felt like he was truly one of them.

Marcus exhaled through his nose, remembering how he spent so much time with them, yet even in the military he'd never truly felt he belonged anywhere. And now that lack of belonging was empowered by Marcus's sense of purposelessness. It wasn't that Marcus didn't want to dream; he just didn't have one. There was nowhere that he wanted to go and nothing that he wanted to do. He had always wanted to slay evil and protect people. He got his fill of evil and more in the prior wars but even now, as demonstrated by those four thugs, evil still existed. All the world did in the wars he fought in was destroy itself. And what did it accomplish? The world was now in a famine for resources, entire countries were destroyed, entire populations displaced, and cultures wiped out from the face of the planet. Marcus knew there was dwelling hatred. Hatred that would sprout one day and cause a great evil. But who knew if he would be alive to fight it?

What do I do now?

Marcus sighed. "I wish Carmen were here. She would know what to do. Or even Dad."

He wanted to cry but couldn't, leaving him with the lack of feeling he'd always felt since he'd joined the wars. It triggered his yearning for his family. Marcus leaned his head back as his heart cringed in pain. The loss still fresh in his heart, longing desperately for their love. "Dad . . . Carmen . . . I miss you guys."

Marcus inhaled and calmed himself, still longing for his family. But he couldn't see them, even if they were alive, at least not until later. Knowing he would have to wait years to see his loved ones again was torture. The impatience boiled in his veins. It pained Marcus to think about his past, but he had to hold onto it because if he let it go, he would get lost in the turmoil.

Marcus closed his eyes and threaded his hands in prayer. "God, what do I do now? What do you want me to do?"

He waited in silence but received no answer. The fury from the lack of a response roused a fire within Marcus. He knew God could answer his prayer, so why wouldn't he just tell him? It was a simple thing to do and it would save Marcus a lot of pain.

But Marcus also knew that God had a way of testing him and developing him through pain, so he doused the emotional anger and moved on. Marcus continued to pray until the morning light came. He opened his eyes, still sleep-deprived, and said, "Another day," dreading the repeat of another day of wandering.

CHAPTER THREE

OLD SCARS

*"When the dust settled and the world was at peace again, everyone
asked themselves the big question . . . What now?"*

—DREW HAX, CITIZEN OF LAYTHIA

Laythia

09:01 hrs, 18/04/2258 (13 days A.F.)

Marcus watched the citizens enter and exit the gate, some happy, some sad, others not caring. He leaned against a tree and tried to decide whether to go into town or not.

Marcus had opened his eyes today to find that his jacket was torn. He could repair it himself, but he needed a needle to do it, and he was sure he could find a needle in the city. Marcus assessed what would be counted as currency in his inventory, but he had dwindled down the tradeable items he had with the young merchant. Any more and he would leave himself exposed to danger.

Marcus was reluctant but he had to search anyway. Keeping his weapons close, he snuck past the guards and stepped into the city, looking around for small merchants trading sewing items. The shops around him were rough but at least they formed some small sense of economy, and a booming one at that. Marcus saw roasted animals, cockroaches on a stick, and some famous tizwa slow roasting. There were people selling clay plates and pottery, and other worn-out booths advertising medicines that Marcus knew weren't safe to drink. In a way, it made him happy to see some normalcy return to these people. Most of their lives had been in war like his had, so to see people enjoying life with no major enemy was a blessing. He'd never realized that about peacetime. The lack of danger was beautiful.

What bothered him the most were the open brothels and how there was no lack of prostitutes roaming about. Every city had its sin and Marcus wasn't angry, but he felt bad that young women had to grow up and survive in that sort of way. Then again, some of them chose to go down that route because they liked it. It just showed the moral decay of the city. Marcus glanced around and realized how worn the buildings were. Every building needed immediate repair, with clear signs this place had seen action in the previous war. But no one had bothered to fix them, so life continued on despite the conditions.

Marcus lowered his eyes to assess the crowds, checking for weapons or any ill intent. He stayed close to the alleyways, avoiding the large groups. He never did well with crowds, and he never wanted to be in the middle of them. It caused him extreme anxiety because he'd had too many bad experiences with crowds. They were too open to bomb threats. But he had to go into the city in order to get materials. He didn't have money, but he needed to try. Things wouldn't go his way until he did. Marcus had thought of going to the city lord and offering his services, but he decided against it. Being the hand of some dictator was not the life he wanted. He was not a hired gun.

He stared at the crowd before him, observing their clothing and their style of fashion. Most of the clothing was just a mishmash of whatever people could find. Anything from animal skins to leather jackets was prevalent. Most of the people wore old-fashioned tunics and simple clothing. There wasn't much of a choice in fashion these days, although he noticed a few people walking around in fancy clothing that signified there were some forms of textiles operating in this city. Some women even wore burqas, which he found curious given the style of culture this city emanated. It reminded him more of a medieval city rather than a collection of towns. Its guards patrolling the walls in their brown leather clothing made Marcus feel like he was in a completely different world.

Marcus brought his attention back and spotted a sewing shop across the way, but it was behind a massive crowd of people flowing past him like a freeway at rush hour. Instinct told Marcus to evade the crowd, so he took the long way, going around, avoiding every person he could. His anxiety kicked up from a seven to a nine the deeper he went. His eyes repeatedly scanned the crowd for weapons or suicide vests. He hated suicide vests. Every instinct told him this was a bad idea but he pressed on regardless. Marcus wormed his way through the edge of the crowd until he approached the sewing shop.

Cotton, sewing needles, all sorts of mismatched buttons, and even some broken toys were on display. Linen and newly assorted goods were pinned and held out for all to see. A gray-haired woman with a couple of warts on her nose looked up from her chair. She was clearly old, too old to be running this shop on her own. She squinted at him. "We don't accept your kind here."

"Do you accept customers?" Marcus replied, used to people saying that to him.

"If you've got the coin," the woman said.

"I don't," Marcus said flatly.

The woman craned her neck forward. "Then why are yous here?"

"I wanted to see if you had anything I desired."

The woman grinned. "Sorry, sonny, I'm too old for yous."

Marcus said flatly, "Sewing needles, ma'am."

The woman brightened. "Ma'am? I like the sound of that." The woman looked at him longingly, taking in the sight of Marcus's dense frame and strong muscles.

Marcus asked, "Do you need help around the shop?"

The woman shook her head. "No. I can't take your kind. People would kill mi business if they saw yous working here."

Marcus sighed. He was getting sick of this. "Is it that obvious?" he asked.

The woman tilted her head and cocked an unsurprised eyebrow. "Sonny, I could tell just by looking at yous."

Marcus grunted, feeling neither happy nor sad about that comment. A young boy ran into the shop playing with a wooden plane. The woman turned. "Arthur! I told yous not to play in the shop!" she snapped, but the boy kept playing. Marcus found some relief in watching the boy. It was nice, watching kids be kids.

Arthur tripped and the plane came tumbling forward until it smacked against the table, breaking the turbine on the front. The boy saw the broken toy and began to cry. The old woman turned and smacked the boy with her cane. "Now stop your yapping, boy! I told yous not to play inside the shop."

Marcus wanted to help but he didn't know how. It was one of those things he didn't know how to approach. He had seen hundreds, if not thousands, of men cry on the battlefield, but children were different. They required a special touch. Marcus wanted to fix the broken toy, but the propellers were completely broken into four pieces.

The old woman eyed him while Arthur cried in the back, and said, "Look sonny, if yous ain't gonna buy something, then just get going. I've got enough things to worry about."

Marcus bowed slightly with his arm across his chest. "I wish you good fortune, ma'am."

The old woman waved him off. "Yeah, yeah."

Marcus walked away feeling helpless, wondering how he could have helped that boy. It was one of those rare times when Marcus didn't know what to do. He wanted to fix that boy's toy, but how? He didn't know how to make toys in the first place. His transcendent failure ate at him as he left the city, returning to the woods where he felt calm again, his anxiety dropping to normal levels.

《——·——》

Marcus held his sword at the ready, flexing his wounded shoulders. The thin Kaisk tree stood before him like a white pencil. It was not as tough as an oak, but they were more numerous than oaks were. Marcus frequently took the time to practice his swordsmanship. He had plenty of time so he could blow off a little steam, plus he needed to relax. He hadn't felt fully relaxed since he left the military, and practicing with his sword and training was one of the few ways he felt some peace.

Marcus danced around the trunk of the Kaisk tree, swinging and pivoting, making sure his movements were suave as he had to retrain with his wounded shoulders. Raising his arms was difficult but doable. He had gotten better in the past couple of days, and with the medicine he'd crafted with the Vistra, he was able to stop any infection in his wounds, so in time he'd be back to normal. Marcus tried to not look at the cuts on his left forearm, the arm he'd both accidentally and purposefully cut.

He could feel the nightmares coming at him as he swung, the ghosts and voices of his past calling to him like a massed choir, all of them in desperate need of help. Marcus could feel his frustration boil, thinking of that kid who fell and broke his toy, and of how helpless he'd felt.

Marcus pivoted around the tree, finishing with his blade level with what would be the head of an opponent. He wanted to relax but couldn't. Normally this routine would help him calm down but nothing was working. He thought of that bald man who shot him with the arrow, then the four thugs, and finally that stupid merchant.

They hate me. Marcus's anger grew. *They hate me.* His breathing increased, with more fire in his breath. The question booming in his mind was, *What do I do now? What do I do now?* The question repeated over and over, giving rise to Marcus's anger. His anxiety increased to a nine out of ten. He was sick of being anxious, he was sick of being mistreated, he was sick of being rejected, he was sick of not knowing, but most of all he was angry at God for not telling him where he should go. Marcus snapped and let loose on the Kaisk tree, slicing through it with his sword quickly and efficiently as the tree crashed with a loud thud.

Marcus breathed with fire. "Why won't you tell me, God?" He stood up straight, looking at the sky in anger. "What am I doing here? What do you want me to do?"

There was silence, and that silence only enraged Marcus more. In his anger, he sliced another tree next to him, then another one, then another, and another, until more than a dozen Kaisk trees lay fallen on the ground. Marcus's pent-up anger had regressed but his anxiety and lack of purpose remained high.

"I can't live like this!" Marcus thought about what the rest of his life would look like, living on some farm, working some field to raise vegetables, in a world with people who hated him. He thought of living a long life and it sounded like pure torture, having to live with no purpose and with hatred from others, accomplishing nothing.

Marcus missed war. There he'd had a purpose, an objective, a reason to keep going, to one day achieve peace for others. He'd never expected he would survive it all. That was part of the reason why he never dreamed of anything. He hadn't expected to see tomorrow. And now, with tomorrow being all that he had, he felt trapped in a world of pointless activity. *What's the point of working some job, raising a family, retiring, and then dying if it doesn't mean anything?* Marcus had never craved riches. Never wanted to live a fat-happy life like most. What he desired was purpose, and without it, what was he? Dead, and he knew it.

Marcus cooled off and let his anger subside, but he still felt taut like a piece of wire. He dreaded the night coming, knowing he wouldn't get any sleep like every other night. Marcus sagged onto one knee. "God, what do you want me to do? Please use me."

But again, there was no answer. He knew God was there, he knew God was listening, so why was he staying silent? Marcus knew God had his reasons, and knew that for something like this to happen there was some good to come out of it. He just didn't know how or when it would occur. That left Marcus with only one option: faith.

Marcus shook his head. "Sometimes I wish you would tell me what you wanted . . . but, thy will be done." And just like that, it was over. Marcus gathered some of the Kaisk trees for firewood and walked back to his campsite.

The longer he lived on his own, the more he began to feel the need for community. The only conversations he had were with people who hated him. Marcus put the firewood in a neat pile next to the firepit and sat down, leaning against his rucksack. He was starting to smell and would need to bathe soon. He preferred to bathe regularly, but he knew that was a luxury and had grown used to not bathing over the years due to extreme periods of prolonged combat. The fire crackled and sputtered under the wood. Marcus's eyes hung heavy, dreading the nightmares to come while yearning for sleep all the same. He chuckled.

"It's funny," he said, winded. "I got more sleep in war than I do in peacetime."

Marcus fought as hard as he could against the urge to sleep, even praying that God would prevent him from sleeping, but he failed and drifted back into the nightmares.

Noralthra

16:48 hrs, 27/01/2248 (10 B.F)[8]

Cold, sharp air exited his lungs. Marcus stared down the scope of the rifle atop the four-story building. He was able to see everything around the two-story grid-structured city, all the way up to the massive capital building. Temperatures had dropped to -20 degrees Celsius[9], and his Konig M98 sniper rifle stared down the streets as the protests raged on toward the capital of Noralthra. The crowd was getting hot despite the cold. The famine throughout the land was causing the citizens to revolt against their government, a government that pledged loyalty to Aquila. But that's not why Marcus was here. He was here because the splinter cell group called KSP was taking advantage of the chaos in the country, and Marcus knew this was a prime time for chaos.

Marcus stared down the scope. His breathing was calm as he slowly

---

8. B.F (Years Before The Fall)

9. −5 degrees

scanned the rooftops and the crowd below for any signs of trouble, but there were a lot of windows, too many for him to track. The radio hummed on his right shoulder. "This is Eagle 9 to Overwatch 6, over."

Marcus thumbed the radio. "This is Overwatch 6, go ahead Eagle 9."

"Tensions are heating up despite the freezing temperature. No one's going home today. Perfect site for a bombing."

Marcus was not amused. "Copy that Eagle 9."

"Roger that Overwatch 6, Eagle 9 out." The radio went silent.

What's the point of warning if it's already obvious? Marcus knew the KSP would make a move today; it was too good an opportunity to pass up. At least he would take some of their lives and prevent them from harming others. That thought brought him some comfort in the cold.

Marcus heard chanting beneath him. Down in the streets was a massive mob of people with torches heading slowly toward the capital. Marcus's consciousness shook its metaphorical head. *Here comes trouble.* He thumbed the radio again. "Eagle 9, this is Overwatch 6, massive crowd approaching the capital with violent intent." Marcus heard the radioman swear.

"Copy that Overwatch 6, look for hostile candidates and take them down at your discretion. We need to keep this government intact, over."

"Roger that." Marcus shook his head. *If this government can't even handle a riot, how are they supposed to handle the KSP bombing their cities?*

The approaching crowd slowly merged with the already massive protest, creating an unstable and violent beast of flesh and anger. Hunger can drive a country to the brink if handled improperly. Marcus checked the leaders of the crowd, as the ones arousing the masses were possibly secret members of the KSP, creating their opportunity. Marcus slowly gritted his teeth. *This is not good.*

The crowd of roughly twenty thousand people merged with another rally and became fifty thousand strong. The packed streets reminded Marcus of the French Revolution. There was no way for Marcus to track any hostile now. All they had to do was strap on a suicide vest and walk amongst the crowd.

"Overwatch 6! Overwatch 6! Vehicle inbound from the east!"

The van was going seventy-five miles per hour on what was most likely a suicide run, aiming to plow through the crowd and then detonate. Marcus shifted slowly, pacing the van. It was going to run into the crowd in ten seconds. Marcus's finger gently caressed the trigger, controlling his breathing, inhaling slowly and deeply.

Nine . . . eight . . . seven . . . (exhale), six . . . five . . . four . . . (sights lined up on the driver), three . . . two . . .

Marcus squeezed the trigger. The Konig M98 was a semi-automatic anti-materiel rifle. It fired a .50 caliber BMG 12.7x99mm cartridge, so even if he missed the driver, the round would still stop the engine of the van. The round traveled at 850 meters per second,[10] with a firing range of 1,800 meters,[11] until it punctured the windshield and struck the driver in the neck, ripping through muscle, tendon, and bone like they were paper and nearly taking the man's head off. The van slowed and a moment later exploded a hundred feet away from the crowd, devastating two blocks, shattering concrete and windows in tandem.

The entire crowd turned in panic as people ran for their lives from the devastation. Some people were wounded from the explosion, but better to be wounded and live, than to die for nothing.

Then Marcus spotted a man with an RPG rocket launcher coming onto the rooftop from the west, aiming at the crowd. Marcus swiveled in time and sent the man into the afterlife, as the man's body tumbled out of sight in a spray of blood. Marcus watched as the crowd began to disperse until it dramatically stopped moving when one man held up a hand, hoisting a child in the other. The man was wearing a blue coat and held the child up as a shield, yelling something in a language Marcus didn't understand. But one thing was clear. The man had a bomb strapped to his chest, threatening to blow himself and everyone within a two-block radius.

----

10. 2,800 ft/sec

11. 1,970 yds

Marcus didn't even hear the shouting of Eagle 9 on the radio as he centered his sights on the hostile. But the kid was squirming, blocking the shot. Marcus tried to go for the harder target and hit the man in the head, but there was too much motion from the kid and the target was shifting too much. He could hit the man, but striking him in the chest would ignite the suicide vest and kill hundreds of people. Marcus aimed for the head, praying for the right moment, but there was no clean shot. The kid kept fighting, trying to get away from the clutches of a man who wanted only to do evil. Despite the cold Marcus could feel himself sweating. He could hear his heartbeat, which was elevated but calm. He waited for the right moment. The only reason he was using the M98 was because of its impressive range, but the use of its rounds was not as clean due to its velocity. It was powerful but messy. He had no choice.

Marcus controlled his breathing, checking his heartbeat for the right moment, his finger slowly thumbing the trigger, his sights centered on the target's head. At the right moment, the kid pitched to the side.

There.

Marcus pulled the trigger as the world entered slow motion. He could see the round distort the air as it broke through wind and snow, right toward the target. But the boy shifted over towards the center in less than a second, right in the pathway of the incoming projectile. Marcus's eyes widened in horror.

No.

The terrorist pulled the kid dead center and the round struck through the boy's skull first, then blew the terrorist's head off next. The man dropped the detonator and both lives were ended instantly. All Marcus could see was the torn flesh of what used to be a boy's head as he felt his own heart stop.

《━━》

Marcus snapped out of his dream in a cold sweat. His adrenaline was pumping like a racehorse inside his chest. The memory was still fresh in his mind, despite all the years that had passed. All the horror, all the loss. Marcus put his hand to his face, lowered his head, and tried to cry, but no tears came forth. He wanted to feel something but couldn't. All he could feel was his pain. So, he stared at the fire before him until it slowly died out, waiting for morning to come.

CHAPTER FOUR

YOUS GOT A TALENT

"That constant frustration of asking yourself,
'What now?' is enough to drive a man insane."

—MARK HOBLE, FORMER VETERAN OF LAYTHIA

Arghast Forest

01:49 hrs, 19/04/2258 (14 days A.F.)

Marcus sighed. He had the magnum in his left hand, checking the weapon. Then he spun the cartridge, raised the barrel towards his head, and pulled the trigger. *Click.* Marcus spun the cartridge again, hearing the sizzle of it spinning. He put the gun against his head and pulled again. *Click.*

This time Marcus opened the cartridge and checked the ammo count. Five rounds in the chamber out of six. Marcus fumbled in his pocket and inserted the final round in the chamber. He did one final check. Six rounds in the chamber, a full cartridge. He raised the barrel to his head again and pulled the trigger. *Click.*

Marcus lowered the gun and sighed. He looked over at a nearby Kaisk tree and pulled the trigger six times. Thunder boomed in the forest early in the morning as six rounds fired through the trunk of the tree, causing the trunk to collapse to one side.

He sighed. "You still have a plan for me." In boredom, he glanced around, needing something to do, something to occupy his mind since he wasn't going to sleep. Marcus noticed some of the extra chunks of Kaisk wood lying around and grabbed one. He pulled out his long kukri and started whittling the wood down until it became a sharp stake.

As Marcus whittled, he felt a sense of calm descend upon him, almost like he was falling into a lull. His focus was drawn completely to this piece of wood in his hands and for once, he wasn't thinking about anything else. The activity relaxed him somehow. When he was done, Marcus held up the finished stake, inspecting its use as a weapon.

But then his thoughts drifted toward that boy from the city, and he thought of his broken airplane. Marcus looked at the stake and tried to imagine the wooden airplane inside of it. He then cut off the sharp end, making the wooden chunk into a block again. He tried whittling down the wood to create roughly the same figure as the airplane the boy had been playing with.

After a couple of hours, Marcus was left with an awkward-looking figure. It was ugly but it wasn't too bad. It reminded Marcus of a slow PIGZA Mk VI plane, a propeller-type plane mounted with a heavy machine gun to provide air support. The plane was highly expendable and easy to shoot down, but they could swarm a place in large numbers, were cheap to make, and were easy to pilot. Only armies that couldn't afford the technology of modern warfare used them, mainly because they lost so many in battle. But they still made a difference, some of them even carrying a single bomb on their bellies.

Marcus added a few final touches to the PIGZA and crafted a propeller. He held up the finished product and wasn't sure what to do now.

It's not a weapon. So, what do I do with it? He remembered passing by lots of civilians in the countries he fought in, and how many kids would have toys they cherished, things to remind them of their childhood. Suddenly Marcus remembered something from his own childhood. He'd had a small toy car, a red one that his father had given him. He would play with that thing all day with his friends and never grew tired of it. He slept with that car. Marcus remembered how that car made him feel, how happy he was to have it. It was a feeling he had long since forgotten. One from a previous life he had left behind.

Marcus lowered the wooden plane. "Perhaps I should give this to that boy Arthur?" Marcus checked the horizon and saw that the sun was rising. He had stayed up the whole night working on it. He knew the boy would be at the sewing shop, as he probably didn't have anyone else to live with except his grandmother. He was probably destined to run that shop when he grew up. He had to be no older than seven. Too young to understand everything that's going on.

You were younger than that. Remember. Marcus stared into a dark memory of his past. He looked in the direction of the town and took his first step.

Laythia

12:41 hrs, 19/04/2258 (14 days A.F.)

Marcus's anxiety kicked in as, once again, the Townsquare was packed. The massive crowds terrified him. Bad things always happened when he was in crowds. So, Marcus kept to the side of the alleys and buildings, always making sure he had an exit, never venturing into the mass of people. He hugged the wall until he made it to the same shop. The old woman sat there, the same as before. She sized up Marcus again. "Well, if it ain't mi favorite customer."

Marcus checked over his shoulder, making sure he was a couple of feet away from the flowing crowd behind him. He looked at the old lady. "Is Arthur in today?"

"Yeah, he's in. What's it to yous?"

"I'd like to give him something."

The woman scowled. "Eh, fine." She turned around. "Arthur! Yous got a visitor."

Arthur came skipping forward, both eager and wondering why his grandmother called him. The boy looked with curious eyes at his grandma and then at the stranger. Marcus towered over the boy, looking like a giant compared to him. He knelt down and held out the roughly carved PIGZA Mk VI airplane. The boy looked at the airplane, confused by the design. Marcus could tell he had never seen this kind of plane before, let alone any real plane for that matter.

Marcus said, "I wanted to give you this."

The boy looked up at Marcus with pearl blue eyes; Marcus could see the innocence in the boy, much like the one he'd shot. Marcus started shaking and he tensed up, trying to control his speaking and keep his calm. "Take it," he said.

The boy looked up at him in awe. His round freckled face asked the non-verbal question: *Can I really?* He took the plane and ran off smiling. Marcus brought his hand back quickly and needed to get away.

Images of the boy he'd shot flashed through his mind, crowding his thoughts with the sight of the life he took, as well as the villain he'd shot. Voices began calling in his mind, voices of all the dead shouting to him, both the good and bad.

Marcus! Help me!

Save my child, please!

You're a killer! And nothing but a killer!

Murderer!

Baby killer!

Marcus's heart rate shot up, thumping like a racehorse. He stood up straight and the old woman glanced at him with a puzzled look as he took off. Marcus pushed his way forcefully through the crowd, ignoring everyone's rude calls. He approached the gate and was greeted by the same guard he had punched in the abdomen.

"Hey, sonny! We never finished our unfinished business," he said, poking Marcus in the chest.

But Marcus wasn't paying attention to him. He was looking over the guard's shoulder, his mind retracting into a memory from the past. He fought to keep himself in the present, but his body was quickly going into fight or flight mode. Tick . . . tick . . . tick . . .

The guard threw a punch in slow motion at Marcus. Marcus didn't even think as he pivoted, grabbed the guard's arm, then stepped, grabbed the man's tunic by the collar, kicked his leg out from under him, and threw him to the ground before beginning to punch him mercilessly. The man was out in seconds, his arms and legs limp, left with a bloody face that wouldn't be getting any women any time soon.

The entire crowd surrounded them and stared at Marcus in horror before he blinked himself back to reality. He saw the guard on the ground and quickly took in the situation.

Marcus sighed and lowered his head in shame. *I'm sorry, God. I lost it again.* Other guards came rushing to the scene, but Marcus darted through the crowd, avoiding the guards as he escaped through the front gate and back into the forest.

≪━━≫

Marcus had his fist to his head, catching his breath and contemplating what happened. "Lord, I'm not in a stable mind right now. My past is haunting me, and I can't function inside a civilized society. I need help."

The frustration from the guards and the psychological effect of the wars wasn't helping. Marcus thought about the trigger, when he'd looked Arthur in the eye. That was when he'd started to lose it. He hadn't thought, he'd only reacted and let his training take over.

Marcus felt the silence of the forest surrounding him, the peace of the trees, the falling leaves, the lack of activity, and the sun shining through the cracks in the foliage above. He wasn't used to it. Marcus was used to bomb shells and gunfire throughout the night. He was usually able to handle silence well, but now that he was on his own, everything was crashing down.

Marcus had his hand to his face. "God, I need help. I need help, Father."

He looked up towards heaven. "Father, please heal me. Please give me peace of heart, soul, and mind. Lord, I need sleep."

But as usual, the prayer was met with silence. Marcus recited some Scripture. *"Weeping may last through the night, but joy comes with the morning."* Saying the words aloud calmed him, allowing his breathing to stabilize and his heart to slow. Marcus let the peace drape over his shoulders and down his body. He took one final breath and relaxed. "Thank you."

"Hello?" a voice rang out.

Marcus whipped around, magnum in hand and sword ready.

"Hello?" the voice called out again.

Marcus took cover behind a tree and realized it was Arthur and his grandmother. He checked the surrounding area for a possible ambush and waited for them to approach his camp before he revealed himself. Arthur was elated to see him, while his grandmother grunted. Marcus was still a bit out of breath and could hear the voices crowding his mind again as he tried to keep focus on the present. He sheathed the blade but kept the magnum ready. The boy didn't seem to mind and glanced up at Marcus with happy eyes.

Arthur held up the wooden PIGZA plane and said, "I never got to say thank yous, mister!"

The grandmother chimed in, "That's a nice plane yous gave him there." She eyed him and asked, "Where did yous get something like that?"

"I made it," Marcus answered.

The woman seemed surprised. "Yous made it?"

Marcus nodded. "Yes, ma'am."

"Well," she said. "That's some pretty fine work yous did there."

Arthur chimed in, "It's really good, mister! I ain't never seen a plane like this here." The boy looked from the plane to Marcus. "Yous got a talent, mister!"

The compliment sent a ping of emotion through Marcus's chest, like a ripple in a pond, melting the ice in his heart. If Marcus weren't so stoic, he might have shed a tear. But it was enough to hear something good said toward him after all the ridicule and hatred he'd experienced for so long. Marcus straightened, put his right arm across his chest, and bowed slightly. "Thank you, young man," he said.

The boy mimicked Marcus's bow. Marcus raised his head and the grandmother stepped forward and put her hand in a pocket behind her. Marcus braced himself for a weapon of some sort, ready to attack if the old woman played any tricks. But she pulled out a small sewing needle and a band of thread.

She said, "Here, yous earned this with your craftsmanship." The woman laid the needle and thread in Marcus's hand and closed his fingers around them. Then she looked up into Marcus's deep black eyes. "Thank yous for making mi grandson smile." The woman turned and said, "Let's go, Arthur."

The boy waved and said, "Bye mister!" as he ran off with his grandmother.

Marcus held the thread and needle in his hand with slight awe. It had been a while since something had surprised him. That boy's simple thank you had brought Marcus a feeling of joy he hadn't felt in a long time. Not since he'd liberated the Graft Kal Len from the Perion Empire. It sent a flutter of joy through Marcus's chest, filling him with hope and love. He looked at the departing couple and then back at the needle.

Perhaps . . . perhaps I can do other important things in life than just kill. The thought seemed so foreign. Marcus had never imagined he would think something like that. All his life he had been a soldier, fighting bad guys, and he had never quite settled on what he would do now that the wars were over.

Marcus looked up at the clear blue sky and asked, "Is this what you want me to do?"

This time, the clouds parted and a ray of light shined through, as Marcus stared in awe at the sight.

CHAPTER FIVE

A New Profession

"We may not realize it, but God is leading us exactly where we need to be."

—THE SAINT

Arghast Forest

08:03 hrs, 20/04/2258 (15 days A.F.)

Marcus finished his hour-long prayer in the morning and opened his eyes. He was refreshed a little after finally getting some sleep and cleaning himself. He felt good today. He always felt better after he prayed. It relaxed him and brought him back down to earth.

Marcus got up and headed into town. He approached the buildings surrounding the outside of the city gates, noticing how all the houses were beaten down and broken. Marcus approached a butcher working outside his shop as he was trying to cut some meat. Marcus started shaking as he neared the man, but he pushed through his reluctance and said, "Excuse me."

The man chopped the head off the pig he was butchering and then looked up. "Can I help yous?" he asked.

Marcus looked up at the man's shop and noticed the ceiling of the front porch was about to come crashing down. He said, "With respect, do you need help fixing your roof?"

The man looked up at the rotting rooftop and sighed. Marcus could tell he had been aiming to fix it but hadn't gotten around to it. "Agh, yous right," he groaned. But then he shifted his attention back to Marcus and noticed the small book Marcus carried in his jacket pocket at all times. Immediately, the butcher's shared frustration changed to skeptical hatred. "But why would yous help me? Given you're a believer and such."

Marcus answered, "Because I want to love the way my God loves, loving my neighbor as myself."

The man still seemed skeptical but eventually agreed. "Fine. Yous can start whenever yous want, just don't get in the way of mi customers, a'ight?"

Marcus replied, "Yes, sir."

He turned as the man called out, "Sir? I ain't no sir!"

《——一》

Marcus returned to the butcher's shop with an armful of chopped-up lumber from the Kaisk trees. The butcher noticed Marcus didn't have a cart but didn't say anything. Marcus bent over and laid the wood down, pulling out his kukri to whittle the blocks until they were perfect squares.

The butcher watched Marcus work for an hour before he said, "Yous know that if the guards find yous, yous gonna be in serious trouble."

Marcus didn't look up from his work as he replied, "I know."

The butcher saw Marcus working on the blocks one at a time but was bothered by how he was doing it. He went over and grabbed a small hatchet. Marcus looked up immediately and got into a defensive position. The butcher tried to speak calmly to Marcus, saying, "Whoa, easy there."

Marcus defused and inserted his kukri back into its sheath. "Forgive me; I have a bad habit of people attacking me." The butcher approached Marcus and handed him the hatchet peacefully. Marcus took the hatchet and said, "Thank you," giving a slight bow.

The butcher waved him off. "Eh, don't worry about it. Just get that there roof fixed." Marcus almost smiled but he held off.

Marcus took the hatchet and began splitting the pieces of wood into proper pieces. If he had some measuring tape this would be a lot easier, but that was a rarity, even in these days. Marcus also realized he needed a hammer and nails to accomplish this. He hadn't thought about that until now. Marcus asked the butcher, "Excuse me, do you know where I might find a hammer and nails?"

"Ask the blacksmiths if they got a spare hammer to lend yous; nails will have to be made since the materials are so rare these days."

Marcus nodded in understanding. "Where might I find the blacksmith?"

The butcher pointed. "Yous gonna have to go into the Upper Districts for that. And it ain't cheap."

Marcus bowed. "Thank you, Mr. . . . ?"

"Hax. Drew Hax." Hax offered his hand, reluctantly, but still offered it. Marcus grabbed it and gave it a strong shake. The two strong men felt a connection develop between them, reminding Marcus of the comradery he'd had in the military. Marcus felt a small part of himself warm in response. He hadn't felt that way in a long time.

❮—∙—❯

The blacksmith hammered consistently on the new sword as the stranger approached him. The man said, "Hello, I need a hammer and some nails if you have any."

The blacksmith didn't look up. His charcoal-covered hands were crisp with muscle after pounding metal all day every day for ten years. "Metal doesn't come cheap, mi friend," he said.

The blacksmith looked up at the stranger and saw the guy was just as built as he was. Both men measured each other as they stood at the same height and weight. The blacksmith wondered who would win in a fight, but then he saw the sword and weapons on the man's back and knew the answer. *This man is a soldier,* he thought, *and has been for a long time.*

The stranger said, "I don't have any materials to offer."

The blacksmith cocked an eyebrow. "Why come to a place if yous know yous can't pay for anything?"

The man said, "I want to see your inventory. Check out your abilities."

The blacksmith said, "Ah, yous just want to see mi shop and how much

I've got." He stepped closer to the stranger with an intense glare. "Yous planning on robbing mi?"

The man didn't move. "No, sir."

Definitely a soldier.

The blacksmith returned to his work. "I don't have the materials you're looking for. There's a mine a few miles out that has the metal I require to make them but it's dangerous going out there. I hear there's a fort run by the Kotang clan on the mountain. Those Kotang are no joke. They run a multitude of forts throughout the countryside and I hear they are one thousand strong."

"I can make it," the man said flatly.

The blacksmith eyed him. *He's a strange one.* He could tell this man was made of thicker stuff than most and wasn't the type to be bullied by anybody unless he allowed it. The blacksmith said, "Alright friend, if yous get mi the materials from the mine, then I'll craft a hammer and some nails for yous. Deal?"

"Deal."

The blacksmith exchanged a handshake with the soldier and he was off. The blacksmith knew the soldier was wanted in the city and wasn't sure how he got inside without alerting the guards. Whatever. All he cared about was getting the metal from the mine to boost his business. He did shoot one last glance at the stranger before he disappeared. *There's something different about that man,* he thought.

Deep within the Arghast Forest
12:13 hrs, 20/04/2258 (15 days A.F.)

Marcus was glad Hax allowed him to borrow a wagon. It helped make the trip to the mine much easier. But Marcus was going into dangerous territory on his own. He'd asked around, trying to get as much information as he could about the area. People kept telling him to buzz off, but he did overhear that the mine was in bandit territory. Marcus sighed. *Great.*

Marcus had some experience riding animals in the wars, so driving a cart was no problem. Marcus looked up and took in the surrounding area. He was heading back into the forest where he knew the terrain would get rougher the closer he got to the mine, and he was likely to get ambushed on the way there, so he had a few tricks in mind.

Marcus heard a creak in the forest and pulled the cart to a stop. He bowed his head and prayed, asking, *Anything I should worry about?* He waited a few seconds and then saw a figure shift in the shadows. "Bandits."

"You hear that? That's a fresh pickin' for us," Angsley said as he and his crew got in their usual positions, with bowmen on both sides backed up by one man each with a small blade in his hand. They waited as the lone cart approached their normal path. Angsley smiled. *This is too easy*, he thought.

But his smile faded as he realized no one was driving the cart. The donkey pulling it came into view and slowly stopped right in the kill zone of the bandits. The donkey stood there motionless, and curiosity got the better of the four thieves. Angsley sent Gordon to check it out while one of the bowmen stayed with Angsley and the other bowman remained hidden in the forest.

Gordon approached the cart, expecting to find someone inside. Hopefully, a young woman so he could have his way with her. He jumped up in the cart but found it empty. He scratched his fuzzy blonde hair, the sun gleaming off his white skin. Gordon looked at Angsley and then back at the positions of the two bowmen on each side. Then his head exploded as he wheeled back and dropped dead into the cart. His brains splattered all over the donkey. Angsley and the rest of his crew ducked down in cover.

Oh quoitzka! That kinzka has a gun! Angsley hugged the nearest tree. All he had was a sword, so he was relying on the two bowmen to take out the shooter. But the round appeared to have come from a short ways off. Angsley tried to stick his head out in short tangents to avoid getting it blown off, and then he saw the position of the shooter, saw the barrel of the high-powered rifle nesting in a tree about thirty feet away. Angsley motioned his bowman and said, "Cover me," as they spread out in the forest in the direction of the shooter.

They approached the position until they were a few feet away, hopping from tree to tree, hoping the shooter wouldn't get a shot if they moved quickly enough. But nothing had happened since Gordon was killed. It was too quiet. Angsley circled around until he was at the rear of the shooter's position, realizing his bowman had fallen behind in an attempt to be quiet on his approach.

Angsley was alone and only a few feet away from the shooter's position when he realized there was no shooter. Only the gun was left in position. Fear coursed through Angsley's veins like ice. *Where is the shooter?*

He didn't even see the sword plunge through his heart as a hand gripped his mouth, preventing him from screaming. Angsley felt the sharp blade cut through his body like butter as all his strength faded. He was slowly lowered to the ground as the hunter removed the blade from his back and closed Angsley's eyes.

All Angsley could think about was how this hunter had outwitted them. How the man had deliberately shot Gordon to draw them out, then intentionally left his position to set a trap for the approaching group. Then he snuck around and eliminated the group one by one. Angsley thought, *He has to be the sharpest man I've ever met and the last one I'll ever see. What a shame. He would have made a good thief.*

‹‹—•—››

Marcus shifted his head and saw the two bowmen approaching. He hid in the shadows of the forest, waiting for his opportunity. The last thing he wanted was for the two of them to go back-to-back. But he had a little something planned in the direction they were coming from.

The two bowmen paired up and approached the shooter's position. They hadn't heard or seen Angsley and were getting worried that he'd gotten himself killed. Who was this hunter? And what was he doing out here?

Marcus waited, camouflaged as the two bowmen approached the position of their fallen comrade. The bowmen saw the corpse of their fellow bandit and panicked. "Oh my—" They never saw Marcus jump down from a nearby tree, and plunge both his sword and kukri into their hearts. The bowmen could only look at each other as their lives ebbed out of them.

All they heard was, "Hostiles eliminated."

《—■—》

Marcus stared down at the dead bodies all lined up. He wanted to feel something, but staring at the corpses reminded him only of the grimness of this world. He looked at the thief whose head he shot. There wasn't anything to identify him by now. Then he looked at the cart and realized the mess he had made. The brains from the thief had splattered all over the donkey and blood had spilled inside of the cart. He would have to clean that up before he returned it to Hax.

Marcus got to work cleaning out as much of the blood, brains, and skull from the cart as he could using the clothes of the thieves, but without proper soap and water, he knew the cart would be permanently stained with blood. *Sorry, Hax.*

Marcus then went and buried the thieves, giving them small graves next to the road and carving out crosses to place at the head of each one. *Four more hostiles eliminated; four more lives lost.* Marcus didn't feel shame. He didn't want to think about them. But he tried to remind himself they were human so that he didn't forget that he was human.

After Marcus finished burying them, he moved on toward the mine, hoping he wouldn't encounter more bandits on the road.

Laythia

10:10 hrs, 22/04/2258 (17 days A.F.)

Hax's brow furrowed as he saw Marcus approaching with the cart. He was a few days late, but Hax was surprised Marcus had come back at all. The mountain was filled with bandits and no one dared to go up there unless they knew what they were doing. Apparently, Marcus knew what he was doing.

Marcus waved unsmilingly as Hax approached his cart. He smelled blood and looked inside but couldn't see any trace of gore underneath all the mined ore. Hax looked at Marcus skeptically. "Did anything happen while yous were up on the mountain?"

Marcus said flatly, "Not much, sir."

Hax still smelled the strong scent of blood in the cart. He glanced at his mule Robert and saw that he was washed down and cleaned. *That's strange,* Hax thought. *I swears I can smell blood.* Hax looked at Marcus and said, "Well, take this up to the blacksmith and you'll get your materials."

"Roger."

‹‹—·—››

The blacksmith was equally surprised by the gift the soldier had brought. A cart full of metal ore shocked the whole city as it pulled up to his shop. The blacksmith, Kester, knew he had a massive supply now, and judging by the eager looks on everyone's faces, he had a demand.

Marcus jumped down from the cart and said, "Here are your supplies."

Kester creased a smile. "I appreciate the service."

‹‹—·—››

Marcus returned with the supplies and got to work on Hax's shop, hammering nails into the roof, fitting the boards and planks appropriately, making the roof look better, and equipping it to handle the rain more efficiently. Hax stood watching with his hands on his hips, amazed at the soldier's talent. "Hey fella!" he called out. "Where'd yous learn to be so good crafting things and such?"

"I just work hard," Marcus said, resuming his work.

Hax laughed. "Ha! Well, yous got a talent there, mister."

Marcus paused. *"Yous got a talent there, mister"* repeated in his mind. They were just like the words Arthur had said to him.

At dusk, Marcus stepped down from the ladder after hammering in the final nail. He stood next to Hax as they both surveyed the roof. Hax was surprised as he looked around the shop, getting a full picture of the work Marcus had done. The old, withered blocks of wood that had shrouded the building were now replaced with stronger wood planks. What had once been an old grumpy-looking shop was now a premium log cabin, ready to withstand any weather.

Hax said, "I gotta say, yous did a fine job."

Marcus looked at Hax and felt a stirring in his soul. He looked back at the new rooftop he had made and then down at his hands. *I didn't make this. God did.* Marcus said a silent prayer. *Thank you, God, for using me to make this.* He'd had to fight some thieves to get the materials to build this, but Marcus felt something new stir in him. It was . . . hopeful. Marcus looked at the new rooftop, the finely shaped wooden boards nailed together with perfect precision. It was the first time in his life that he realized he could help build something rather than destroy.

Is this what you want me to do, Lord? He felt a warm shift in his heart as if the Holy Spirit inside him was stirring at his comment. Marcus could feel a smile building inside him. It didn't reach the surface—he still had some more healing to do to get there—but it was the start of something he'd never felt before.

CHAPTER SIX

RECONSTRUCTION

"We don't realize how talented we are until we find out much later."

—THE SAINT

Laythia

11:47 hrs, 24/04/2258 (19 days A.F.)

Marcus was reluctant to go, but he knew he had to get this done. He approached the gate where the guard with the triangle beard stood with an arm wrapped in a bandage and his face pummeled. Marcus's war buddies would have laughed at the man for how he looked and cracked some crude joke. He could imagine Caleb making a serious but witty comment about the man's beard. It almost made Marcus smile.

The man instantly recognized Marcus and went to draw his weapon. Marcus raised a hand calmly and said, "I'm not here to fight."

"Yous should have said that the last time," the guard replied in anger.

"I want to see the king."

The guard looked at Marcus with one eye. "Yous wants to see the king? Yous crazy?" Marcus said nothing and stared at him, deadpan. The guard smiled. "Fine, if yous wants to see the king, then it's your funeral." He laughed.

He gestured to another guard to take his place and took Marcus toward the Great Hall of the city. The bearded guard approached two guards standing at the entrance to the Great Hall with Viper 6 submachine guns and said, "This man wants to sees the king."

The two guards frowned at him. "Gobbie, whats you doing?"

"What?" Gobbie asked.

One of the guards, who had an X tattoo on his arm, pointed at Marcus. "You wants to take a man to sees the king and you haven't even relieved him of his weapons?"

Gobbie tried to smile and shrug it off. "Yous sees here . . . uh . . ." Then he lowered his head. "I guess I didn't thinks about that."

The guard looked at Marcus and asked, "What's your business, stranger?"

"I'd like to offer my services," Marcus said.

One of the guards whispered to the other. Marcus could hear him mention how he saw Marcus beat Gobbie. The guard to the right had a tattoo of a blade under his left eye and said, "Weapons off. Then yous can see the king."

Marcus expected that answer. "My weapons stay with me," he said.

An air of tension loomed between them. Gobbie looked at Marcus as if he were crazy.

The guard to the right leaned forward and said, "No weapons, no entry."

"No," Marcus replied.

The main guard eyed Marcus with strong silence before saying, "Fine. You may sees the king, but we all will have our weapons drawn on you."

The whole group took aim at Marcus as they approached the Great Hall and opened the massive wooden doors. The Great Hall was about two hundred feet long and twenty-five feet wide. At the end was an older man, perhaps in his sixties, sitting on a wooden throne with twin Viking-like dragons carved into the arms. The king had long golden hair and a beard, with a red cloak behind him. He reminded Marcus of something of a Viking king from the Medieval Ages.

Standing next to the king was his personal Honor Guard, a man with a darker skin color than the citizens of Laythia, dressed in golden robes and wielding a golden spear. Marcus was impressed with the weapon's craftsmanship as well as the warrior who wielded it. The Honor Guard was clearly a foreigner like himself, and Marcus took one look at him and knew he was a seasoned warrior.

The king stood up and abruptly the chatter from the guards died down. "So, you're the one I've been hearing so much about," he said. "You've been causing me a lot of trouble lately."

Marcus could tell from the man's accent that he wasn't from around here either, but it was best not to mention that; he didn't want to provoke the king. Marcus put his arm to his chest and bowed slightly as he said, "Forgive me, Your Grace. I didn't mean to cause you any problems."

The man stepped down from his throne. "Why have you come here? And why is he armed?" The king glared at his guards. They all shied away.

"I've come to offer my services," Marcus explained.

The king gave a wicked smile. "Oh," he said, unsurprised. "I've heard about your skills. I hear that you took out a band of thieves on your way to mine some ore from Gin-Seng Mountain." Marcus didn't ask the obvious question and remained stoic, but the king answered his unspoken query anyway. "Your friend Hax told me all about it. No man could have gone up to that mountain without encountering some resistance."

But Hax didn't know about the thieves. Marcus eyed the king and knew this man was connected to someone with information. What he was curious about was how well that someone was monitoring his movements.

The king smiled giddily. "I would love to have you in my ranks! With you, we can expand and conquer new territory."

Marcus responded, "Forgive me, Your Grace, but those are not the services I was talking about." The king looked at him quizzically. Marcus continued, "I would like to offer my services to help rebuild your city."

The king was bemused. Then an idea hit him.

He looked up and groaned. "Ah, that's what you're talking about. Yes, I see, the city has been under construction since the Great Wars ended."

He hasn't been constructing anything. Only building his armory, Marcus thought.

The king looked back at Marcus intelligently. "Do this one job for me and I will give you all the supplies you need."

"Such as?" Marcus asked deadpan.

"Go up and slaughter all the thieves on the mountainside and I will give you the supplies."

Marcus replied, "Forgive me, Your Grace, but I must decline."

The king frowned. "Why not? You are a killer, are you not?"

That comment offended Marcus, making him even less interested in the proposition. "I'm not a killer," he said.

"Oh, I disagree. Any man with your talents and skills is clearly a killer. Why, I'll make you the richest soldier in the city if you become my right-hand man."

An enforcer. Marcus tucked his hands behind his back, straightening his spine. "With respect, I must decline."

The king cocked his head sideways quizzically. "I don't understand."

"I don't kill for my own benefit," Marcus answered.

The king narrowed his eyes, stepping down from his stairs and meeting Marcus eye to eye. The king leaned forward. "You are a peculiar one." The guards stood closer, hands drawing to hilts and triggers. "Might there be anything that could change your mind?"

"No," Marcus answered.

"Not even, let's say . . . a woman?"

"No," Marcus answered without hesitation.

"Two women?"

"No."

The king stepped back, flashed his eyebrows up, and smirked. "Ah, how about seven women?"

Marcus lost all interest in the conversation. "No," he replied flatly.

The king showed a flash of anger. "Fine. If you want to waste your talents building houses nobody cares about, then by all means, go ahead." He looked to the guards. "Faal." The Honor Guard stepped forward. "Give this man whatever materials he needs to rebuild the city." Then he looked at

Marcus and added, "But give him forty days to complete the entire city, and he has to find his own workforce, or I'll have him killed."

Marcus just stared at the king, bored and unafraid of what he had in store. It wasn't the first time someone threatened to have him killed. The king waved him away, saying, "Toodle doo!"

Marcus held back rolling his eyes, glad that the conversation was over.

⊁—⊱

Marcus surveyed the buildings all around the city. There was a total of five hundred homes in the city, and around two hundred of them were in need of dire repair. The prior war had left its wounds here, some of them still fresh. The sight of it all gave Marcus pause. *What is the world coming to now? What are the main driving factors? Is the entire planet simply in a state of calm and peace?* But Marcus thought of the thieves on the road, the gangs roaming about, and shook his head. *No, this is just the interim.* He gazed toward the horizon, where storm clouds were brewing behind the mountain. *Something is coming. Something big.*

Marcus took his gaze off the horizon and brought himself back to the task at hand. He had over two hundred houses to fix and no workers. He thought of the logistics; he would need wagons, axes, plenty of wood, and a lot of nails. Which would mean he would have to go back to the mountain. He didn't mind that. He hated being in the city. Hated being engulfed by walls with no open space and surrounded by hundreds of people. He'd had enough bad experiences with cities and preferred being out in the open country. Marcus sniffed the air and could smell the stench of feces and urine spread out in the street due to the poor sewage system in the city. *Disease will break out soon.*

Alongside him walked the Honor Guard, whose name was Faal-li-Nam. Marcus knew what a warrior looked like, and given Faal's looks and accent, he was clearly a seasoned warrior from another country.

Marcus brought his attention back to the city. He noticed a large number of orphaned children roaming the streets, some in burlap, some wearing whatever clothes they could find or steal. Marcus wished it broke his heart to see the kids all left to die, but it didn't. Although there was a deep place in his heart for the orphans of the world, he had seen so many of them that they no longer affected him.

Marcus remembered a verse from Scripture. *"Love your neighbor as yourself."* He didn't think of the verse to feel its calling to him, but it reminded him of when he gave Arthur that toy plane and how overjoyed the boy felt. Marcus usually kept his distance from children and crowds, which was why he was reluctant to be in the city in the first place. He still hated crowds and didn't want to be anywhere near them, but his work in the city brought him out of his comfort zone and forced him to interact with the locals.

He saw a kid sitting half-dead against a broken shack. The boy looked up, a skeleton in his skin, and saw Marcus kneel down. Marcus foraged through his pocket and pulled out what looked like some berries. He gave the berries to the young boy, who stared at him with wide eyes and then down at the food. The boy held the berries in his hands like they were gold and started to cry.

Marcus felt something strike his heart, chipping away at the stone inside. He had forgotten the joy of giving to others. He would always help kids during the wars, but after the recent conflicts, Marcus had stopped giving to the youth.

More children came when they saw Marcus handing out food, but he backed away and was on his way before they could get to them. Marcus felt his heartbeat increase and his anxiety kick in. He recited Scripture in his mind to calm himself. *"'For I know the plans I have for you,' declares the Lord, 'plans to prosper you and not to harm you, plans to give you hope and a future.'"* Marcus recited the verse and felt its assurances calm him.

Faal watched Marcus with an eyebrow cocked. Marcus met his gaze. "Forgive me. I . . . I don't handle children well."

Faal said, "You have scars, believer, as we all do. But you carry more than most."

Marcus wanted to feel amazed at Faal's wisdom, but he didn't. He suddenly felt very tired.

Marcus resumed his focus on the task at hand: fixing up the houses. After he counted each of the buildings and assessed the amount of lumber required for each of them, he calculated how much time it would take to chop all the wood and bring it back to the city, as well as the cost for the workers to achieve this. The only problem was that there were no workers. Marcus was starting this project all on his own.

Marcus turned to Faal. "Faal, do you know where we can hire some workers?"

"Best go to the taverns and simply ask."

"Where are the taverns?"

"Follow me." Faal led Marcus with his spear in hand to the rougher side of town. The conditions of the city deteriorated, and Marcus could sense evil brewing here. Faal gestured to a rough-looking establishment that was only two stories high, but still taller than any other building around. It had a large lounge on the first floor and a square roof, allowing the guests to eat and dine atop. Faal gestured towards its door. "You'll find your workers in there."

Marcus went in alone. Faal stayed outside, watching Marcus's figure disappear inside the establishment. Soon there was the sound of a massive scuffling, glasses being broken, a knife thrown, and eventually a gunshot. Marcus came out seconds later and said, "They said no." Faal was unsurprised and the two of them walked back.

They spent the rest of the day looking for workers to hire but no one in the entire city agreed to help. Marcus sighed and said to Faal, "I'm going to take some time to pray. I'll be back tomorrow so we can begin."

Faal nodded but did nothing. It wasn't his job to help build the houses, only to watch this stranger who just so happened to walk into this city with a strange set of skills and values.

⁂

Marcus returned to his camp in the forest, the sun setting and the approaching stars gleaming in the distance. He sat in front of the fire with his hands crossed and head down. He remained there for over an hour asking the same thing, "Father, please, provide me workers to complete this job. Father, please provide me workers like you did with Nehemiah. Please."

Marcus felt his body grow calmer than it had felt in a while. He felt his mind elevate and his soul lift. Other than battle, prayer and talking to God in silence were the only things that seemed to relax him. He stilled his mind, calming it to a smooth pond with no wind. His body settled and grew comfortable in its position. Marcus felt a slow and comfortable rush of peace course up from his heart and smooth over his shoulders. He kept his hands clasped together, continually praying, "Father, please provide me workers."

He took a breath before continuing. "Yet I want your will be done." He accepted the decision of whether God would provide workers or not. If God chose not to, then God had a very good reason. And if he chose to, then Marcus would accomplish his goal.

Marcus didn't think much about the king's threats. He didn't find them credible in any sense. So, he continued on, remembering them but not letting them block his efforts.

He prayed again, going for another hour, and afterward, he was able to fall asleep and rest through the night.

While he slept, Marcus saw a giant red tide coming up from a small lake. The water gushed out from the lake's boundaries. Marcus watched overhead as the bloody water spread in all directions with immense speed. Embedded in the lake was the symbol of an iron red cross. Thorns and beautiful flowers grew from it, planting in the soil wherever it stretched, growing strong trees despite there being no water. The overwhelming tide encroached upon everything it touched until it had its sights on Marcus.

The bloody lake transfixed Marcus. It reshaped into three figures and a body. It almost looked . . . familiar. The three figures were a bear, an eagle, and a rose. At the top of the body was a snakehead, a figure Marcus didn't recognize. But it knew him. The red figure as a whole stretched its arms out and welcomed Marcus. But Marcus knew it was a lie. He knew this coming tide would mark assured destruction wherever it went as fire reigned and burned down everything in the world. The red figure shouted in a multitude of voices, voices that Marcus recognized, "THEY ARE COMING! THEY ARE COMING!"

Marcus awoke from his dream, neither sweaty nor fearful. But this time he felt he should be. This dream felt like something else. *A vision, perhaps?* Marcus glanced up at the night sky, the world still turning. *Father, was that a warning?*

Marcus received no answer, but he knew that dream meant something. He didn't accept it as a direct answer yet, so he held the dream in the back of his mind, having a feeling it would come back to him later.

Tettenhall, Gin-Seng Mountain

19:28 hrs, 24/04/2258 (19 days A.F.)

The fort roared with applause and laughter. Willow sang with his fellow bandits with a large pint of ale in his hand as the hall was filled to the brim with Kotang members. He stepped outside to catch some air, taking in the sight of the rest of the massive square fort of Tettenhall. The party was just as loud outside as it was inside. Nowhere in the fort was there a quiet moment that was not full of celebrating.

Willow looked around at the partying fort, observing the massive thirty-foot walls made of wood, iron, and steel. He observed the catwalks stretching all around the sides of the square fort, built into the side of Gin-Seng Mountain, and the massive firepower they had built up. There were huge light machine guns around all the sides, and even some cannons they were able to forge. They may be thieves, but they were good craftsmen as well.

He half-drunkenly went up the steps to the higher levels of the catwalk toward Commander Margo Vincent's office, who was not partaking in the party. Running a massive gang was no easy feat and as second in command, Willow would ensure things went smoothly . . . in the morning, of course.

Willow laughed to himself and took a big swig from his stein. He approached the door to the commander's office and slammed it open, finding a somber environment waiting inside. The room was candle-lit and warm, protecting them from the freezing air outside. Willow saw the faces inside, his good friend Welsh who was third in command, along with Mak, the fourth in command, standing next to him. Welsh had fine white hair and a fairly strong body, as did Mak, who stood there with a shaved head and a grim goatee. But neither of them could compare to the commander of the Kotang sitting in his chair behind his desk. The mere sight of the desk and the massive man behind it emanated power, power that Willow would like to command one day, should his commander have a tragic *accident*. But for now, he would play the puppy and adhere to his commander's orders.

Willow quickly took in the atmosphere of the room and realized it was grim. Before Willow could ask, Commander Margo said, "Ah Willow, perfect timing. I was just about to send for you."

Willow was a bit confused as he studied the faces in the room and realized he was about to be hit with something serious. In the flash of a moment, Willow sobered up and asked, "What is it, Commander?"

Margo stood from his desk, observing Willow and his Prince-Charming-blonde hair. Margo said, "We've been receiving reports of some of our lesser groups being ambushed and killed."

Willow tilted his head at that last word. *Killed?* Willow asked, "Are you saying there's someone out there hunting our men?"

The commander nodded. "Yes. And we need to kill this kinzka so that he stops impeding our efforts. It makes the Kotang look weak."

Mak spoke up, though it wasn't his place to. "What should we do, Commander?"

The commander said, "We've received a tip that he is in Laythia."

Willow smiled wickedly. "Ah, the Laythians, our longtime enemies. What do they want with this man?"

The commander said, "You know what they want."

Willow grinned wider. "As you wish."

CHAPTER SEVEN

THE WORKERS

"Sometimes you need to just start working to get something done."

—THE SAINT

Laythia

08:18 hrs, 25/04/2258 (20 days A.F.)

Marcus approached the gate to the city, still avoiding all the people, and found Gobbie standing there bored. Gobbie raised an eyebrow. "Yous gonna start the works on the buildings and whatnot?"

Marcus answered, "I'm starting on your house today."

Gobbie tilted his head in confusion. "What?"

Marcus asked, "Do you mind showing me to your home so I may begin?"

Gobbie appeared reluctant, his goblin-like face and nose shriveled. "Eh, a'ight." He looked at the other guard. "Bo, take over for mi."

Gobbie showed Marcus through the city streets to his home. Gobbie had a two-story house that he shared with a lot of family members. Kids were running about and his parents were still living there. Marcus sized up the building and knew this was going to be difficult given the height. Having a two-story home in Laythia symbolized wealth, as most homes were one-story high. The building was also perched on the hillside, so working on the roof would be challenging. Marcus hoisted his pack and got out the tools the blacksmith had offered him, as well as all the spare nails he'd been able to craft from the huge metal deposit Marcus had brought back.

Gobbie introduced Marcus to all of his family members living in the house. "This is Billy, Billy Joe, Billy Joe B., Billi with an 'I', Billy Joe B. Jr., Billy Joe B. Senior . . ." Marcus remembered the names of everyone in the family. The age range went from newborn to sixty. Quite the family to have. The parents were in their mid-sixties and looked to have worked their entire lives to raise a healthy home. Gobbie introduced Marcus to his parents and said, "This man has come to improve our home for the time being."

Gobbie's father, Lucious, flared with anger. "Improve! Nothing needs to be improved." Gobbie looked up and saw different. The roof looked like it was ready to cave in from a raindrop, but Gobbie's dad waved him off.

Marcus spoke calmly, lowering his voice, "Forgive me, but I have to get this done."

Gobbie's father squared up to Marcus. Marcus was easily a head taller than the overweight man, but Gobbie's father responded, "Oh yeahs? And why might that be?"

"I have my reasons."

Lucious scoffed, "Well, it looks like we got ourselves a Saint here!" He aimed his rage at Gobbie. "Who is this man yous got involved with? And why is he offering free work?" Luscious chided with a mock smile, "Heh, maybe he's one of those believers Gob, don't ya think? Them believers are the ones who started all those wars in the first place.

Gobbie looked at Marcus, but Marcus was stone-cold and unreadable. He waited for Lucious to finish his rant until he finally stormed off, telling the rest of the family about the man working on their home. They all gave Marcus death stares, some looking like they would actually attack him. Marcus paid no attention to them and focused on the roof.

Gobbie said, "Yous got your work cut out for yous, Saint."

Marcus stared at him a moment too long, as if he had seen a ghost. Gobbie was getting a little uncomfortable from the pause and wondered what the man was thinking.

"Good luck," Gobbie said as he departed.

He heard the Saint respond, "There's no such thing as luck."

«——·——»

The evening sun cast the world in shades of orange and yellow. It was always a beautiful sight to watch the sunset from the hillside of the city. Once evening had fallen, Gobbie returned home and looked up to see the Saint's progress. The whole right side of the house had been replaced with a new set of light brown boards, which looked much better compared to the bland, dark brown boards they'd previously used.

"Wow," Gobbie said. "This is some nice works, Saint."

He could see the Saint at the top of the ladder, hammering in the final nails for the right side of the house. The Saint knocked a spare hammer and it fell to the ground. For some reason, Gobbie went over and picked up the tool.

The Saint called from above, "Could you hand me that, please?" He shifted over, opening up the ladder.

Gobbie saw the opportunity and decided to go with it. He hoisted himself up on the ladder, stretching out his muscles after standing the whole day watching people enter and exit the city. Gobbie carried the tool to the top of the ladder and handed it to the Saint. The Saint took it and said, "Thank you."

Gobbie surveyed the work up close and saw that it was going to keep the roof from leaking like it had in the past. It was well done.

He nodded and said, "Nice job here," and that was the truth. Gobbie was legitimately impressed with the Saint's craftsmanship. But he looked out at all the sides of houses the Saint needed to fix and knew there was too much work and not enough time for him to complete it alone.

The Saint said, "Thanks," and got to work on the other side.

Gobbie stopped him. "I think that's enough for now."

The Saint nodded. "You're right. I don't want to bother your family when they're sleeping." The Saint followed Gobbie down the ladder and picked up his things. "I'll resume this work tomorrow. Farewell, Gobbie."

Gobbie cocked an eyebrow. "Yous too."

Laythia

10:31 hrs, 26/04/2258 (21 days A.F.)

The next morning the Saint came back and got to work on the other side of the roof. Gobbie saw the progress the Saint had made in only a couple of hours when he stepped out to relieve himself. He was nearly done.

Gobbie looked up at the Saint as he worked on the final board near the front of the house. It was dangerously close to the ledge. The Saint was having some difficulty getting the final board planted and holding himself up. Gobbie watched him struggle and called out, "Come on, Saint, yous ain't gonna gets that final board if yous gonna keep hanging like that."

The Saint said nothing and continued. He tried hoisting himself up with one arm while holding the last plank in place, but that left him with neither hand free to hammer the nails in. The Saint eventually dropped the board, letting it fall next to Gobbie. Gobbie laughed and picked it up.

"Haha, I knew it. Yous needs help, don't yous?"

The Saint answered his question casually, not offended at all at his asking. "Yes, I do."

For some reason, Gobbie brought the final plank back up to the Saint as he perched on the second floor of his house. He stood and watched the Saint try again, but this time Gobbie found himself intervening. Why Gobbie was helping, he didn't know, but he said, "Here, I'll hold this here plank down and yous hammer it in, got it?"

"Yes, sir," the Saint said.

The Saint hung from the ledge, hammer ready, while Gobbie put the plank down and held the nails in place. He realized that he was trusting this stranger next to him to hammer the nails in when he could hit him at any time. Gobbie remembered the last couple of times when the Saint had punched him and both were not fun. He held the nails nervously in place while the Saint, as if not noticing Gobbie's thoughts, said, "Keep the nails still."

Gobbie held the nails in place as the Saint hammered them in, not missing a single mark. As the final nail was inserted, both Gobbie and the Saint stepped off and observed their work. Gobbie looked up at the roof and realized something. *I was a part of that.* He stared at that last board he had helped put into place. The Saint wouldn't have been able to do it on his own. Gobbie felt a sense of pride in having helped with the last plank. He knew it was stupid to feel that way, but he couldn't help but feel like he was part of something greater.

"Wow," he said, surveying the completed triangle roof. "It looks great."

The Saint had his hands on his hips. "It sure does," he answered, grabbing Gobbie's shoulder and giving him a shake. Gobbie chuckled at the comradery. The Saint said, "Thank you for helping me. I couldn't have done it without you."

Gobbie felt a rush of joy flood his heart from that compliment. It was a compliment that gave him purpose and touched his very soul. Gobbie turned back to the house. "Nah, yous did most of the works."

"Maybe," the Saint said. "But I still needed help." He looked up and added, "Time to get to the next one."

He headed toward the house next to Gobbie's and laid his tools out. Gobbie thought for a moment about joining him. He could help the Saint rebuild the houses in the district. He thought about how monotonous his job of standing guard at the Main Gate was and how a change of pace would be good for him.

Bo would have him covered anyway. Gobbie walked toward the Saint and said, "Got room for one more?"

The Saint looked at him, almost seeming happy. "Of course. You are free to help out if you'd like."

The same process repeated, this time faster. Gobbie handed the Saint the pre-cut pieces of wood and helped him nail them into the rooftop of the next house. Instead of taking a full day, it only took half a day. When they were finished, both Gobbie and the Saint surveyed their work. The light brown wood frames on each triangle house were dramatically improved in both their quality and weather protection.

Gobbie nodded. "These are some nice houses," he said, feeling that same wonderful accomplishment as he had with his own house. It flooded his heart and filled him with purpose.

The Saint turned to Gobbie and said, "Nice job. You did well today."

Gobbie was surprised and impressed with this man's gratitude. Gobbie remembered treating him harshly at first, and now he found himself receiving compliments about working hard. It sparked a feeling he wished he'd received from his father. Gobbie was still in his twenties, but the Saint had a look to him that made him seem neither young nor old, making it impossible to tell his age. But Gobbie could tell that the Saint was at least older than himself. It felt almost like the Saint was a lost older brother to Gobbie.

Gobbie gave a soft smile. "Thanks."

The Saint broke a tiny sliver of a smile. Gobbie saw it and was surprised. *Wow, this guy does smile.* The Saint's stoic demeanor made him look stone-cold, appearing expressionless the majority of the time. But for this moment, the Saint was happy, however little he showed it.

A question formed on the roof of Gobbie's mouth. "Can I ask yous a question?"

"Ask away," the Saint said, rubbing his hands free of dirt.

"Why are yous doing this?"

The Saint answered, "Because it's what God would have done."

Gobbie wasn't ready to get into a religious discussion, and he was initially skeptical about this fellow because he was a believer in a god. These days, people didn't like anyone who believed in a higher power. They blamed the believers of any god for the start of all the wars in the past, so there was much persecution of believers. Gobbie had never entertained any questions of religion before, but after meeting this stranger, he was curious. "What do yous mean?"

The Saint answered, "God would have helped because that's what life is all about. Loving God and loving others."

"I don't understand."

"It's simple, life is not about you. You can have all the things in the world, but in the end it's all worthless. The only thing truly important is loving God and loving others."

Gobbie shook his head. "I'm not sure I believe yous."

The Saint shrugged. "That's your choice."

"But I don't understand. What is it yous are trying to achieve?"

Marcus didn't answer. "You wouldn't believe me if I told you. For now, trust that I am doing this because I want to do the right thing."

Gobbie didn't have the words to answer. He had never heard someone speak like this before, so he let the conversation die. The Saint understood the discussion was over, but it had ended in a healthy way. The Saint picked up his tools and said, "Thanks for the help today. I deeply appreciate it." He strode off to work on the next house, leaving Gobbie's heart in wonder and with a whirl of questions.

Laythia

16:56 hrs, 27/04/2258 (22 days A.F.)

The following day was the same. Gobbie helped the Saint with another house and felt that same feeling. The joy of serving. It happened day after day, leaving Gobbie with more questions than before.

Gobbie was on his way home from work. His absence from his position at the front gate was catching up to him, but he strolled through the city, going nowhere. He didn't want to be at his house right now. All the drama from his family drove him insane. He liked walking through the city when it was calm, just to think and enjoy the peace of the world.

Gobbie strode through a random street and to his surprise found the Saint standing there overlooking some hungry children.

Gobbie watched the Saint reach into his pocket and pull out a small chunk of bread. The children wowed in awe at the sight of it. It made Gobbie himself feel hungry. *Where in the world did this man get bread?* The Saint then broke it apart to give a piece to each of them.

They waved their friends to come forward until more children came rushing up, quickly surrounding the Saint, but the Saint gave them the rest of the bread and backed off before the crowd of children could overwhelm him. Gobbie found that reaction curious, but he couldn't shake the feeling that there was something different about this man. That he had something no one else had. His only question was, what was it?

CHAPTER EIGHT

A Helping Hand

"Help can come from the most random of places. But it's welcome all the same."

—THE SAINT

Laythia

12:19 hrs, 29/04/2258 (24 days A.F.)

Gobbie sat at lunch with his best friend and fellow guard, Bo, at one of the local taverns. But Gobbie wasn't eating. For the first time in his life, he wasn't hungry, and he wasn't sure whether that was a good or bad thing.

Bo stared at him curiously. "Something wrong with the food?" he asked cautiously. The sight was new to him as well.

The two of them sat there in silence for a minute before Gobbie spoke.

"Yous ever wonder why a person is kind?" he asked. Bo only tilted his head in confusion. "I mean like, have yous ever had a person be nice to yous when yous weren't nice back?"

Bo raised his head. "Yeah, I have. It was this one time when I went to mi cousin Dickory's house and I accidentally spilled their dinner all over the floor and they still cleaned it up and ended up giving mi the best foods for some reason."

"Did they ever tell yous why they did it?"

Bo shook his head. "I just brushed it off and assumed they're nice peoples and such."

"Huh." Gobbie lowered his gaze to the table. "That must say something about a person if they can do that."

Gobbie lowered his head even more. He knew he would never have the gall to do that. To forgive an enemy. To Gobbie, that was one of the hardest things a fellow could do.

Gobbie thought about the work the Saint had done on his house, and how nice it looked once it was all finished. He thought about the other houses they'd worked on together and how that made him feel good. Then he remembered the Saint talking about how life was all about loving God and loving others. Gobbie wasn't sure if what that man said was true, but he couldn't deny that the Saint was right on how it felt good to be nice to people. Gobbie had never really been nice to anyone since no one had been nice to him, especially his pa.

Gobbie looked up at Bo, who still had that worried look, and said, "I think we should help the Saint out more with the repair job."

Bo was sipping his drink as Gobbie spoke and choked. He smacked his chest and buck-shot vapors from his mouth. Gobbie laughed hard at the ale splattered all over the table. Then Bo wiped his face and said, "Yous crazy? Why would we do that?"

"Because I said so, yous buck-toed idiot." Gobbie got up and went to the door, grabbing his bread to go. "Now come on, we got work to do."

❮——❯

Marcus brushed the sweat off his brow and looked up at the half-finished house with the sun beaming overhead. It had grown hot over the past couple of days and Marcus still wasn't done with more than ten houses. Only one-hundred and ninety to go. But he was getting faster. He drank some water out of a nearby bowl and splashed some on his face.

Marcus looked down the road and saw Gobbie walking by with one of his fellow guards. The two of them approached Marcus and laid their weapons aside. Marcus said nothing as Gobbie rolled up his sleeves and his friend did the same. Gobbie tried to stand up straight and perk his head up. "We're here to help yous," he said.

Marcus continued toward the opposite side of the house and said, "Let's get started." He wanted to feel happy but no emotion came forward. Deep down he was pleased, but he didn't recognize it. Marcus was skeptical. He didn't always trust people when they offered their services for free. Regardless, Marcus would appreciate their help.

They got to work and were making steady progress. It was much easier having two people than one, and three were better than two. It reminded Marcus of a saying in Scripture. *"A person standing alone can be attacked and defeated, but two can stand back-to-back and conquer. Three are even better, for a triple-braided cord is not easily broken."*

It brought Marcus joy to be working with others again. It reminded him of his time in the military, of the close bonds he'd felt with his comrades in combat, how they'd saved his life and he'd saved theirs. But he also remembered the cost that came with war. The loss of life, the loss of dreams, and the people who would never go home again. Every time Marcus had lost a friend, he'd lost a part of himself. It was hard in war. It brings you to your limits and even then, it still pushes you further.

As the three of them were up on the roof, Marcus heard someone call, "HEY!" He looked down and saw it was Arthur and his grandmother. The ginger-haired boy came to them with sweets in his hand, wrapped in a handkerchief. Gobbie and Bo were more than eager to climb down to receive some treats, as desserts were a rarity these days. Marcus came down too and found Arthur and his grandmother had baked a batch of fruitcake for them. Gobbie and Bo were already digging in, although they looked guilty about diving in before Marcus.

Marcus stepped down and asked, "What's all this?"

Arthur said, "We heard yous were fixing up the town so we wanted to give yous this." He gestured to the half-eaten fruitcake.

Marcus was skeptical towards the free gift but he saw that Gobbie and

Bo were eating it, so it must be ok. Marcus took a bite and let the fruity dough sag in his mouth.

Marcus swallowed and bowed slightly. "Thank you. That's very kind."

Arthur handed the rest of the cake to Marcus and ran off. His grandmother passed by and said, "Just be sure to give him another toy when yous comes by."

Marcus bowed his head. "I will."

The grandmother strode off, mumbling as she vanished into the city with her grandson, "And what's with all that bowing? So formal all the time."

Marcus knew it wasn't much, but the fact that he was working in a city of people and was able to have conversations and work with others again was remarkable. He had some more fruitcake, feeling the rough and cakey dough stick in his mouth, as he let the fruity taste soak his tastebuds.

Is it possible that I'm feeling . . . good? Marcus felt his senses enhance and he checked his surroundings. It was strange to be living in a time without war. To live in a small world with no conflict. With no rush to do anything. To just live life and be. It had always been go go go for Marcus and he hadn't known how he would ever adjust to civilian life. But here he was now, working with two coworkers and engaging with a young boy and his grandmother. Civilians had always been far away from the warzone, at least those who could get out of it. Marcus usually just passed by and let them be or would tend to their wounds when he had the time or resources, although he did try to interact with them wherever he went because it was important to get to know the community and share the love of God with them.

Even when the project was over, Marcus could envision himself doing this again, going around, fixing up the world after it had been broken, and sharing the love of God. He nodded. *That would be nice.*

But he remembered that dream. That dream of that flooding lake, which he knew was evil, but what was it truly about? Marcus didn't know. But this dream gave him a feeling that he couldn't shake. A feeling . . . that something was coming, something *terrible*.

<< —•— >>

The group finished a couple of houses in one day rather than half a house. The team congratulated itself and high fives were given. Marcus thanked Gobbie and Bo for helping out, hoping they would stick around.

Even though he didn't show it, Marcus didn't expect Bo and Gobbie to show up again, this time with more of their work buddies. The next day turned out to be more productive, and they were even more productive the following week. Marcus couldn't help but feel excited about the progress they were making. If they were lucky, their force would continue to grow until they completed all the houses before the deadline.

CHAPTER NINE

SETBACK

"Would you still do the right thing if everyone hated you for it?

—THE SAINT

Laythia

13:38 hrs, 30/05/2258 (55 days A.F.)

Marcus and the group of now ten workers made steady progress on the following houses. The growing heat was not helping, but having the extra hands did. More and more people were joining the movement every day and it was looking promising that they were going to finish by the end of the month. They had completed over one-hundred and eighty homes, with the additional ten Marcus had completed initially, and they still had five days left.

Marcus took a break and went down to grab some water. The rest of the men were working on the house when suddenly the streets cleared. The other working men didn't see the change, but Marcus noticed right away. This sort of thing would happen when he was deployed in foreign cities dealing with local militia and terrorist groups. Marcus heard a rumbling in the distance; after so many years of combat in the dark, his ears had honed themselves to pick up sounds most people wouldn't. Marcus tried to decipher what each sound meant. *Two . . . three . . . carts. Carts?* Then it all clicked.

Marcus yelled, "Get down!" but the three carts, all driven by wild donkeys, pulled up as masked men exploded from the backs and fired bows,

Barista FKs, and Viper 6 submachine guns at Marcus and all the workers. Bullets pinged and flew everywhere, ruining the house and mortally wounding nine out of the ten workers.

The weapons quickly went silent as they ran out of ammunition. Marcus unholstered his magnum and withdrew from cover, spotting the closest cart and firing three rounds into the back of it. His rounds caught two of the attackers, ripping the arm off one and burrowing a deep hole in the chest of the other. The three carts drove off in haste as Marcus threw his SR75k over his shoulder and clambered to the roof of a building. He ran to the highest point, getting an overview of where the carts might be going. He spotted one heading west and followed it on the rooftops, jumping from building to building in hopes of catching up to it. When he came to the edge of the district he stopped, looking over the most open space in the city.

He spotted a single cart heading west and loosed his rifle from his shoulder. Marcus controlled his breathing, expanding and clearing his lungs with full control. He inhaled through his nose and exhaled through his mouth, hearing the thump of his heart as the world faded. His only focus was on the driver in the cart. He lined up his sights and inhaled, hearing only the sound of his own heartbeat, then exhaled into his natural respiratory pause. *Thump thump . . . Thump thump . . . Thump thump . . .* The cross reticle focused on the head of the driver. His finger subconsciously thumbed the trigger, until the world froze at the perfect moment.

The barrel of the rifle exploded as the .50 caliber round fired at 850 meters per second,[12] striking the skull of the driver and splitting his brain into a thousand pieces like a watermelon. His body went limp and the cart slowed as the driver barreled over. Another assailant took the reins of the cart and vanished into the city.

Marcus returned to the crime scene, only to find the dismay he always found. Nine of the workers had been successfully hit; the assailants had

____

12. 2790 ft/s

taken their time to effectively plan this attack. Marcus found Gobbie holding Bo as he bled out in his arms. Marcus didn't need to be a doctor to know the boy was done for. So, he knelt and waited for Bo's end to come.

Gobbie cradled Bo's head and cried, begging his friend to keep his eyes open. Marcus saw Bo's wounds; the boy, roughly twenty years old, had four bullet wounds in his chest and two arrows in his stomach. Marcus kept quiet. Gobbie begged his friend, "Bo! Bo, please don't die!" He crumpled forward as he felt his friend fading.

Marcus and Gobbie's eyes met as Gobbie asked him, "Saint! What do we do? How do we fix this?" But Marcus only gave him that same sad compassion he had given to so many comrades. Marcus took Bo by the hand, stepping into his line of sight.

"Bo, do you believe in God?" Marcus spoke slowly and calmly. Bo tried to keep his focus on Marcus and shook his head. Marcus asked him, "Do you know that God sent his Son to come down and die for us long ago in order to bring us salvation?" Marcus waited for Bo to respond, but the boy only had seconds left. Even so, Marcus didn't rush a single moment. "Would you like to accept God into your life and let him forgive you of your sins? Because this is the last chance." Bo only shook his head as he leaned back and felt his life drain out of him.

Gobbie looked at Marcus and was frustrated to see the lack of sorrow in his expression. Marcus wanted to feel sad, but he had stopped feeling that emotion when watching someone die long ago. Gobbie felt his anger boil in his stomach. "Yous. Yous did this!"

He looked at Gobbie with a blank expression. Gobbie couldn't tell whether Marcus felt bad about this or not. "You're why these men died! If yous hadn't butted into our lives, then these men would be alive!"

Marcus only stared at Gobbie with that same blank expression. Gobbie was surprised that he wasn't reacting at all, but Marcus merely stood up and looked over the other dead bodies around the building. All nine workers were dead, and there was no bringing them back. Marcus glared at the sight, comparing it to so many others he'd seen over the years. It was never new. Loss was always loss.

"We need to bury them," Marcus said softly.

Gobbie got up in frustration. "Yous bury 'em! I'll bury mi own. Yous filthy Saint!" Gobbie picked up Bo's corpse and walked away, leaving Marcus alone. He sighed. *Another bloody massacre.*

⸭—⸭

"We shall go after these culprits at once," the king said. "We will not rest until they are brought to justice."

Marcus had heard those words before. He only glared at the king with bored skepticism. It didn't matter. The king was only spouting words as a formality. Marcus knew he would get no justice, and he knew they would come after him again. Let them.

Gobbie stood glaring at Marcus with intense anger. Marcus had seen that anger before, too many times. He hoped Gobbie would calm down after a time, but only God knew what the boy would do. They stood in the Great Hall as the king addressed the current situation. Marcus could care less about what he said. He knew the king would do nothing. He had that look on his face of a politician, a politician who would do nothing except rile up the crowd in his favor, and that could be dangerous. Marcus had to tread carefully because he knew there was more going on than he realized.

⸭—⸭

Hax was busy finishing up the final touches on his work for the day when he saw Marcus looming toward his shop. He took one look at his face and saw a man in gloom. Marcus had a dark aura as he approached the shop and met the eyes of Hax. Hax saw great darkness in those eyes, controlled but ready to be unleashed.

Marcus only said, "I'm going to need to borrow your cart, Hax. Please."

Arghast Forest

23:11 hrs, 30/05/2258 (55 days A.F.)

Willow and his men were stationed on the crossroads, ready for another late-night ambush. As part of the Kotang gang, they would pillage and kill anyone to get their goods. But there had been a slip-up recently that had kicked the hornets' nest. An intruder had gone into their territory and taken metal ore without their knowing. The same intruder Commander Margo said had killed one of their ambush squads and another of their small gangs in a nearby village. The Kotang clan had eventually killed everyone in that village but before the townsfolk were all gone, they said a wounded man had left their town little over a month ago after they refused to help him. They were told he lived in the forest, but by the time they got there, he had moved into the city of Laythia.

Willow, as second in command, swore he would get the kinzka-de-hejo who'd killed their men. Willow had almost gotten him earlier today in the city of Laythia when they did a drive-by. They killed nine of his workers, but they had missed their main target, and as a result two of their men were killed and one lost an arm. Whoever this target was, he was good.

Willow brought his focus back to yet another cart coming down the road, all too eager to spring forth, slice their throat, and take their loot. But Willow and his eight men were surprised when it was an empty cart. The cart came to a stop and the group approached it with caution. They had already lost one group from the intruder and did not want to lose another. That's why they'd reinforced their numbers and weapons. All of them now had automatic weapons and submachine guns, though ammo was short.

One of them approached the empty cart but reared over and vomited on the side. The thief said, "Willow, you're gonna wanna see this."

Willow strode out from the cover of the forest and stepped up into the cart. Written in blood were the words: *I want to meet.* A location scrawled beneath was the village of Elum, at midnight tomorrow. Willow knew the village. It was the same one they'd burned down. It had even had a bald old man who was a good shot with the bow. Willow had killed him without a second thought.

Willow smiled. "Good. Let's go catch a fish."

Elum Village, Arghast Forest
23:00 hrs, 31/05/2258 (56 days A.F.)

Twenty-four hours later, Willow, Mak, and forty men stood in secret locations all around Elum. The village was burnt to a crisp and surrounded by forest, creating perfect hiding places in dozens of locations. Only Willow stood out in the open. He had to sell the act. They'd even brought the cart the stranger had left with the message. Strange thing for a feller to write a message in blood, but then again, there wasn't much else to write with these days.

They waited one hour, then two, then three. His men beginning to fall asleep. Willow constantly had to remind them to keep their wits about or this guy would slit their throats. But even Willow was growing tired of all this standing around. Another hour went by and then another.

In his rage, Willow picked up a broken lantern and chucked it at the ground. "Son of a Chinkza! He didn't show!"

Tettenhall, Gin-Seng Mountain
03:27 hrs, 01/06/2258 (57 days A.F.)

Willow, Mak, and his men returned to their hideout Tettenhall, at the base of Gin-Seng Mountain. Willow was frustrated and tired. That bloody stranger threw them for a loop and did nothing but waste their time. They came to the large wooden gates of Tettenhall and called out, "Hey crackhead!" Silence. Willow called out again, "Hey crackhead! You lousy soap of suds. Open the gate!" No answer.

Willow was out of patience and slammed his fist against the big wooden doors, which opened easily with a creak. Willow and his men were surprised they'd opened. He pushed open the doors and gasped at what he saw. Hundreds of men, the entire force of the fort, were all dead. Small fires fluttered while the main wooden buildings were completely burnt down. Ash was still present in the air as stains of blood pocketed the ground and walls. Bullet holes and slash marks marked the buildings and walls. A few days ago, this place was brimming with life; now it was a hollow shell of the past.

"Who could've done this?" one of Willow's men asked in fear. In the center of the courtyard were the hundreds of bodies, all lined up to form a cross, and at the head of the graveyard was a large wooden cross. Willow approached the cross and found his crime boss Margo nailed to it. His body was stripped and bloody, and he had been brutally nailed to the cross while he was still alive.

Willow wanted to feel mad but he'd hated his crime boss, as had the rest of them. But he still had taken them in and taught them to be killers and thieves, so he had something to thank him for, at least. Willow brushed through his blonde Prince Charming-like hair and looked up, only to find a message written in blood on the wall: JUDGEMENT HAS COME.

"This is punishment," one of the thieves blurted out. "This is punishment for all the sins we've done."

"Pucker your mouth, Chebowski!" yelled Willow. Then it all clicked. Willow kicked a nearby log and shouted. "That Chinkza! He lured us away so he could attack our main fort!"

"What are we going to do, boss?"

Willow faced his remaining forty men. "We are going to kill this Chinkza! Even if it's the last thing I do!"

CHAPTER TEN

RETALIATION

*"It doesn't take much for things to escalate into an all-out war.
Sometimes it's just one event that can start it all."*

—GOBBIE

Deep within the Arghast Forest
08:45 hrs, 01/06/2258 (57 days A.F.)

The lone scouting party was wracked with nerves. Every guard in the party was less than twenty years old with little to no experience of fighting, as all the older men had died in the previous wars. You were either young or very young. The supposed leader of this group was a guy named Little. He didn't like that he had to handle a bunch of teenagers who hadn't even shaved yet and tell them to act professionally. Whatever that meant these days. For the past few decades of human history, there had been so much war that anyone who was a soldier was either maimed or dead.

But his orders came from Faal himself and as captain of the guard, he had control over all the guards in the city. After the attack, Faal had ordered scouting parties to scour the countryside to look for any possible rendezvous site for any enemy to prepare for a possible second attack. Little's men were armed with Barista FK rifles and were told to do scouting only. But Little could already tell that his men, if he could call them that, were either too jumpy or didn't care. They had never heard of an enemy outside their pretty wooden walls that was a true threat. No one had seen the organization of an army since the end of the wars. Most of these boys had enjoyed the relative time of peace since the final shot of the last war, not even know-ing what war was like.

Little didn't need to add that to his growing list of worries and tried to focus on the matter at hand. They were scouting ridge after ridge, trying to find any place that looked like a possible rendezvous site for the enemy. There had been growing rumors in the countryside that the Kotang had assembled an army one thousand strong. Little himself didn't believe the Kotang had a thousand men but he had been wrong before, so he stuffed away his presuppositions and pushed on. The squad of four stayed close as they reared up the top of Homeland Ridge, a short four kilometers away from their city of Laythia.

Little's men were joking as they neared the top of the ridge, when Little thought he'd heard something behind them. He stopped while the rest of his men continued climbing and stared down at the trees of the forest. He waited a solid minute but no sound came from behind, not even the chirp of a grasshopper. *I've got a bad feeling about this.* Despite his better instincts, he turned away and continued climbing with his men.

"Keep quiet!" he whispered.

As they approached the top of the ridge, they slouched to a prone posi-tion overlooking the valley below. There was a wide enough space for an entire football field and on it were one thousand Kotang bandits. A majority of them had weaponry, some handguns, shotguns, rifles, and a few auto-matic weapons. Guns that were far superior to their Baristas and Viper submachine guns.

Little's mind went into a panic. He whitened at the sight of the army, the organization. He was amazed that such a group was able to stand united with such a force in these times. And the road they were on was heading towards Laythia. He eyed the soldiers more and saw that they had a mish-mash of hand-to-hand weaponry. Nothing formalized, but a collection of axes, clubs, swords, daggers, knives, and even some pitchforks. He made a guess that they didn't have much ammunition, but they compensated for that by having bows and arrows in selected groups.

"Whoever these chumps are," Little said, "theys have organization." He tried to stifle the fear in his voice but failed. It spread to the rest of his men as well.

"How the heck are we going to destroy this kinda army?" a bleach-blonde-haired boy asked.

"I don't know," Little said. "But at least—" His words cut off when he found a bow and arrow pointed at his head as several men in hoods appeared around them.

An approaching man with a thin beard and a deep red neck gave a soft wicked smile. Little went pale and nearly soiled himself. But he quickly accepted the reality and sighed with disappointment at his men. "Nobody was watching our backs, guys . . ."

Officer's Barracks, Laythia
12:45 hrs, 01/06/2258 (57 days A.F.)

"What happened to them?" Faal tried to keep his anger contained.

An officer said feebly, "They went missing."

Marcus asked for a map. "Where exactly did they go missing?"

Faal stood with him, calling more of their officers into the meeting. The first officer made a circular gesture with his finger, surrounding an area on the map. "It's hard to say. We don't exactly have a radio to communicate with them. We sent them off about four kilometers but they could have disappeared anywhere in the area."

Marcus looked at Faal. "You sent scouting parties in all directions, correct?"

"Correct," Faal said.

Marcus put a pencil in his mouth and trailed his finger up the map, checking the surrounding terrain. "If only we knew exactly where they were," he said.

Marcus and Faal heard some commotion and turned their attention to the Main Gate. They stepped out and could see the Main Gates open as a twenty-year-old boy, dressed in the leather brown uniform the guards wore, came limping into the city.

Marcus and Faal went over to check the sight, joining a crowd of people standing there horrified. Blood was running down the side of the boy's face. He clutched at his bleeding neck, and he had an arrow in his back and another in his leg.

Little stammered and choked, half-dazed. "Theys coming. The Kotang clan and their army," he said.

Marcus and Faal watched from the side of the developing crowd as Little continued. "One thousand of them. All armed to the teeth with gadgets and guns. Big guns."

The crowd began to surround the boy until Marcus finally noticed the bulge on his chest under his shirt. His eyes went wide and he immediately grabbed Faal and anyone else he could, threw them to the ground, and laid on top to cover them.

All Little said was, "Theys coming," before the vest under his shirt detonated, injuring dozens of civilians and some officers in the crowd. Blood, guts, and limbs sprayed through the air. Marcus tasted gunpowder, dirt, and chemicals as the crowd screamed and ran in all directions. Those who could not run remained wounded or dead. Arms and legs were torn. Ligaments and bones were sticking out. Boys and girls screamed for their parents, crying out in pain.

Marcus shook off the daze and felt his adrenaline kick in. All his instincts became automatic as he checked Faal and everyone else for injuries. Luckily, Faal was uninjured as well as some of the people he'd pulled from the crowd. The rest of them were not so lucky. At least twenty-four people were injured and three were dead. Shrapnel lay everywhere, cutting people's feet as they rushed over to help.

Marcus took command, raising his voice. "Get all these people cordoned off! We need all the doctors and healers you can find. Get them to assess the conditions of the wounded and begin treatment. Start cordoning off some houses for a select hospital and storage of equipment. Let's move, people!"

Instantly, people started acting with more coordination. The crowd was no longer a flurry of chaos and fear, but one of coordination.

Marcus and Faal did what they could to assist the wounded as Faal said, "That was a message."

Marcus nodded. "Indeed."

"They're going to come in force. And they have supplies."

"Agreed."

"So, what do we do?"

Marcus said, "You handle things here. I'll alert the king."

‹‹—•—››

Marcus neared the dainty doors of the hall. A guard named Rorsch was standing there with a grin on his face. Marcus approached and said, "I need to speak with the king."

Rorsch laughed. "The king is busy with his *business.*"

Marcus had no time for this. "I need to see the king now."

Rorsch retorted, "He's *busy.*"

Marcus fought to keep his temper and voice under control. "Tell him that if he doesn't do anything then everyone in this city is going to die." Marcus walked away as Rorsch went pale.

Fifteen minutes later Marcus was summoned into the Great Hall before the king. The king looked frustrated. *Not a good starting point for discussion,* Marcus thought. Marcus knew what he had interrupted but he had no patience when there was a real-life crisis on their hands.

The king sat on his throne glaring at Marcus with anger. "To what purpose do you interrupt my business? I am a busy man, you know."

Marcus waited and then spoke. "Your Grace, I came to w—"

"Now, let's get down to it properly," the king interrupted. "Bow down to me first and then I will hear your request."

Marcus straightened his posture, put his hand across his chest, and gave a most courteous bow. The king looked uninterested. "No, no. On all fours."

Marcus remained stoic and unmoved. "Your Grace, with respect I will not."

The king flung his golden wine cup at Marcus's feet. "You dare defy a king!"

Marcus spoke as if the outrage hadn't happened. "Your Grace, there is an amassing army outside your walls."

The king was stunned and didn't know whether he should be curious or furious. "What army?"

"An army of bandits."

The king rolled his eyes and leaned against one of the arms on his chair, putting his hand over his face. "Yes, there are some bandits outside the walls. So what?"

Marcus remained as calm as ever. "They are amassing as we speak and are preparing to attack this city."

"And how do you know this?"

Marcus answered simply, "A young man had a bomb strapped to his chest and warned the city the Kotang were coming one thousand strong and then detonated. Your Grace, an attack is imminent."

"OUTRAGEOUS!" The king was on his feet now. "I ought to have you thrown into a dungeon."

Marcus kept his cool. "With respect, Your Grace, I am not sworn to you. I—"

"Well, we can change that now." The king grinned. "I see that you have not completed the work on the city and it is nearly the deadline." Marcus stayed silent, but not out of weakness. The king clapped his hands together. "I propose you swear an oath to me, and then I will fulfill your request and complete the work on all the housing in the city. I'll even prepare the army to meet these bandits that are rearing up on our borders. Or else . . . I'll have you killed right here, right now."

Marcus had his hands behind his back. "Your Grace, I am not your enemy."

"Well, you're about to be, depending on your answer."

Marcus said, "There is an amassing army of a thousand bandits about to attack your city," loudly enough for all the guards to hear. "With your walls and defenses, you won't be able to hold them off, and you will not survive with picks and pistols."

"HOW DARE YOU!" the king yelled. He turned to his guards. "Arrest this man and have him tortured!"

But his guards stayed where they were. Marcus nodded at them before turning his back to the king and walked out.

The king yelled after him, "Somebody arrest that man! He's a liar and a thief!" But not a hand was laid on him.

«——»

Marcus approached the camp barracks where the guards of the city were. Hopefully, he would be able to find the officers and convince them to join him.

Marcus came up to the door to the barracks, glanced up, and was disappointed. The barracks were barely a series of shacks housing the guards. There should have been a strong sense of discipline and reaction to the bombing this morning but there was an obvious lack of coordination. He opened the door, further disappointed that the door to what should be a secure military installation was unlocked. Marcus glanced inside and saw a bunch of giddy teenagers wearing armor and playing with their gear. Kids no older than twelve or thirteen years old, and they needed to be turned into soldiers if they were to survive. They didn't even notice him as Marcus closed the door behind him and walked into the main office where he found Faal standing there with a smirk on his face and his arms crossed. "That was quite the show you put on there," he said.

"I had to warn the king."

"I know." Faal relaxed and sat down in his chair. A pot of tea stood on the corner of his desk and he poured each of them a cup. "We have been hearing reports from other towns of the bandits gathering but we never knew they could assemble an actual force. Which means something has happened and the bandits are mobilizing for battle."

"I'm aware," Marcus said, staring down at the tea and then up at Faal. Faal didn't catch his suspicions. "I've encountered them before."

Faal took a sip from his tea. "How much time do you think we have?"

"Not much. They need time to gather their forces and make a plan of attack. This is a city so they will have to plan a way in. It may be a weak city, but there are still some defenses." Marcus met Faal's eyes. "How many men do you have?"

"Five hundred."

"And how trained are they?"

"They're a bunch of lying jokesters." Marcus held his reaction in and gave only a blank expression, but Faal could see the frustration hidden inside. "Meaning, it's not looking good for us."

"No, it is not," Marcus agreed solemnly.

He wanted to know everything to have a proper plan. What defenses they had, what types of vehicles and weaponry, and the experience of the soldiers. "What's your arsenal?" he asked.

"Viper 6 submachine guns, less than a hundred Barista FK rifles, bows, arrows, spears, some swords, and one rocket launcher."

"Ammunition?"

"Low."

That was going to be a problem. Marcus had a plan formulating in his mind. Thoughts connecting. Ideas converging and then disconnecting. He looked up at Faal. "We are facing overwhelming odds here, and if what your reports are telling us, the other scouting parties haven't seen any sign of the enemy. That means they have to be coming in the direction of the lone scouting party that went missing." Marcus pointed at the map on Faal's desk. "Here, northwest of Laythia, following the road up to Gin-Seng mountain. They could be amassing anywhere from here to here." Marcus pointed between two points on the map a couple of miles out from Laythia.

More officers began entering the war room and one chimed in, "Sir, the Kotang have relatively kept to their own territory since the end of the Great Wars. Why would they assemble now?"

Marcus shook his head. "Don't know. But there may be a new head to the snake driving this all together. We just have to figure out where they are and hit them first so we can do more damage before they come here."

Another officer with a blue bandanna said, "We're going to fight inside Laythia?"

"If we have to," Marcus said. "It would be difficult for their forces and would inflict maximum damage. Armies of history typically don't like close-quarters combat. So, we're going to give it to them."

Jaws dropped. Most of the men weren't familiar with close-quarters combat. Marcus looked around, forming impressions of each of them. Every man was hesitant to do anything except Faal. Most of these men were in their late teens to early twenties and hadn't led anything other than their girlfriends to bed. Now they were about to get a taste of real war.

Marcus held his sigh in, knowing some of these men wouldn't be coming back, assuming they survived at all. One thousand versus five hundred. A lot of guns versus not a lot of guns. It was going to be fun.

"So, what do we do?" an officer asked.

Marcus said, pointing at the map, "We have to find their location and then hit them to weaken their attack while preparing defenses here. I'll take a small force of a dozen men and we'll do as much damage as we can. Meanwhile, the main force stays here and readies for the attack. Prepare an exit strategy in case we can't protect the city or its citizens. We need to have contingency plans for this." All the officers straightened, feeling more confident now that they had a plan. "Let's get to work, people. Move."

All the officers went their separate ways, this time with push in their step. Faal seemed to catch wind of this and smiled.

"What?" Marcus asked, focusing more on the map.

Faal tilted his head and crossed his arms, still smiling. "They listen to you."

"I'm just doing what I can."

Faal didn't let Marcus's humility deter him. "You've got a gift for leading. Has anyone ever told you that?"

Marcus looked up from the map and glanced at Faal. "Yes," he said humbly.

Faal detected a hint of sadness in that statement. As two men as old as they were, they both had seen horrible things in the Great Wars and during the conflicts in between. Any man older than thirty was considered old in this day and age. Living to be forty was deemed a privilege, and living past fifty was nearly unprecedented. Anyone who was old enough had fought in the prior wars and died. And for men like Marcus and Faal, they'd had to lead those men to slaughter in constant battle, receiving wounds both physical and psychological. Faal could now see Marcus's wounds from leading men in the past. It was a job he knew Marcus hadn't wanted but accepted regardless of his personal feelings. Faal could see that Marcus understood what it meant to lead men, and what it meant to watch them die at your command. Marcus just stared at the map, trying to play out the various scenarios of how this battle would go down, whether in their favor or leading to their defeat.

"Do you think we'll win?" Faal asked.

Marcus said nothing for a minute. "Hard to say." He looked at Faal. "Whatever God wills."

Faal nodded. "Whatever God wills."

CHAPTER ELEVEN

THE RAID

*"There is a reason why man has always feared the
dark. Tonight I'm going to show why."*

—THE SAINT

Arghast Forest

02:15 hrs, 02/06/2258 (58 days A.F.)

It was reckless to be going out without doing any recon, but they didn't have much of a choice. Marcus needed information on where the enemy was and how to attack them. There was no time to delay. If that army of one thousand was real, then they could attack Laythia tonight and succeed. And if what that boy said was true, then they also had weaponry that the Laythians desperately needed, or else they would be destroyed. Marcus looked back at Laythia, the golden city on the hill. It was a prime target for any army but also a good place for defense. They needed to buy time, or else they would all die.

Marcus glanced at the twelve men with him. One was Faal, and another was named Joax, a tall twenty-seven-year-old with bright red hair and a short beard. Joax had a strong body and was one of the more experienced Laythian guards. The rest of their group were handpicked by Faal for this mission. Marcus was glad to have Faal with him. Another veteran with fighting experience made their unit all the better. But it was still going to be tricky and they had no idea where the enemy was. That would change soon.

Instead of sending scouting parties during the day, they were scouting at night when it was more difficult. It would be hard, but if they were looking for a large force, they wouldn't have to look far. Large forces left big impacts on the land and were nearly impossible to hide. Although, there was one event where one of Marcus's previous generals performed the greatest military trick in the book. General Almsteidt made his entire army disappear and attacked an enemy that outnumbered them three to one and still prevailed. Maybe Marcus would take a play out of his book soon.

They were nearing the location where the Laythian patrol went missing. They slowly approached Homeland Ridge and climbed. Marcus unslung his SR75k sniper rifle, a powerful rifle with a suppressor mounted. These days it was difficult to find ammunition for it but Marcus used it when he needed to, and tonight he definitely would have to. The problem was, though, it was very powerful and very messy. It was not an ideal sniper rifle for sneaking around; it was more of an anti-materiel weapon, capable of punching a hole through a truck and making it stop, but with the suppressor, Marcus could pull it off. Even if things did get a little messy.

The darkness in the forest made it hard for anyone to see, making tripping on tree roots likely to happen. The men with Marcus walked slowly through the forest, covered in shadows. Marcus halted and held up his fist. The group stopped. Marcus remained perfectly still, once again in his natural element of battle and stealth. His ears listened, waiting for any sound, whether it be human or animal. He knelt and the rest of his squad did the same. Their weaponry was different from his. They were all loaded with their Viper 6 submachine guns in case things got hot. They also had a couple of bows with them for stealth attacks.

They hid in the shadows of the trees, the moonlight barely visible through the canopy above them. Marcus waited, hearing nothing. And that was the problem. He heard nothing.

Then a slow rumble sounded in the distance. Marcus shifted focus and followed the sound. A series of three trucks passed by on the road, filling the forest with the rumbling of the mechanical monsters. Marcus let the trucks pass by, heading up the road they were following. They were definitely going to the base, no question.

They picked up their weapons and continued forward up the ridge. They went prone before barely glimpsing over the ridgeline. Down below was a raging camp of one thousand men, all armed to the teeth.

Joax said, "I think we found their base."

Marcus turned to them. "Let's go over our plan of attack."

《——》

From atop of Homeland Ridge Marcus got into position overlooking the entire Kotang camp. He planted his weapon on its bipod and readied his scope on the guard at the first checkpoint, where he could see Faal and the others as they crouched in the bushes. The first checkpoint had only three guards, each placed at certain points. There wasn't much to build on the checkpoint, as it was only a boundary that led to the inside of the camp. There were fires all around the camp but it was difficult to see without proper lighting and electricity. That would work to their advantage.

Marcus checked his magazine before he loaded up; he had ten rounds in the SR75k and that was it. Bullets were scarce these days so using ten bullets in one fight was a rare commodity. But now he was looking at an enemy with access to a nearby armory. That changed the game.

Marcus had told the group to wait for his mark. He targeted the first guard in the shack on the left while the other two stood outside, standing bored in the night. Marcus centered on the first guard's head as the stranger stared into the blackness of the night.

Marcus exhaled slowly and squeezed the trigger as the suppressed rifle blew the man's head off, splattering into the guards' room. Faal and the others unleashed their arrows on the other two guards and dragged their bodies and weapons away. Joax and the others picked up their weaponry, as any asset the enemy had could be an asset for them as well. Marcus could tell the Kotang clan had access to a good armory, given they were using some AX5M assault rifles and shotguns.

Nine rounds left. Marcus centered the scope on the next checkpoint. It was going to get more and more difficult to eliminate hostiles when in the camp. His SR75k would be able to handle the guards, and it could even shoot some of them through the walls due to its power. But it was its power that made the rifle notorious for its ability to break the suppressors mounted onto it. Regardless, Marcus would make do with the suppressor he had and hoped it wouldn't shatter while firing.

Marcus shifted his focus toward the sniper towers on each side of the base. There were roughly four towers and each had only one man on top. They were a rough conglomeration of wooden pillars raised up but Marcus had to admire the enemy's ingenuity. They were quick workers, even if it wasn't quality. Marcus sized up on the sniper closest to Faal and his team, sighted on his chest, and squeezed the trigger. The man fell as Marcus's rifle coughed. Eight rounds left.

He watched the team through the scope and saw them distract a guard and then slice his throat before entering a tent. They came out slightly bloody but alive. Marcus shifted the scope over and recognized an ammo depot on the far west side of the camp. He spotted three guards around it. He shifted his sights over to the three trucks they saw on their way in. The trucks could each hold about a dozen men or more and were useful for loading equipment into harsh weather conditions. Faal was thinking the exact same thing. He shifted over and secured the trucks, gaining the keys and killing any guards around. The rest of the camp was still oblivious, enjoying their quiet evening before marching to victory.

Faal secured the trucks and left one man with them. They were going to need a fast exit and the trucks would be useful to them. Faal and his men almost got caught by a guard before a bullet from Marcus caught the man in the chest and silenced any scream he would have. They dragged the body away while Marcus used his scope to scan the rest of the base, hoping to find any HVTs (High Value Targets).

He spotted an HVT dining by himself in his tent, but without proper radio communication, Marcus could not alert Faal to anything around them.

He let the HVT go but kept him in mind for later. All he could do was cover Faal for now. Marcus knew that the longer they were here, the more likely they were to be discovered. They needed to get out, and soon.

Faal and his men found the ammo depot guarded by three men. Marcus spotted them as they hid in the shadows and waited. Marcus squeezed the trigger twice and two bodies fell while the third was taken out by Faal using a throwing knife. They hauled the bodies into the dark. Marcus had no idea how much time had gone by, but he could take a guess and say twenty minutes had passed. They were bound to be discovered soon.

They began loading as much ammunition as they could onto the trucks, using the darkness to hide their progress.

A large portion of the army was in the northeastern part of the camp, using the area as a large-scale dining hall. Some of the men ate in their tents alone, and those who did found a knife waiting for their throats. *This is going well*, Marcus thought, but he knew it wouldn't last forever. Faal and his men were loading a giant red barrel of gasoline off the side of one of the trucks. Marcus was curious for a moment and then understood what they were doing. They rolled the barrel over to the ammunition depot and threw it on top of a pile of ammunition. Marcus almost smiled.

He shifted his attention and saw a bandit staring at them across the open courtyard. Marcus lined up sights on the man but then realized how young he was. It was a thirteen-year-old kid. The kid stared at Faal and their squad in pale terror. He had an AK84 in his hands as Marcus aimed at his chest.

The kid and Faal locked eyes. Faal shook his head, silently telling him, *Don't*, as the kid froze in terror. It was impossible to read what the kid was thinking. He probably wasn't thinking at all. *Don't do it*, Marcus thought, his finger brushing the trigger. Then the kid raised the rifle at Faal and his men, and Marcus felt his heart twist in pain as he pulled the trigger. The kid toppled back, dead.

Marcus knew that kid was going to haunt him tonight, assuming he got any sleep at all. Faal and his men hid the body, then loaded up as much ammunition as they could into the trucks.

Just then, a guard eating a roll of bread came stumbling out into the courtyard with one of his buddies. Marcus dropped them with speed and precision. Two bodies fell. Two rounds left. The trucks ran through the open checkpoints due to the lack of security and drove into the open road, vanishing into the forest and heading toward Laythia. Marcus had a few minutes before they would return to pick him up, so he scanned the rest of the camp for any extra targets. Might as well stir the hornets' nest.

Marcus brought his attention back to the high-ranking officer he'd spotted earlier dining in his tent. The officer was busy writing something when his chest erupted in a flurry of red and iron. He groaned and crumpled over.

One round left.

Marcus shifted over and aimed at the red barrel next to the giant pile of ammunition in the camp. He pulled the trigger. The round penetrated the red barrel and exploded next to the ammunition, sending bullets flying in all directions like a bunch of fireworks. Some men in nearby tents were wounded by the bullets and started firing back at an unknown enemy. Their undisciplined firing methods ended up hitting some of their comrades in the dining hall, causing the bandits in the dining hall to fire back at those shooting at them. What resulted was a bloodbath of confusion, anger, and iron. Kotang members were turning on their own soldiers in the dead of night, firing at an unknown enemy. Soon a hundred men were dead, either from the exploding ammo or the friendly fire of their comrades.

Marcus let out a tiny smile. He allowed himself that much. Roughly one hundred dead, with more wounded, an ammo pile destroyed, a high-ranking officer dead, and they didn't lose a single man. Not a bad night for a raid.

≪—•—≫

Willow took in the sight of his men panicking and running around like a bunch of ballerinas. He yelled for Captain Welsh, his second in command. "Welsh! Welsh!" Willow turned and pulled the flaps to Welsh's tent. "Welsh where the—" The sight of the fist-sized hole where his heart was said it all.

Willow turned bright red. "How the hell did intruders get into our camp and cause so much chaos!?"

Willow gritted his teeth and felt a vein bulge in his temple. The shouting outside did nothing to calm his mood. He screamed in frustration, stormed outside, found Mak, and yelled, "Get your men in order! I want this place cleaned up and find out what the hell happened!"

A stray round from the burning pile of ammunition shot out and nearly struck Willow in the head. Willow ducked out of the way as the bullet smacked into the wooden pole next to him. "And get that fire put out."

Mak went on his way, trying to calm the troops. Willow knew he was in good hands with Mak taking command. He was loyal to the cause and the men trusted and liked him. He had the talents of a natural leader.

Willow redirected his focus toward the destruction in the camp. He clenched his fist and thought, *Whoever it was that orchestrated this attack is good. Probably the same person who attacked our fort.* "I'm gonna find this man and I'm gonna wring his neck loose!" He swore in the night and watched as his men scurried along trying to get the fire out without getting shot in the process.

CHAPTER TWELVE

THE DAY BEFORE TOMORROW

"We have weapons, ammo, and best of all . . . spunk.
Now we'll be ready for when those Kotang show up!"

—JOAX

On approach to Laythia

05:24 hrs, 02/06/2258 (58 days A.F.)

They brought the trucks into view of Laythia, but the raiding party didn't have any radio communication with the city, so when they approached the Main Gate, the Laythians open fired from the walls. It wasn't until Marcus and Faal stepped out into the headlights of the trucks that they finally stopped shooting at them. One of the guards up top rubbed his head and said, "Uh . . . sorry about that. Come on in." All the men in Marcus's squad sighed.

The big wooden doors opened and they let the trucks through. This time, there was a more appropriate greeting as they searched the trucks for bombs and any other explosive devices.

Faal jumped down from a truck, happy as could be. "We've got gifts for you, Laythia!" he announced. "Ammunition and weapons to go around."

The city guards rushed over, forgetting all about their posts as they tried to get the new weapons for the upcoming fight. They argued over the new AX5M assault rifles and cradled them like a bunch of boys getting new toys.

Marcus dismounted from the truck and watched as the Laythian guards all scrambled over their new weapons. One thought that bothered Marcus was how they hadn't been able to find any prisoners in the enemy's camp. If members of the patrol party that had disappeared were still alive then they would have been able to locate them amongst the Kotang's camp, but to their dismay there had been no signs of prisoners. Marcus wondered about that and found it peculiar, but his attention was drawn elsewhere when he spotted a guard who looked about seventeen sitting on a rock, peering straight down the barrel of one of the guns. Marcus stomped over and snatched the weapon away from the boy's face.

"Hey!" the boy shouted.

Marcus met the boy with a glare that shut him down. He looked at the young guard with anger. "Never look down the barrel of a weapon! Here are a few rules of gun safety. Number one: always treat a firearm as if it's loaded. Number two: always point the gun in a safe direction. Number three: keep your finger off the trigger until you intend to shoot something."

A gunshot rang out and everyone looked over and screamed as another seventeen-year-old boy blew his brains out doing the same thing the first one had. Marcus was the only one in the crowd who didn't flinch. A woman screamed as Marcus handed the weapon back to the first boy. "Or else you'll end up like that."

Despite the small victory, what just happened showed Marcus how much of a problem they still had. Forget about having better weaponry; this city has no fighting experience. They could equal out the numbers but that wouldn't matter if the enemy was better trained.

People crowded around the dead boy. Despite his wishes, Marcus stepped into the crowd, feeling his worries grow again. But he kept them contained, trying to maintain a calm demeanor. He looked at the boy whose brains were splattered over the floor and sighed.

If we hadn't raided that camp, this boy would still be alive.

Stop it. You know you shouldn't blame yourself.

I know. I've got enough on my mind already.

Marcus picked up the boy and took him outside the city. He thought about the Kotang and their forces. Nothing would happen today. He knew the enemy was recuperating, so they wouldn't try anything immediately. Now was a time to rest and prepare. But first, he had to bury this boy.

After Marcus finished burying another soul he stayed out in the countryside for a little longer. It was still dark but Marcus could see the morning dawn lighting the horizon with living orange in the distance. The silence finally gave him time to think. Time away from all the people in the city. Time away from fighting the Kotang clan. Marcus sat himself under a tree and closed his eyes. He couldn't sleep yet, so he threaded his hands and prayed in silence.

Father, yet another kid was killed today. All from a dumb accident. Marcus didn't hate the kid. He just felt pity. But that was the only thing he felt. Apart from that, Marcus felt nothing about the boy dying. He was just another casualty of war. But the memory was still fresh.

Marcus kept his eyes closed. He tried getting his heart to feel again. To feel sorry for the thirteen-year-old boy he'd killed in the camp tonight. Then Marcus spoke out loud. "Father . . . I . . . took another boy's life today. He didn't look older than thirteen." Marcus opened his eyes. "I don't know if that was right or not. I know that if I didn't shoot him, the rest of my team would have been spotted and some of them could have gotten killed. I know that he pulled his gun to fire first but still . . . what bothers me isn't the fact that I killed another kid today; it's the fact that I don't feel bothered by it that tears me up."

Marcus remembered the boy taken hostage during the Hosang Revolution. How he took out those terrorists attacking the mob, but how he'd accidentally killed that boy in the process. Marcus knew it was the best outcome, but even the best outcome was not the preferred one. Marcus wanted everyone to live in that scenario, but if he had to make the choice, he would rather take one kid dead than thousands of people dead. It was just one more victim in the art of war. A sad reality that sometimes the wrong people get killed.

Marcus sighed and closed his eyes again. "Father, I don't know if what I did was wrong or not. If it was, then punish me for it but . . . I don't know.

The sad reality is that I don't feel bad about it. At least not anymore. I don't know if that makes me a killer or not." Marcus felt the words clog in his throat, thinking of all the times he'd had to fire on an armed child. "I . . . I didn't want to kill those kids. I don't want to kill these people. Father, please keep me grounded, and focused on doing the right thing. And rebuke me if I ever do wrong. You may revoke your blessing on me. For you give and you take away."

Marcus felt a wave of relief flush over his shoulders and dribble down his body, relaxing every fiber of his being. The pain and the burden of war that he had been carrying for so long lightened. Marcus felt a tiny drip of emotion ping inside his soul. He tried to remember he was human. He tried to not be a killer.

You're a killer, and you always will be. Marcus's breathing grew heavier.

I'm not a killer.

Oh yes, you are. Just ask that thirteen-year-old boy you shot.

I'm not a killer.

Marcus opened his eyes and felt the dawn come. Another beautiful day. *Let's see if it ends in bloodshed.*

City Streets of Laythia

17:52 hrs, 02/06/2258 (58 days A.F.)

At the end of the day, after training the troops and making preparations for the coming attack, Marcus entered the gates of Laythia and this time was greeted with an open welcome. The people inside were somber but grateful for his work. Some of them even thanked him directly. Marcus wasn't used to being greeted by so many people. A small huddle of housewives admired him from afar. His dense muscles, chiseled square chin, and short black beard. His tall body and handsome form. They giggled, but Marcus felt nothing.

His lack of emotion to their gawking made him question his emotional well-being. It bothered him when he felt nothing when he should feel something. It made him wonder at times if he was truly human.

Some people were dancing and celebrating in the early evening as a lone man played a violin in a tavern nearby. A few couples were dancing together to the soothing music, forgetting the harsh reality they lived in. Marcus saw a man and a woman with black and blonde hair dancing in each other's arms. He stopped and watched them, allowing himself to enjoy humanity for once.

Only God can create something so beautiful. He watched them sway from side to side, holding each other tightly. It triggered a memory of when he was dancing with Carmen. He remembered her sleek blonde hair rolling down her back, the scent of lavender perfume as she passed by, and how she felt in his hands as they danced. Marcus felt a flurry surge in his chest and then fall.

Carmen . . . I miss her so much. The memory was permeated with joy and pain. It hurt to think about her but he couldn't let it go. Marcus went into his jacket and pulled out a picture of Carmen. He held it up in the light to see her face. Her blonde hair and white skin gleamed in the evening lighting. Marcus felt his heart surge slightly with joy, remembering all the good times he'd had back home. *Father, I miss her.* Marcus lowered the picture and stared at it for a little longer. He turned it over and read the handwritten words, "Come back home safe." Marcus allowed a tiny smile on his face, but the bitter reality killed it. *I can't come home.*

He returned his focus to the couples dancing and watched until he forgot the time. It was nice to watch people be so happy. To watch people enjoy life rather than suffer through it.

"What are yous doing, mister?"

Marcus looked down to his left and found it was Arthur. His ginger hair and freckles reflected the evening sun like mirrors. Marcus allowed Arthur to see his smile for a second before it faded.

"I'm watching these people dance," he said.

"But why?"

Marcus returned his gaze to the dancers. "Just enjoying humanity."

"Yous talk funny, mister, yous know that?"

Marcus almost laughed, but he held it back. He looked back at Arthur. "And what are you doing here?"

"I came to find yous."

Marcus maintained his stoicism. "Well, you found me." It was sarcastic but it didn't come across as strongly as Marcus intended.

"So, yous a soldier, right?"

Marcus lowered his head in honest contemplation. "I was . . ."

"Yous ain't now?"

"I don't know." Marcus was curious as he said that. Throughout his entire life, he had never thought of himself as anything but a soldier. Marcus was struck with the question, *What do I do now?* It gave him pause. *Do I stay here in Laythia and fight with these people, or do I continue traveling?* That thought made Marcus pause even longer. He wasn't accustomed to asking these questions. Sure, there was still a fight to be won here, but that wouldn't last forever. Even the Great Wars ended; the world couldn't be at war forever. But what would life look like for Marcus outside of battle? Marcus shifted his attention to all the homes he and the workers built. All the rooftops they'd fixed from the degradation of the prior war. A glimmer of hope slipped inside his heart at the sight of them. *I'm not sure where I fit in this world. I'm not sure if I can live in a world without war. But maybe there's a chance I could belong somewhere . . .*

Marcus was stuck in thought for so long that Arthur was looking at him with an eyebrow cocked.

"Well, what's your answer?" the boy asked.

Marcus returned his gaze to Arthur. "I'm figuring that out."

What was strange was how Marcus hadn't stopped fighting when the Great Wars stopped. Ever since he'd left the military Marcus has encountered rogue bandits, thieves, gang attacks, fought the guards of Laythia, and now this Kotang clan. Even though the wars stopped, the world was still rampaged by constant conflict, just on a smaller scale, leaving Marcus to wonder where his place was in all this. He glanced up at the sky and prayed in his mind, *What do You want from me?*

The boy ran off, yelling, "I've got to go now. Bye."

Marcus waved goodbye as he took off into the streets. He enjoyed the sight of the boy looking so happy. It always brought him joy to see other people happy, especially when so young. The boy was about seven and he hadn't even seen the world yet. It warmed Marcus's cold heart to see a spark shine so brightly in this dark world.

Faal stepped out from the shadows and greeted Marcus. "Are you ready?" he asked.

Marcus nodded and followed Faal back to the Barracks Headquarters. They returned to a room full of officers and whatever maps they had of the surrounding area. Faal spoke up, splaying his hands over the table. "We stole over one hundred guns and five thousand rounds of ammunition. That has improved our fighting force dramatically when we get into an open firefight."

Five thousand rounds, Marcus thought. *Not enough ammunition.* He remembered how quickly soldiers could burn through ammunition. With about five hundred men fighting, each with ten rounds, that equated to only a few minutes of firefighting. *That's not enough.* Marcus could tell it was quickly going to turn into a sword fight, which was why he would prefer for the battle inside the city to be a last resort. The enemy still had better weaponry but after their raid last night, they would be in the same boat as them with ammunition. Who knew how long they could last with their ammunition before the fight suddenly turned quiet? Triple Click, as they called it in the final years of the Great Wars, when both sides would run out of ammunition and the battle turned from a gunfight into a close-quarters brawl.

Marcus pointed at the map. "We have to start the battle outside the walls and then successfully retreat back into the city where we'll have the advantage of the hillside when it turns to hand-to-hand combat."

Faal nodded. "Agreed. But we have to last that long and maintain a proper force until it happens." He looked up. "If we have less than two hundred men still standing once they enter the city, we won't be able to put up much of a fight. Even I know you can't win a sword fight of a hundred men against a thousand."

Marcus said nothing and peered at the map, looking for anything that could give them the advantage. He made one last decision. "We need to start setting up traps as well. That will help delay our opponent and make it harder for them to attack."

All the officers and Faal nodded. Marcus saw their approval and said, "Let's get to work."

Temporary Kotang Campsite, Arghast Forest
17:52 hrs, 02/06/2258 (58 days A.F.)

Willow had been furious the night before, but his fury had festered into a rageful weapon he'd honed and intended to unleash on that worthless town of Laythia. His army had been disorganized and wounded from the night raid, but they had reformed and were all fit with rage. He could feel it in his men when he walked by them as they stood at attention. Despite being a band of rogue thieves, they were still an army, and one with slight organization at that. That would give them an advantage against the untrained troops of Laythia.

But he had a surprise for Laythia too, something not many people could do these days. He grinned wide as he looked toward the direction of the city, rearing to unleash his fury upon those people. "We're coming for you Laythia." He grinned. "And there will be no escape!"

Laythia
19:52 hrs, 02/06/2258 (58 days A.F.)

They had less than a day before the Kotang clan would be there, and they made use of every moment. It was the calm before the storm that Marcus hated. He disliked waiting for the bullets to fly and the day to be pumped with adrenaline, screaming, blood, and fury. It would come. He had waited through days like today more times than he could count. He knew they would attack at dawn; knew they wanted to bring them out of the city and into the surrounding forest.

But that would come tomorrow. For now, evening lay and the night settled, and the town relaxed into a semi-active sobriety of work and calm. The defenses had been laid with what time and resources they had. Marcus tried not to worry about having fewer resources than he'd like. He remembered, *"And this same God who takes care of me will supply all your needs from his glorious riches, which have been given to us in Christ Jesus."* The Scripture relaxed him and he was able to settle into the moment again. Everything was in place. All he could do now was wait.

After Marcus had finished his evening prayer, he went to check on Gobbie. He hadn't seen the young lad recently and was curious what his frame of mind was. Marcus walked through the city streets, still avoiding the large crowds gathering at taverns. He still struggled to fit in with the citizens of the city, and his prior PTSD was preventing him from interacting well with them. He'd have to work on that, given time. Marcus walked through the gravel streets, surrounded by houses made of Kaisk wood and Meeraith trees. The city reminded him of a medieval castle, only the castle was made of wood instead of stone. Too prone to fires.

What was once a lively city was now a terrified shell of itself. Most of the streets were abandoned and the people were in their homes waiting for the battle that would determine whether they would live or not. They had prepared an exit plan for the civilians to filter through the back of the city, through the mountain, and out into the hillside behind where hopefully they would be safe. The city of Laythia was surrounded by forests and a mountain at its back, but what made it so pragmatic was its defensible position. The city was in a bowl called the Bog, surrounded by hills. In those hills were thick forests, and then the city rose in elevation up the side of

Hillsong Mountain. But Marcus knew a safe box was no different than a coffin. And a defensible position can easily turn into a kill zone. He brushed those thoughts out of his mind for now. The battle would come.

Marcus approached Gobbie's two-story home, finding only a few candles lit and the activity inside low. He knocked on the ragged wooden door, almost getting a couple of splinters from doing so. Gobbie's father answered with a machete in his hand. The man's defensiveness was defused when he saw Marcus and he opened the door further, calling, "Gobbie! Your friend is here, the Saint."

Marcus paused. Even now he still heard that nickname. He thought that since he wasn't in the military anymore that nickname would vanish, but somehow it stuck to him like a tattoo.

He brought himself back to reality as Gobbie answered the door. His eyes were red and swollen, and Marcus knew he was still mourning Bo's death.

"What do yous want?" Gobbie asked impatiently. Marcus could still see the hatred in his eyes. Hatred pointed at him.

Marcus measured his words and spoke calmly. "I wanted to check on you. See how you were doing."

"We're fine. Okay? Now bugger off and get to defending the city. And take your stupid faith with yous."

Marcus whispered, "I just want to make sure you're okay."

Gobbie snapped. "Well, I'm not okays! Ever since yous came to this here city, there's been nothing but trouble. You're like a magnet for conflict. It finds yous whether yous go looking for it or not. I thought yous were kind at first, but then mi friend Bo was killed because of mi stupidity for wanting to help yous. Now I've learned that yous have to be selfish in this world to survive. Because being unselfish just gets yous killed, and those yous love killed. So, in order for mi to love, I have to not love. Okay? Now bugger out of mi life before I kill yous."

Marcus knew there was no changing his mind. He knew a stubborn man when he saw one. Gobbie went back inside and slammed the door, waking some of the neighbors. Marcus took that as his cue to leave and pondered Gobbie's response as he walked back to the barracks.

Part of him is not wrong. But he's not entirely right. While it is safer to not love others and to simply care for yourself, that doesn't mean life will get any better by doing that. If you choose to not love, then you are still hurting others. While it may keep people alive, it also keeps them stuck in fear. And that is not a proper way to live. You have to love, even when it hurts you. For choosing not to love is to deny the purpose of living. Marcus thought back to the look in Gobbie's blue-black eyes. Eyes of hatred. Eyes of vengeance.

Marcus thought of an interesting question. *Would you do the right thing, even if it hurt those around you? Would you still love, even if someone got hurt because of it?* Marcus's default answer was yes. Because if you do nothing, then people will still suffer, and it takes the responsibility off of you because you did the right thing. It removes the judgment from your shoulders, even though it still hurts sometimes.

Marcus wondered if things would be better if he'd never come to this town. As Gobbie said, he was a magnet for conflict. That had been a fact since he was born. No matter what Marcus did, the fight would always find him. He never had to go looking for it. It had found him before, and now it had found him again, and this city was about to be destroyed by a rogue gang that was one thousand strong.

It's all your fault! If you never came to this city then all these people would still be safe. His mind pictured Bo's pale face, bleeding on the ground as it stared at him with contempt. *He would still be alive if you'd never come.*

Marcus shook off those thoughts and kept his mind on the present task: defending the city. He tried not to blame himself but sometimes he couldn't help it. It felt like he was pounding himself with an anvil to justify his actions. Now that the wars were over, Marcus wondered more about what he did during them and what he'd gone through. Whether it was all worth it or if he was just another killer out there destroying the world.

Marcus shook his head. *No. Those wars weren't for nothing, even if they seem like they were.* He thought of the men he'd served with, all the greatness and courage they embodied, both his men and the enemies he'd fought. Marcus had some admiration for his opponents. Even though he beat them he often wondered if in another life they would have been good friends. "Most likely," he said as he strolled down the empty road in the dark.

But the deeper he thought about it, the more sullen he became. All those men and women he'd served with were now dead. And all those wars he fought before didn't matter. *So what was it all for?* He thought. *What was the point of all that death and destruction?*

He briefly looked up at the sky and thought, *There had to have been a point to it all. It couldn't have all been for nothing.*

Suddenly, Marcus could feel the Spirit rising within him. Warning him. *"Stop."* Marcus stuffed his thoughts away when he suddenly stopped and felt the still air around him. There was no activity this late in the night. All the houses were filled with people, as no one dared to go outside. The city of Laythia emanated a ghost town feeling. He felt his hair stick up as he suddenly realized he was being watched. He didn't have his rifle with him, but he had his handgun, sword, and kukri.

Three figures suddenly dashed out of the midnight darkness with gleaming blades directed at him. One thrust from behind aiming for his back, while the other two attacks came at the same time, trying to pin him into a triangle of blades. But Marcus sidestepped, whipped around and kicked one of the blades away, using his hands to grab another attacker and pull him in front of him. He impaled the second attacker with the blade of the attacker from behind. Marcus saw they were all wearing dark cloaks and had been hidden completely in the night.

Marcus sidestepped and threw the second attacker aside, knocking the blade of the third attacker down and grabbing the man's throat. The first attacker came back to his senses and tried to strike Marcus while he still held the third attacker. Marcus shifted his weight and kicked the first attacker aside, who tumbled and fell into a bale of hay. Marcus reaffirmed his grip on the third attacker's neck, lifting the man off the ground with one arm. The third attacker tried to grip another blade but Marcus kneed the man in the groin, causing him to drop the blade out of reaction to grab his privates. That kicked out any air left in the man's lungs as Marcus gripped the man's trachea, digging his fingernails into the man's skin. The attacker croaked in pain as Marcus gripped as hard as he could, ripping the man's trachea out from his throat. Blood spurted and the man dropped to his knees, gargling and choking on his own blood.

Marcus turned his attention to the final attacker, grabbing him from the haystack and throwing him aside onto some nearby stonework. The man's head struck the stonework and his body went limp from the impact. Marcus grabbed the man by the collar, checking him for weapons, as he pulled the man closer. But the man's eyes would not meet his own, as the man's soul departed from this world. Marcus let the man go and overlooked the three bodies, frustrated he wouldn't get any answers.

CHAPTER THIRTEEN

THE BATTLE BEGINS

*"This is bullshieska! There are a 1000 men coming
to kill us and I have to be at the front?!"*

—JOAX

Arghast Forest

05:45 hrs, 03/06/2258 (59 days A.F.)

Joax didn't like being on the front lines because they were the first point of contact. He wished the Saint was here, but he needed to stay back to lead the defense at the city with Faal. So, Joax was hereby determined to be the third in command. *Great . . . I'm the point guy, the one most likely to die.*

The Saint had volunteered to lead the guerilla group, but Faal and the majority voted against it. Instead, Joax was given the responsibility of slowing the enemy down. He shrugged his shoulders and accepted the responsibility. *Oh well, at least I get to be a pain in somebody's kinzka and get paid to do it.* But that also meant he was most likely to get killed. Joax sighed. *Whatever; let's just get this over with before I'm sprinting back to Laythia with my tail between my legs.*

Joax looked over the one hundred men under his command, who were spread throughout the west side of the forest. One hundred men to fight an incoming force of one thousand, although after their raid, the Saint had said the enemy was whittled down to roughly nine hundred. But still, that was a superior force to deal with.

Joax crouched in the forest, the leaves squishing under his boots, the soft ground providing moist comfort. It was a good season for spring. Maybe it would all turn orange in the summer, assuming he lived that long. Joax cradled his AX5M assault rifle in his hands. The AX5M was a newer model of weapon developed by the country Aquila; it was very versatile, capable of being used for close quarters as well as long range engagements. It had a range of 500 meters and fired 5.56x45mm ammunition at a velocity of 910 m/s[13] with a magazine capable of holding thirty rounds. Unfortunately, they only had ten rounds per man, so this was going to be an initial attack and then a quick retreat. After they ran out of ammo they would switch to bows and arrows and try to hold out for as long as they could. Joax smiled, ready to run. "Here we go."

He heard movement coming through the trees. Joax peered slightly over his little ditch toward the main road and saw the marching men. They were goading each other and laughing, having no idea what was waiting for them.

They're arrogant . . . good. Joax almost smiled. He looked at his fellow Laythians all spread out in a thin line throughout the trees. It was his job to buy the city as much time as possible. Dawn was about to break. Joax calmed his men and told them to keep quiet. One of the guards next to Joax stared at him with sweat and terror. Joax just looked at him and shrugged his shoulders.

"I guess it's time we start shooting," he said. He leveled his AX5M on the first bandit he saw. The rest of his men did the same. *Save your rounds, Joax. Don't fire blindly.* The rifle was set to semi-auto to preserve his ammo and make every bullet count. "Let's get hot!"

Joax squeezed the trigger. The brass round fired at the walking band of flesh at 910 m/s and struck the first bandit in the lower stomach. The man heaved forward, the gunshot echoing through the forest.

It has begun.

The rest of Joax's men open fired, ambushing the dark figures in the

---

13. 2,970 ft/s

early dawn as bullets ricocheted off tree limbs and the air filled with gunpowder and sulfur. The enemy returned fire, with more power in their punch. Joax and his men's position were peppered with bullets, forcing their heads to go down behind the mounds of dirt protecting them.

A few minutes passed by and at least three of Joax's men were killed in the firing. Some quickly shifted to bows and arrows after they ran out of ammo and fired as best as they could while the rest of them retreated. The rumbling of the constant gunfire echoed throughout the entire forest. Joax knew everyone in the city was hearing this.

Joax and his men fired back with bows until they quickly realized they were out of arrows. *Quoitzka!* He threw the bow down and began to run back to the city, shifting up and down and using trees for cover to avoid getting shredded by the gunfire.

Joax ran for his life, as did the rest of his men. Everyone else in the city was about to have a big eye-opener today.

Laythia
05:45 hrs, 03/06/2258 (59 days A.F.)

Marcus knew he wasn't going to get any sleep tonight, so he relinquished himself to a long session of prayer. Finding a quiet spot near the walls in the city where no one would find him, he prayed, "Father, I know the battle is coming. Please protect the citizens of this city. May we survive the coming day. I want to pray for victory for our side, but whatever happens, I want Your will to be done and not my own. I don't know exactly what You want from me, but Lord, please use me for Your purposes."

Marcus kept his eyes closed, sitting on a patch of grass, meditating on Scripture in pure silence. Prayer and meditation always helped him with his PTSD. They helped him remain focused on the present and feel calm at all times. It was one of the benefits of having God in his life; allowing him to cope better with the troubles of the world.

Marcus finished off with an "Amen," and opened his eyes. He stood and headed to the catwalk of the city walls. He looked out over the Bog, waiting for the enemy he knew would come. As part of the defenses, they had broken down any houses that were outside the walls to create a clear line of fire and prevent the enemy from having extra cover when they attacked. They had also placed a guerilla unit in the forest to try and delay the enemy, and when they started shooting, they would know the enemy was approaching. But the guerilla unit was only about one hundred men. The only instructions those men had were to run and shoot, to delay the enemy as much as possible. They didn't even have the ammunition for that kind of strategy. Marcus knew it would devolve into swords and bows; it was only a matter of time.

He stood on the catwalk and scanned the horizon with the guards. He stared toward the forest in the early light of dawn. It would begin soon. He could feel it.

Pop. A lone gunshot in the distance. *Pop, pop.* Heads were starting to rise, and lights inside homes were doused. Figures in the night approached the walls, all looking in the same direction.

It had begun.

Marcus could hear the gunshots in the distance. First, there was a quick series of gunshots going in both directions, then a one-sided argument as men began running through the trees back to the city walls. Marcus wasn't looking so much as to where the men were running, but rather where the gunfire was coming from. *Our men ran out of ammo.* It hadn't taken long, and he only hoped they'd inflicted damage on the enemy before they ran.

Marcus did one final check of his body before the fight began. He rolled his shoulders, both of them still sore but ready for action. It had been a short period of time since Marcus had been in a major conflict such as this, although the definition of a major conflict has changed nowadays. Regardless, it was time for the second line of defense. The men rushed inward toward the city, taking slow steps to avoid falling as the gate closed slowly to allow the surviving men to enter. It felt safe behind the large wooden doors, but they wouldn't be safe for long. Marcus stood atop the catwalk, hugging one of the wooden barriers. The sun was rising and the warm rays heated his skin. He'd already begun to sweat. It was going to be a hot day.

The next line of men hugged the walls as well, and Marcus was ready to get off this catwalk as soon as possible. The wooden walls could hold against small arms weaponry, but anything larger would easily penetrate them like paper. They may be wood, but they wouldn't hold out forever against bullets.

Lines of vision ranging from the downhill portions around the town up to the forest lines were beginning to clear. The area in front of Laythia was labeled the Bog because it contained a series of cut tree trunks and open ground. Given its open nature and lack of cover, it was an ideal kill box with a few surprises laid inside.

Marcus said, "Snipers at the ready."

Pairs of bowmen hugged the squads of snipers on the wooden catwalk, ready to fire when they were reloading. They didn't have much ammunition, so they had to see how long they would last. Marcus hugged the wooden wall, his SR75k in his hands, ten rounds for his magazine, and the remaining ammunition distributed to the rest of the army.

It was quiet for a long moment until Marcus saw movement in the tree line. Men dressed in red outfits began pouring down the rim of the Bog, down into the bowl in front of Laythia.

Marcus called out, "Target the men on the sides, make sure they funnel straight at us." The men on the catwalk beside him nodded. Pairs of men seated together, one with a rifle in hand, the other with a bow and a stack of arrows placed next to each position.

Marcus lifted his SR75k and took aim at the first attacker. With his scope, he was able to see the sweat on the man's face as well as his ugly pimples. Marcus whispered, *"Be strong and courageous. Do not be afraid or terrified because of them, for the Lord your God goes with you; he will never leave you nor forsake you."*

Marcus felt a sense of tranquility flow over him, as he squeezed the trigger and the first man instantly became a fountain of blood. The rifle thundered, overshadowing any gunshot fired in the arena. Marcus had taken off the suppressor for his rifle, wanting a more psychological effect in battle. He wanted men to hear his thunder and fear it, knowing every time he took a shot, another of their comrades died and they could be next. The effect worked wonders in the fight, but the Kotang were still charging toward the city.

The Laythian guards along the city walls open fired, targeting just as Marcus had instructed, keeping the Kotang funneling toward the front of the city by attacking the sides of the charge and not the front. Arrows and bullets flew through the air as the Kotang and Laythians unleashed hell upon each other. It brought Marcus back to his natural state of calm when in battle. Marcus aimed down the sight, now targeting the front of the Kotang charge as they were starting to pour down the hill into the Bog. Marcus's rifle thundered again, taking another life with deadly precision.

The Kotang found the open area of the Bog against their wishes, as the chopped tree stumps were the only source of cover along with some tiny holes for them to hide in. Therefore, there was only one way to reach cover . . . forward. But Marcus had anticipated this and it's exactly what he'd wanted.

The red horde of Kotang was charging down from the rim of the hillside when suddenly men began dropping and shrieking in pain, clutching their legs. Dozens of men tripped and fell as they charged forward, finding their limbs injured and punctured as the ground betrayed them. At least eighty men fell into Marcus's traps before the Kotang realized what was happening. Another twenty fell in spite of jumping over their comrades. Even if he wasn't dead, an injured man could no longer run, meaning he was out of the fight and left to die of infection.

But the Kotang were like a giant horde, unable to change course despite the front's recognition of the problem. Instead of changing their strategy, they continued to charge forward into the center of the Bog toward Laythia, firing their weapons high up at the defenders, only to find their legs giving way to a series of sharpened stakes.

Marcus saw at least a hundred and fifty of the horde fall into the hundreds of traps he'd taught the Laythians to create. Marcus and the Laythians had accomplished getting the Kotang to charge straight at them, using their arrogance in numbers and weaponry to fuel their demise. The Kotang continued to fire, disregarding their wounded comrades and charging forward. Some of them stopped, trying to find cover while firing back. But Marcus and the Laythians were also pouring some heat of their own. Using their high ground and the cover behind the walls, the Laythians had a clear view of the Kotang charging at them and were firing their own weapons, causing more enemies to fall over their brothers and into the traps they had set. Marcus fired his weapon again and again, each thundering round giving some Kotang pause as they switched tactics and sought cover instead of charging to their deaths. *That's exactly what I want you to do*, Marcus thought.

A mixture of bullets and arrows flew from both sides, but the Laythians were better protected and were raining fire on the charging Kotang coming at them. They were able to chop their numbers down from nine hundred to seven hundred using both the traps and returning fire. This evened out the odds little by little. That advantage would only last so long, however, as Marcus knew the Laythians were quickly running out of ammo and had started using more bows and arrows to target their opponents. But most of the Laythians weren't as proficient with bows as they were with guns. Guns were easier to wield and took less skill to fire than a bow, and some of the Laythians were taking casualties despite their cover on the walls. Marcus knew the Kotang still had more ammunition than them and despite the Laythians' good head start, the battle was to be determined by endurance. Either the Laythians would outlast the Kotang, or the Kotang the Laythians.

The Laythians on top of the wall ran out of ammo and were now relying entirely on bows, arrows, and even some rocks to chuck down at their invaders. The Kotang were gaining ground despite their slowed charge, and had managed to clear most of the traps now, and the distance between them and the wall was diminishing. One of the Laythian guards next to Marcus shouted, "We're running out of ammo, sir!"

Marcus fired his last round and dropped down into cover with him. Marcus maintained an absolute calm, speaking above the din of the battle. "We're going t—"

Marcus heard it immediately. His head shot up like a dog sensing a squirrel. He focused on the slow but massive rumble of an approaching beast. The metallic shriek and rumbling crunch of a being long since dead. Marcus's mind went into flashbacks as he recognized the sound of the vehicle instantly. A tank slowly revealed itself from the shadow of the forest, aiming its massive cannon toward Laythia.

Marcus looked at the Laythians hiding behind the wall and shouted, "GET OFF TH—"

The main gun open fired. The whole front gate exploded as wood and shrapnel cut through the air. About thirty Laythian men were immediately vaporized while the secondary M2HB heavy machine gun on top of the tank opened up on the rest of the walls of Laythia. About twenty Laythian guards were caught in the hail of bullets. The FMJ rounds from the heavy machine gun punched through the wood like it was paper. Marcus and the rest of the men jumped down, taking cover in the homes or on the ground behind the wall. The M2HB continued to fire non-stop, peppering the entire wooden wall with .50 caliber rounds. The main gun opened up once more and fired another massive hole into the northwest side of the city, then another round into the southwest side. The barrage took out another fifty Laythian guards who couldn't find cover in time. The M2HB continued to fire in concert until the gun stopped and the tank was finally silent.

Marcus had leaped off the catwalk and down into the buildings. He felt the impact on his back, sending a stunning ache throughout his body like lighting as he fell again and landed on the ground. He might have heard a pop if he was listening hard enough. Miraculously, he hadn't broken or dislocated any joints upon his fall, and he was amazed he was able to stand.

He made a quick prayer of gratitude before he stood up again. But when Marcus looked over, he realized most of the other Laythians hadn't fared so well. The catwalk proved a deathtrap in itself, with some men falling either with the steep drop or staying to only get shredded by the .50 caliber rounds. Most of the Laythians who had jumped the wall were now clutching at their broken legs and backs, unable to stand up and fight.

Marcus waited for the tank to pour on the artillery but it remained silent. *Conserving their ammo. They want to save their bullets for the final act.* That was fine. Marcus didn't need to deal with a tank now. But the silence begged an opportunity.

Marcus could hear the angry Kotang yell, "CHAAARRGE!" as hundreds of men poured up from the Bog toward the open holes in the city wall. Instantly, the charging Kotang lost their discipline and ran forward spraying the city with bullets. They breached the gates of Laythia and were now charging toward the dozens of wounded Laythians spread about, giving them the fate of a bayonet to the stomach.

Marcus unsheathed his sword and magnum, shouting, "FALL BACK! Get to the next line of defense at the Townsquare!"

Men began charging in, firing wildly at anything that moved. The Kotang were running into houses and ending anyone who had dared to stay behind in what were once their safe homes. Meanwhile, the Laythians were retreating as fast as they could, trying to bring their wounded comrades, only to receive a gunshot in the back if they did.

Marcus held his ground and defended against the Kotang entering the city. With his magnum in his left hand and his black sword in his right, he was ready for close-quarters combat. Some of the houses inside Laythia were catching fire, filling the area with smoke as the Laythians continued their retreat. Six attackers came at Marcus as he stuck to cover, trying his best to slowly retreat while buying the Laythians time to regroup. Marcus found himself in an alley as six attackers approached. One of them tried to take aim at him, but Marcus was able to move quicker with his sidearm than the man could with his assault weapon, putting a massive hole in the man's chest while the thunder from the magnum drew the attention of the other five Kotang. They charged at him with bayonets, knives, swords, clubs, and anything else they could get their hands on. Marcus whipped and dodged, using his sword to parry while using his magnum to club enemies who got too close, only firing when an opponent dared to fire at him first to conserve ammunition.

Marcus whipped the magnum and clubbed an attacker, breaking the man's teeth and nose. The man fell to the ground as four more attackers pounced. One of them swung a metal club at him. Marcus parried it with his sword, using his leg to kick one attacker into another while swinging his magnum at a different target, striking the man in the temple and shattering his skull with a loud crack. The man fell to the ground. What was once a group of six was reduced to two in three seconds. Marcus readjusted his footing and sliced his sword against the metal-clubbed attacker's back and then thrust through his back. Marcus quickly retrieved his sword in a fluid motion as if the blade were passing through butter.

The remaining two attackers didn't have time for fear as Marcus approached them. They swung their attacks wide, not coordinating. Marcus was able to parry and dodge them before he removed their hands with deadly efficiency, their weapons dropping to the ground as the two attackers stared in shock at their severed limbs. Marcus swung his sword and relieved them of their suffering . . . and their heads as well. The bodies fell to the ground, squirting fountains of blood as they tumbled over.

Normally that would be the end of the violence for the day, but just as Marcus took down six men in ten seconds, another dozen flooded the alleyway. He retreated slowly, and only after he had taken another three men with him as he backed out into the main street, joining the horde of chaos rushing through the burning roads of Laythia.

Marcus continued his tactic and kept chopping at the charging Kotang, reducing their numbers and firing on them if they dared to fire on him. He quickly ran out of ammo for his magnum and didn't have time to reload it. So, he placed the weapon back in its holster on his left thigh.

Marcus continued to use his sword as well as every limb on his body as a weapon. He was surprisingly agile for a man of his size and build, which only made him more dangerous. Marcus even had to use some of the throwing knives on his belt to hit distant attackers.

Eventually, Marcus made it back to the Townsquare, where the remaining Laythians were present for their final defense. The three hundred and fifty Laythians remained centered in the Townsquare as the surviving five hundred Kotang charged through their city, burning and killing anything and anyone they set their eyes upon.

Marcus saw the Laythians were on the verge of panic. He could see the thoughts running through some of their minds, the idea of surrender. But Marcus knew the truth. There would be no surrender. Not to these people. The Kotang would surely kill them if they laid down their arms. This was to be a fight to the death.

Smoke began to fill the city as buildings caught fire from the sparks of the shell casings. Joax glanced at him and cried, "Sir, we are about to die! We're getting overrun!" But Marcus stood there stoically, listening to the sounds of the battle, interpreting what they meant.

Why are their men continuing to charge instead of running for cover? His thoughts ran to Blitzkrieg in a war a long time ago. *They're trying to overwhelm us with speed, that's why they don't stop.* Marcus could hear it now, the decreasing sound of gunfire, as well as the slowing of the rushing tide.

Smoke was beginning to permeate the entire city. The sounds of choking and gasping filled the courtyard. Marcus paid the smoke no attention, accustomed to the smell of sulfur and gunpowder. Then, just as the sound of gunfire was slowing down, it immediately stopped. Marcus heard the gunfire from his men turn into a click, click, click noise, and from the opposing side came click, click, click. *Triple Click*, Marcus thought. *No ammo.*

Marcus unsheathed his kukri, raised his sword, and yelled, "CHARGE!"

sprinting toward the enemy. His courage infected the remaining Laythians, causing them to charge at the Kotang despite their fear. Marcus ran downhill into the mass of bodies, sword and kukri ready, slicing and stabbing any enemy he encountered.

Marcus and the Laythians slammed into the red Kotang bandits, and just as he surmised, found they were exhausted from all the sprinting and shooting. Marcus had deliberately held their forces back until the enemy had exhausted both their guns and their physical stamina. The smoke offered perfect protection for close-quarters combat as the battle quickly devolved from guns to knives. Whether it was day or night didn't matter, as the smoke from the fires made it nearly impossible to see any ally or enemy outside of a five-foot radius. Most men were choking on both sides, with those still standing using what little energy they had to fight.

The battle quickly turned brutal as men clashed with each other. They charged, their screams and yells increasing until they became a uniform voice as hundreds of men plowed into each other with flaming rage. No mercy, no hesitation, just hundreds of men slamming into each other, all with the intent to kill.

Skulls slammed, swords sliced, knuckles smashed, arrows flew, necks broke, skin tore. Men fought with their bare teeth as weapons when they had the chance. Those who held onto their remaining bullets used them, wrapping up a few extra kills before their guns clicked empty and turned into bludgeons. Men choked, stabbed, punched, kicked, shot, and smashed with anything they could find.

Marcus knew he had to cause as much chaos for the enemy as possible, but even if he killed their commanders, it wouldn't take much brainpower to find the enemy standing in front of you and kill them. The men didn't need leading; the battle was an all-out brawl. Marcus ran through the smoke, ripping apart whole groups of men as he swung through. Using both his sword and kukri, Marcus became a dancer of blades as he sliced through mass after mass of hostiles.

He ran into a group of four men, each armed with a different weapon.

Marcus whipped around and stabbed the first man in the throat with his sword, shifted his weight, and threw the dead man into the others, dwindling the group to one opponent. Marcus slashed him across the man's stomach three times with his kukri with such speed that the man barely had time to react. He fell over clutching his bleeding stomach while Marcus turned and finished off the other two, who were pinned under the dead man.

Sunlight shined down on Marcus as he moved from group to group until he realized he could see the sun through the smoke. *We're visible.* Marcus's thoughts shifted to the tank on the hill as he turned and saw it lower its turret amidst the chaos of blood and knives. The tank steadied on its position and froze. Marcus took cover, trying to scream amongst the hundreds of yelling men as their position exploded in a mess of gunpowder and sulfur. Limbs, splinters, shrapnel, and blood flung over the area where the HE shell impacted.

Marcus was grabbed by the arm, but before he could whip around and stab the intruder, he saw it was Faal, drenched in sweat and blood. "We need to destroy that tank my friend, or else none of us are leaving here alive!"

Marcus saw the battle whittling down. It wasn't looking good for either side.

He glanced at the tank. *They have a Type 12 H6 tank. Range: six thousand meters, track-based, fires 120mm HE rounds, accompanied with an M2HB heavy machine gun, capacity: two thousand .50 caliber rounds . . . that's not good.*

Marcus looked at Faal and asked, "Do you have any ammunition?" Faal pulled out a single round. Marcus handed Faal his SR75k rifle. "Be ready." Faal knew his instructions.

《———》

For a man charging into battle, this was not what he'd had in mind. He'd imagined a white horse available from the king, but instead, Marcus charged out of the city riding on a donkey. The donkey probably wasn't used to being ridden so fast and was having difficulty listening to Marcus's instructions as it avoided the traps. Marcus had ridden horses before but never a donkey. *This is humiliating*, he thought as he charged up to the lone H6 tank.

A tank was nearly impossible to destroy these days. He only had one rocket and it was an old design. But one shot was all he needed. The only problem was that he needed to get close enough to fire it.

One of Faal's officers had shown the rocket launcher to Marcus and he'd hidden his reaction to prevent the group from realizing how bad their situation was. The rocket launcher was an old 88 Cymba model from over seventy years ago. The only reason they had it was because they'd found it in an old archeology site next to the city. Marcus severely doubted the thing would even fire. For all he knew it could kill the person firing it.

The main gun on the tank couldn't go any lower unless it went down into the valley toward the city. But the M2HB on top was able to, ready for the enemy to make a counterattack against their trump card.

Marcus hefted the 88 Cymba rocket launcher. The eyes of the gunner outside manning the M2HB widened at the sight of the rocket as Marcus aimed at the underbelly of the tank. The gunner was stunned by the sight and reared to fire. Marcus closed his eyes. *God, I know you're in control.* The gunner's head exploded and he toppled over. Marcus exhaled. *Thank you, God, and thank you, Faal.* He turned and gave a nod to Faal's location on the last remnant of the wooden catwalk still standing.

Marcus now had a clear shot at the underbelly of the tank. He hoisted the rocket launcher up and clicked the trigger, but the rocket didn't fire.

Marcus's eyes shifted to the rocket launcher and immediately threw it aside as the launcher exploded and sent shrapnel into his right leg. The donkey toppled over from the explosion, making Marcus's wound even worse. He groaned from the pain, but it wasn't anything new.

Marcus got to his feet and coughed up blood as he stood before the tank. Marcus limped over and climbed on top of the tank, his adrenaline from the fight earlier draining, but he shrugged off the pain in his leg and climbed upwards. The tank made no motion to back up as a man with white-blonde hair came out from the open hatch.

The man stood on top of the tank, stuck his arms out wide, and said, "So, you're the one who's been killing all my men." Marcus said nothing. The man looked at him with brilliant blue eyes. "I see you've got an injury there. So sorry. Does that hurt?" He waddled his voice to sound like a baby. Marcus paid no attention.

The man unsheathed a sword from his belt. "You want this tank?" he asked. "You'll have to go through me."

Normally Marcus would just shoot this man and be done with it, but he had used up all his ammunition during the fight back in town. All he had were his sword and kukri. But the only way they were going to win this fight was if they had the tank. Marcus didn't take his eyes off his target, knowing that the man could easily have a handgun somewhere. The two men stood atop the tank ready to duel.

Marcus didn't take out his sword yet and stared at the man. Then he pulled his magnum out of the holster. The man was shocked that Marcus had a gun and reached for his. But Marcus threw the magnum faster than the man could anticipate, causing him to lose his balance and opening him up for the perfect opportunity. Marcus unsheathed his sword in the blink of an eye and brought it down on the man. The man reacted just in time to block it, but not quickly enough to prevent Marcus from wounding his left shoulder.

Marcus then kicked the man off the tank and he smacked the ground flat on his back, losing his firearm in the process. Marcus jumped down and went for the final blow. The man rolled and recovered his footing as Marcus planted his sword in the ground.

Marcus and the man squared off, blades in hand, circling each other, while the rest of the battle raged on in the city. Two men representing each side, ready to duel. Marcus knew not to underestimate his opponent and that the injury on his leg would hinder him, but he'd have to tough it out and keep fighting or else they would lose this battle.

Either way, it was time to strike. The man inspected his own sword, clearly taken from somebody else. "You know, this sword has taken many lives. Like you." The sword was long and had a slight curve to it. It had a gold hilt, providing great protection to the holder in case a sword struck their hand and was longer than Marcus's so getting close was going to be difficult.

The man swiveled around, lowering the sword in a blank stance but ready to strike at any time. "I can tell just by looking at you that you're a wounded warrior. A man looking for a purpose in a purposeless world. Why not come work for me?" Marcus said nothing. The man recognized Marcus's silence. "Ah, my apologies. I believe it is time for proper introductions." The man bowed. "I am Willow Catzby, previous second in command, now the current leader of the Kotang clan. And you are?"

"Nobody important."

Willow smirked. "Ah, a humble man who doesn't want people to know who he is. Really, why do you fight for these people? Why not come work with me? You'd be welcomed among brothers. We even have some men with prior military experience who have joined our ranks."

"No thanks. I'm no killer."

Willow flattened his brow and looked at Marcus quizzically. "Now, that's a strange answer. For a man who has just fought through an entire battle, taking dozens, or even hundreds, of lives, you still claim that you are *not* a killer. Most curious. I have to say, though, you've been a thorn in my side, especially since you killed my officer Welsh back at the camp."

Marcus said nothing. This was starting to grow old.

"I'll give you one last chance," Willow said. "Join us and the battle will be over. I'll call off my men and we will work together."

"Forgive me, but I must respectfully decline," Marcus replied. "Because that would be wrong."

Willow was angered. "Wrong? Wrong? What is right and wrong?" He pointed his sword at Marcus. "You're a man who's got nothing to live for, and yet you choose to deny yourself the good life and live as a rogue, with no place to go and nowhere to belong." Marcus said nothing, giving Willow an unreadable expression. "WHY? Why do you insist on living this purposeless life where you have nothing to live for?"

"Because," Marcus said, "it's not purposeless." He met the man's eyes, allowing Willow to see his pain. "With God, there is purpose in living. Even if I don't know right now what my purpose is exactly. I will live out my calling, however painful it may be, until I accomplish what I was set out to do."

Willow tilted his head quizzically. "My my, you are a strange one. Now, enough talk. Let's fight."

Willow lunged forward, bringing his sword mere inches from Marcus's face. Marcus parried the swing just in time, tossing the man aside and letting him tumble into the side of the tank. Marcus went after him, but Willow recovered and defended against his strikes. Marcus slashed overhead but Willow blocked and let the steel clash.

Willow stepped back as Marcus's blade slashed into the side of the tank, leaving a massive cut in the armor. Willow was surprised to see Marcus's sword had been able to slash through the armor of the tank. He noticed Marcus's blade looked different. The sword Marcus wielded was pitch black, not like the silver steel Willow carried.

Marcus charged at Willow and the two exchanged equal blows. Willow tried his best to dodge, parry, or block most of Marcus's attacks, but Marcus was more skilled in sword fighting. Willow had to take a couple of slices on his face, shoulder, leg, and even a few punches to the gut. Marcus on the other hand received a few cuts on his body and a kick to his wounded leg. It took everything he had not to scream from that kick.

After ten whole minutes of clashing, both men were exhausted. Willow was surprised Marcus had lasted this long, especially since he had been fighting all morning inside Laythia. Marcus measured Willow and saw he was catching his breath too.

Willow noticed again that something was different about Marcus's sword. The edges of the blade were red hot while the main body remained black and cool. The clash of their swords had caused the black blade to heat up.

The two men regained their breath and continued their dance. Marcus noticed that Willow was getting more and more physical with his attacks, using his body with more agility now, changing his technique and tactics. But Marcus caught the man mid-transition and kicked him in the stomach, sending Willow falling against a Kaisk tree behind him. The impact knocked the wind out of Willow as he lay against the tree.

Marcus didn't hesitate and brought the sword downward. Willow held up his sword with one hand as a last-ditch effort to block the attack. The two swords collided but Willow's fear came true. The red-hot edge of the black blade was so intense that it burned through the steel of his sword, snapping the blade and cutting deep into his right shoulder. Willow shouted in pain as the blade burned through his skin.

It was over. Any chance Willow had of winning was gone.

Marcus removed the sword from Willow's shoulder, causing an eruption of blood from the open cavity in his flesh. Willow put his hand to his wound, trying to literally hold himself together. He coughed up blood as one of his lungs collapsed. Marcus held him at sword point, the searing edge of the blade only millimeters from Willow's throat.

Willow sighed. "Dang . . . I guess this is it for me." He looked up at Marcus with contempt. "This would have never happened, you know, if you never attacked our fort. We would've stayed complacent and never left those walls."

Marcus tilted his head quizzically, lowering his brow. "I never attacked your fort."

Willow coughed up more blood. "What?"

"I never attacked your fort."

"That's impossible," Willow said. "The entire fort was destroyed, and everyone was dead in the courtyard, and up top, there was this big red cross, and next to it were the words JUDGEMENT HAS COME."

Marcus seemed more interested now. "A big red cross?"

Willow nodded; he was dying anyway so what was the point of holding back? "Yeah. We heard rumors of a lone man traveling the countryside with a strong faith. We thought we had tracked him down to the city of Laythia. That's where we first targeted you."

"I'm aware," Marcus said. "But I didn't attack your fort."

Willow's strength was fading. "But if you didn't attack our fort, then who did?"

Marcus took his eyes off Willow and looked at the horizon, watching the sun rise high in the sky. "Someone very dangerous."

Marcus knew this had something to do with the vision he saw. He remembered the gigantic flow of red scouring the globe at great speed. It was already happening; he just hadn't known it, or where it would begin.

Marcus looked back at Willow and tossed him some bandages. "If you're still alive let's meet again. But don't come back here."

Willow sighed with blood in his mouth. "I won't . . . assuming I don't die right now."

Marcus left Willow there and shifted his sights toward the tank.

"One last thing to do."

《——》

Marcus entered the tank and seated himself in the main gunner's seat. He peered down the scope and extended the magnification until he could see everything clearly in the town. The battle was not going well for the Laythians. They were down to two hundred guards and the enemy still remained strong at about four hundred. They surrounded the Laythian guards and had them trapped.

Marcus centered the main gun on the largest group of hostiles he could find and clicked the firing mechanism. The tank shuddered backwards then recentered. The 120mm HE round fired at 1,600 m/s,[14] sending a canister made of sulfur, shrapnel, metal, gunpowder, and other chemicals into a

---

14. 3,579 miles per hour

group of fifty hostiles. They vanished in the blink of an eye, the shockwave turning the sights of the others toward the tank. Marcus reloaded and fired again, killing another fifty hostiles.

Marcus clicked the firing mechanism again but the tank ran empty. "Out of ammo," he said. "Figures." He shifted into the driver's seat and revved the tank forward.

The destruction of a hundred men in less than a minute shocked the Kotang forces. The remaining two hundred Laythians rallied and were performing a last-ditch effort. But they were still surrounded by three hundred Kotang. Marcus drove the tank as fast as he could into the city, ramming through the broken gates and bringing it directly up to the encircled Laythians.

The Kotang forces looked confused when their tank pulled up, and were even more confused when Marcus popped the main hatch, pulled the M2HB from its mount, and pulled the charging handle. He stood atop the tank and fired into the air, the gunshots silencing any further slicing from the blades and blunt weaponry. The whole town quieted.

Marcus aimed the M2HB at the Kotang forces. "Stand down." He spoke sternly. "Or I'll mow you down."

One guy charged at Marcus, but he reacted quickly and gunned the man down with a quick burst. Marcus aimed the gun back at the rest of the Kotang forces. "Drop your weapons now!"

It would have been suicidal to charge the tank with nothing but swords, so all the Kotang forces dropped their weapons. The Laythians cheered in victory as the Kotang forces went on their knees with their hands up.

"This battle is over," Marcus announced.

The king stepped out from his shelter in the Great Hall, his sword shiny and new, having avoided all bloodshed. "Well done. Well done!" The king joined the men, acting as if he had been there the entire time. "We have successfully defeated the enemy!"

None of the men cheered. All of them just glared at him in awkward confusion. Marcus kept his reaction to himself, although he would roll his eyes when he had a moment alone.

The king came forward and pointed his shiny new sword at the neck of one of the Kotang prisoners. "Now, what shall we do with you?" He toyed the edge of the blade against the man's flesh, one swipe away from ending his life. The sunlight gleamed on the blade as the man soiled his pants.

Marcus stepped down from the tank. "Tie them up and lock them away."

The king looked up at him in surprise. "I beg your pardon, sir, but shouldn't we end their lives?" he asked.

"No," Marcus replied sternly. "The battle is over." He turned to Joax, his brown tunic spattered with ash, mud, and blood. "Joax, take the prisoners and get them bandaged and healed. Have them fed as well, but keep them tied up and separated."

Joax stared at Marcus for a moment, then he nodded in understanding and escorted the prisoners off. The king was outraged. He stormed up, his nice leather boots scratching the brown gravel and grass stubs up to the tank. "What is the meaning of this? We should kill these prisoners as judgment for what they've done to our city."

Marcus stepped down from the tank. "They have been beaten and the battle is over, Your Grace. While they deserve punishment, we can think of other options."

"Killing them *IS* our only option!"

Marcus looked over at the three hundred Kotang prisoners being led away, then surveyed the destroyed city. Marcus turned back to the king. "What if you use them as a laboring force to rebuild the city? Station them with armed guards and have them work to repair the destruction they brought. That would help rebuild the city and improve the defenses in good time. And it would help prevent other hostiles from attacking the city in a time of weakness. Wouldn't that be beneficial, Your Grace?"

The king stared at him, red hot with anger, but his eyes gradually defused as he thought about the idea. Then his face brightened with a smile. "Yes! That is a wonderful idea. They will be our slaves!"

"No," Marcus interjected. "They will serve as your indentured servants for ten years. But after they shall all be released as free men."

The king was baffled. "I do not believe I am hearing this. That is far too kind to this enemy."

Marcus showed no sign of compromise. "Treat your enemy the way you would want to be treated. These men deserve to pay for what they have done, and they should seek to rebuild what they have destroyed. Then they shall pay in servitude to your people and be freed later."

Marcus turned to the Laythian guards and said, "Is that satisfactory?"

They all nodded in agreement. One of the guards said, "We agree to the terms, and promise to keep them."

The rest of the Laythians said, "Aye!"

The king planted his feet, his brown leather boots crunching the gravel. "This isn't over," he said before walking away in frustration.

Faal stepped up, his golden robes ruined from the fighting. "You know, you are walking on thin ice," he told Marcus. "The king does not like to be insulted or commanded. I suggest you watch your back." Faal went to return to the works on the city, leaving Marcus to contemplate his warning.

Marcus looked toward the destruction of the city, the black and white clouds of smoke from the fires breaking, revealing the hidden sun. "I know," Marcus said. "I know."

CHAPTER FOURTEEN

PRISONERS

"We can live as kings in one moment, then as slaves the next."

—THE SAINT

Laythia

08:05 hrs, 03/06/2258 (59 days A.F.)

The three hundred Kotang prisoners were separated into three camps throughout the city. Each company was kept under constant guard by Laythians wielding a loaded AX5M and bows. The Laythians had scoured the battlefield and recovered what ammunition the fallen Kotang members had and were able to create a small stockpile. It wasn't much but it was enough to keep the large group of prisoners under control with a small guard population.

Marcus had to contemplate the tank and whether to leave it with the Laythians or to destroy it. He glared up at the giant beast shining in the sun and decided to leave it be. It was harmless now that it was out of ammunition.

Marcus surveyed the destruction from the battle as he walked through the city. Almost every single one of the five hundred houses was damaged or pocked with bullets. The rounds from the tank had decimated the wooden wall surrounding the city and destroyed dozens of homes. Over nine hundred bodies were spread throughout the streets, both from the red Kotang and the brown Laythians. Blood ran down in small rivers from the base of the Townsquare to the lower basin in front of the city, creating small pools in the Bog.

The battle had raged for only a few hours but that was enough to change everything. The Laythian people had already been a weak population of two thousand, with only five hundred men to fight. Now, the Laythians only had two hundred men who could fight. The rest were mostly women and children.

The enemy had suffered as well. The Kotang took tremendous losses from their charge tactic. Beginning with an overwhelming force of nine hundred, they had been whittled down to three hundred.

The victory did nothing to stifle the hate the Laythians held toward the remaining Kotang. Marcus noticed harsh looks from the Laythians toward the Kotang as they already started mocking their prisoners. Marcus understood their anger. A group of people declared war on them and nearly eliminated their entire city.

The Kotang's feelings were no different. After losing the battle with what was supposedly an overwhelming and technical advantage, they were now reduced to servants to a people they hated.

Marcus stood at the Townsquare overlooking the whole city. Smoke billowing from some of the houses. He knew winning the peace was going to be a lot harder than winning the war, so he took a deep breath and said, "Let's begin the reconstruction."

He nodded, "We'll start with the bodies." He turned to Joax, who had returned from escorting the prisoners, and said, "Take some men to guard the new prisoners and escort them as they bury their dead."

For a moment, it looked as if Joax was going to say something, but he held back and kept his words to himself. Marcus looked around and thought, *There's so much destruction to fix. Not just in material buildings, but in hearts as well. It could take decades before things settle down here.* But Marcus wasn't one to sit and doddle. He took his first steps forward and walked down, doing the job nobody liked but that had to be done.

He didn't have to look far to find the bodies. Layered around the Townsquare were hundreds of bodies, both Laythian and Kotang alike. He always hated this part of war, the remains afterward. Both the physical wounds and, more importantly, the psychological ones, would fester and could grow worse over time from the aftermath.

Marcus immediately joined a group of Laythians as he helped them put their dead on stretchers and carry them out of the Main Gate toward the Bog. The bodies would have to be buried out in the Arghast Forest, so they had to go up and down the hill to bury them. Marcus didn't complain and got to work helping the Laythians put away their dead.

Marcus could see the looks on the Laythians' faces. There were grim expressions and hardened sadness, sadness minted with a cold fury at those who attacked them. At the Kotang. Marcus had seen these faces before, many times over. He knew it could overtake a people and drive them to madness with rage. He had no idea how the Laythians would react, but one thing was for sure, they weren't the defenseless cattle they were prior to this battle. He could see it in their eyes. Eyes that had seen the darkness of the world come to their doorstep. In a way, it could be seen as a sense of maturity, one that Marcus shared, but he also knew it could lead to deep bitterness and hatred if left uncontrolled. They were no longer kids, but seasoned killers. After fighting a harsh battle, they were no longer the young dumb guards of Laythia. They knew what war was and it had changed them.

Marcus worked with the Laythians, some of them offering him a scarf to put around his face, but Marcus went into his rucksack and pulled out a red scarf he had taken from one of the dead thugs before he came to Laythia. He used the red scarf as a mask as he stooped down to pick up the remains of the dead. Very soon the bodies would start to decay and bulge with maggots and decomposing gases. Worms would come up from the ground and flies would permeate the bodies quickly. Flesh would decay and what were once living beings would become nothing more than rotting flesh. Memories and life that were there less than a few hours ago were gone forever. Personalities and dreams gone. Nothing but meat.

The scent of blood and gunpowder filled the air. Smoke and ash filled most of the city, covering all the Laythians and Kotang in a mild layer of black ash, along with the scent of sweat, urine, and feces. Marcus found a majority of the Laythians had soiled themselves at the start of the fight and were only now realizing it, those who lived anyway, as the rest who had died were now corpses lying in their own fecal matter, unable to understand how awful they smelled. The sight of it all would have made anyone heave their guts out, and a few of the Laythians and even the Kotang did, but to Marcus nothing about this was new. This was home.

Soon, they recovered all the bodies of the Laythians and brought them safely through the Bog and into the Arghast Forest. Marcus and his party were able to acquire some tools from the blacksmiths in Laythia and were busy chopping down trees to create a cemetery.

After all the Laythian bodies had been taken, Marcus saw the Kotang begin recovering their dead as well. They were under guard from the Laythians, who did nothing to help the Kotang recover their own and merely stood and watched, already hurling insults at their new captives.

"Not as fun now, is it?" one of the guards yelled, "having to pick up so much of your own dead."

Marcus did nothing for the time being. He'd known the Laythians would have hatred toward the Kotang. It was already happening.

Once they had cleared most of the Townsquare, Marcus shifted his efforts to cleaning up the remaining bodies from the rest of the city. He didn't stay with just the Laythians and to the surprise of many, he joined the Kotang and helped them recover their dead.

Marcus approached a group of Kotang, under the watch of Laythian guards, and brought a stretcher to help them. One of the Laythian guards charged at him, demanding, "What are yous doing? We don't offer stretchers to those scumbags!"

Marcus eyed the Kotang for a moment and then looked back at the guard. "Using the stretchers will help remove the bodies quicker," he answered.

The guard retorted, "Not for those murderers! They don't get to use stretchers. They have to use their bare hands to carry out their dead."

Marcus stood up to the guard and said, "The stretchers will help." His tone was firm but it wasn't commanding. He was trying not to fan the flames of a recent battle.

But the Laythian guard planted himself in front of Marcus. "No. I will not permit the Kotang to use any stretchers." Marcus turned and saw that the other Laythian guards agreed.

He looked over at the Kotang behind him, careful that they didn't stab him in the back, before turning and kneeling in front of one of the bodies. He abandoned the stretcher and looked at the Kotang across from him. "Pick up his legs," he directed.

The closest Kotang bandit looked at Marcus for a moment, then back at the Laythian guards. He hesitated for a second then followed Marcus's orders, picking up the body's legs. The other Kotang members did the same with the bodies around them, heaving the bodies upwards and walking them out of the city. The Kotang around Marcus didn't know what to think. None of the Laythians were helping carry out the Kotang's dead, and Marcus was the first person to offer his assistance to the prisoners. Without looking he knew their thoughts. They were wondering what to think about him, whether he was still a foe or not. Marcus could sense a slight change in atmosphere with the Kotang. His actions created a slight sliver of pause among the former bandits.

The rest of the cleanup continued with the tiring efforts of clearing the bodies from both inside and outside the city. There were even a few accidents from the foot traps laid out in the Bog, claiming a couple of Laythians as well as Kotang. Marcus did his best to help prevent as many people from getting hurt as he could but even he knew he was powerless to stop everyone from hurting themselves. He knew where all the traps were so those who followed him were on the safest path. Marcus led the Kotang members out through the Bog and into the Arghast Forest to create their own cemetery. The only problem was that the Laythians did not permit the Kotang to use any shovels as they could be construed as weapons. So, Marcus and the Kotang workers had to use their hands to dig up any open ground to bury the dead.

Marcus didn't care whether they were his enemy or not. The words *"Love your neighbor as yourself"* echoed in his head as he buried the Kotang, men he was fighting very recently. Now, he was giving them a proper burial with the tools he had. Marcus was permitted to still use his weapons and used his kukri and sword to slice tree roots so they could dig properly into the ground.

After a couple hours, the bodies were finally all placed in the ground. Marcus had started working with the Laythians and had ended working with the Kotang. He finished burying the last Kotang casualty in the ground and realized he was surrounded by three hundred Kotang prisoners in the middle of a newly cleared cemetery.

Marcus fashioned hundreds of crosses for the bodies and their graves. The Laythians protested when Marcus performed such a gesture to their enemies, but Marcus continued regardless. The Kotang didn't know what to think of the crosses at their graves, some of them were still shaken by the attack on their fort and the red cross that had killed their brothers.

But the Kotang didn't seem too shaken up about their comrades dying. Marcus observed their faces as they stood in the meadow, overlooking the six hundred dead bodies buried in the ground. Marcus wondered if they'd even liked their fellow compatriots or if they were glad they were gone. But one thing was for sure: the Kotang were defeated.

Laythia

12:12 hrs, 03/06/2258 (59 days A.F.)

When they were finished burying the bodies, Marcus went down to Faal's office in the Barracks HQ, the building pocketed with holes and barely standing. Faal was trying to figure out which maps were destroyed and which he could still use. Meanwhile, Gobbie stood there with a decorated ribbon on his chest and a new green uniform. He had recently shaved his head down to a buzz cut as well as his beard, revealing more of his round head and making him look more mature. But that look of maturity was actually grimness overshadowing his face. Gobbie had the look of silent hatred, a look Marcus was all too familiar with.

The remaining officers were there as well. Faal looked his way and said, "Welcome. We were just discussing what to do with the new 'work detail.' "

Marcus said nothing and kept his thoughts to himself. Gobbie stared at him with skepticism. Marcus ignored the glare and met Faal's eyes.

Marcus said, "I came here to offer my services."

Faal tilted his head. "Oh? What services?"

"I'd like to oversee the work detail and participate in the cleanup and repair of the city."

Faal relaxed a bit. "My friend, you have done enough for this city. Why don't you find a nice spot of land and settle down?"

"I may do that one day, but for now I'd like to participate in the reconstruction."

"With the prisoners?" Gobbie inquired.

Marcus nodded. "Yes. I'll oversee them and assist them in cleaning up the city."

Gobbie was flabbergasted but Faal merely shook his head and smiled. "It seems you have found your work detail, Saint." Marcus didn't react and kept his face blank. "Very well. I give you the authority to assist and command the work detail."

Gobbie interjected, "Sir, shouldn't we delegate this responsibility to somebody else?" He glanced in Marcus's direction. "We wouldn't need him to oversee the entire operation. It's too critical."

Faal gestured to Marcus. "Even before the battle, this man was working on repairing this city. You were one of his workers, were you not? You of all people know that he is a capable craftsman. He will do nicely."

"But—"

"End of discussion," Faal finished. He looked at Marcus with his brown and blue eyes. "You are free to command the repair detail in any way you please."

CHAPTER FIFTEEN

A LITTLE OUTING

*"Those men deserve to be punished! They tried to kill all
of us, so it is only logical for them to suffer."*

—GOBBIE

Laythia

09:35 hrs, 04/06/2258 (2 months A.F.)

Marcus overlooked the sorry bunch of prisoners. Some of them had fresh black eyes. *The locals aren't treating their prisoners well. Although, I did make them servants for the next ten years. So, I understood they would be mistreated even if the locals promised not to.* Marcus tried to feel compassionate for this sorry bunch of bandits but couldn't, no matter how hard he tried. Not because he hated them but because his heart was so broken.

Marcus observed the conditions of the prisoners. About a hundred of them were chained together in a big, long link. The blacksmiths had been busy forging chains. He checked their physical conditions, seeing the bruises, bandages sprayed with blood from the recent battle, and that some of them didn't even have shoes. A few weeks ago, they were living in their fort with all the resources in the world. Now, they were slaves to a people that hated them.

Marcus looked up, the weather growing hot as the sun beamed down on them, making them all sweat just from sitting there for a few minutes. He stood on the main gravel road in front of the Main Gate outside the city. It was the primary line of traffic that connected the outskirts of the city with the wooden wall. They had cleared the main path from the traps laid but now there was no wooden wall, and there was no shade for anybody.

Marcus shifted his attention and scanned the eyes of the prisoners. Eyes that had come from all different kinds of backgrounds, only to be homeless and enslaved now. Eyes that held one emotion: defeat. The defeat gave Marcus pause. *Was ten years of servitude too much of a punishment for these men? Should I have made it shorter? Or was servitude even the proper choice?* Marcus thought about it longer. They couldn't just let them go, or else what justice would there be for their attack? They could maim all of them, but Marcus wondered if it was cruel to maim three hundred men and then release them. They would be likely to die on their own if they were wounded. There was also no special place to house all the prisoners, and given the decreased Laythian population, it was difficult to maintain a strong defense force to keep the prisoners in check. The Kotang still outnumbered the guards, but it was a matter of hands versus guns. The time for conflict might come, but for now, Marcus could see only defeat in these bandits.

Marcus checked the sun again; it was still early in the morning and it was already blazing hot. He looked around at the destruction. The first thing they needed to do was rebuild the walls around the city.

Marcus addressed them. "Alright. We're going to begin the repair of the city walls and then work on the city buildings themselves. You men were part of the attack on this city, so now we're going to fix it." None of them reacted. Marcus saddened. *They don't care. The defeat is so heavy they don't care anymore.* Men he was fighting roughly a day ago were now on their knees in the heat with no cover. "But first, we'll need lumber, and lots of it. We're going to head out into the forest and chop down some Kaisk and Meeraith trees. Then we will bring the lumber here and begin rebuilding the walls of this city. Understand?" Most of the eyes ignored him. Some complied and nodded, while others just didn't care.

Marcus had a total of ten guards with him, overlooking the one hundred prisoners. There was always the risk of the prisoners overthrowing the guards. Marcus kept that thought in his mind as he led these men. He took one last glance at the sorry faces, sighed, and put his hands on his hips.

"Look, I'm not one for speeches but this is your time for a second chance. Your old life is over, but your life isn't finished. This is the time to pay back the wrongs we've done." Marcus included 'we' to resonate with the attackers. It seemed to work. More heads looked up and gave him their attention. "So, let's finish working on this city." Marcus looked towards the forested hills. "Move out."

The prisoners began to stand one by one and moved toward the Arghast Forest. Marcus and the Laythian guards walked them out in a straight line toward the shade of the trees. The blood from the recent battle was still prevalent, giving some of the prisoners looks of dread and hatred. Marcus could see it all and understood how familiar it felt. It was never pleasant to lose a battle, especially when you were the expected winning side.

The Kotang prisoners marched into the shade, relieved to be out of the blazing sun. They marched deeper and deeper into the forest, their ankle chains making a symphony of drudgery. They each had a chain around one of their legs, making their movement slow. It would be especially difficult to escape given that they didn't have iron weapons, but it wasn't impossible, and Marcus knew that thought was coursing through their minds.

They approached their first position where a pile of axes lay. Marcus knew it was a bad idea to be arming these prisoners with bladed weaponry, but they wouldn't be able to work efficiently if they didn't have tools. That's why the Laythian guards were armed with bows and automatic weapons to kill any prisoner who tried to take advantage of them. But it would have been easy for a larger prisoner to physically overpower a smaller guard. Brute force had its uses. And Marcus still wasn't confident in the fighting ability of the Laythian guards. A majority of them were young boys claiming to be men holding guns like they were kings of the world. But Marcus had to bite the bullet and take the risk.

Marcus faced the prisoners and said, "Alright, now begin chopping down the trees until you have decent-sized lumber. We will have carts ready to bring the materials back to the city by the end of the day. Get moving."

The prisoners picked up the axes, feeling a sense of empowerment as they hefted the weapons. Some of the men got to work while a handful of others merely stood there with the weapons in their hands. Marcus saw the look in their eyes, the thoughts of escape and revolt coursing through their veins. He approached this group and said, "Get to work," in a calm but stern manner. The leader of the group looked to be a thin man with a short beard and dark brown hair and eyes. He looked at Marcus, glaring at him with silent hatred that he tried to conceal. Marcus glared back at him and the man reluctantly fell into line.

To most of their surprise, Marcus picked up an ax too, and got to work. He stood alongside the Kotang as they slowly looked his way. Most of their faces showed surprise that this man was working with them, while the Laythian guards just looked at Marcus with disgust. Marcus paid no attention to the Laythians' glaring and focused on the work at hand. Some of the Kotang exchanged looks, unsure what to think of this man who worked beside them. They all continued their work in silence as the day dragged on.

An hour passed and the men were making steady progress. There was some difficulty for some of the Kotang handling the ankle weights of their shackles but it wasn't enough to impede the whole process.

One of the Laythian guards stood with his rifle up, watching the Kotang prisoners with glee as he said, "Now don't yous get no splinters, boys, or else we gonna be picking up some bruises for laters. HA!"

Marcus saw the guard cheer and jibe. He let the comment go and resumed his work. The thick sound of chopping wood filled the air. The scent of pine and Kaisk filled the area with the growing pollen from the surrounding plants, causing some of the men to begin sneezing.

Marcus eyeballed some of the men, his attention focusing on one man who was sneezing very heavily. He sneezed over and over until he fell to the ground. Marcus stepped over to check on the man when he suddenly swung the ax at Marcus's abdomen. Marcus had suspected this and dodged it accordingly. It was the same man with dark brown eyes and hair who had stared at Marcus earlier.

Marcus quickly found himself surrounded by ten men with axes. The Laythian guards raised their weapons, ready to kill any man who made the first swing. But Marcus remained calm as ever, as if there wasn't a threat to begin with.

Marcus called out to the Laythians, "Stand down." The Laythian guards looked at each other in confusion as he assured them, "I'll handle this."

Surrounded by ten men armed with axes, Marcus glared at the leader. Marcus had his .44 magnum strapped to his thigh and his kukri behind his back but he never considered using them. Marcus looked at them all and said with an edge of warning, "Don't do this." The leader swung first. Marcus stepped aside and threw the man to the ground without much force. He barely touched him. The rest of the ten men joined in the fight, each swinging at Marcus with fury and desperation to escape. Marcus dodged and parried them all with just his bare hands, never breaking a sweat.

One of the prisoners swung at him and Marcus dodged and jabbed his fist into the man's throat, making him choke on his own air. The man fell to the ground clutching his throat. The other nine attackers resumed their barrage. Marcus dodged another attack at his head, grabbed the ax of one of the attackers, and wrenched it free from him. Against his best instincts, he forced himself to use the non-bladed portion of the ax handle and smacked it into the face of the attacker, breaking his nose and sending the man tumbling down. Marcus shifted and parried another attack, smacking the non-bladed end of the ax into the temple of the next man, knocking him out cold. Seven attackers left.

Three men attacked him at once. Marcus swung the bladed side of the ax wide to create space between the group, and then threw the ax and smacked it into the ground next to the foot of the attacker in the middle. Just as he planned, the attacker flinched, and Marcus used that opening to tackle the man and steal his weapon.

Marcus was on his feet in a blur with a new weapon, smacking the tackled man with the handle and knocking him out. Marcus swung the ax behind him and stopped two axes from plummeting into his back. He wrenched free from the two attackers and made quick work of them. They fell in seconds. Four attackers left. Marcus turned to them. Their determination was waning. One man charged him blindly and Marcus merely sideswiped, knocking the man out cold before he even hit the ground. Three attackers remained. Marcus stared at the remaining men. The fear was ever-present in their eyes.

One of them took a step back, but Marcus shook his head. *No, there is no escape.* Marcus charged forward, this time with more ferocity and using the bladed portion of the ax to break the defense of one of the prisoners, snapping his ax handle in two, barely missing the man's flesh. Marcus jammed the butt end of the handle into the man's face, breaking his nose and sending the man tumbling to the ground. The second remaining attacker swung the ax at him, but Marcus spun and parried the bladed portion with his blade, the gentle yet sharp *TING* filling the air as Marcus flipped the ax and hit the man with the blunt portion of the weapon, sending him flying into a nearby tree.

Marcus shifted his attention to the last attacker, the leader. The man stared at Marcus like he knew death was coming. He stood there in fear, his hands shaking with sweat. Marcus looked the man in the eyes and whispered, "Drop it."

But the man somehow found his courage and resumed his attack. He charged forward at Marcus, swinging wildly. Marcus dodged every attack with ease as if this was more of a dance than a swordfight. Even the blade of the ax missing Marcus's body by mere centimeters didn't cause him to flinch. Marcus used the leader's momentum to parry the weapon and thrust the blade into a nearby tree, chopping the tree down and causing it to fall. Marcus used the butt of his weapon and smacked the leader in the face; the man stumbled back into a tree, and Marcus whipped the bladed ax around and smacked it deep into his abdomen.

The man's eyes went wide as he shouted in pain from the blade in his stomach. "AGGGHHHH!" He slid down against the tree stump, the ax still in his abdomen, blood spilling from the wound as the strength slowly ebbed from him. The man's head lowered as the life drained from his body until there was nothing left. He was dead.

Marcus turned and saw the other nine attackers groaning in pain, lying with broken noses and concussions. The remaining ninety prisoners surrounded the area and looked at Marcus in fear. Instead of a speech, Marcus chose to say nothing, letting the results speak for themselves.

The other prisoners went to tend to the wounded, pulling them back with total fear in their faces. One of the prisoners asked in fearful reverence, "What are you?" Marcus didn't answer.

He removed the ax from the dead prisoner, the blood and intestines pulled from their rightful place in the body. Marcus wiped the blood off the blade with the dead man's clothing and then placed the ax aside.

Marcus looked to Joax standing nearby and said, "Joax, pick three men to help me bury this man. Then you overlook the rest of the detail."

Joax nodded and shouted out to the group. The rest of the workers picked up their wounded and got back to work. The remaining Kotang prisoners were terrified of how Marcus was able to take down ten men without much effort at all.

Marcus hefted the dead body as three prisoners joined him. Their chains had been released, but it didn't matter. He knew they wouldn't run after that, and if they did, he'd shoot them.

Marcus and the three prisoners walked a ways out into the woods until they found an open field that broke the forest. Marcus looked at the prisoners behind him and saw the looks of defeat plastered over their faces. *No way they'll run now.* Marcus stopped in the field, the grass stretching waist high, and said, "We'll bury him here."

One of the prisoners, with a bald head and a brown goatee, said, "But sir, we don't have shovels."

Marcus replied, "We're going to use our hands." The prisoners sighed.

Another prisoner, this one missing a tooth and with a split lip, said, "And you just gonna watch us, huh? Typical."

Marcus said nothing, knelt down, and started digging. The prisoners looked at him awkwardly. "What are you doing?" one asked.

Marcus answered simply, "I'm helping."

The prisoner missing a tooth asked, "But why?"

Marcus answered, "Because if I were you, then I would want some stranger to help me."

The third prisoner said, "And what about that guy you *helped* kill?"

Marcus didn't answer and kept digging. He didn't feel any shame over taking the man's life. He didn't feel any shame over harming those other prisoners either. To his sadness, he didn't feel anything, and that bothered him the most. He should at least feel something.

Marcus felt his knees soak from the moisture beneath, the hum of the grass brushing in the wind and the scent of pollen and starch filling his nostrils. Marcus mentally checked himself, feeling his body and soul tight as wire. He hadn't fully relaxed since the battle ended, but it hadn't been very long. Hopefully, he would relax in time . . . hopefully.

He and the prisoners finished digging a small hole then hoisted the body inwards and covered him with dirt. Marcus stood, used his kukri to sharpen a cross out of some wooden sticks, and placed it at the head of the grave.

The prisoners looked at him with curiosity. "Why are you doing that?" one asked.

Marcus answered, "Because that man was a child of God." The prisoners looked at each other in puzzlement and then shrugged their shoulders. Marcus placed the cross in the dirt and looked at the prisoners. "Did any of you know him?" he asked.

The third prisoner, who had no scars on his body and looked to be quite young, said, "He was my father."

Marcus wanted to feel shame at that statement but to his lack of remorse, he didn't. He understood that every man he killed had a family. With every life he took, there was some mother out there who had lost her son forever. But Marcus had killed so many it didn't bother him anymore. He had gotten used to it.

Marcus lowered his head in an attempt to spark some shame inside him as he said, "I'm sorry." But the prisoner didn't look at Marcus with the usual glare of hatred, only looked down at his dead father's grave.

"I hated him, but at least you gave him a proper burial." The prisoner turned away and said, "Let's go back."

The other prisoners followed him and Marcus observed the group. He took one last look at the grave beneath him and wondered, *Should I have killed him?* Marcus thought about how he'd disarmed those other nine men. But did he really have to kill this one man? Marcus added it to the growing pile of questions he had for himself, but for now, he had to get back to work. He would question himself later when he prayed that evening.

They had finished chopping down large portions of wood and shaped them into pillars of timber for the wall. The prisoners left the forest drenched in sweat, returning to the outskirts of the city where tents and other guards waited. Some Laythian civilians stood on the side of the main road, men and women alike, shouting insults at the defeated prisoners as Marcus walked alongside them. The Laythians were looking cheerful as they shouted:

"You baby killing monsters! You deserves this!"

"This is what was coming to yous!"

"What a waste!"

"Worthless human lives!"

"Yous don't deserves to live!"

The insults grew louder and louder until Marcus approached a small group of civilians who looked his way and greeted him with joy. "Ahh, the hero, the Saint!" one man wearing a flimsy hat called out to him. "Come to join us? Send an insult their way. It's fun."

But Marcus only glared at the lead man, shooting him a look of intimidation that would silence anyone. The man sweated in response to Marcus's glare. Then Marcus simply said, "Back off."

The whole crowd was silenced and Marcus returned to the prisoners. Some of the prisoners had stopped and witnessed the whole thing. Marcus paid them no attention and continued walking.

One of the prisoners, a man by the name of Mak, said, "You see that?"

The prisoner in front of him was the young man whose father Marcus had killed. "Yeah, I saw it," the young boy, who was named Noah, said paying little attention.

Mak looked at him and said, "He stood up for us."

Noah didn't have the energy to entertain this conversation, but Mak was curious. He looked at his fellow Kotang and saw some of them were thinking the same thing. A hint of respect evolved between them and this Saint figure. He kept walking forward as Mak said, "Now why did he do that?"

Edge of Arghast Forest close to Laythia
18:39 hrs, 04/06/2258 (2 months A.F.)

Dusk fell over the hills of Laythia. Marcus sat atop the hillside on the edge of the Arghast Forest overlooking the city as the prisoners prepared to end their day. He watched as the daylight fell and the night came, the sky overhead changing from an effervescent orange to a humming indigo blue. The bodies had been buried and the repairs were underway. Now the hard part began. Winning the peace.

Marcus leaned against the stump of a broken tree, watching the sunset. He felt better now that he was alone. He had been fighting and working for the majority of the week, and his bones and muscles ached from all the exertion. He rolled his shoulders, loosening the muscles and tendons within. His shoulders seemed okay and were back to normal after their earlier injuries, but Marcus still felt pain from where the shrapnel had been implanted in his right leg. It had taken hours to remove and it was excruciatingly painful, but at least he was able to still use his leg to a certain degree.

Marcus exhaled, basking in the feeling of being alone for once. He had lived through yet another battle. Another battle of hard fighting and misery.

"When will it end, God?" He knew it was a rhetorical question but he had to ask it. Marcus put one arm on his knee and let his other leg spread out as he leaned against the tree stump. He knew there were going to be problems between the Laythians and Kotang for years to come, but God only knew how long that would last or whether Marcus would be here for it.

Marcus thought about that man he killed today. The rebel leader. Without his knowing, the emotions all came boiling to the surface.

You didn't have to kill that man. Marcus paused for a long second. He thought about how he told the man to drop the weapon but he didn't. Marcus could have disarmed him, but would that have stopped him? If he continued to live, he might have inspired more rebellion. Marcus sighed. It was one of those grey areas where he didn't fully know what was the right answer. So, he closed his eyes and prayed to God. "Father, was that wrong of me to end that man's life? Should I have merely disarmed him and knocked him out?" Marcus knew it was a possibility but he also doubted it. He took another breath and shook his head. "I don't know if what I did was right or wrong today." He would have to be more careful as to who he decided lived and who he decided died.

Marcus leaned his head back against the brown tree stump. He wasn't God. He was just a man. But a man who'd had to make hard decisions, no doubt. "God, I don't know if everything I've done was right or wrong. I know there was certainly some evil that I vanquished along the way, but in war, I know that not every enemy is entirely evil, as I am not entirely good either." Marcus looked up to the indigo sky, now filling with stars. "Father, I've tried to be a good man. I've tried to follow your commands, but I can't help but doubt myself and wonder if I truly am being a good follower like your Son. With all the lives I've taken, were they all evil?"

Marcus thought about that and came to the understanding that a majority of them were. He did not regret ending lives that were truly wicked. It was the lives he took that weren't totally evil that haunted him. There were so many enemies whom he'd fought and found a shaking resemblance with, yet he'd taken their lives regardless because they were born in different places or circumstances.

Marcus shook his head slowly. He didn't have all the answers, and maybe he never would. That was one of the things he hated about war; that it wasn't all black and white. He wished war was simpler. Bad guys were evil, good guys were not. But Marcus was not naïve enough to believe that. He knew humans were a combination of both good and evil, and whether a person chose to fill their life with good or evil determined how Marcus fought them. So, what was it? Did the man he killed today choose to fill his life with good or evil? Did simply standing against Marcus make someone else evil? He knew this debate would go nowhere, as it always had.

He put his hands together, closed his eyes, and lowered his head. He remained there for over an hour, praying silently to God. Praying for those he lost. Praying for the Kotang members and their fallen comrades. Praying for the Laythians and their families, as well as the king and Arthur and Gobbie.

Marcus remained in prayer for as long as he needed. He felt the presence of the silence surround him and relax him a bit. It helped quiet his raging thoughts and relax his ever-tense body. "Thank you, Father," he prayed. When he opened his eyes, he found a crisp Milky Way galaxy stretching through the night. Its splendor enveloped Marcus with growing awe. "I never get sick of that sight, God. Never." He felt his heart cleanse and as the night came, he allowed himself to sleep.

Marcus awoke to warm light penetrating the trees and birds chirping. He allowed the beauty of nature to fill him with peace, letting its soothing feeling flow into every part of his body. His body wasn't as tense and his breathing was calm. Allowing the sun to shine down on him, warming his skin, Marcus exhaled in a whisper, "Thank you, Father."

He thought of his family, thought of Carmen. The warm morning reminded him of the scent of her lavender perfume. Thinking of her beautiful face, Marcus's peace faded slowly, as his warmth remembered the pain of the past and the sad reality he was in.

Marcus put those memories aside and focused on the world around him. He didn't look at the city but focused on the surrounding nature. The forest shrouded him in a small but beautiful world. He took in a deep breath, feeling the oxygen fill his powerful lungs, enjoying the trees in bloom and the sunlight that radiated between them. There was no motion in the forest, only a slight breeze.

Marcus breathed and enjoyed the stillness of it all. He nodded slightly and said aloud, "The world is still turning, regardless of everything that's happened." He was just glad to find some calm among all the chaos. To find places like this that reflected God's beauty gave Marcus a lasting sense of peace, filling his wounded heart with a hint of joy and warming it to new levels he hadn't known were there.

"Thank you, Father." Marcus lifted his eyes to the beautiful blue sky. A few cirrus clouds streaked the air in dozens of curved strips. There was no sense of rain coming any time soon, but the clouds would provide some shade during the heat of the day. Marcus thanked God again and felt his mood improve.

Marcus stood up from his spot against the tree trunk, feeling his back and muscles sore from the weeks prior. He stretched out in the sun and inhaled the pollen-filled air. "Let's get to work."

CHAPTER SIXTEEN

GOLDBERRY LAKE

"I can see a lot of potential in these Kotang men. With the way they work, they definitely have been showing some improvement."

—THE SAINT

Wall Construction Site, Laythia

14:40 hrs, 04/07/2258 (3 months A.F.)

Marcus pushed forward, pressing with all his might as they lifted the giant tree trunk into place. The large square log stretched up thirty feet and was four feet thick and four feet wide. They were cutting down trees whole and shaping them into the new wall. That kind of work took a lot of manpower.

Marcus and ten prisoners pushed the log upwards until they planted the wooden pillar upright and cheered when they had done it successfully. Marcus had taken off his jacket and was dressed in his black undershirt with nothing but his kukri blade on him. Every other man was in the same boat, sweating like a dog in the heat.

The Kotang on both sides of the wall cheered with Marcus. The prisoners gathered around him and they all hugged each other, matching their cheers with the same manly tone. Marcus received pats on the back and other hugs and congratulations as he still clasped onto the kukri blade behind his back. Marcus felt their happiness and reciprocated their joy at the hard work's success. He patted each man on the back and complimented them on their good work.

"Good work, men," Marcus said, feeling the mood of the Kotang prisoners brightening. "You've all done well today."

The men nodded, some of them giving Marcus looks of eagerness for what to do next. Marcus looked up at the sky and saw it was the middle of the afternoon. A good time for a break. He checked the wall and its progress and saw they had finished the construction for the entire new wall. They were making good progress for being only a month in. The next project would be repairing all the homes inside Laythia.

Marcus shifted his attention back to the men and saw the Laythian guards standing behind them, holding their rifles, shooting him looks of contempt. Marcus ignored their negative looks but remembered them for later. *They're not interacting with any of the prisoners. They're only isolating themselves and sowing seeds of hatred.* Marcus had a feeling that would be a problem later, but for now, he brought his attention back to the prisoners.

Marcus stood atop a lone boulder and looked over the men as he said, "Line up." He didn't need to shout. He wasn't the shouting type unless he needed to be heard in battle. It was one thing for men to listen to him when he was shouting, but it was better when men listened to him when he wasn't. The men lined up without question, looking more like soldiers than defeated bandits. Marcus suppressed a smile and killed his joy.

"Follow me." Marcus led the column of one hundred men out into the Arghast Forest with the Laythian guards trailing them on all sides. The men picked up their axes, prepared for more work, but when they approached the fork in the road, instead of turning left deeper into the woods, Marcus turned right, going into Trapper's Pass. The men looked confused as they followed but they didn't defy Marcus's orders.

He led them down the path for miles until they stopped at a beautiful place called Goldberry Lake. Joax had told Marcus about it and how it was a known water source nearby that they could travel to. With the growing heat, it was a popular spot for the Laythians to retreat to escape the sweltering weather. If Marcus had known about the lake sooner, he probably wouldn't have come to Laythia in the first place.

Marcus stood with hands over his hips, watching the sweating men catch their breath. Even the Laythian guards were surprised they were here. Marcus suppressed another smile, knowing it was dangerous for him to be happy, and said, "Because of your hard work, we will not be doing any more labor for the rest of the day."

The Kotang prisoners all lifted their heads like a bunch of prairie dogs, their eyes wide and ears sharp, as if they couldn't believe what they were hearing.

Marcus continued, "As a reward for your efforts, I am allowing you all to bathe in the lake." The looks on all the men's faces were shifting to surprise. "One more thing." They all quieted. Marcus turned to the Laythian guards. "Release them from their shackles for the time being."

The Laythian guards stood there in angered shock. Marcus nodded as if answering their hidden questions. Reluctantly, they complied and released every prisoner from their chains.

Marcus gave one final warning. "But remember, any man who is not present at the end of the day, I will hunt down myself. Do not take advantage of my kindness."

Marcus expected fear from the men, but they only looked like a bunch of eager kids ready to play in the summer. They stood in a line and all looked at him with the same question, *Can we really?* Marcus allowed a tiny smile to break on his face, then nodded. The men looked at each other, checking whether it was truly okay for them to go forward. They looked at Marcus for another signal but Marcus just stood there.

Then one man stepped forward, testing the boundaries. Marcus made no gesture to stop him as the man walked slowly by him and stepped into the refreshing clear water. More men trickled by as Marcus made no gesture to stop them either. Soon more prisoners followed until every man charged into the water. Marcus stood there with his hands on his hips. The Laythians held their guns ready, concerned that the swarm of the one hundred prisoners was about to overwhelm Marcus, but they merely passed by him and ran into the refreshing water with their clothes still on.

Marcus turned and watched as all one hundred prisoners splashed and played in the refreshing lake. The heat from the summer was hot and bearing down on all of them, making even Marcus want to take a dip. But he remained planted and watched the men, knowing he still had a responsibility to follow. If even one man was missing there would be a problem. But Marcus had a feeling that wouldn't be the outcome.

The Laythian guards merely stood there in contempt. Joax leaned against a nearby tree, unsure how to feel. He was slightly angered by Marcus's generosity but he also admired the man for being so kind to a former enemy.

Marcus stood there in the sun, watching the men from the edge of the lake, as they swam, played, wrestled, and enjoyed life. The image stirred a memory within him, reminding him of all his military buddies after the battle of Guadaluca, how they'd all swam in the ocean and played after the horrors they'd endured. Watching their comradery brought a sense of joy to Marcus's heart. Despite how horrible it was, there were still some good things that came out of war. The comradery between brothers was something Marcus would cherish forever. These prisoners were his enemy a short while ago, but Marcus could see the same comradery in these men, even if they did lose the battle.

Marcus was standing at the lip of the lake, watching, when one of the prisoners splashed him with ice-cold refreshing water. Marcus didn't even blink, feeling the cold water soothe his sweating skin. Some of the other prisoners stared at him in fear, wondering what he'd do. They didn't know whether Marcus would shoot them or join them. To their luck, Marcus smiled. It was small but enough to raise their spirits.

The older-looking prisoner Mak said, "Hey Saint! You gonna join us?"

For once, Marcus wasn't taken aback by hearing that nickname. He had received that epithet everywhere, whether he intended it or not, yet hearing it now didn't bother him. Marcus felt his heart ping with a feeling he hadn't felt in a while. A yearning for brotherhood. He could feel the cold water soak into his clothes and cool his body. He desperately wanted to go in, but he had a job to do.

Mak, the leader of the group, stepped forward and said, "Come on. You know you want to." Then Mak turned and chanted, "Saint, Saint, Saint," with the other prisoners joining in until the whole company was chanting. "Saint! Saint! Saint!"

Surprisingly, Marcus rolled his eyes, but it was not from annoyance, and stepped in the water, soaking his boots and clothes with the ice-cold water. The whole company erupted with cheers and splashed at Marcus as he stepped into the lake. Marcus killed his smile but the Kotang knew he was enjoying this. They greeted him as if they had known him for years, forgetting about the battle a month ago, now reveling in the joy of today and the kindness he had shown them. Sowing the seeds of brotherhood.

Laythia

19:04 hrs, 04/07/2258 (3 months A.F.)

The Kotang prisoners returned from their "work outing" with gleaming smiles and high morale. Marcus could feel their morale influence him as well. He knew they were prisoners but they were feeling less like that every day.

Marcus and the Kotang members approached the Main Gate, the guards at the top glaring at them with angry faces. Marcus looked up and called out, "We are returning from our work duties in the forest."

The Laythian guards rolled their eyes and opened the gates, only to reveal a crowd standing there, all with angry faces pointed toward Marcus. Marcus cooled his emotions and maintained proper etiquette. "Is there a problem?" He knew the answer but he asked anyway.

All the guards and their families stood glaring at Marcus. One of the guards shouted, "What are yous doing with those prisoners? Aren't yous supposed to be working thems into the ground?"

Marcus knew it was best to keep a cool head and respond calmly to hostile crowds. He had done it before when dealing with panicking civilians in deteriorating countries but he was never really good at it. He was better a killing people than making them feel better. He quickly thought of a verse from Scripture to help keep his emotions cool. *"A hot-tempered person stirs up conflict, but the one who is patient calms a quarrel."* Marcus felt the Scripture ground him and relax his body, cooling his rising temper as he resumed more control over his voice.

"We have accomplished our duties for the day." Marcus gestured to the completed wall surrounding the city, the proof itself.

The guard who'd spoken was silent, but a woman stepped forward, shouting, "Yous shouldn't be spending your time with those murderers! They attacked our city no less than a month ago, and yous are going out theres and being all buddy-buddy with them is sickening! You're no Saint. You're the Devil!"

Marcus felt almost bored with the conversation. He didn't show it but the emotion was there. He had been called the Devil before, as well as a plethora of other insulting names, so this didn't surprise him at all.

Gobbie stepped forward, and Marcus couldn't help but feel a sense of betrayal stab him. Gobbie stood there in his new light green guard uniform, saying, "He's no Saint! He's only come to destroy us!" His words ramped up the crowd.

Marcus bowed and spoke calmly. "I assure you I have no intention of creating conflict. I only want peace." But the crowd didn't listen to him, and Gobbie's infectious anger was only making things worse.

Gobbie pointed at him, taking advantage of the distance between Marcus and the crowd. Marcus knew anything he said wouldn't make a difference, but to his surprise, Joax stepped forward and spoke to the gathered people. "I know everyone is ramped up right now. But please remember that this is the man who helped save our city. We wouldn't be here if it wasn't for him. And I remember every day his heroism and kindness. Did we forget that this man worked to rebuild our city even before the attack began?"

Joax's words calmed the crowd and some were even nodding. Marcus was grateful for Joax stepping forward. The people seemed more apt to listen to one of their own. But it only proved they viewed Marcus as a foreigner still, even if he had fought for their city.

But Gobbie stepped forward again. "Don't listen to that man!" he shouted, now pointing at Joax, "He's been corrupted by the Saint's false religion!"

Joax lowered his brow and tilted his head quizzically. "Corrupted?" He looked at Marcus and then back at the crowd. "Are you lumping me in with this guy's religion?" He turned slightly and whispered to Marcus, "Sorry."

Marcus shook his head and mouthed, "It's fine," finding no offense.

Then one of the prisoners, Mak, stepped forward. "I know you think of me as an enemy," he said. The crowd quieted, their rage shaping their silence. "But please remember," Mak gestured to Marcus, "this man is not like most men. He has the ability to forgive his enemies and treat them with kindness." Mak looked at Marcus with his brown eyes and shaved head. "I have nothing but the utmost respect for him."

This only enraged the crowd even more. Marcus knew Mak didn't intend for it to go that way but he was still grateful to have his support.

The crowd started throwing insults at Marcus again, their anger fueled by Gobbie.

"Murderer! Killer!"

"Why don't yous go back to where yous belong?"

"We don't want yous here!"

"Yous won't convert us to your false religion, Saint!"

"Devil! He's the Devil incarnate!"

Marcus had heard all these comments before and wasn't surprised. *They could at least come up with some better insults,* he thought comically. But Marcus only turned the other cheek and went back out from the city gates toward the Kotang prisoners, who stood there with concerned faces. Some of them wanted to touch Marcus and comfort him but held back, still giving him looks of concern.

Marcus ignored the angry crowd behind him and addressed the prisoners. "That's enough work for today. Return to your tents and we shall resume in the morning." The gleam of dusk over the horizon showered the valley with orange translucence as the day ended.

The Kotang prisoners only looked at Marcus in puzzled concern. "That will be all," he told them as he departed into the forest to pray.

CHAPTER SEVENTEEN

WHAT COMES NEXT . . .

"When does an enemy become an enemy and when does an enemy become an ally?"

—ANONYMOUS

Kotang Holding Camp, Laythia

21:48 hrs, 04/07/2258 (3 months A.F.)

Mak sat perched next to his tent by the fire. All the prisoners were spread out in the Bog on the outskirts of the city, under guard from all sides by Laythians. Mak didn't mind it, though. He was just glad for the fire. They weren't given much from the Laythians but at least they were given tents and some firewood.

Mak had heard the other companies of prisoners weren't doing well. He'd heard they were under strict management from their Laythian keepers and took a lot of beatings, which was why he was grateful to be under the Saint's leadership. What surprised Mak the most was when the Saint put his weapons down, aside from the .44 magnum and kukri on his back, and joined the Kotang prisoners in their work. For whatever reason, this attitude defused Mak and made him feel comfortable around the man. He had even heard that the man apologized to Noah for killing his father and that Noah accepted his apology with no grudge. That mere statement had surprised Mak beyond belief.

The rest of the Kotang and even some people from Laythia had given him the nickname the Saint. Surprisingly, it fit; for a man who was so good at war, he was remarkably kind, even if he didn't show much emotion. Mak still liked him, though. He was glad to be treated under the Saint's conditions, even if they were to be prisoners for the next ten years. It was a tough reality to swallow but Mak could at least feel safe knowing it wouldn't last forever.

But would that really happen? Would the Laythians really honor their word and release them after ten years? Mak froze and pondered that, staring into the fire, the wind blowing the heat sideways, away from him. *No, he thought*, the realization hitting him slowly. *They're never going to let us go. We attacked them blind and now they hate us for it.* Mak stared in shock, but deep down, he'd already known. *They're going to keep us as slaves forever or kill us. They have no reason to let us go.* The new reality sank in, draining Mak's previous good mood. It made sense. It was perfect logic. *The Laythians hate us. They want to see us suffer.*

Mak wanted to say something but couldn't. He just let the reality sink in, wondering what he was going to do. Would he stay here for the rest of his life as a slave, trying to repay his debt for his past actions? He let the thoughts slip for now; he would have time to ponder these things later.

Mak was sitting beside the main road on a log. The camp hummed with low activity but it was alive, nonetheless. He looked up and surprisingly saw the Saint walking through the camp. More heads popped up and noticed him too. His darkened figure was difficult to spot in the night, but Mak could still tell who it was.

As the Saint walked by, Mak said, "Hey Saint, care for a seat?"

Mak watched him contemplate the question, but only for a brief second. Mak brought out another block of wood and the Saint took a seat, the two of them staring into the fire. Mak heard more activity and some other prisoners came over and joined them. Pretty soon there were about half a dozen people sitting around the small fire. Mak surveyed the faces of all the Kotang around him. Most of their morale was pretty high, especially after the swim today, so he saved his grim realization for another time, not wanting to ruin their good day.

Surprisingly, the Saint was the first to speak. "You men worked hard today. Good job."

Mak stared at the Saint in admiration. The man's words sent encouragement to his grim heart, melting away the sadness like soap on a dish. The man had a way of defusing others. Mak stared into the fire, watching its orange and red flames dance before them like a show. He could tell the Saint's positive enthusiasm infected them all, making their morale higher. Mak forgot about his previous reality and enjoyed the moment.

Mak observed the age range of the Kotang members surrounding the fire. Most of them looked to be in their early twenties, one in their teens, and a few in their early thirties, while Mak was in his mid-thirties. Mak shifted his attention to the Saint but had a hard time determining his age. The man could be in his early thirties, but the lines on his face could mean he was in his forties as well. He had the type of appearance that made the man's age impossible to gauge. But one thing was for sure, the Saint was older than all of them. Mak continued to stare at him.

He was going to say something but then a teenager in the group by the name of Ollie asked, "Excuse me, sir?" The banter around the fire quieted. "Why do you spend your time with us? You could be with the Laythians, you know, people you fought for and all."

The Saint replied, "You guys aren't so bad." This raised the spirits of the Kotang even more.

"I've got a better question," Mak said. The whole group shifted their focus. "Why do you act so kindly to us when we were your enemy?"

The Saint answered, "Because Jesus forgave me and showed me mercy, even when I didn't deserve it."

Mak didn't realize how much of an impact those words had on him. He felt his whole heart flush and felt showered with relief and forgiveness, relieving the massive burden on his chest. He hadn't even realized how much regret he had over attacking the Laythians until now. Before Mak had attacked people with no problem, but this was different.

Tears spread from the eyes of the Kotang members around the fire. Nearly all of them were crying, trying to hold back their manly tears. Mak himself was crying and he didn't even realize it. Only when he felt the teardrops patter his trousers did he notice.

Mak felt a powerful rush in his heart, touching that emptiness he'd felt since he was a boy. He'd tried to fill it with pleasures, only to feel it grow and consume more and more of himself until there was nothing left. But meeting this man now made Mak hope again that life was not all suffering and evil. That he could actually be a good person despite his shortcomings.

Mak shook his head in bemusement. "I don't know what to say."

The Saint gave no visible reaction as he said, "You don't have to say anything." Then he stretched his hand out and put it on Mak's shoulder, and the warmth in his touch was unlike any warmth Mak had experienced. His hand was warm but not burning. Then he asked, "Can I pray for you? All of you?"

Mak nodded without thinking about it. It seemed the proper thing to do, and the rest of the Kotang members did the same.

The Saint closed his eyes and prayed, "Father, I know we have done evil. We have broken your laws, but Jesus please forgive us for our sins. Please forgive me for the people I've hurt and please forgive these men for whom they've hurt. Please forgive us for the things we've stolen. Please forgive us for the pain we've caused. Father, please renew us and let us repent of our actions and choose to live our lives for you. In Jesus' name, I pray, amen."

Mak opened his eyes and was still crying, but he didn't fight it. The words this man said over him were like nothing he'd ever experienced. It was like this man was God in the flesh.

The Saint then went around praying for all the members around the fire, not looking at them as enemies or Kotang, but as fellow human beings who were hurting people. He prayed with them, listened with them, and comforted them. He heard all they had to say and prayed over their troubles and trials. Hope was brought to their weary hearts through this man's kindness.

Mak took in the sight and could not believe this was real. These men were all murderers and thieves, decked out with tattoos and teardrops, but now they were healing, becoming something better. In a world where kindness was rare and goodness was killed, this man stood above it all and continued on despite the hardships. It amazed Mak down to his soul that a man like this existed. He wanted to learn more, to understand why this man loved his enemies when he had no reason to. Any other person would tell Mak to hate his enemies, but here was a man living by example by literally loving his enemies.

But who was this man? Was he truly a man? Or something else?

CHAPTER EIGHTEEN

CHOOSE A SIDE

*"I hate them . . . I hate them all! I want to kill every
single one of those Kotang murderers!"*

—GOBBIE

The Great Hall, Laythia
11:49 hrs, 05/07/2258 (3 months A.F.)

Marcus stood before the king, who had elevated his seating more by adding additional stairs since the last time Marcus had been in the Great Hall.
Marcus tried with all his might not to roll his eyes. Even in other kingdoms,
doing so would get you beheaded. So, Marcus restrained himself and killed
his emotions, being all business all the time.

The king sat on his throne with Faal next to him, looking down at
Marcus and grinning. Marcus hated that grin and could feel his blood boil
in response. Then the king's grin died and he said, "I'm sure you're wondering the reason why I've called you here."

Marcus said nothing, as usual. The king stood up from his throne, his
plush red and gold clothing and long blonde hair making him look like an
emanate figure. The king stepped down a couple of steps before stopping
on the last one, standing just slightly taller than Marcus so Marcus would
have to look up at him. Marcus knew it was the king's vain attempt to grab
power. To muzzle this stranger whom he could never control.

The king stuffed his hands into his fancy robe. "It has come to my attention that you have been showing kindness to the Kotang invaders," he said.

They're not invaders anymore, Marcus thought.

The king asked, "What do you have to say for yourself?"

Marcus knew it was a rhetorical question. He knew the king was testing him. He tried to deflect the topic slightly by saying, "If you are asking about the progress we've been making then I would say that over the past month, we have completed the process of rebuilding the wall. Very soon we shall be getting started on rebuilding the homes as well—"

"Yes yes, that's all said and done," the king said dismissively. "I'm talking about the rumors I hear about you treating these insects with kindness."

Insects, he noted. Marcus chose his words carefully. "I have treated them accordingly to their work conditions, Your Grace. They have proven to be valuable workers."

The king raised a crooked smile. "So I've heard. And what do you plan to do with them after they have completed all the work?"

Marcus answered honestly, "Honor the punishment and release them after ten years." He paused, knowing what he said next would infuriate the king. "Perhaps in a shorter time given their behavior within the community."

The king turned bright red, barely containing the anger in his voice. "And you dare to treat these invaders with such kindness?"

Marcus nodded once. "I do."

The king looked ready to pop. "What reason do you have to release these men under a shorter period? Wasn't their attack against our beloved city wrongful enough?"

Marcus answered honorably, "The term stands, Your Grace, but given their work on the city walls as well as their behavior, I have seen no reason to punish these men further. Ten years is enough."

The king's anger transformed into an evil grin. Marcus never liked it when someone gave him that look. "What if I tell you that I don't plan to release them after ten years?" the king asked. Marcus said nothing, only glared at him. The king saw his chance. "I don't intend to release them. I would say that putting them in indentured servitude for the rest of their lives seems a proper punishment for their crimes."

A life sentence, Marcus thought. *Either kill them or use them as slaves for the rest of their lives.* He had a feeling this would happen. He should have thought of a more fitting punishment for the three hundred prisoners rather than ten years of servitude, but that was void now because the Laythians didn't intend to honor their promise.

Marcus had to fight it now or he would lose any chance of appeal. But if he did, he would lose any faith this king had in him. Marcus knew, however, that he'd never had any faith from this king to begin with. He was only a tool that the king knew he could not control.

Marcus stood up straighter and spoke as calmly as he possibly could. "Your Grace, with respect, that will not go well with the people. The prisoners will feel mistreated and it will likely sponsor a revolt."

"Good," the king said. "I want a reason to shoot them all." The king looked aside. "But then again, I don't really need one. I could have them all killed for being traitors and invaders."

Marcus said, "Your Grace, I am warning you. If you intend to harm a wounded enemy, it will not end well for you."

But the king seemed uninterested in Marcus's warning. "Yes yes, Saint, your words have been heeded," he said as if he had never heard Marcus. The king finished his thought and clapped his hands. "It is settled! The moment all the buildings are finished, I shall host a public execution for all the invaders for their treachery against Laythia."

This time Faal interjected, keeping his voice calm as he spoke. "Your Grace, executing the prisoners may prove to show insecurity in your power. Perhaps showing mercy may be a more admirable attribute to demonstrate as a king to your people?"

The king looked to Faal with disgust. "You're repulsive, Faal, and so are your ideals. I will execute them once their work is done. There is no point in feeding extra mouths if they are all evil anyway." The king looked at Marcus and squinted his eyes. He stepped forward, now ground level with Marcus. "And what will you do?" He began pacing around Marcus. "How do you take this news?"

Marcus said nothing. His face was blank and expressionless. The king had a frustrating time reading him until he stepped directly in front of Marcus, raising his eyebrows in expectation of an answer. The smaller man demanded the larger man to answer to him. But Marcus remained stoic and silent.

The king's anger flared. "Well? What's your answer?" he demanded, raising his voice a little too high. Marcus still said nothing. The king stepped forward. "You give me an answer right now or I swear by the heavens I will have you killed." The king looked straight up at Marcus now.

Marcus met his eyes and said, "Do not swear by the heavens; you don't believe in them."

The king took a step back. "Well then, let's see who ends up where. Which one of us will end up in heaven and which one in hell?"

Marcus said, "It doesn't have to be either or."

The king sneered. "You continue to despise me." He stepped back, speaking louder for all to hear. "So, what's your answer? Do you agree with killing them, or not?"

The whole room went silent. Faal tried to step in, saying, "The king is very tired. Perhaps we should all resume this with cooled heads?" He put a hand on the king's shoulder.

The king threw off the hand and said, "No! I want to hear what he has to say." He stepped right up to Marcus's face. "Are you with me or *not*?"

The room fell silent once again. Tick, tick, tick. Marcus looked down at the king with a calm demeanor and said, "I am not."

The king's anger finally burst. "TRAITOR!" He turned. "Guards! Kill this man!"

The six armored guards in the room drew their weapons and approached Marcus slowly, while Marcus stood there calm as ever. The six guards approached Marcus with their AX5M assault rifles aimed at him, set to full auto, but Marcus did not move. The guards all sweated in intensity as the man who saved their city was now their enemy. They were all aware of his abilities with a blade so they approached him with caution.

Marcus ignored the danger and looked down at the floor, as if ashamed. "You don't want to do this," he said. It was more a warning to the guards than to the king.

The six guards hesitated and looked at each other, giving Marcus the opportunity he needed. Marcus drew his sidearm and fired on the three guards in quick succession. The .44 dropped all three men with fist-sized holes in their chests. Marcus then grabbed the weapon of the guard on his right. The guards attempted to fire but Marcus had already overpowered the guard and used him as a shield, firing his .44 magnum over the man's shoulder, taking out the other two guards before they could fire.

Marcus fired his last round in his .44 into the man he was using as a shield and the man's body dropped to the floor. Gunpowder and the taste of blood filled the air as Marcus stood with six guards lying dead at his feet.

The king stood atop his staircase as Faal wielded a spear in his hand. He shouted, "Faal! Kill this man!"

Faal spun the spear like an expert. Marcus didn't show any reaction but he was impressed with Faal's moves and experience. He was clearly a man who'd disciplined himself and was a master of both war and the spear. Marcus was out of ammo and it would take time to reload his .44, so he holstered his sidearm and unsheathed his sword, shifting his sword into his left hand. The two of them squared off in the Great Hall, the king watching with glee in the background.

Marcus knew he was at a major disadvantage here. He may be good with a sword but a spear had the advantage of distance in this battle. And in this empty hall, there wasn't much to impede Faal's efforts. Nevertheless, Marcus had to fight him.

Faal spun the spear around his body like it was an extension of himself. Marcus backed up, away from the center of the hall. Faal thrust so fast that Marcus almost didn't block the blow in time, leaving a cut on his cheek. Marcus parried the spear aside and held the sword at the ready. Faal retreated then came back again, this time thrusting for Marcus's stomach. If Marcus didn't time this right he would be impaled for sure, but the thrust didn't come as quickly as he'd expected. He deflected the weapon with his sword, grabbing the spear and trying to wrench it from Faal. He spun the spear around and threw Faal into a nearby wall, but Faal never let go of the spear, the two of them trying to wrench the weapon free from the other. Faal was not as big as Marcus, but he was still very strong, although he didn't show it under all that fancy fabric.

Marcus kneed Faal in the stomach and spun the spear around again, slamming him into a nearby door. Faal recovered, abandoning his grip on the spear, and quickly clapped Marcus in the ears, stunning him briefly and allowing him to wrench the spear free before slamming the butt end of it into Marcus's stomach and then swiping the bladed end toward his face. Marcus held his sword up to deflect the attack but the force sent his own weapon toward him and briefly cut his forehead, spilling blood into his right eye. *Better a cut forehead than a severed head.* Faal regained the advantage of distance while Marcus retreated, blocking as well as he could while staying close to the walls and entrance to the Great Hall.

The king chuckled in glee as he watched the two men fight. Marcus was stronger than Faal, but Faal was quicker. Marcus waited for Faal to tire and to his luck, he did. Faal slowed down, allowing Marcus a chance to come at him. He charged forward but Faal had feinted and used the spear as a pole and kicked Marcus in the face. The pain was blinding for a split second. Faal then sent another kick to his abdomen and Marcus felt the air leave his lungs as he was sent flying out the entrance of the Great Hall.

He came tumbling down the steps before he found his feet again, only to look around and find a massive angry mob standing outside the Great Hall with torches and pitchforks. There at the front stood Gobbie, holding his AX5M as Faal came out of the Great Hall.

Gobbie grunted in contempt. "Well, Saint. You've got a bit of a reputation around here's." He grinned.

Marcus took the time to get back on his feet and recover his lost breath, only to face the massive mob in front of him, never forgetting Faal standing behind him. He still held onto his sword, as he was surrounded by hostiles, all of them wanting him dead. The crowd was armed with any pointed weapon they could find. They carried the classic spears, pitchforks, and torches, as well as anything else that could kill a human. The main threats were the ones with guns, but thankfully only Gobbie and a handful of other Laythian guards were armed with them.

Marcus caught his breath as Gobbie got the crowd fired up. "What do yous say, people? Should we rid this filth from our streets?" The whole crowd cheered in an uproar. "And what do we do with filth in our city?"

The crowd shouted in unison, "KILL THEM!"

Marcus really wished he had his SR75k, but he would have to make do. He used his right hand to grab a throwing knife behind his belt and struck Gobbie in the arm before he could take aim at Marcus. Gobbie screamed as the knife penetrated his bone sending searing pain into his arm. He dropped his weapon, which Marcus happily picked up.

He held his sword in his left hand, using his arm as a bar to hold the gun, and flicked the weapon to semi-automatic, firing on the guards with guns. He quickly took the guards down and then thrust the butt end of the gun into Gobbie's face, making him tumble over in pain.

The rest of the crowd wasn't deterred, though. Despite Marcus having a gun they didn't run. Marcus checked for Faal behind him but he was nowhere to be found. He brought his attention back to the crowd that was slowly encroaching upon him.

Marcus backed up against the stairs, saying, "Back away. I don't want to fight you."

An old woman with an evil grin smiled at him with broken teeth. "We don't care," she said.

Marcus flipped the catch to automatic but that still didn't deter the crowd from slowly approaching. There had to be two hundred people in this mob, all of them armed with blades and blunt weaponry. There was a variety of ages. Anyone from the age of thirteen to forty was involved in this group, all of them wanting his blood and blaming him for bringing all the troubles to their city.

Marcus wondered why the crowd kept approaching until he remembered that all guards in the city had a limit of ten rounds of ammunition per gun. Marcus had shot six guards, firing eight or nine rounds.

The crowd continued to come forward. *Father, please help me*, he prayed silently. The crowd was now stepping up the stairs. Marcus had no choice. He fired on the wicked woman, splitting her skull open like a watermelon with the 5.56x45mm rounds. The crowd stopped, the shot echoing in the valley. They all stared at the woman for a second but then approached once more.

"Don't do this," Marcus said.

Gobbie stood back up behind the crowd, shouting, "Kill him!"

Marcus clicked the trigger but the clip was empty. The whole crowd glared at him with wicked smiles. Marcus tossed the gun aside and unsheathed his kukri, switching both blades back into their appropriate hands as he slowly backed into the open entrance of the Great Hall. Faal was still nowhere to be found and Marcus found that odd as he stood there, weapons drawn.

Marcus prayed silently to himself. "*The Lord is my light and my salvation— so why should I be afraid? The Lord is my fortress, protecting me from danger, so why should I tremble? When evil people come to devour me, when my enemies and foes attack me, they will stumble and fall. Though a mighty army surrounds me, my heart will not be afraid.*"

Then he whispered, "The Lord is my strength and my song; he has given me victory."

The crowd slowly surrounded him, a hateful grin shared among all their faces. Silence filled the Great Hall until all two hundred people began laughing wickedly. Marcus remained frozen, ready. They laughed for what felt like an eternity, grinning with evil as they stared at their prey. Their laughs mixed until they became one uniform voice as if it were coming from one person. Marcus stared at the crowd, waiting, and everyone abruptly went dead silent.

Marcus's senses were heightened to their limits, with threats from all sides waiting to attack. The silence lingered as the sweat slowly dripped from his body. He breathed slowly, feeling his knuckles turn white as they gripped the hilts of his weapons. His blades calm in his hands as he stared at the crowd.

Then Marcus closed his eyes and remembered a verse.

"Don't be afraid, for I am with you." Hearing the verse rejuvenated Marcus, filling him with renewed strength. Marcus inhaled, and then, with a deep breath, he exhaled sharply and opened his eyes in total peace.

The crowd suddenly charged him. With his sword in his right hand and his kukri in his left, Marcus quickly became a dancer of blades, slicing at all attackers. They really were trying to kill him with all their intent. They may be inexperienced but they had numbers. It was two hundred against one.

The crowd continued to charge him, and Marcus held nothing back. Slicing through necks, arteries, arms, legs, groins, and hearts, he became a force of nature as he whipped around attacking, dodging, and defending all at the same time, using his body with agility like an Olympic gymnast. The crowd kept charging using whatever weaponry they could, but Marcus was so deadly with his sword and kukri that no numbers mattered against him. He sliced through bones and limbs, with anyone daring to come close losing life or limb. Screams of rage quickly filled the hall. All these people were charging to try and kill a man they had no quarrel with. Marcus didn't have time to think about the morality of it all. They were trying to kill him and he was trying to survive.

The circle quickly became difficult to stand in, as the ground became ridden with blood and bodies. People were slipping over the blood of their neighbors and tripping over the bodies of their children, but they were still charging him nonetheless. Marcus made use of this, well aware of his surroundings. He stuck his sword through the neck of a man before he removed the blade and threw the body at two charging women, making them trip and fall before him so he could plunge his blades into their backs. The two women screamed in pain as their lives left them. Marcus turned, now covered in blood, as more and more people surrounded him. He didn't care how many there were. He would fight them all if he had to. His blood-soaked appearance, skill, and rage deterred his attackers from being as effective in battle. Marcus screamed his battle cry, terrifying the people and demoralizing them, but they still came at him.

The Great Hall was filling with bodies, the floor now completely covered with blood. Marcus kept slashing, parrying, dodging, and taking some blows from a few lucky attackers. The crowd just kept coming, until the two hundred whittled down to one hundred, then fifty, then twenty. Marcus was completely soaked with blood and guts. His black sword now brimming red with heat.

The final twenty attackers had the choice to leave but they chose a darker fate instead. But this time, the remaining hostiles became tactful. The mass of twenty charged him all at once, abandoning all sense of injury. They were going for the charge to pin Marcus down and kill him but Marcus had planned for this. The circle had opened up behind him and he now stepped atop the piles of bodies around him, using it as a hill to stumble their attack.

Marcus kicked the closest attacker and he went tumbling down the small pile. The bodies continued to trip the remaining attackers, allowing Marcus a couple of free kills before they could regroup. One of them grabbed Marcus's left hand holding the kukri, but since Marcus was wielding two weapons, he easily chopped the man's hand off, regaining control of his weapon and plunging his kukri into the neck of an attacker and slicing outwards, sending the man's blood into the face of another attacker, blinding him. The attacker dropped his weapons and put his hands to his face. Marcus plunged the kukri into the man's chest. The blade entered his body, slicing through organs and bone like butter.

Some of the attackers managed to land a couple of cuts on Marcus's arms and punches to his face, but Marcus was familiar with pain and understood that no battle was left without scars. One man managed to cut his right forearm with a small blade, but Marcus ended his life quickly by slicing his leg in half and then slicing his head off as he fell to a knee.

There were now ten attackers remaining. Marcus was nearly out of breath and misplaced his footing, causing him to come tumbling down the small hill on the other side, into the presence of three of the ten attackers. Marcus tucked with the roll and sliced the legs of the attackers at the bottom, quickly ending their pain and getting back on his feet. One of the attackers wielded a spear and threw it toward him, but due to his lack of training the spear missed and landed harmlessly beside Marcus. Marcus sheathed his kukri with his left hand, picked up the spear, and threw it back at the attacker, striking him through the chest as the man vanished behind the pile.

The remaining six attackers surrounded Marcus, one of them rearing to throw another spear at him. Using his open hand, Marcus threw a throwing knife at the armed attacker, sending the blade into the man's head. Wielding only his sword and surrounded by five attackers, it quickly turned into a symphony of blades. Marcus used every body part to get an advantage, his agility proving useful in this scenario as he kicked, dodged, parried, and attacked, often at the same time. He sliced through the abdomen of one attacker, grabbed the man's spear, and used it to block another's attack, then thrust his sword into them.

Three hostiles remaining. Marcus sheathed his sword and was now barehanded. One attacker charged at him with a hook-shaped sickle sword. Marcus sideswiped, grabbing the man's arm after he missed his attack, spun the weapon around, and sliced the man's throat with his own sword.

Marcus faced the two remaining attackers, one of them with a double-ended spear and the other with a chained mace. The spear attacker went first, jabbing at Marcus but trying to maintain his distance. Marcus merely backed up until the man tripped over a body and fell onto the other bladed end of his spear, impaling himself. Marcus looked at the man quizzically, then shifted his attention to the last attacker.

That mace is going to be a problem, Marcus thought. With his bare hands, he picked up a nearby body and hoisted it as a shield as the attacker with the mace swung it toward him. The mace smacked into the body he was using as a shield, breaking bones in the process, but not enough to wound Marcus behind it. Marcus threw the body toward the attacker, pinning the man to the ground and causing him to lose control of his mace. Marcus picked up the weapon and spun it around. The mace felt natural to him, despite him never wielding it before. Marcus spun it around his body like he had been training with it for years, then swung at the final attacker's knee. The knee inverted and the man shrieked in pain as he tried to grab his broken limb, but Marcus spun the chain and smacked it into the man's chin, shattering bone as he fell backward. Marcus swung three more times until the man's skull shattered brain and bone, continuing until there was nothing but mush.

There were some small moans of pain amidst the crowd as Marcus looked over the horror he'd created. Two hundred people lay dead, wounded, or dying. Many were hacked to pieces. Limbs, blood, and guts were spread throughout the Great Hall. Teenagers to middle-aged men and women lay spread across the hall, all of them without life or a soul. Their blood stained Marcus's hands as he caught his breath and checked for more hostiles. The hall was empty except for a few wounded people.

Marcus cleaned off his weapons and took the time to reload his .44. He would need to learn to reload it quicker in order to fire in quick succession. But it packed such a punch that one bullet was enough to kill a man.

Marcus was drenched in blood, most of it not his, and he caught his breath as he walked through the horror scene that was the Great Hall. One young woman who looked to be in her mid-twenties and was missing a hand looked up at him and said, "You're the Devil Saint. The Angel of Death sent to cleanse the wicked."

Marcus looked at the wounded woman and saw she was buried under a plethora of bodies. He went over to check her for weapons, but before he could she reached under her coat and pulled out a grenade with no pin.

"See yous in hell!" she said as she grinned.

Marcus kicked the grenade under the woman and dove for cover, grabbing a body next to him as a shield. The grenade went off with a loud *BOOM!*—sending blood and limbs everywhere. Remarkably, he wasn't injured by the grenade and knew he had to use better judgment when assisting the wounded. It had happened like that before in prior wars, which was why Marcus had a hard time taking prisoners. He wanted to be kind and take prisoners alive but previous wars and even this recent event showed him that it was dangerous.

Marcus looked out toward the opening of the Great Hall and stepped outside, planning his next move. He could tell as he exited the Great Hall that the rest of the city was on alert. The remaining two hundred Laythian guards would be on the prowl looking for him and they would shoot to kill given that Marcus had just killed two hundred of their people. There was no way he would be permitted to come back here again. But Marcus's priorities shifted to the next target of concern: the Kotang prisoners.

The prisoners were being held on the outskirts of the city in tents in front of the gates. Marcus wanted to curse that they'd finished the city gates, meaning he would either have to climb over a thirty-foot wall and then run across open ground or he would have to find another way out the city. He had left his SR75k rifle back at his camp outside the city and the rest of the Laythian militia would be armed with the ammo and weaponry left from the previous battle. But Marcus knew there was more than one way out of this city. During the previous attack, the Laythian people had sent their women and children into underground caverns built into the mountain. They had a network of tunnels and most likely an exit.

Marcus knew he would have to come back for the Kotang prisoners before the Laythians executed them, but for now, he needed more supplies and he needed to get out of the city. Marcus went past the Great Hall, now a massive graveyard, and toward the buildings built into the side of the mountain. He headed toward the east side of the city, climbing in elevation until he was at the entrance of one of the escape routes that led into the tunnels.

The brightness of the sun vanished as Marcus took a torch and headed into the heart of the mountain.

«— —»

The king was furious. Gobbie stood angered as well. The two of them were speaking inside the king's private quarters behind the Great Hall, tormented by the fact that not even a crowd of two hundred people could kill this man.

Gobbie asked, "What should we do, sire?"

The king responded with an outburst. "I know exactly what we are going to do! We are going to find this man and kill him!"

Gobbie sighed. He knew the king was a complete buffoon.

The king asked, "Where was he last spotted?"

"Heading into the caverns, sire," Faal spoke up as he entered the square room.

The king lowered his voice, understanding what the Saint's plan must be. "He's trying to use the caverns to escape the city. We must stop him!" He turned to Gobbie. "Send our units to block the passage leading toward the exit of the mountain. Send men down into the caverns. Find him and kill him. Then round up those Kotang members. If he escapes, we'll have something to bring him back."

Gobbie grinned. "Count on it."

But before he could go, the king said, "And one more thing." Gobbie turned. "You have been promoted to the new captain of the guard."

Faal stood to the side, spear in hand, slightly disappointed. The king turned to him and said, "Since you failed to kill this man you have been demoted."

Gobbie grinned at him, but Faal stifled his emotions and kept them to himself, saying nothing, while Gobbie said, "Right away, sire."

«——»

The Laythians never found the Saint in the catacombs, and the day ended with the Great Hall covered in blood and the king infuriated with the failure of his troops. Yet not all was lost, as the king prepared for tomorrow and the wicked joy it would bring.

CHAPTER NINETEEN

THE EXECUTION

*"Do you know how you draw a rat out? It's easy really. All
you need is to set out some cheese and a trap."*

—THE KING

Laythia

05:59 hrs, 06/07/2258 (3 months A.F.)

Dawn approached as the sun rose over the horizon. The king stood over the
town courtyard surrounded by fifty of his guards and the other hundred
fifty dispersed throughout the city and on the wall. He welcomed the new
day, the beautiful orange sun gleaming over the mountain, warming his perfect skin under his blonde beard.

The king inhaled and said, "It's a fine day for an execution." He scanned
the sky, saw there were no clouds in sight, and reveled in the beauty of a new
day. Behind him stood Gobbie in his green uniform, wielding a new AX5M.

The Townsquare had been transformed into a gallows, ripe for a hanging. The crowd began to fizzle in. After hearing the news that the Saint had
killed over two hundred people the entire city was in uproar calling for the
man's head. Unfortunately, the man had escaped, but nothing a little bait
wouldn't do to bring out a rat. The king smiled. *He'll come. It's part of his nature.*

The king clasped his hands behind his back and looked over his shoulder. Faal was nowhere to be found but that was to be expected. He did
demote him the other day, so it would make sense that he didn't want to
be here.

The crowd of the remaining families left in the city trickled in until they surrounded the Townsquare. They were settled until the king brought out the prisoners. Seeing the Kotang inside the city walls created an uproar throughout the crowd. Seeing their murderers chained up, ready to be hanged, brought a strong sense of vengeance amongst them. The king saw their bloodlust and welcomed it. It would make it all the more difficult for the Saint when he returned to save his beloved murderers.

The king spotted a brief flicker of light coming from the woods overlooking Laythia. He found it peculiar, and almost had a thought as to what it was but disregarded it. He had never felt more secure in his life having all his guards armed with full weaponry.

The king allowed the crowd to become a little more intoxicated with bloodlust before he stepped forth and addressed them. "My fellow subjects. We are gathered here to administer justice. Justice against the fiends who sought to ravage our beautiful city and destroy our way of life!" The crowd cheered with hatred, just the way he wanted. The king strolled the gallows. "These men have been found guilty of supporting the Saint! They are guilty of their actions and they all plead to be hanged and die with no regrets about the horrendous battle, in which our brave citizens fought to repel the invaders. So now we, the people, united as one, will hang these traitors for their crimes against our city and against humanity!"

The three hundred criminals were lined up and chained behind the gallows, the hanging ropes ready for use. The king looked out at the tree line beyond Laythia and saw that same flicker of light. He paused for a moment, finding it peculiar again, but he resumed his performance and played it well. "Bring the prisoners forward!"

Mak, Noah, and another prisoner were brought forward. The king watched as the ropes were placed around each man's neck and tightened. The king took his leave and stepped back up to the upper courtyard to watch the performance, knowing that at any moment the Saint would show himself. Even if he didn't, the king would order the prisoners to be shot on-site. That would make it one and done, but he had to make a show of it. And the show was about to begin. To the east behind the mountain, the sun continued to rise over the valley.

The king noticed that some of his guards were wearing green marks on their arms. It was slightly different than the usual brown leather uniforms all the Laythians wore. He wondered about that for a second but then pushed it away.

The executioner stepped forward and gripped the handle, ready to pull, the drums rolling fast, until suddenly thunder cracked as the executioner rocketed back like he had been hit by a cannon. The entire city went silent. Mak stood there dumbfounded as the whole crowd tried to register what just happened.

The screams signaled the beginning of the chaos. The citizens scrambled away into their homes after seeing the dead body of the executioner on the ground with a massive hole in his chest. The fifty guards surrounded the king, searching frantically for where the shot came from. The prisoners began scrambling as well, trying to undo the chains they were attached to, but it was no good. They were stuck and couldn't move.

The king was about to yell orders to execute the prisoners when the guard standing closest to him suddenly exploded, snapping back. Then the guard to his right looked out to the tree line before he exploded as well. More guards scrambled for cover, but even through the wooden buildings men suddenly found their lives ended. It was like someone had a cannon out there and it wasn't stopped by any barrier it met.

The king felt like he was quickly losing control now that the crowd had dispersed, leaving only his guards remaining. But they were all just as confused as he was. None of them knew where the shots came from. One of them made a break for it across the courtyard trying to find cover, but half his back was ripped in two. The young guard was dead before he hit the ground.

The king was pulled to cover, back towards the Great Hall, watching as more guards exploded before his very eyes. He shouted, "Kill the prisoners! Kill them all!" But none of his shouts were heard over the thundering of gunfire. Six more guards exploded as if in fury, the courtyard now stained with tiny bits of brain and organs.

There was a brief lull. The silence lasted only five seconds before another round of thunder began and eight more guards fell. Whether they were in cover or not, no one was safe. The morale of the guards was decreasing and most of them were starting to scramble for safety.

The roughly thirty personal guards remaining were trying to get themselves and the king to cover when five of them suddenly turned and began firing on their coworkers. Joax was one of them and he and his troopers fired on the remaining guards, dwindling their numbers down to twenty before they ran out of ammo and disappeared.

The king could feel his whole world crumbling. What was supposed to be a perfect ending was now in shambles. All he wanted was to end that Saint's life but now he was losing the very people he'd had control over. The courtyard was left with the prisoners still struggling to get their shackles off. Silence loomed as the thunder stopped and the city froze.

The king watched as white mist clouded the valley below and filled the city with opaque fog. He went back into his Great Hall as his remaining guards led him into the secret throne room for his safety. It was all crumbling before his very eyes. His kingdom. His life.

‹‹—‒—››

The fog proved very beneficial. Marcus had to change tactics but this only worked in his favor. He looked up at the clouding sky and said a silent, *Thank You.*

He brought his focus back to the city. Marcus could now approach the walls without being fired upon. Of course, that was if he played this right. The guards on the wall—the very wall Marcus had helped create—were on lockdown. The fog made visibility short to only a few meters. The guards themselves were terrified atop their wall, in fear of another's presence, even if it was one of their own.

Marcus shuffled through the lower valley, moving slowly. He froze when he thought he might be spotted and moved when it proved appropri-ate. He had exhausted all his rounds from his SR75k, using the .50 caliber rounds to rain havoc on the Laythian guards. Joax and some of the men who'd proved loyal to Marcus had painted themselves with green markers so he could distinguish friend from foe. It was most useful.

Marcus knew it wasn't the best tactic, but after praying the night before he'd received the impression to go through the front door. The doors were massive and were probably locked but Marcus trusted the impression he'd gotten and followed it.

He shifted from stump to stump, the fog proving extremely useful for hiding his movements. He could hear the men atop the wall but they were well out of sight. Marcus didn't bother trying to find them visually; all he needed was to hear them. He made it through the Bog without being spot-ted and finally came up to the Main Gate. He approached when the guards weren't looking and stepped up to the entrance. He put his hand against the big wooden door, the very door he had created, and prayed, *Father, I ask that the doors be open. Yet I want your will done.*

Marcus pushed gently, knowing these massive doors would likely be barred and locked, but the doors opened without a sound. Marcus smiled. *I can always trust you, Lord.* The doors parted and Marcus vanished into the white fog. The city was open.

≪—•—≫

Benny never knew which side to join. He hadn't heard much about the other guards revolting but after what happened today, he was ready to wet his pants. Benny stood atop the wall, AX5M in hand. His sweaty hands were gripping the weapon like a baby holding onto its mother for dear life when he suddenly heard a scream coming from inside the city. The scream was quickly silenced.

Benny looked at his officer, who was another guy in his early twenties. His officer tried to maintain a semblance of authority and composure but the man was failing badly. Benny saw the man had already wet his pants. He was about to say something when he heard another scream that lasted 1.2 seconds. He had almost recognized that scream when he heard some shuffling in a nearby building.

Benny looked over to his officer. "Hey, is that—" He stopped speaking when he saw a tall figure shrouded in black standing with a knife in his officer's throat. There was no sound. Benny thought it was a demon. The man ending the life of his superior didn't even look human. Benny ran for dear life, adrenaline pumping through his body like a racehorse. He hadn't even heard the figure coming up the stairs. It was like this Devil Saint made no sound whatsoever.

Benny screamed and tumbled down the stairs, forgetting about his weapon and pissing his pants as he found a corner in the wall and hid there. He closed his eyes and put his hands to his ears, but that was pointless, as they were unable to block the rhythmic screaming and sound of occasional gunfire rising and then quickly dying. The city slowly felt quieter and quieter. The Angel of Death had come.

《—●—》

Marcus removed his blade from the officer's throat, lowering the body to the ground gently. His body made no sound whatsoever. It was like all his movements were muted and he was a figure of death passing through this world.

I need to free the prisoners. Marcus stood atop the catwalk along the wall, looking inwards toward the city. The whole area was shrouded in deep fog, providing the perfect atmosphere for Marcus's stealth assassination approach. He knew the prisoners would be at the Townsquare. He had to play this right to maintain the advantage.

Marcus dropped from the catwalk, landing and rolling silently on the ground to curb the fall. His black jacket made him look menacing. He wore no mask or helmet, but his figure was covered in blood and black paint he'd created the night prior. To the average person, Marcus looked more like a demon than a regular human. The Devil Saint was coming.

Marcus vanished into the fog and kept to the alleys, approaching the main square. The whole city was silent. A patrol of four guards in the street came towards Marcus, who hid in the alley and let them pass. He knew they were going to come back and one less hostile was one less problem. Marcus unsheathed his sword and waited until he was behind the patrol. They were on edge; Marcus would use that to his advantage.

He made his move, coming behind the rear guard, the fog masking his approach. He put his hand against the guard's mouth, rearing him back and slicing the man's throat. The man made a muffled grunt, but no sound left Marcus's hand. The other guards were so on edge they didn't even notice their comrade dying right behind them.

Marcus lowered the body and vanished into the mist. The other three guards eventually noticed the fourth guard's absence and all turned around to check on him. The moment they turned, Marcus appeared from the other side and struck the nearest man behind the other two guards, taking him down without a sound.

Two hostiles remaining. Marcus unsheathed a throwing knife from his belt and approached the two remaining guards with a silence that was unworldly. The ground was gravel but his feet made no sound. One guard turned in time to see Marcus jam his sword into the neck of his comrade before Marcus threw a throwing knife into his eye.

Hostiles eliminated. Marcus retrieved his blade and continued forward toward the Townsquare. He took care of a couple more patrols, but the resistance was growing light. Marcus made sure not to lower his guard, however. It was always when things started going his way that they were most likely to spin out of control. He crouched behind an empty barrel, the fog lifting to provide visibility of five meters. He was able to see the long line of prisoners shackled together, unable to leave the gallows.

Suddenly a flare was fired into the air, the red smoke reverberating off the fog, bright enough for everyone in the city to see. Marcus knew that would attract the remaining guards in the area, so he had to work fast. He approached the group of prisoners and found Mak and the others waiting.

Mak looked at him with warm surprise. "Saint!" The other prisoners rose to their feet as Marcus approached. They were all smiling. Marcus held back his emotions and focused on the mission. He pulled his sword and cut the ropes off Mak, Noah, and the other prisoner on the platform then started slashing the chains off the legs of each prisoner, taking care not to wound their feet. But he quickly realized that this would take time, and it was making a lot of noise.

He looked around and saw the fog was clearing. *Not good.* He handed Mak his sword, directing, "Cut the rest of the prisoners loose. I'll cover you."

Mak took the sword and went to work while Marcus picked up one of the AX5M rifles and checked the magazine. It only had four rounds but that was enough for the time being. He unbuttoned the .44 holster, ready to draw it at any time, and vanished into the fog again, using whatever advantage he had.

⸎—•—⸎

Mak was busy working on getting the chains off the rest of the Kotang prisoners but the work was taking longer than he'd expected. It was tiring swinging the sword down through heavy metal chains. He had to put all his might into the weapon to get the sword to cut through and even then, the blade was getting duller with each strike.

Mak looked around and said to the men he had already released, "Look for some weapons so we can shoot off the chains from the other prisoners."

The freed prisoners ran to look for weapons on the guards the Saint had shot. They had tried earlier to grab some weapons off the dead guards but they were all out of reach. Mak looked up, sweat dripping from his face, and realized the sun was coming out, breaking through the clouds. *That's not good. We're losing our cover.*

Mak's worst fear came true when he saw a guard standing on a rooftop aiming down at him. *No.* But the man was interrupted when a blade pierced through his neck, leaving Marcus standing there like an angel of death in his black jacket, covered in blood. Mak froze for a moment, knowing that death had nearly claimed him. The thought struck him that only a short while ago he was trying to kill the Saint, but now the roles were reversed and the Saint was fighting to save their lives.

Mak shook himself out of his reverie and returned to freeing the prisoners. But it was still taking too long. There were three hundred prisoners total and they were all chained together. Another guard reared over a building on the opposite side, but his head exploded after the Saint fired a round into his skull. More guards followed the sound of gunfire to the Townsquare. The Saint fired two more times at an enemy Mak couldn't see and then tossed the gun aside.

He dropped down from the building and threw over his .44 magnum to Mak. "Keep going!" he yelled.

The Saint ran forward, picking up another weapon as Mak went to work firing the six rounds in the chamber to free six more prisoners. The gun clicked empty too soon and he returned to swinging the sword. About one-third of the prisoners were free and the others were picking up weapons and using the guns to break off their chains. That sped up the process until the guns quickly ran empty. Mak cursed.

Man, I hate how there are so few bullets these days! Mak heard more gunfire, this time closer and in quick succession. Men screamed and the fog lifted, the clarity of the city revealing to Mak the horror he couldn't see before. Overlooking the city from the Townsquare, he could see dozens of dead bodies spread throughout the area. Blood filled the streets as Laythian guards were killed with bullets and blades and worse. Mak shifted his gaze to the Saint, watching him fire at the approaching enemy. *This man is something else.* It horrified Mak that he was once an enemy of the Saint; woe to any who opposed him. The man had more skills than everybody in the Kotang clan combined. He was a one-man army, a Rambo, as they say. But a few guards were approaching and were breaking through. Some of them spotted the freed prisoners and open fired, taking a few of the Kotang down in seconds. The rest of the prisoners scrambled and fell to the ground, trying to find cover and evade the bullets and arrows.

More and more guards were coming, this time firing more rapidly, their guns apparently having more ammo after looting their dead comrades. One man armed with a hundred rounds can be more effective than a hundred men with a single bullet given the right situation. And that situation was evolving the longer the battle went on. The fewer men there were, the more ammo was prevalent, and the more dangerous a person with a gun became.

The fog had lifted completely and Mak could see the bright blue sky and the rising sun. He looked to his right toward the warehouse on the north side of the city when he heard what sounded like a roaring engine. A large truck came out of the works and approached them.

The truck pulled up in the middle of the Townsquare and in the driver's seat was Faal. The man stepped out and shouted over the sound of gunfire, "Get your men on the truck now!"

Mak sheathed the sword in his belt and helped get the freed men onto the truck while the remaining prisoners tried to get free of their chains. More and more bullets were flying now and pinging off the side of the truck. Mak realized that there was just the one vehicle.

He looked to Faal and said, "There's not enough room!"

Faal replied, "We know! But it's all we have right now; the rest of you will have to run back through the city gates. The Saint will cover you."

"Why don't we just go through the catacombs into the mountain?" Mak asked.

Faal explained, "Because the Saint escaped the same way yesterday, so they bolstered their defenses. If we do that then we'll be cornered and killed. So, the only way out is through the front door."

Mak gritted his teeth but he knew the logic was sound. He turned and saw the Saint coming back, smelling of blood and gunpowder like he had taken a bath in charcoal.

The Saint stood there calm and in total authority. "Get the weakest prisoners on the truck; the rest will stay with me and we'll escort them out of the city," he ordered.

Mak nodded and obeyed the man without question. It felt natural to listen to him as the Saint had a strange sense of calm amidst battle, which made nearly every man around him automatically listen to him. Twenty prisoners loaded into the truck, filling it to the brim. Faal stepped back into the driver's seat.

Mak turned and the Saint handed him his bandolier. The belt contained roughly forty-eight .44 caliber rounds. Mak looked up as the Saint said, "Use this to cover the truck as it leaves. I want you in there providing suppressive fire."

The Saint handed Mak another AX5M rifle before stooping down and picking up a 6MY Gonta rifle for himself. The rifle was good for only twelve rounds but was devastating at long range. It had a scope up top and was good for open areas. It also had an iron sight built into the side to provide use in close-quarters combat. The Saint ran over and stood atop one of the roofs to provide overwatch. "I'll cover you as you guys head out," he called.

Mak nodded and hopped in the truck, reloading the .44 as quickly as he could, then hoisting up the AX5M and switching it to semi-automatic. He sat in the open backseat with Noah as the truck charged forward with no intention of slowing down. Mak was jumbled about and then saw two guards come out of nowhere, ready to gun down the prisoners in the back. He open fired with the AX5M, taking one guard down, but the other had the advantage of distance and time. But the second guard found a couple of rounds suddenly placed in his chest and he dropped to the ground.

The truck charged through the city as more guards came out of the woodworks, the lack of fog stimulating their recent low morale. Men felt better when they could see. And now they had a big fat target. Mak handed the .44 to Noah and the two of them provided cover fire as the truck rampaged through the city. Bullets and arrows pinged off the sides and some of the prisoners suffered wounds, but the guards were suffering heavier losses as the Saint's overwatch protected them.

Mak heard Faal yell from the front, "Buckle up! I'm ramming the gate!"

Mak's eyes went wide. "What?" He didn't even have a seatbelt.

Mak gripped the side of the truck and held on until his hands were white. The Laythians had realized their escape plan and had bolted the Main Gate shut. So, Faal put the truck in gear, charging at full speed. The truck rammed the gate but it came to a full stop halfway through the door. The gate had broken but so had the truck.

Mak craned his head back in pain from the impact. Looking toward Noah, he asked, "They couldn't have come up with a better idea?"

Noah shrugged and the men stepped out, crawling through the openings in the broken gate. Mak looked over and saw that Faal was unconscious in the driver's seat.

Mak helped him out and was tending to the other prisoners who were injured when he heard a gun click and saw three Laythian guards with weapons pointed toward them yelling, "GET ON THE GROUND!"

Mak tried to open fire on the group, but his gun clicked empty and Noah didn't have time to reload either. The three guards grinned and were about to open fire until they were cut down by bullets from both sides. The three bodies dropped and more Laythian guards stepped out. Mak tried to reload in time but knew the new guards would fire on them any moment. The new guards were calm, however, and didn't raise their weapons. They had green paint marking their shoulders which Mak found curious. Then he recognized one of the guards. "Joax?"

Joax responded, "Good to see you too."

"Where have you guys been?" Mak asked, looking at the other guards warily.

Joax shrugged his shoulders. "Oh, you know, causing mayhem, creating chaos, rescuing princesses."

Mak scoffed and smiled. *Kinzka.*

Joax took command. "We need to get you out of here!" he shouted.

The Laythian rebels helped get the wooden gate open for the rest of the prisoners. Another guard stood on a rooftop and aimed but was taken care of when the Saint shot him in the chest. The gate opened with their combined efforts and the doors to freedom were ajar. Mak and the others ran, trying to get away from this crazy city before it killed them. Mak turned and saw the other prisoners following right behind. The Saint had covered them well enough to get them to the front gate without incident. Mak and the others ran through the little camp outside the walls and then looked up to the hills surrounding the bowl they were in.

Then Mak heard a massive metallic roar coming from the heart of the city. The others turned and saw the tank come raging out of a warehouse atop the hill near the Grand Hall and point down at them. The prisoners all ducked for cover as the tank opened up and killed dozens of people with its fire.

The Saint regrouped with Mak, and the two of them ducked for cover as the tank stood atop the city like a giant turret, killing anybody who dared to escape. The Laythian guards were charging through the streets, ensnaring the prisoners in a trap, preventing them from running back into the city. They were blocking even the sides that led to the mountains. The only way out was up towards the forest, but the prisoners would have to make it across open ground up a hill in sight of the tank and its weaponry.

Mak put his head down in the dirt as the tank open fired, sending blood and limbs into the air. He yelled, "We have to take care of that tank or else none of us are leaving here alive!"

The Saint lifted his head, covering the back of it with his hands to protect it from the falling debris. "I'll take care of the tank," he said. "You and the men be ready."

"Saint!" Mak handed him his sword and .44 back. "You're going to need this."

The Saint accepted the weapons with a thin smile. "Thank you."

Mak saw the Saint contemplating his next move. He looked toward the city as over a hundred armed Laythians approached. Mak's fear at the force turned his face pale, but then he looked toward the Saint who was as calm as ever. *How can this man be so calm?*

The Saint lowered himself to one knee and put his hands together in prayer. Mak was so bewildered by the action that he forgot he was being shot at. It was like the man was in a completely different place. After what felt like an eternity, the Saint opened his black eyes and looked at Mak. "I'm ready."

Mak had no response to what he was about to do, so he yelled, "Good luck!"

The Saint replied, "There's no such thing as luck," before he ran out into the midst of hot lead and gunfire.

«——»

Marcus ran up toward the Main Gate where Joax and Faal were pinned down. The Laythians were preventing them from escaping into the city and were slowly encroaching upon the Kotang members. The Kotang were fighting back with whatever they had, but the battle had turned to quick potshots from the Kotang while the Laythians were advancing upon them.

Marcus approached Joax, who yelled to Marcus through the gunfire, "We're pinned down here in the Bog and can't get through. That tank at the top is preventing us from leaving lest we want to find an early grave. We've got all the Laythians coming down on us and we have no route of escape."

Marcus said, "I'll handle the tank; you just be ready to get these men out when the time comes." Marcus took a flare gun from Joax's belt. "I'll fire this to signal that it's time to leave and the tank is destroyed."

"How are you going to get out?"

Marcus patted his shoulder. "You let me worry about that."

It was hard to hear with the gunfire, but Joax complied. He handed Marcus his AX5M and said, "Here's a couple of extra mags. This is most of the ammo that we've gathered so far, and you'll have four full magazines."

Marcus took the gun graciously as well as the four magazines. He smiled as if the ammunition and weapon were an old friend.

120 rounds. Nice.

He looked to Faal, who was clearly concussed from the gate ramming. He tapped his shoulder and said, "I'll be back! You get yourself clear!"

Faal didn't have the brainpower or energy to respond as Marcus left. Marcus checked the AX5M rifle, feeling its metal as he slammed a fresh clip into the weapon and pulled the charging handle back, racking a fresh round into the chamber. Marcus smiled. He had missed having extra ammunition, and now, he would wreak havoc. He clicked the weapon to semi-auto. Marcus leaned against the wall, the potshots taken through the massive doorway filling the ground next to him. He closed his eyes and remembered a verse.

"The Lord is my shepherd; I shall not want." Marcus felt the words reinvigorate him, instilling him with an energy he had lost before. His heart was calm and body prime for a fight. He felt his skin warm and his hair stood up, a welcome feeling. Marcus took a deep breath and exhaled. Time for war.

He whipped around the corner and spotted the first hostile. Aiming down the iron sights of the AX5M, he sent two rounds into the hostile's chest.

For some reason, Marcus's gun fired louder than the others. It interrupted the whole battle and the entire Laythian force stopped firing for a second as if stunned.

Marcus bolted into the open space, firing rapidly and efficiently at whatever contact he spotted. His body moved on its own, with speed that didn't register with a regular human. Marcus was firing and shifting so fast that five hostiles were down in seconds. He pushed forward, not stopping his advance. He kept firing, taking down more hostiles as bodies fell from the rooftops.

Marcus didn't slow down; he had to get to that tank and stop it before they were overwhelmed. He cut through a building into a shop filled with nice China, but that beauty was interrupted when three guards approached from within, Marcus fired a quick succession of rounds and dropped the guards before they could even react to him. He reloaded.

Ninety rounds remaining.

He pulled back on the charging handle, racking a fresh round in the chamber, and pushed up the street. Marcus continued forward, hugging a small house. He fired and took down a guard atop a building, then fired at a guard passing in the street, and then at two more guards who were following. Men were falling left and right as Marcus dodged and shot. He stopped behind another house, feeling the incline of the hill finally reach him.

More guards were yelling in his direction, warning the others of the approaching menace. A squad of guards ran into Marcus in a nearby alley. They were all so close that they panicked. In a quarter-second, Marcus switched to full auto and pulled the trigger. He sprayed the five guards as the recoil pulled in a diagonal direction. All five guards fell with three rounds each in their chests as Marcus cleared the alleyway.

He wanted to curse but held it back. He dropped the mag and inserted a new one. *Sixty rounds left.* He wanted to vent over using too much ammunition but it was the heat of the battle and things changed in an instant.

Marcus pushed up the hill, the firing of the Laythians slowing. Marcus kept moving, making sure not to stay in one place for too long, as speed was his best friend in this fight and if he got bogged down and cornered by a larger force, he would be dead. He heard the tank fire at a group of prisoners trying to escape up the hillside. The prisoners were vaporized in an instant. Nothing remained. The tank fired again, blowing a hole in the wooden wall protecting the Kotang. Marcus looked at the gaping hole and sighed. *I just fixed that.* The tank fired for a third time.

Marcus wanted to feel surprised but he wasn't. *They must have found a nearby armory or raided the Kotang camp after the battle last month, securing more ammunition for the tank.* The rest of the Kotang members hugged the ground as the tank rained fire on them. Marcus had to move and take out the tank now. But how? He didn't have any anti-tank material to destroy it with. He would think of that later; first, he had to get to the tank. Marcus rushed out after the tank had fired, shooting at four guards as they saw him approaching.

Surrounding the tank were some twenty guards. Marcus got pinned down approaching and shifted to guerilla tactics, taking shots at the guards surrounding the tank and then shifting position. He funneled down their numbers until they were down to ten, then five, then one.

Marcus squatted inside a building and checked his ammo count. *Three rounds left.* Those twenty guards had proved most difficult and took up too much ammunition. The tank stood unmoved by the approaching threat. Then the top hatch popped open as Gobbie stood up and pulled the charging handle to the M2HB with gritted teeth, shouting, "Son of a mirakunzka!"

Marcus dove to the ground as Gobbie fired in anger at all the surrounding houses, tearing through the wood and brick like they were paper. Marcus found himself under a couple of broken logs and pushed them aside as Gobbie looked over the destruction.

Gobbie yelled, "Did that kill yous yet, Saint? Are yous satisfied with the destruction yous brought to this city?" Marcus got up and repositioned himself while Gobbie vented. "It was all your fault that these Kotang members came here! It was your fault that mi friend Bo died! And it's all your fault now that this city's burning to embers! Are yous happy with yourself? It would have been better if yous had never come here at all!"

Marcus closed his eyes, catching his breath. Hearing Gobbie's words struck deeper than any knife. He had never wanted any of this to happen. He never wanted to seek war or conflict. He only wanted to live in peace. But worldly peace was never granted to him, and everywhere he went, people died. What hurt the most, though, was Gobbie's betrayal. The young man who used to work with Marcus now hated him due to misplaced blame. It broke Marcus's heart.

Marcus exhaled and accepted the fact. He would deal with his demons later, but for now, he killed his emotions and focused on his current priority, destroying the tank. Marcus rounded a corner, aimed at Gobbie, and fired his last rounds. But Gobbie saw his attack coming and ducked down into the tank. The first two shots missed, but the third shot skimmed his forehead.

Marcus's gun clicked. *Empty.*

Gobbie put his hand to his forehead in frustration. He screamed and thumbed the trigger on the M2HB again, peppering the house Marcus was using for cover with rounds until it was a heap of rubble. Gobbie gritted his teeth in rage as the bullets flew hot all over the place, tearing through the brick and dirt, and then fired on the rubble remaining.

Marcus slowly rose from the pile of rubble, covered in blood and dirt but not wounded. Not even once. Gobbie was angrily amazed as he centered the gun on Marcus.

Marcus approached the tank slowly, a limp in his step but with no weapon in his hands. Marcus saw Gobbie grin. "How does it feel to have everything ripped from yous?" he asked. "To know that you're helpless to defeat us?"

Marcus stood, blood trickling over his forehead and into his eyes. He looked up at Gobbie, exhausted. "If I'm being honest . . ." He paused, catching his breath. "It's all too familiar."

Marcus pulled his .44 from its holster lightning fast and shot Gobbie in the shoulder, sending him tumbling over the side of the tank. Marcus spun the .44 until it landed perfectly back into his holster. "Way too familiar."

Marcus looked over and saw Gobbie clutching the wound on his shoulder before he passed out. Marcus kicked away Gobbie's weapons and inspected his body carefully for any others. Gobbie made no resistance as Marcus disarmed him.

Marcus took off a small satchel full of hand grenades from Gobbie and looked towards the tank. He popped open the hatch, pulled the pin off one of the grenades, and tossed the satchel in. He heard a muffled scream before a mute explosion filled the cabin of the tank. Black smoke pillowed out as the inside of the tank was disintegrated."

Marcus fired the flare into the air, the bright red aura signaling the Kotang.

Marcus then tended to Gobbie's wounds with some bandages, preventing him from bleeding to death. Luckily, Marcus hadn't injured him too badly, but the wound left by the .44 would take some time to heal. Gobbie would have a scar across his left forehead but women would find it attractive.

After Marcus tended to Gobbie's wounds, he looked over the city to find it burning. The gunfire died down as Marcus caught his breath. He took in the sight of the destruction he caused.

"What was all this for, God? What was the point of all this?" Marcus looked up to heaven, desperate for an answer. "I don't understand why you let this all happen."

As usual, Marcus was met with silence. He heard gunfire again, though it was too low and spaced out to be considered a threat. Then he saw the Kotang prisoners fleeing the valley and into the woods. Watching the sight of the men escaping gave Marcus a small booster to his morale. *Maybe that's enough for now*, he thought. He stood up, feeling every bone and muscle in his body ache with pain. He had suffered no major injuries, but he still had a limp. Marcus turned toward the Great Hall. One more thing to do.

The king hid in his bunker, eager for news of the battle outside. He heard gunfire outside but it was dying down. He marched across his white carpet into his library. It was a place few people had access to. Books were rare these days so having a bookcase was meant to display one's wealth.

The king had just stepped into his library when a black sword was put to his throat. The Saint stood there, bruised, cut, and bloody, but no less intimidating. The king saw the sword and the massive man standing before him, ready to end his life. The Saint backed the king into the bookcase until the king was flush against it.

"It's over," he said.

The king wet his royal robes. The urine seeped through the fine red and white cloth onto the white carpet. The Saint kept his eyes on the king's face and commented, "That's going to stain." If it were any other situation the king might have laughed, but now he was riddled with fear. He feared his life would end right here at the hands of this foreigner.

The Saint held the sword, now coated black, against the king's neck. The cool steel pressed against the man's throat, welcoming the blood underneath.

"It was you," the Saint said. "You ordered the hit inside the city walls." The king said nothing, his lip quivering. The Saint pressed the sword closer to his neck. "Don't deny it."

The king exhaled. "Fine. You got me." Then the king spoke with more determination in his voice. "I ordered the hit. They were meant to take you out and the workers."

"Why?" The Saint already knew but he asked anyway.

The king looked at the Saint with more fire in his eyes. "Because you were in the way. I've no place for you or your dead religion in my city. Your actions were stirring up my attention so I wanted you gone."

The Saint replied, "You used the Kotang and allowed them to enter the walls for the strike, making it look like it was an outside organization that caused the attack."

The king nodded. "Yes, I did. It was all too easy. And as a bonus I even got Gobbie to hate you with a passion." The king shrugged his shoulders. "I didn't even have to do anything with that. It was child's play."

The Saint reaffirmed his grip. "After all this, you still don't regret your decisions? Even after they caused a war that ended in hundreds of people dying?" The Saint's tone was cold. He knew the answers to all these questions; he only wanted to see what the king had to say in regard to his actions.

"They're *my* subjects. What I do with them is my business. Don't bring your religion and morals into this. This was meant to be a perfect society, but then you walked in with your righteousness and screwed it all up." The king saw he was gaining the upper hand in the conversation. He grinned. "But my hands aren't the only ones who are bloody. Yours are just as dirty as mine." The Saint didn't answer, and the king went on. "You are now responsible for killing hundreds of people in Laythia. That crowd that Gobbie stirred up. Woah. What a shocker!" The king chuckled. "It was too much! I was enjoying myself because I didn't even have to stir up my subjects to hate you. All they had to do was be themselves, and because of that, you killed them. Those two hundred people, all dead because of you."

The Saint didn't move. He knew his actions had been in self-defense. He did not want to kill all those people but they'd struck first and they wouldn't stop.

The king lowered his grin and spoke more solemnly but with a slight taste of wickedness. "But I guess that's all I can do for now. I suppose *he* will want to meet you later."

The Saint's interest peaked. "He?"

The king raised a wicked smile. "Oh yes. He is aware of you."

The Saint drew closer. "Who is *he*?"

"The one who represents darkness. The one who will bring true salvation to this world."

The Saint narrowed his eyes. "So, you're a follower of his?"

The king nodded. "Yes, and he has many people under his thumb. And he has been gifted, like you . . . You fight for one side, and he fights for another. You're practically twins. But don't worry. You'll meet him one day, whether that be tomorrow or in ten years. He will come, and he will find you."

"I'm looking forward to it." The Saint pulled his sword back and let the king go. "Did you hear enough, Gobbie?"

Gobbie stepped into the room holding his wounded shoulder. His anger had diffused somewhat but was still present. "I heard enough." Gobbie looked toward the pitiful king. "So, yous killed Bo, huh?"

The king looked up with a beggar's face. But Gobbie was finished with anger. He turned and left the room, and the Saint followed. The king sat there on his knees as his attackers vanished into the hallway, left alone to his failures.

《— —》

There was still some gunfire as the Saint and Gobbie left the Great Hall and approached the Laythian forces by the gate. The Saint was holding Gobbie with his arm over his shoulder when Gobbie yelled, "STAND DOWN!"

The Laythians at the gate turned and saw the Saint and Gobbie. They lifted their weapons at him, but the Saint made no gesture to attack. Gobbie shouted, "I said stand down!" The men looked at him in confusion, some of them still aiming at the Saint. "It's over," Gobbie said, lowering his voice. "It's over."

The guards lowered their weapons. Gobbie looked toward the Saint and said, "Mi men will help rebuild this city. But yous might need to consider your position. If yous stay, I cannot guarantee that mi men won't attack yous, and if yous leave now, yous will be safer out theres."

The Saint understood the predicament. Blood was still boiling and tensions were high. He had wiped out a majority of the Laythian military and those who remained knew of the Saint and his deadly skills. Most of them were still angry that he had killed so many of their comrades and relatives. The Saint looked over the men, finding their faces, checking their eyes for what they thought of him. Most of them were just tired while some were angry. He had seen those eyes before.

The Saint turned to Gobbie and said, "Give me time to think about it." Gobbie understood and allowed the Saint to leave.

One of the guards spoke up, "Sir, are we's just going to let him walk out?"

Gobbie didn't look at the man, paying more attention to the Saint's departure. "Yes," he said. It was like the old Gobbie who was once a proud and arrogant little brat had changed into a hardened young man. He was different after the battles. He stood watching as the Saint walked out the front gates, already observing the damage done to the walls.

Tettenhall, Gin-Seng Mountain
15:05 hrs, 07/07/2258 (3 months A.F.)

Mak and the Saint stood at Tettenhall, the fortress of the Kotang members, with their hands on their hips, observing the reconstruction of the fort. Mak answered the Saint's unspoken question, saying, "We'll be sure to get this place up and running again, but we won't be the same as we were before." Mak looked up at the potential this fortress had, the things they could do, and the good they could bring. He nodded. "Yes, as of today, we'll be something different. Instead of being bandits and robbing people, we'll work to protect them from invaders and gangs." The Saint glanced at Mak. Mak returned the glance with happy assurance. "Don't worry, we won't revert to our old ways. You've made sure of that."

The Saint merely stared at him with a blank expression for a long moment. Mak saw this and said, "Listen, Saint, we watched you fight like that, against hordes of people trying to kill us. *Us.* The Kotang. We were liars and thieves beforehand, robbing anyone we got our sights on. But after watching you, we all felt a change. We all see how different you are and we want to be like you. We recognized our current state of life and weren't fulfilled with how things were going." Mak paused. "I don't know how we could ever repay you."

The Saint said, "You don't have to repay me."

Mak looked at him, wanting to give the Saint something. "Then what can we do to thank you?"

The Saint shook his head. "Don't. It was a gift. I saved your life because Jesus saved mine."

Mak marveled at the man. "I don't think I've ever met a man such as you who would refuse payment for something. Especially after you risked your own life to save us."

Mak put a hand on the man's thick shoulder. "Take care, my friend. You do not need to worry about us. I give you my word that we will be different from now on. Better, even."

The Saint nodded, "I appreciate that."

Mak felt the moment change and he knew it was time. The Saint and Mak clasped forearms. "If you need anything, my friend," Mak said, "just ask."

"I appreciate it, Mak." The Saint turned and approached the massive gates of Tettenhall. The giant wooden doors opened before him, letting the bright sun shine on the Saint. Mak didn't fully believe it, but he could have sworn that he saw the Saint glowing in the light.

The Saint departed, straight back to Laythia.

CHAPTER TWENTY

WOUNDS

*"I can't believe everything that's happened. Everyone dying and for what?
What was the point of it all if the Kotang were just going to get away?!"*

—DANTE, FELLOW GUARD AND FRIEND OF GOBBIE

Laythia

07:58 hrs, 09/07/2258 (3 months A.F.)

Gobbie stood at the top of the wooden catwalk, overlooking the Bog beneath the city as the sun rose over a new day. The catwalk was barely standing since the tank had fired massive shells through the wall. Only three days ago there had been a bloodbath and an unnecessary one. But today was something new. Something welcome. The sun shined over Gobbie's face. His features were young; he was barely twenty-five years old and now Captain of the Guard for the city of Laythia.

Who would have thought that in the past two months things would have gone from bad to worse? The city had lost about half its population in the fighting, with families struggling to grieve the losses that were still fresh in their minds. Removing the bodies from the most recent bloodbath was challenging. Some of the dead were still spread around the city, as they were having difficulty due to a literal lack of manpower. The remaining guards were all exhausted, especially those staying up on the night shift. Gobbie made sure he took the first watch, knowing he was no better off than his men. He may be young but the men respected him now. He had served in two battles and had fought both with and against the Saint himself and lived. Not bad for his reputation.

Gobbie stood staring towards the tree line of the Arghast Forest. His eyes widened when he saw a man walking down from the forest toward Laythia.

Gobbie could not believe it. There was the Saint walking towards the city like nothing ever happened. Even the other guards were surprised. Some of them shot him angry looks, and one of them even took aim at the Saint as he approached. Gobbie gently put a hand on the gun. The Laythian looked at him with red eyes, a clear sign of fatigue, lack of sleep, and anger.

The Laythian glared at Gobbie. "What do yous think you're doing? This is the man responsible for all the death in our city."

Normally, Gobbie would have wanted a man like that dead too, but right now he only felt bitterness mixed with a sense of remorse. He had wrongfully blamed this man for the death of his friend Bo, so now Gobbie felt a slight sense of debt to the Saint.

Gobbie said, "Stand down."

The Laythian looked at him bewildered, hurt, and lost. He wanted vengeance, but Gobbie knew being controlled by anger wouldn't lead to fruition. The guard was breathing heavily, wanting to exact some last bit of revenge, especially when their previous opponent was so out in the open, but Gobbie wouldn't let him. So, the man relinquished his aim and lowered the rifle. Gobbie saw another emotion in his eyes. A look that Gobbie himself was familiar with. Fatigue. Everyone in Laythia was tired of fighting. The exhaustion from the battles had settled and now everyone just wanted peace. They wanted an end to the war that had ravaged their city.

Most of the guards were surprised the Saint came back at all, knowing he was putting himself at risk by staying with the people he was fighting less than three days ago. The sight was unbelievable.

The Saint stopped at the gates, his black jacket covering him from the hot morning sun as he looked up. "May I enter, please?"

The guards looked at Gobbie, bewildered. Gobbie never took his focus off the Saint. He stared hard for a long moment then said grimly, "Open the gates."

"What?" the guard next to him exclaimed.

Gobbie took his arms off the wall and walked away. "Open the gates." The words were like a bitter pill he had to swallow.

The doors opened reluctantly as the Saint was allowed to enter the city of Laythia.

《——》

Marcus entered the city and glanced around at the faces of all the guards looking at him with mixed reviews. A majority of the faces were of hatred, others of indecision. Marcus knew it was awkward, with the memories of the dead still fresh in their minds.

Marcus looked around and saw there were still bodies lying nearby. Even after three days the Laythians still hadn't been able to clean up the rest of their dead. Marcus saw the reason immediately. The city around him was quieter than usual. There was less activity, but most of all, there were less men to go around. Most of the men in the city were guards, but Marcus knew that out of the five hundred Laythian guards that existed two months ago, only one hundred were still alive. And not only that, but two hundred additional townspeople were dead because of the massacre in the Great Hall. The city had experienced a massive demographic change and was suffering the consequences of it. Since there were fewer men, not as much physical labor was being accomplished, and, as a result, bodies were still laid about in the city, left to rot.

We need to get rid of the bodies or else disease will spread. Marcus pulled out his red scarf and wrapped it around his face. He knew it wasn't an ideal mask but something was better than nothing. Marcus looked up at the catwalk that ran along what remained of the city walls and saw Gobbie and a city guard glaring at him with contempt. He knew he was being watched but he continued anyway. He had to tread carefully as anything could spark the festering hatred that all these people shared toward him.

Marcus looked over and saw a pile of bodies laid out next to the main road in the city. No one was trying to clean them up except for a lone woman who struggled to pull one of the bodies away. Marcus approached the woman and knelt to help her pick up the body. The woman saw the help and looked up with gratitude. "Oh, thank yous, sir—" Her smile quickly soured as she recognized who she was speaking with. Her face turned grim as she stared in contempt at Marcus. "What are yous doing here?" she asked with venom in her voice.

"Would you like help, ma'am?" Marcus asked.

The woman shook her head. "Not from the likes of yous."

She continued to try and pull the body of one of the dead men, but she struggled and only managed to move it a few inches before stopping. Without saying anything Marcus picked up the body by the legs.

The woman lifted her attention to him again. "I told yous I don't want your help!"

She tugged on the body but Marcus waited patiently and did not make a move. She pulled on the body again, and this time Marcus moved it with her. The woman stopped again. "I said I don't wants help!" she shouted.

Marcus remained as quiet as a statue until the woman realized they had moved the body without her noticing. The woman looked into Marcus's eyes and saw the saddened pain etched into them. She could see the genuine side of the man truly wanting to help, even if it was painful for him.

For some reason, Marcus's eyes defused the woman slightly, and her bitterness lessened a bit. She looked aside and grunted. "Fine. Yous can help."

Marcus only stared at her with a blank expression. The woman resumed her efforts and this time did not fight Marcus helping her. They continued to lift the body and carried it out to the Arghast Forest. They laid it down and went to retrieve other bodies as well. The project took a couple of hours but they were finally able to remove the pile of bodies from the main street of Laythia and give them a proper burial.

Marcus performed the digging for the graves as the woman curled backward, attempting to stretch her back. Marcus finished digging five graves while the woman watched. He noticed the woman wore a white outfit, with a white cloth draping over and around her head, but the white was covered in dirt and old blood that shaded it into a dark velvet brown.

Marcus helped lower the bodies into the graves and spread dirt over them. After he finished, he waited a moment, holding the shovel while the woman looked down at the resting places of what had been her family. Her eyes were red and dried out from excessive crying. Marcus did nothing and waited. The woman finally looked his way. He could see the hidden gratitude etched in her face, but it was hidden behind the bravado of bitterness she held toward him.

For Marcus, that was enough. She didn't have to say it. Marcus then looked down at the bodies of the five men he'd buried and wondered if he was the one who killed them. It struck him as peculiar. Not uncomfortable, but peculiar. A few days ago, he and these men were trying to kill each other, and now here he was helping this widow when he was probably the one who killed these men. Marcus tried not to dwell on how fast life changes, but he couldn't help but feel . . . peculiar. He didn't feel uncomfortable or apologetic. It just felt weird, being at war and then not so dramatically. What bothered him the most was that he didn't feel remorse over what he'd done. These men were acting wickedly by trying to execute the Kotang and had attacked him as well. Still, though, it felt strange to kill a man and then spend time with his widow shortly after.

After a long moment of silence, the woman turned to him and said, "Thank yous." She couldn't look him in the eyes but it was surprising she'd said anything nice to him at all. Marcus didn't show any surprise, however, and merely bowed his head. The woman continued, "I had been trying to bury thems for the past three days but no one has been able to help mi. It only got harder once their bodies started to decays and the maggots settled in."

Marcus didn't say a word, knowing it was better to say nothing in these kinds of situations.

"So, that's it," she said.

Marcus saw she wanted to say thank you again but she held it back, knowing she had already given him too much. Marcus didn't want to press the woman further so he left the shovel in the dirt and left the woman to be by herself. As he retreated, he heard her moan and cry in the forest behind him.

《—▬—》

The Saint continued to help with the clean-up efforts, burying the bodies around the city of Laythia. The people were distasteful toward his arrival, but gradually they grew to accept his help whether they liked it or not. And after a couple of days, the city was finally clean.

CHAPTER TWENTY-ONE

ROAD TO RECOVERY

"The road to recovery is long and hard, especially after losing a war."

—THE SAINT

Laythia

16:01 hrs, 11/07/2258 (3 months A.F.)

Marcus returned from his final burial trip in the forest. The sun was low but he still had a few hours of light left before nightfall. Marcus stood back at the main road inside Laythia. The bodies may have been cleaned up but Marcus could still see the degradation done to the city. The houses and walls were utterly destroyed and burned. He looked around and saw that the citizens were not even trying to rebuild due to the emotional devastation they had suffered. But the destruction of the homes didn't draw his immediate concern.

Marcus noticed a woman in a white dress wearing a brown overcoat passing by, holding her arm awkwardly. Marcus deduced the woman was injured. A stray round had probably struck her as she and her family were hiding among the chaos.

Marcus approached the woman and said, "Excuse me, ma'am." The woman stopped, clutching her arm cautiously.

Marcus pointed. "May I take a look at that?"

The woman stood there unsure of what to do. She was fearful of the Devil Saint who'd attacked her city but she didn't run away. Marcus stepped slowly, allowing her the choice to walk away should she want to. But the woman stayed where she was. She looked pale, too pale for her own good. She resumed her focus on the pain in her arm as Marcus gently grasped the injured limb, the woman moaning in pain from the gentle grip, causing the attention of others to shoot his way.

Some guards were hot in their heads and yelled, "Hey! What are yous doing with that there woman?"

Marcus replied calmly, "Just administering medical treatment."

He brought his focus back to the woman's arm and slowly unrolled the bandages. He saw the open wound, a mixture of broken bone and blood. It was miraculous her arm wasn't severed. But the bone was pointing in the wrong direction and it was likely infection would settle in soon. Marcus peered deeper into the wound and saw a stray bullet lodged there. He looked up at the woman and asked, "Is there a doctor you can take yourself to?"

"Not many," the woman replied. "Theys aren't that reliable and I don't have the money to pay them."

Marcus made a low grunt to himself. "The bullet is still in there."

The woman said nothing. Marcus looked at her, his face stone cold but he tried to weaken his tough gaze. "Would you like me to remove it and treat the wound?"

The woman looked at him with both a mixture of concern and fear. She looked at the other guards, who were all glaring in their direction, but she brought her gaze back to Marcus and saw his softened expression, even if it was only a slight difference. The woman cautiously nodded, pain shooting through her arm.

Marcus sat her down at a nearby table. "I'm going to need some proper tools before I can operate on your arm," he told her. "So let me talk to the blacksmith and see what I can get, and then I'll be back to treat your wound."

The woman nodded, her face growing pale. Marcus noted the severe lack of color and knew he would have to hurry if the woman was going to live.

Marcus came back shortly after speaking with the blacksmith and obtaining some medical tools they had on hand. He saw the woman was paler than before. This time her husband was standing over her with concern. The man looked at Marcus with anger and asked, "What did yous do to her?"

Marcus neatly laid out the proper tools on the table and pulled out some crafted medicine he had made from Vistra in the Arghast Forest. He answered, "I need to pull the bullet out and splint her arm. Otherwise, she won't be able to use it again and may die from infection."

The man backed off, surprised with that real of an answer. He stepped away and let Marcus operate. After a short bit, Marcus had removed the bullet and applied proper medicine and a splint to her arm, saving the woman's limb and her life in the process.

The man stood there wearing grey dungarees and asked, "Where did yous learn medicine?"

Marcus kept his focus on the final wrap around the woman's arm as he answered. "In the military, we didn't always have medics around. So, in battle, you had to learn how to operate on your fellow companions to save their lives."

"So, yous were a soldier before?"

"I was."

"What are yous now?"

That question gave Marcus pause. The Great Wars were over, but he was still fighting in smaller conflicts. He was a soldier with no army. No nation to belong to. Marcus looked up at the sky and then back down. "I don't know."

The man looked at him, unsure of what to say. "Well . . . thank yous, for treating mi wife."

Marcus looked up at the man, feeling a sliver of hope in his heart. He looked down at his hands, seeing how bloody they were. He was used to his hands being covered in blood, and this wasn't the first time he'd had to operate on someone to try and save their life, but Marcus didn't realize just how useful his skills from the military would be in this new world. He looked at the woman and saw the color finally return to her face.

The man helped his wife up and walked her back towards their home, saying, "Thank yous, Saint."

Marcus felt another flicker in his heart because of that. For once, he hadn't used his skills to destroy. This time, he'd used what he had learned to help people with their wounds, despite the many he carried himself. It brought Marcus a sense of relief. There was fulfillment in watching others' lives be fixed and seeing them benefit because of his actions.

Marcus looked up at the sky and prayed, keeping his eyes open. *Is this what you want me to do, Lord?*

He brought his attention back down when a person with a wounded shoulder suddenly came up to him and said, "Please sir, are yous a doctor?"

Marcus answered, "I'm not a doctor, but I know how to treat wounds."

The man lowered himself. "Please sir, I am in pain and I don't knows how to treat this. Could yous help me?"

Marcus felt happy to have the opportunity and said, "Of course, sir." The man sat down and Marcus started treating his wounds. After he finished, Marcus went into his rucksack and saw that he was starting to run low on Vistra plants. He looked over his shoulder and realized a line of people had developed who had wounds or family members with wounds that the doctors in the city could not cure. Marcus realized he was going to need more Vistra plants as well as medical equipment. And he had an idea of where to get them.

Tettenhall, Gin-Seng Mountain
11:07 hrs, 12/07/2258 (3 months A.F.)

Marcus approached the massive gates of Tettenhall on a donkey. The woman he'd helped bury her family had offered him her donkey for use and with it, Marcus was able to make it to Tettenhall in good time.

Marcus saw a sentry atop the massive walls who shouted, "The Saint has returned!" He vanished behind the walls, repeating his statement. The massive doors opened and Marcus slowly entered.

He stopped in the middle of the courtyard and Mak, the new Commander of the Kotang, came down from the main office and joined him. Mak, with his shaved head and a gruff brown goatee, extended his hand as they clasped forearms.

Mak smiled and said, "My friend! What can I do for you? What brings you back so soon?"

Marcus got right down to business and said, "I am in need of medical supplies. Would you have any here I could purchase?"

Mak raised a hand. "Say no more." He turned to Noah and said, "Noah, get a wagon ready and fill it with all the medical supplies we can spare."

Noah looked at Mak and nodded. He didn't share that same look of hate the Laythians had toward Marcus. Marcus was curious as to why the boy had never liked his father, but he assumed the relationship wasn't a healthy one. The rest of the Kotang followed Mak's order and scrambled with eager haste.

Marcus was impressed as the Kotang quickly filled a cart with medical supplies. The cart pointed like a mountain as the medical supplies were piled on. Marcus saw the massive amount of supplies and was a little surprised with how much the Kotang had, but also how willing they were to give it. Medical supplies in this world were a rarity, and to give them away so freely was even more uncommon.

The Kotang finished loading the cart as Mak turned and asked, "Will this suffice?"

Marcus tried not to stare in amazement at the pile and said, "Yes." Marcus turned to the small pouch of coins he had and said, "I'm not sure I have the means to pay you for all this."

But Mak raised his hand again. "Consider it a gift."

Marcus was caught off guard but he didn't show it. It had been a while since someone had done something so kind to him and without charge. To have someone do something nice to him brought warmth to Marcus's heart. He felt a comradery between himself, Mak, and the other Kotang.

Marcus bowed his head slightly. "I cannot thank you enough."

"No." Mak bowed his head, as did the rest of the Kotang. "*We* cannot thank you enough, Saint. For saving our lives, this is nothing."

Marcus didn't know what to say. He looked around and could see that the expressions on all of the men around him were genuine. Each of these men truly wanted to repent for what they had done. It brought a sense of wonder to Marcus's cold heart as he was amazed a band of thieves could show such promise.

"Thank you, my friend," Marcus said. "I won't forget this."

"And we won't forget either," Mak said. "If you need anything, don't hesitate to ask."

Marcus bowed and clasped arms with Mak again. "You are a good man, Mak."

Mak's eyes widened as tears welled up in them. He quickly blinked them away. He faltered in his words as he said, "I'm not a good man."

"Neither am I."

Mak looked at Marcus, dumbfounded. Marcus put a hand on his shoulder and said, "But with God, you can be." Mak didn't know what to say, and Marcus took the silence as his cue to leave. "Take care, my friend," he said, as he mounted the wagon full of supplies and yipped at the donkey to start going.

Marcus left the gates of Tettenhall behind as Mak and his fellow Kotang stared in amazement at the departing Saint, wishing the man would return soon.

Laythia

10:05 hrs, 13/07/2258 (3 months A.F.)

Gobbie sat atop the remaining catwalk overlooking Laythia. He and his fellow guard Dante were biding their time, sipping on warm coffee in the cold morning. The sky was an ocean of blue, etched with a sense of peace and tranquility. Gobbie appreciated the quiet. It had been so hectic over the past couple of months that he was ready for a long quiet life.

Gobbie sipped his coffee, his mind brought back to his current emotional state. He stared at the black liquid, thinking about his misplaced anger. He had let his emotions get the better of him and because of that, he'd fueled an entire crowd to attack the Saint which only got more people killed. Those deaths weighed on Gobbie, as he knew he was responsible for fueling the flame of the people's hatred all because of his own. But that hatred had accomplished him nothing. It only caused him more pain.

He wondered if the Saint felt the same way. Having hatred but nowhere to point it. Gobbie could feel that what was once a burning furnace inside him was now nothing but smoking embers. He had burned out and didn't know what to do with his emotions. He refused to let himself become engulfed by his feelings. He wouldn't let that stupidity happen again because he got emotional over some misplaced blame.

In reality, Gobbie was just avoiding blame. Deep down he knew the Saint had nothing to do with the death of Bo. He just didn't know how to grieve or direct his anger about it. He hated the Kotang as much as anybody in Laythia, but he also couldn't deny that the Laythians had been the ones who were controlled by their anger and tried to become the murderers they so hated.

Gobbie lowered his head, abandoning the endeavor of trying to figure this out. His head felt like it was spinning. His buddy Dante nudged him and said, "Hey, Gob, check this out."

Gobbie looked over at what Dante was pointing at and saw a cart approaching in the distance. It was filled with supplies and slowly went down into the Bog. Gobbie saw that it was the Saint driving the cart as he pulled up to the Main Gate.

The Saint looked up and said, "I bring medical supplies for the people of Laythia. May I have entry, please?"

Despite Gobbie's misplaced feelings, he still felt some sense of hatred for the Saint. He didn't like how perfect he was or how righteous he appeared, no matter what happened to him. It bothered him that a man like this existed, and yet the man was not to blame.

Gobbie said, "Open the gates."

The gates opened and the Saint brought the cart in. Dante said, "Would you look at that?"

Gobbie looked down and saw a line of people standing in front of a table before the Saint. The man was treating injuries from the previous conflict with medicine and tools. Gobbie suspected the Saint got the tools from the local blacksmith, but Gobbie didn't mind that. There weren't many doctors around these days and the Saint was treating patients regularly. Gobbie didn't fight it. They needed doctors who knew what they were doing, not those false-nosed people who called themselves doctors but were just trying to scam a profit.

Gobbie had thought the Saint was supposed to be fixing up the walls of the city, but he figured that could wait. The wounded came first and people always welcomed a doctor. Gobbie heard one woman ask the Saint, "Where did yous learn how to practice medicine?"

The Saint answered, "From the wars, ma'am."

The woman was delighted that she was under the practice of a man with experience. Gobbie rolled his eyes. Dante looked at Gobbie and asked, "Captain, should we do something about this? I mean, the man was attacking our city a week ago."

Gobbie didn't look at Dante and answered, "If the man can offer medical treatment, then let him stay. It doesn't hurt to patch up our wounds after a long fight."

Gobbie overheard another conversation from below. This time it was a little boy asking the Saint, "Were yous the squad medic in your group?"

The Saint shook his head. "No, but I did have to operate on some of my buddies when they got hurt." Gobbie almost thought he heard the man chuckle as he added, "They would get hurt a lot."

The young boy chuckled and the Saint held his smile back. Gobbie saw the line of patients grow larger as the day went on, and even some of the guards went up and received aid from the Saint. Some were reluctant to go, but when they left the Saint's treatment, they were always better than before. Other guards looked down at the man in hatred, but everyone was so tired from fighting that the looks of hatred never lasted.

The Saint even sent some of Gobbie's men to look for Vistra flowers. They were prevalent throughout the Arghast Forest so the men went out at once. They were the youngest men of Gobbie's guard, the most naïve out of them all, but it was their naivete that allowed them to forget about the horrors of the past few days, so maybe that was a good thing.

When the young guards came back from the forest the Saint taught them how to grind the materials and craft them into a healing ointment. Some of the guards accepted his teaching and began treating other people as the Saint guided them in medical practices. With the extra help, they were able to set up a hospital and treat nearly everyone in the city, even the guards the Saint had fought against. It was a sight to behold, and a strange one at that.

Laythia

16:41 hrs, 13/07/2258 (3 months A.F.)

Gobbie approached the officers' lounge on the south end of the city. He found three of his companions sitting in the lounge around the fire with a discussion going on. The lounge wasn't the typical indoor room with air conditioning but was instead a room crafted out of brick and stone that had somehow remained standing after both battles in the city. It had a stone firepit in the middle and an open ceiling with blocks of wood and chairs around the fire, along with a small table with a jar of water and some clay cups. It was a place where officers would spend time together and take breaks when off duty to play cards and such.

Gobbie entered the room, tired after another long day of work. He poured himself some water and joined the three guards seated around the fire in their brown leather uniforms. Dante noticed Gobbie's cup and asked, "Hey, you be drinking water?" He took Gobbie's cup and exchanged it with his, saying, "Here, have some ale."

Gobbie didn't fight the exchange and even gave Dante a smile. He sat down on a small block of wood and stared into the fire as the three continued with their discussion.

Gobbie's eyes centered on the fire, not paying much attention to their current conversation. The three guards were Dante, a man with short black hair and a handsome face, Evans, one of the older guards who had blue eyes and numerous scars across his forearms from the recent fighting, and Chris, a man with an amber-brown beard the size of Batman's cape. All three were holding their clay cups, sharing their thoughts on the current subject. Gobbie's eyes drifted upwards and saw the confusion from his men. "What's the issue?" he asked, the question sounding more like an order.

Dante and Evans exchanged looks of concern. Their egos were deflated, their tempers calm. "Well sir, we're just not sures how to go with this," said Dante.

Gobbie took a sip from his ale. "What do yous mean?"

Evans spoke up, "Sir, that man there was fighting us only a week ago. It's been nice and all that he's been treating the people but . . . is that really . . ." Evans fumbled for the right word. "Proper?"

Dante picked up where his friend left off. "What we're saying is . . . well, it's weird. Weird that a week agos this man was killing our folk and now he's fixing us up like nothing's happened. We're just not sures how to react to it."

Gobbie held the clay cup, staring down into the fire. He understood exactly where they were coming from. A stranger who was their ally, then their enemy, and now their healer, all within the short span of two months? It was strange, and people didn't know what to think of it. Gobbie understood those feelings because he had worked with the Saint before. He thought of the children he fed and how happy they seemed, the action giving him pause. Gobbie's shoulders relaxed. He knew the man was trying to be good, even at his own expense. It just surprised him that the man was back so soon and was helping the people who'd tried to kill him.

"I know how yous feel," Gobbie said, lifting his eyes to them. He straightened up and took a sip from the ale. "He's a strange fella, ain't he?"

Evans and Dante nodded, both unsure of whether to feel reassured or concerned about how to react next. But Chris had another thing on his mind. He put his clay cup down and crossed his arms. "I think yous are fools," he said. Neither Gobbie nor the others were offended by Chris's statement. "That man killed our buddies and now we're just gonna let him walks back in like nothing happened?"

Evans replied weakly, "But it ain't like we didn't try to kill him too."

Chris looked at him, his amber-brown beard and round chin adding to his bulkiness. "That ain't what I'm saying." Both Evans and Dante nodded. They understood Chris's frustration. They had felt it themselves, but they were too worn out from fighting to care right now. Chris continued, "He should be hanged for what he did."

Evans spoke up again. "But he did save our city once."

Chris fired back, "Only to come back a month later and save the very ones who tried to kill us."

Evans retorted, "If you want to try and kills him, be our guest. But look where that gots us."

"The king said—"

Gobbie cut him off. "The king is a liar." All their heads turned toward him. Gobbie met their surprise with a determined look of his own. "I overheard what the king said. He was the one who allowed the Kotang to perform the hit-and-run that killed Bo and the others. He confessed it himself."

The others stared at him in silence.

"Is this true?" Dante asked.

Gobbie nodded. The king had recently been deposed but none of the Laythians knew where he was. They all assumed he'd escaped through the catacombs of Hillsong Mountain.

Evans swirled his ale in his cup. "So, what do we do now? I mean, what was it all for?"

"I don't know." Gobbie shook his head. "What happened before is in the past. Let's focus on rebuilding today. So, from now on, I don't want none of yous trashing on the Saint, yous got that?" They all nodded, even Chris. "Good." Gobbie gestured his hand toward Dante. "Now, if yous don't mind, I need more ale, and a lot of it."

Dante creased a smile and stood up happily. "Yes sir!"

CHAPTER TWENTY-TWO

An Apology

"You can harbor resentment in your heart if you want, but all it will do is eat you alive."

—THE SAINT

Main Gate, Laythia

08:07 hrs, 14/07/2258 (3 months A.F.)

Gobbie was reluctant to proceed but he knew it had to be done. His shoulder was killing him and he couldn't find a better doctor in the city. The Saint wasn't doing anything fancy, but still, someone with some medical practice was better than nothing. It was humiliating to ask him for help but Gobbie swallowed his pride due to the pain in his left shoulder. Reluctantly, he got in line and waited for his turn. He was hoping one of the other Laythians the Saint had trained would treat him, but Gobbie had a feeling it wouldn't turn out that way.

Most of the people in line were injured like himself, but Gobbie had more than just physical wounds that needed healing. The line shortened and it was his turn to step forward. The Saint sat at a small table and saw Gobbie. He motioned for him to approach. For a moment, Gobbie remained where he was. He remembered the fire within him, but with the confession of the king, that fire was pointless. He gritted his teeth and stepped forward.

He sat down and the Saint stood up from his chair, ready to inspect him. "May I?" he asked.

Gobbie gave him permission and the Saint got to work, unwrapping the bandages over his wound. The shoulder the Saint had shot was not doing well and was giving Gobbie a lot of pain. He tried to keep it contained when he was around his fellow guards but he needed to see a doctor, and for right now, the Saint was it.

The Saint held up a needle and said, "I'm going to inject you with a painkiller."

Gobbie didn't refuse and the Saint inserted the needle into his arm. He squirmed a bit until the needle was fully in. It took a moment before Gobbie could feel its effects, and then the Saint began his work on Gobbie's left shoulder. It had hurt like a son of a kinzka when the Saint had shot him with his .44. Gobbie was surprised that he survived the encounter at all. Given the Saint's skills, finding any survivors was a miracle.

The Saint stood over him, working on Gobbie's injury while Gobbie sat there with his shirt off. Gobbie was staring forward when the Saint said, "I'm sorry . . . for everything."

Gobbie wanted to lash out in anger, but that anger had accomplished nothing. To his reluctance, he spoke the truth that was on his mind. "It wasn't your fault . . ." He paused, knowing the words he was about to say were going to hurt, but they were the truth. "It was mine." He paused again. "I stirred up those crowds to hate yous out of misplaced blame. Yous had nothing to do with Bo's death. Yous were just trying to do something nice."

The Saint said nothing.

Gobbie continued, "I still hate the Kotang for what they did. They still killed Bo, but the king was also responsible." Gobbie expected a response but got none. The Saint just continued to work, so Gobbie went on. "It wasn't wise of mi to let my anger control mi. And because of that, I gots a lot of people killed."

"Don't be so hard on yourself," the Saint replied.

Gobbie tried to look over his shoulder but the pain prevented him, even with the painkillers. He was forced to listen to the man's words. "You're not the only one who's made mistakes that have gotten people killed," the Saint told him.

Gobbie found resonance with that. He may not know this man's past, but he knew he was telling the truth. And that truth disarmed him, draining away the broken hatred he'd kept within himself.

"I'm sorry," Gobbie said.

"You're forgiven."

Gobbie tried to turn around again but failed. "Just like that?"

"Just like that," the Saint replied.

Gobbie lowered his head, nodding. He accepted the man's apology and was grateful to receive forgiveness without any judgment. It felt like a bitter part of him had finally died and Gobbie could move on a little. He still hated the Kotang, and that would be a mountain to climb at another time, but for now, he could at least forgive this man.

He sighed. "And I forgive yous too. So . . . don't beat yourself up too much."

Gobbie didn't know it, but his words were a huge help to Marcus. Marcus kept his emotions close and didn't let Gobbie see while Gobbie kept his gaze forward, relieved to finally be moving on.

❦

With their combined efforts, nearly everyone who was wounded in the city was treated, saving some people from illness and infection. The Laythians gained a little respect for the Saint, but it wasn't enough to eradicate all their hatred.

❦

Marcus finished the final touches on a woman's injured arm. "There you go, ma'am. All done."

The older woman looked at her bandaged wound and brightened. "Thank yous, Saint!" she exclaimed.

The woman got up and walked off into the city. Marcus stood from his medical table and looked over the street. The sound of crunching gravel and clopping hooves filled the city as people passed by continuing with their business. Marcus felt happy that the city was coming alive again, especially after the horrors that had encompassed it.

Once Marcus finished healing the rest of the wounded, he looked to see the current status of the walls and the houses. There was a lot more room since the population had, quote on quote, "declined." But the horrors of war leave deep wounds. Marcus could clearly see the wounds left on the city that he had both defended and attacked.

He tried not to think of that, of how shortly before, he was both an ally and then an enemy to these people. Marcus knew he wasn't entirely safe but he wasn't entirely in danger either. The war was over and everyone just wanted peace. Or so he thought. Marcus knew well of the desire for revenge. Losing a war never ends well, and those who lose are left with deep scars. After trying with all your might to win, being overcome by another force stung deep. Marcus had seen it before. How people formed insurrections and guerilla units in response to another nation taking theirs over. Marcus had been part of some of those occupying forces before, but for good reason. He was never part of an ill-conquering nation.

Marcus saw a young boy held by the hand of his mother as they picked out fruit in a nearby market. It reminded Marcus of his own family.

Carmen . . . Dad . . . I miss you so much. It was bitter to think about, so he brushed those thoughts aside. Marcus lifted his gaze to the massive gate on his right, looking over the wood pocked with bullet holes. The walls had received a lot of damage from the Laythians when they were shooting at the Kotang from behind the gate. The gates themselves were not much protection, the tank had proved that, but it was a beneficial overlooking position to those who were defending, especially if the attacking force didn't have any vehicles.

But one thing that bothered Marcus was the man both the king and the former Kotang leader had mentioned. A man with power, able to destroy an entire fort and leave it to rot. Marcus had no confirmation whether this was related to his dream but he knew enough about dreams to know that when they were unique, they were something to remember.

Marcus felt the sun glaze over him, his skin absorbing the warming rays, stretching his arms out from his black jacket. *Thank you, Father, for this warming sun.* Marcus opened his eyes and focused again on the damage to the city. Most of the homes were riddled with bullet holes and some were burnt down. Now that Marcus had treated all the wounded, he could begin working on the houses and walls again. But he would need supplies, again, and it would take time to rebuild, especially if he ran into resistance. Marcus shrugged his shoulders. *I'm going to need some help. And I know just who to ask.*

CHAPTER TWENTY-THREE

NEW ASSISTANCE

"Sometimes an opportunity to forgive is presented to us.
It's our choice of whether we want to though."

—THE SAINT

Tettenhall, Gin-Seng Mountain

20:41 hrs, 14/07/2258 (3 months A.F.)

Marcus neared the gates of Tettenhall. The ominous square fort perched against Gin-Seng Mountain was menacing to anyone who approached it. Marcus rode forward on the small donkey that Hax had lent to him. He dismounted and stood before the gate, where a guard from above recognized him and said, "It's the Saint! He's back again."

The doors parted and Marcus entered the square yard brimming with activity as the Kotang trained and worked throughout the fort. *They're improving their fighting abilities. Not bad.*

Commander Mak looked at Marcus from the balcony of the third floor, embedded into the side of the mountain, and smiled. He came down and greeted Marcus with a warm hug. Mak broke away and said, "What can I do for you, Saint? You're back so soon."

Marcus said, "I've got an opportunity for you. Want to hear it?"

"I'm all ears," Mak said.

Marcus settled and his tone became somber. "I want to rebuild the walls of Laythia again, and I'm going to need help. Will you join me?"

Mak paused for a long moment, then he looked up and yelled, "Sound the bell!"

A man working on the wooden balcony on the second floor heard the command and rang the large bell inside the fort. All the Kotang members stopped what they were doing and assembled in the main courtyard. Marcus monitored their reaction speed to the call. *Not bad.* They might prove to be worthy soldiers in the future.

Mak had Marcus follow him up to the second floor as he addressed the men. "This may come as a shock to some of you but I am going to tell you anyway." The Kotang members looked at each other quietly while Mak continued. "The Saint has come back and is requesting service from us to help rebuild Laythia." Mak let the message sink in, knowing this would cause some unrest. "I know that some of you may feel conflicted about this decision, so I'm going to give you a choice. You can choose to help out and rebuild Laythia, or you can remain here and continue training." Mak gestured to Marcus. "This man wants to do right by the people of Laythia, and it is our duty to pay for our sinful actions. It was our sin and our fault that we attacked Laythia first and brought harm to their city. We must therefore repay the wrong we have done."

One of them shouted, "Why should we care for the Laythians? They were going to execute us right on the spot." Some of the men nodded in agreement.

Mak had expected this sort of response. "Never forget, my friends, that it was us who attacked them first."

Another man shouted, "Who cares whether we attacked them first or not? We lost and they tried to kill us."

Mak remained calm and controlled. "Need I remind you who saved us?" The men went silent. Mak gestured to Marcus again. "This man fought for the Laythians, but he also chose to do the right thing and save us from execution. I will not lie to you; after all that's happened, I am indebted to the Saint, who took the time to forgive an enemy and save us. You may harbor ill feelings towards the Laythians and that is fine. It's to be expected. But never forget the man who saved us and taught us the right path." Then Mak put his hands on the wooden balcony and spoke genuinely. "Men, aren't you tired of living like thieves? We may have been rich but I felt like I owned nothing. We were killers only living for ourselves. Is that truly a life worth living?"

Marcus saw that Mak was wooing his men very well. The man had a natural talent for speaking. He was able to speak honestly and openly to all his men. Marcus almost envied the man for his talent to address crowds, a talent he lacked.

Mak put a hand to his heart. "Men, I am tired of living a hollow life. The Saint not only saved us from physical harm but also from spiritual damnation." More men were looking up from their shame at Mak's hopeful words. "No longer shall we be killers, but protectors. We shall live a life of honor as this man does," he gestured to Marcus, "and seek to love others above ourselves the way the Saint has." Mak paused for effect. "But no one will force you to come. I ask for volunteers. Who will help us rebuild Laythia?"

Almost immediately, nearly every man stepped forward, and even those few who initially stayed back stepped into line reluctantly. Mak turned to Marcus with a smirk. "You have your workforce."

Marcus had come there hoping to receive a few workers, but he never imagined every man in the Kotang clan would join him. Deep down, Marcus felt a slight spark in his hardened heart. It felt like he was back with his fellow soldiers again. Good men. Men he could trust and who were strong in the faith.

"Very well," Marcus said. "Let's get to work."

CHAPTER TWENTY-FOUR

UNLIKELY HELP

*"It's easy to say we will forgive others; it's harder though,
when someone just murdered your whole family."*

—THE SAINT

Laythia

05:59 hrs, 15/07/2258 (3 months A.F.)

Gobbie and the rest of the guard watched on top of the Main Gate as the morning sun rose. He welcomed the morning light and was happy that the landscape provided a sense of peace after the previous horrors that ravaged the city.

Dante approached Gobbie, rifle slung over his shoulder and sword sheathed at his side. "All quiet, sir."

Gobbie returned his gaze to the landscape, staring at the Arghast Forest and the hills surrounding Laythia. The Saint hadn't been around yesterday and Gobbie was starting to wonder what he was up to.

It started as a slight flicker, but then Gobbie saw movement in the tree line. His instincts told him to get down and that's what Gobbie did. Gobbie slung his rifle from his shoulder and took cover. Dante followed and pretty soon the rest of the guards around the walls had taken positions on the catwalk overlooking the Bog. The Laythian guards had been taken advantage of too many times, which is why Gobbie had instructed those remaining to improve their combat effectiveness and drill constantly to maintain strict discipline.

"What do you see, sir?" Dante asked, breathing heavily.

Gobbie peeked his head over the wooden cover and saw more movement along the road from the Arghast Forest. He looked around to spot any snipers who wanted to take a shot. After the Saint reigned literal hell on the Laythians from that very tree line, they knew they were not to be taken advantage of again. Then he heard marching and saw what appeared to be hundreds of men coming toward them. The mere sound of marching frightened Gobbie. Marching meant an army, and an army meant a disciplined fighting force.

"Oh no," Gobbie whispered. "We're going to have to fight again." He lowered his head in distress. *Not again. I can't take another battle.* But suddenly the marching stopped.

Gobbie looked over toward the main road leading to Laythia and saw hundreds of men standing at the tree line. Gobbie couldn't believe it. The Kotang members were going to exact their revenge on the Laythians. He gritted his teeth in painful regret. *I knew we shouldn't have let them go.* But he had let them go under the Saint's supervision. Did they rebel against him?

Dante looked at him with pale terror. "What do we do, sir?" he asked.

Every man was lined up along the wall, surrounded by wooden cover and sandbags, peeping through firing holes, ready to take a shot at the coming invaders. Gobbie saw that some of the men welcomed the fight; they wanted to exact their revenge for the loss of their comrades in the previous battles.

Gobbie yelled, "Hold your fire!"

The men heard him, but eagerly held their fingers on their triggers, ready to fire at the first opportunity. Gobbie peered over the cover to look again and realized that this time the column approached not with weapons but with shovels, axes, and crafting tools. Gobbie even saw two carts full of large logs. However, although there were no weapons among the men, that didn't dispel the idea of suicide vests.

Gobbie yelled again, "Hold your fire!" He could see the fear in his men, but also the anger. All it would take was one shot and the conflict would reignite.

The column of Kotang came to a stop, now in the middle of the Bog before the massive gate. Gobbie stood up, revealing himself to the approaching column. He saw the Saint leading the men. All was quiet; only the sound of the wind filled the air.

The Saint raised his hands and announced, "We do not mean to fight, and we leave ourselves at your mercy."

Gobbie said nothing, staring hard at the Saint. He could not believe it. The very men who were slaves to this city less than a month ago were back, but this time of their own volition. Gobbie could have them all killed right here, right now. But maybe that's what the Saint wanted, to give Gobbie that power as a sign of trust.

The Saint continued, "We only ask that we're allowed to help rebuild the city we destroyed."

"And what do yous want in return?" Gobbie asked.

The Saint shook his head slowly. "Nothing."

Gobbie frowned, pondering the Saint's request.

Dante approached him and whispered in his ear, "Sir, we can end this now. Give the order and every man along the wall will end these thieves and traitors."

Gobbie glared hard at Dante and said, "I've been acquainted with being controlled by mi anger. I let it drive me to do horrible things, but I will not permit yous, nor any other man, to do the same." Dante was left bewildered as Gobbie turned to face the Saint beneath him. "Yous will all be searched before yous enter this city, and yous will be watched twenty-four-seven," he said. "Yous may carry no weapons as yous work inside the city and if a single man is found with one, or if any hostile fighting breaks out, yous will all be exiled from the city or detained. Am I clear?"

The Saint straightened as if talking to a superior officer. "Crystal, sir."

Gobbie took his hands off the balcony wall and said, "Open the gates and search them."

Dante stood bewildered. "Sir, are we just going to let them in again? After all that's happened?"

Gobbie looked at him as they walked down the stairway and said, "Yes."

Dante couldn't believe his ears. Men were stationed in every direction as the Kotang workforce stood before the open gates. Gobbie stood with men on each side, every one of them almost eager to fire their weapons at the coming oppressors. The Saint unsheathed his sword and surrendered it to the nearest guard. The rest of the Kotang members lowered their tools to the ground and stood in a straight line behind the Saint.

One guard searched the Saint for any bomb vests before relieving him of his weapons. Gobbie gave the all-clear to approach, while the rest of the Kotang members were searched one by one, with nothing found but the tools they had brought with them.

The guard who had disarmed the Saint brought his sword over to Gobbie and held it in front of him. Gobbie took the Saint's sword and observed the black material, then looked back at the Kotang members. *Like cattle to the slaughter.* He eyed the Saint with a hard stare. Gobbie handed the sword to Dante, who took it and walked back to safety behind the other Laythian guards.

Gobbie sighed and turned to his guards. "Watch them inside. Allow them to begin their work and prevent any civilians from interacting with them. If anyone tries to harm them, protect them." The order sent a shock through his men as they looked at each other in confusion, each one hoping to find some reassurance in the man standing next to him. Gobbie said, "Mi order stands. But do not interfere with their work or I will have yous punished, understand?"

The men straightened. "Yes sir!"

"Good." Gobbie turned back to the Kotang members as they entered the city. He checked their tattooed faces and saw most of them had grim looks of shame. Gobbie's hard expression faltered. *Are they ashamed of what they did?* The question made Gobbie's frustration increase. His heart turned into stone at the sight of the killers.

The Saint approached Gobbie and said, "Thank you." Gobbie tried to relax his heart.

He replied, "There's still a lot of bad blood between us Laythians and the Kotang. I may have forgiven yous. But don't be thinking our two peoples will be all buddy-buddy now. Yous won't fix everything just by rebuilding some houses."

The Saint looked away and nodded. "You're right. You're exactly right." That admission disarmed Gobbie for a second. He wasn't expecting the Saint to agree with him. He brought his gaze back to Gobbie and asked, "With your permission, may we help rebuild your city?"

Gobbie was reluctant but said, "Permission granted."

The Saint saluted Gobbie, catching him off guard with the gesture. Gobbie returned the salute and felt a level of respect connect the two. Gobbie lowered the salute and returned to his men.

Gobbie sat on a wooden bench and watched with three other guards as the Kotang members spread out and got to work on repairing the wooden walls. The Saint approached them again, this time followed by a man wearing a big coat, a brown beard, and a round head. His face was not too threatening but Gobbie could tell the man was clearly in charge. The Saint gestured to him. "This is Commander Mak of the Kotang forces. If you have any questions, please be sure to ask him."

Mak bowed slightly and held out a hand, saying, "Sir." Gobbie took it but didn't hide his reluctance. The man was a decade older than him, maybe more, but he acknowledged Gobbie as an equal. Mak said, "If there is any problem with my men then please speak to me about it. I will handle it with due diligence."

Gobbie bowed his head and the two men broke away. Surprisingly, the Saint and Commander Mak took off their heavy overcoats and went to work with their men. That sight made Gobbie curious. He had to admit it was impressive that even the commanders did the dirty work.

Gobbie scratched the growing stubble on his chin. He had shaved his beard after the first battle and was now letting it grow out again. He continued to watch with perplexity and suspicion as the men who were once their enemy were now willingly rebuilding their city. The whole situation made Gobbie's head spin. He couldn't make heads or tails out of this matter. He wasn't sure what was right and wrong anymore. All he did know was that the Kotang were rebuilding Laythia shortly after they'd attacked it. And he couldn't make sense of that.

CHAPTER TWENTY-FIVE

PROGRESS

"Life can change within an instant. One day you are killing your enemies. The next, you are sharing a meal with them."

—FAAL

Wall Construction Site, Laythia

17:47 hrs, 18/07/2258 (3 months A.F.)

Marcus and the other workers hefted a large wooden log thirty feet in the air. Men on the other side lifted the log by the ropes tied to it while the men on the inside pushed it upright. "Push!" Marcus chanted.

The men hefted the heavy log into the air until it stood straight up and planted it into the ground. They cheered, slapped hands, and congratulated each other on their hard work. They'd had to tear down the old walls of the city first and then rebuild it with a more detailed structure in mind, one that would brunt the attacks of bullets. Unfortunately, they wouldn't be able to stop a tank but that was a rarity, even in this part of the world. Marcus and the Kotang members hefted more logs until they were able to lay the base foundation for the Main Gate.

Marcus backed off and observed the work they'd completed. His shirt was stained with sweat, but he didn't mind the sweat or working in the heat. He was glad to be working on something important rather than destroying things. The Kotang members looked at each other in congratulation, clapping shoulders and arms. The sight of it triggered a small smile from Marcus. It reminded him of the soldiers he'd fought with in all the wars, but also of the enemies he'd fought. Even Marcus had to admit there were occasions when he would bond with the enemy whilst fighting them. It reminded him that even though they were his enemy, they were still human. Whether a person was his enemy or not, they were still going through the same hardships he was, and that caused Marcus to relate to them, whether they were his own men or the people he was fighting.

Marcus looked up and saw dusk setting. The yellow-orange sun gleamed past the forest, fading away into the night as indigo took over the sky. Marcus felt his sweat turn cool as a nice breeze brushed past him. He brought his gaze toward the Laythian guards glaring at them, watching with both hatred and curiosity. Some were more interested than others. Some were just angry. Marcus had given them a good reason. He had probably killed a couple of their buddies a short while ago and in a city this small, everyone knew each other. He saw their expressions, small daggers of anger meant for him. But Marcus had become so accustomed to that look that it no longer bothered him. He couldn't make everyone happy and there would always be people who hated him, some even for no reason. Marcus didn't feel shame about saving the Kotang prisoners and fighting the Laythians. He'd saved lives when they were going to execute all of the Kotang after they had promised to release them after their ten years of indentured servitude.

It was strange to Marcus how quickly the world changed. How things went from crazy to calm to insane in the blink of an eye. Trouble would always find him, and Marcus accepted that. It had been like that since he was born.

Marcus took his gaze off the guards and went back to join the Kotang members. The Main Gate opened and all the Kotang departed out into the Bog, placing their camping supplies in the same spots from when they were held in captivity. Some of the Kotang chuckled and cracked jokes. "Heh, back to work I see, might as well have never left." Some of the men cackled, the laughter infectious. It didn't reach Marcus but he was glad to see morale was high despite the previous horrors.

As part of their agreement, Marcus and the Kotang members had agreed to camp in the Bog and be under watch from the Laythians until their work was finished. The Laythians didn't want any Kotang members roaming the city without supervision. The Laythian people might revolt and kill them if they did or vice versa.

They were now squatting among tents and small fires, some heating up food in pots and pans and distributing it amongst the others. Marcus sat on the edge of camp and watched from a distance, still not sure whether he was part of them or not. He watched the cheeriness and enjoyed the sight of his men feeling happy. *My men?* That thought surprised him. It had been a while since he had led men into battle. *How long has it been now?* It had been some time since he had left the military, and now he was making his way in this new but strange world. Still fighting, but that wouldn't change for all of history. Humans would always have conflict with each other no matter where they were.

Marcus lit a small fire for himself and pulled out his book of Scripture to read quietly. Allowing the firelight to illuminate the pages, Marcus read in silence while the Kotang camp cheered and jibed, reminding him of his days of soldiering. It almost made him smile.

Mak came by holding a stick of meat in his hand and asked, "May I sit with you?"

Marcus gestured for Mak to take a seat and he pulled up a nearby rock to sit on. The two sat around the fire in silence as Marcus read while Mak ate. Mak held a piece of deer meat toward him. Marcus grabbed the stick and took a bite. The stingy meat coursed through his rough teeth as he chewed and swallowed, relishing the blessing of having meat. He swallowed before speaking. "Thank you."

"Don't mention it," Mak returned. He stared into the fire while Marcus kept reading. "Quite the sight huh?"

"Uh-huh," Marcus said, not looking up from his book of Scripture.

Mak said, "I never thought we'd be back here so soon."

Marcus lowered his book and followed Mak's gaze towards his men. "Yes," he said.

"Who would have thought the Laythians would let us back in their city?" Mak looked at Marcus in amazement. "I never would have believed they would let us back in. I for sure thought they were going to kill us."

"Maybe they will," Marcus said, returning his gaze to his reading. Mak's enthusiasm deflated.

"You know, you really are strange," he said. Marcus lowered his book again. "To think you would be back here so soon after fighting both sides. Must put you in an odd position, don't you think?"

Marcus lowered his gaze and thought about the statement. Mak wasn't wrong. Marcus did feel a little awkward working with both sides now, after previously fighting for each of them. It was one of the strange things about life that Marcus had come to accept. That yesterday's enemies were today's allies, and today's allies could be tomorrow's enemies. Alliances and loyalties shifted so much that Marcus had a hard time keeping track of it all. So, he kept his focus on the present circumstances and thought about the rest later. But when he did think about it, it surprised Marcus how quickly things changed in such short periods of time. How strange was that? But that's how things went and Marcus worried little about the past and focused instead on how to deal with the present.

He glanced over at the Kotang members, their cheery moods infecting each other. When humans were happy amidst this harsh and cruel world, Marcus was happy. Deep down, he wanted everyone to be happy. He knew this world was going to end one day, and the new world would come. He only had to wait and complete his mission until then.

Marcus shifted his gaze toward the new wall they were building for Laythia and saw the guards watching them, their faces hidden in the darkness. Eyes of hatred peered toward the Kotang. Marcus could sense some hatred from the Kotang as well, but those wounds would take time to heal, and even if they did, there would still be conflict. Humans have a long track record of carrying grudges and holding the next generation accountable for them. He hoped that wouldn't happen here but Marcus had no control of it, so he surrendered it to God. *Thy will be done, Lord.*

This time Marcus spoke up. "I do wonder," he said. Mak turned, surprised Marcus initiated a conversation. "I wonder how the world will turn out, after all that's happened."

Mak leaned back. "Ah, you're referring to life after the Great Wars, huh?" Marcus nodded. Mak shrugged his shoulders. "Who knows? The world is constantly changing. Just look here and you can tell that things are already different."

Marcus knew what he meant. With so much happening in so little time, the demographics as well as the political climate of this region had changed forever. Whether it had been destabilized by the warfare or was prone to grow in industry because of it, Marcus could only guess what the future had in store.

Mak asked him, "So, what were you before all this happened?"

Marcus answered, "A soldier."

Mak nodded. "That explains much." His voice was gruff as he took another bite of deer meat. "And now what are you?"

That question gave Marcus pause. There was nothing Marcus wanted to do or accomplish with his life except to fight evil. And he had done that ten times over throughout his lifetime, fighting empires, insurrections, and terrorists alike, all of it buried in the past with nothing to show for it. Now, Marcus had all the time in the world but no purpose to follow. He was facing a new reality, one most soldiers have to go through once they exit wartime: the question of what to do now that the wars are over.

But Marcus knew the wars were far from over. The world just got smaller. The warfare was still there and it always would be, but Marcus had to figure out where he fit in this new world. What would he do for the rest of his life now that he had no country to belong to?

He could feel war boiling in his blood. The adrenaline rush and purpose it gave him, preparing him for battle, were all he knew, so now what? Marcus had never believed he would survive all the wars. He believed he would die on some battlefield for something noble, but now there was nothing noble to fight for. So, why fight? Why continue?

To survive? But what was the point of surviving if you didn't have anything to live for?

Marcus leaned back, putting his hands in his lap and looking down into the fire. He still wasn't sure exactly what he was fighting for. He could fight for God, but what does that mean in this new world? How was he to live for God? Marcus looked around at the Kotang members and all their cheerful smiles. He knew these battles occurred for a reason. They didn't happen for nothing. He just didn't know what that reason was.

Marcus said, "I've traveled the world and fought in many different countries, but now that the wars are over, I ask myself, 'What do I do now?'" Mak kept silent, allowing Marcus to speak. "For my entire life, I attributed my identity to that of a soldier. I've never considered I would be anything but that. But now I wonder if perhaps I'm something else. If I am more than just a soldier?" He looked at Mak. "I know that my true identity is I am a child of God. But am I meant for just one thing? Or am I more than that?" Mak nodded in understanding. Marcus asked him, "Did you serve?"

Mak nodded again. "Under General Fortworth in the Gregocian military." Marcus nodded. He had fought against the Gregocians and understood them as a difficult army to defeat. They were tough; even if you put five bullets into them, they kept coming. "But after the war, I drifted for a while and ended up at Tettenhall, where I joined the Kotang and fell into a life of thievery and robbing. I put my skills from the military to use but I felt empty while I was doing it. I had wealth but I had nothing. It was hard for me to figure out who I was after the wars ended, and I still don't know the answer."

"I'll tell you." Mak looked up as Marcus said, "You're not just a thief and a murderer. You are more than your mistakes. For you are a child of God."

Hearing those words shook Mak to his core. "Saint, you really are something else." Mak blinked to prevent tears from coming out. "I ain't never heard anybody say that to me before."

Marcus suppressed a smile, hoping to not get too attached to these men. But he couldn't help the connection. It was a human thing to do, although Marcus wished it didn't always happen. His joy faded. He hid his emotions from Mak, allowing the man to recover.

"And you really believe in this God of yours?" Mak asked. "You know, like a supreme being in the heavens and such?"

Marcus nodded. "With all my heart."

"Do you think . . . that a scumbag like me could be forgiven?" Marcus nodded. Mak lowered his head. "I've done a lot of things wrong in my life. Much of it can't be taken back. I've killed women and children. Murdered husbands and took their pride and joy away. I've robbed the poor and killed the weak, all for my own self-gain. Do you really think a murderer like me can find forgiveness?"

"Yes," Marcus answered without hesitation.

The direct answer shocked Mak, coiling his head back. He wasn't expecting an answer like that. Marcus knew Mak was striving for redemption. All his actions so far had confirmed it, as Mak strove to repay the wrongs that he'd done in his life. That was why he was so eager to help rebuild the city. Because for the first time in his life, he was feeling guilt for what he'd done.

Mak immediately broke into tears. The massive man hugged Marcus, in need of comfort. Marcus sat there, unsure at first at the sudden comradery, but then put his hand on Mak's shoulder, allowing him to cry.

CHAPTER TWENTY-SIX

BRIDGING THE GAP

*"While we may be rebuilding the walls for Laythia, it's the relationship
with the Laythians that we need to rebuild most of all."*

—THE SAINT

Wall Construction Site, Laythia
09:38 hrs, 20/07/2258 (3 months A.F.)

Marcus and twenty Kotang hoisted up another massive log to finish yet another piece of the wall. The log finally planted into the hole and stood tall and strong. Nobody was getting through that . . . unless they had a tank, a heavy machine gun, or explosives.

Marcus looked to his left at the number of wooden logs they still needed. They still had a ways to go, so in a month they should be finished and could work on the houses next.

Marcus and the Kotang workers shifted as they heard a gang of Laythian guards approaching with long sticks in their hands. Trouble was brewing. But violence had been forbidden between the two groups. Marcus stepped forward and said, "I'll handle this," fully aware that fighting was likely to happen.

Four Laythian guards, all looking to be under sixteen years old, hefted sticks in their hands like baseball bats, trying to look intimidating. They may just be sticks, but they could pack a punch if used properly. Marcus approached them and stood in between both groups. The Kotang were watching him nervously, knowing they had no weapons or means to defend themselves inside the city.

Marcus stood on the gravel between them and asked the Laythians, "Can I help you?"

The four boys grinned. One of them approached him with an evil look in his eye, about to do something devious. "Oh, not really," he said. "Just wanted to check on your progress, that's all."

The boy hefted a stick half the thickness of a baseball bat to Marcus's chin. It took all of Marcus's willpower to maintain self-control. He knew what was coming and he would bear it, doing the one thing he hated doing: not fighting back. The Kotang watched him, ready to fight should they be called upon. They understood when a bunch of young dumb bucks were abusing their power.

The young leader lowered his stick and walked over to the wooden wall. "Yous have done a good job." Knocking on the wood, he added, "Real sturdy." He positioned the stick over his shoulder. "But yous see, we got some beef with yous and I can't really hold mi-self back."

One of the Kotang spoke up. "Say the word, Saint, and we'll back you up." The rest of the Kotang readied to fight, fists raised.

The other young Laythian guards squared up as well, but Marcus said, "Stand down."

The Kotang were bewildered by Marcus's response. "What?" one of them asked.

"Stand down." Marcus kept his voice low and cool. He refocused on the leader. The young boy was sweating through his white undershirt and was wearing brown pants, with blue eyes and bleach-blonde hair. Marcus looked at the boy and said, "You have anger inside you, and you need to get it out. Take it out on me."

The young leader eyed him. "Oh, I intend to," he said. The boy backed off, then frowned solemnly. "Mi dad was a guard to this city. He died when yous shot him with a sniper rifle. Barely recognized the body. Could only recognize him by his feet."

Marcus looked straight at the boy, trying to imbue his eyes with as much compassion as he could, but there wasn't much. "I'm sorry."

"Sorry doesn't get mi dad back!" The boy slapped Marcus across the face.

The slap was sharp and loud, loud enough for the other Kotang workers along the wall to notice what was going on. More Kotang began filing in the background, but Marcus said, "Stand down," as if nothing had happened. The Kotang members stared in bewilderment as Marcus stood there. The young guard then punched Marcus in the stomach, but the boy only hurt his hand when he realized Marcus was built like a rock. He backed off, tending to his wounded hand, while the other young guards stepped in.

One of the Kotang shouted, "Saint!"

But Marcus repeated, "Stand down," his voice as calm as ever. The Kotang members stared in complete amazement as he stood there while the four guards smacked him with sticks. Marcus made no effort to fight back, allowing the four boys to take their anger out on him.

"Yous like that?" one of the guards shouted, smacking Marcus across the face with his stick. The blow left a red mark on Marcus's right cheek, but he took it like it was nothing. One of the guards smacked the stick into Marcus's leg, leaving a massive purple bruise, but Marcus remained standing, unmoved. The guard who had thrown the blow backed off in surprise. But Marcus remained steadfast like a statue.

The other guards went crazy on Marcus, striking, punching, and spitting, taking all their anger out from the loss they'd experienced in the recent battles. The courtyard was filled with the sound of smacking sticks and striking flesh. The Kotang were unsure of how to even comprehend this situation. The four guards kept striking, punching, and kicking until they were too tired to stand. They lowered themselves to the ground exhausted, catching their breath. The Kotang watching were amazed at Marcus's level of self-control, as the man stood there bloody and wounded, but unshaken.

One of the Kotang whispered, "How . . . how is he able to do that?" The rest of the Kotang looked at Marcus in disbelief, wondering how a man like that existed in this world, and how he could choose not to fight.

The young leader of the Laythians lay on his back against a nearby pile of hay, looking up at a bruised and bloody Marcus, but the man was still standing, nonetheless.

Marcus looked at the young leader and said, "I'm sorry about your father, and I am sorry about what happened to your city. Will you forgive me?"

Marcus bent down to one knee, hearing a crack and pop in his joint as he lowered himself. He held his pain in and looked straight into the boy's blue eyes. The boy leader was bewildered and replied angrily, "No, I will never forgive yous for what you've done. You took mi father away from me's."

Marcus only looked at the boy with grim sadness. He stood up and walked away, saying, "I'm sorry."

He returned to the Kotang workers with a massive limp. A man handed Marcus a rag to wipe his bloody face. He had suffered multiple blows to his abdomen, back, chest, legs, and face. His face was bruised, cut, and spit on, and his left eye was swelling up entirely. The Kotang took Marcus by the arms and hefted him up as Marcus's strength gave out and he collapsed. "Holy Quoizka! This guy is heavy!" one man shouted.

The Kotang workers guided Marcus to the Main Gate. More Kotang came out to check what had happened as they laid him down on a nearby pile of hay.

They all looked at him, surrounding the beaten and bloodied Saint. Marcus had both eyes closed and whispered, "Did I win?"

Slowly, the Kotang began to chuckle. Their chuckles turned to small laughs, which turned into contagious laughter that spread to every man around until all the Kotang were laughing uncontrollably and patting each other on the back. Marcus couldn't see but he could hear their laughter, and he felt its contagion spread to him. He laughed as well, his ribs aching from the joy as he said, "Please stop. It hurts to laugh." That only made the Kotang laugh even harder, all of them smacking each other on the back.

One of the Kotang caught his breath in between laughs and said, "Yeah Saint, you won."

Marcus merely raised his fist in the air, causing the laughter to start again. He received numerous pats on the shoulder despite not being able to see who gave them. A Kotang said, "You're alright, Saint. Keep this up and you'll be our leader for sure!"

The laughter erupted again. Marcus laughed as hard as he could, which was only a slight breath or two, but he enjoyed the comradery nonetheless. He may be hurt, but he had never felt happier than he did right now being surrounded by a bunch of good men. *Good times*, he thought, *good times.*

≪—•—≫

"This guy is the strangest man I have ever met." Joax stood with one arm on his knee, watching from the catwalk as the crowd of Kotang surrounded a beaten and bloodied Saint, all laughing their hardest at something he couldn't hear. "What do you think?"

Gobbie stepped next to Joax and peered down at the activity. Gobbie used to be laughing and lighthearted himself, but after the battles of Laythia, he had become stone cold. "He always confuses mi," he said.

Joax nodded, stroking his ginger beard between his fingers. "I ain't never seen anything like that before. And the man was still standing. What do you think it means?"

"That man is something else," Gobbie replied.

Joax nodded, then chuckled, and suddenly he was laughing. Gobbie looked at him and couldn't help but laugh too, breaking through the thick hatred in the air and replacing it with joyous mirth. Soon Gobbie and Joax were laughing uncontrollably, and the other Laythian guards saw them and couldn't help but start laughing too until every Laythian guard on the wall and Kotang worker in the city were laughing as hard as they could for no reason at all.

The Kotang looked up and saw the Laythians were laughing and were surprised by that. But neither side aimed to stop. They all laughed together like they were all one big broken family. The Laythian guards smacked their knees and the Kotang shook each other in response.

Then the Kotang and Laythians suddenly looked at each other, their laughter dying. It took both sides a moment to realize it, and when they did, the laughing stopped. They looked at each other in curiosity rather than hatred, looking at each other as human beings.

One of the Kotang members raised a hand amidst the crowd and waved at the Laythian guards above. For a moment there was a long pause between the two groups until a hand stretched over the catwalk and a Laythian waved back down at the Kotang. The two men waved at each other, the other Laythians and Kotang looking at their own awkwardly. The waving stopped and the sides gradually retreated back to their business. But one thing was for sure, something had changed between the two groups.

CHAPTER TWENTY-SEVEN

AFTERMATH

*"What a strange event. I've never seen a man take a
beating for nothing and still look like he won."*

—NOAH

Laythia

13:14 hrs, 20/07/2258 (3 months A.F.)

Marcus awoke on a haystack set up in the officers' lounge on the south end
of the city, far away from the Main Gate. Marcus opened his unbruised eye
to find Mak, Gobbie, Joax, and Faal standing there watching him. His left
eye was so swollen he couldn't see through it. He scanned their faces, all of
them smiling for some reason.

"How long was I out?" Marcus croaked.

"A couple of hours," Gobbie said. "Yous took a mighty beating."

"All from a couple of kids," Mak added.

The rest of the group laughed. Marcus smiled too. At least he still had
his teeth. He felt the result of the fight. His ribs were sore, which would
make it painful to stand, let alone to breathe. His groin was sore and his left
eye was completely swollen. Marcus felt tremendous pain in his legs, which
were bruised purple the whole way down. He had been in worse shape
before, though. He tried to sit up but struggled. Everyone stuck their hands
out to keep him down.

This time Faal spoke up. "My friend, do not overexert yourself."

Marcus groaned, forcing a painful breath through the fire in his stomach from the bruised ribs. "But I need to get back to work."

"The work will get done," Faal said. "Do not worry. We shall take care of things."

Marcus looked from left to right, noticing the other figures in the room. The Kotang leaders were standing alongside the Laythian leaders. The four men leading the two groups were all cooperating. Marcus leaned back against his bale of hay. *Those kids pack a punch.* It wasn't anything new to Marcus. He was used to this kind of persecution, but he didn't like the state he was in. All he could do now was wait.

So, Marcus rested in the hay, not happy about going to sleep because of the nightmares that awaited him. but he knew he needed to rest. He slowly closed his eyes and his mind drifted into the unknown.

Laythia

05:48 hrs, 21/07/2258 (3 months A.F.)

Marcus awoke from his slumber on the bale of hay the next day. He arched forward, feeling the cuts and bruises still present on his body. He still wasn't able to see out of his left eye but he had his other one to spare. His ribs were bruised so he had a hard time breathing. Marcus shrugged it off. *Rub some dirt on it,* he thought and pushed forward. It was still dark out but he could see the eve of dawn just over the horizon.

Marcus limped along the catwalk. He could see the Kotang stirring on the other side of the wall, getting ready for another day of hard work in the heat. Two Laythian guards approached Marcus, rifles slung over their shoulders. They stared in disbelief as he limped past them.

One of the guards said, "Whoah, I thought yous were dead." Marcus said nothing.

Then the other guard spoke up. "I gotta tell ya, I ain't never seen anything like that before. Yous taking a beating and still winning. Blows mi mind every time I thinks about it."

Marcus merely nodded and continued forward. The sun rose as he walked down the stairway toward the Main Gate. He picked up where he'd left off and got to work on the next pillar, going slow, but still making progress.

More and more of the Kotang members came into the city after being searched at the Main Gate, only to stand there dumbfounded when they saw Marcus already working.

Marcus tried hoisting a new log into place but faltered while trying to lift it. The weight was too much. The Kotang looked at each other and then helped out. Marcus said, "Thank you," as they hoisted the log into the air and put it into place.

They got back to work, resuming their normal pace on the wall. Marcus and the Kotang members were working on another log when they saw the four guards from yesterday approaching in shame.

Marcus faced them, the rest of the Kotang hanging back as the leader of the young guards said, "We're being punished for our actions yesterday, so we're required to help yous until the city is finished."

Marcus held no negative feelings toward the young leader or his little group and held out his hand. "Welcome aboard."

«— —»

Lunchtime came and the Kotang and Marcus sat in the shade of the wall eating bread the Laythians had prepared for them. As an offer of goodwill, Gobbie had orchestrated some of the Laythian people to bake freshly made bread for the Kotang and Marcus. It was a mighty generous offer since food was rare these days. Marcus and the Kotang accepted the gesture as an offer of good faith. They sat there on the grassy side facing outwards towards the Bog, using the shade from the wall while they took a break.

Marcus took a bite of his bread and noticed the young guards from the other day. He still wasn't able to see through his left eye, and his ribs and knee hurt like hell, but he was able to move better.

The young Kotang Noah was sitting next to Marcus as they ate their lunch in the shade. The boy had a baby face, long black hair, and hazel green eyes, as he studied Marcus up and down. Marcus saw the look and didn't say anything, waiting to see what the young man would say.

Eventually, Noah asked, "Have you been feeling alright?"

Marcus answered, "As well as I can. Why?"

"Your face, it looks . . ."

"Better?"

"Awful."

Marcus chuckled. He brought his attention over to the Laythian workers who sat a short distance from the Kotang. *Of course they would be sitting over there. They're the ones who attacked a close friend of the Kotang, so if they came nearer, they could get killed.* Marcus noticed how the young group was squatting in the sun and how they had no food to eat.

Marcus stood up for a second, but his legs gave out from under him. He fell back down, then asked Noah, "Do you mind helping me up?"

The young Kotang obliged and struggled to help Marcus to his feet. Even wounded, Marcus still weighed nearly a ton, but the lad finally got him to his feet and helped him toward the young Laythian guards with one arm over his shoulder.

Marcus clutched his bread as they approached the guards, the four of them looking down in defeat as they sat in the sun sweating like dogs. The young leader met Marcus's gaze, his blue eyes showing defeat and humility. "I'm sorry for attacking yous," he said. He gestured to his men. "We got punished and now we aren't given a food ration or nothin'. Plus, they told us to sit in the sun and not work in the shade, so yeah."

Marcus extended out his arm holding the small loaf of bread. The young leader pointed to himself. "Really? For us?"

Marcus nodded. The young leader took the loaf and distributed it among his compatriots. The young leader lowered his head in shame as he said, "Thank yous, mister. I appreciate it." Marcus merely nodded and Noah helped him back toward the shade.

As they walked back Noah asked, "Why did you do that? They were your enemy, right? Don't they deserve what's coming to 'em?"

Marcus responded, "The same way *we* deserve punishment?"

Noah didn't know what to say. Marcus looked at the young Kotang and said, "God commands us to love our enemies. Therefore, I will be generous to them as I would want them to be generous to me."

"Even if they don't treat you kindly back."

Marcus nodded. "Especially if they don't treat you kindly back."

Noah said softly, "You know, you really are something else." The young Kotang gestured to the rest of the workers. "We all look up to you. Even though you were our enemy we still look up to you."

Marcus bowed his head. "I appreciate it."

"No problem," Noah replied, helping Marcus sit back down.

Marcus enjoyed the shade and sat back watching the grass flurry in the wind. *What a wonderful day, Lord.*

CHAPTER TWENTY-EIGHT

UNDESERVED KINDNESS

"It's so backwards. Turning the other cheek. It just doesn't make sense. Wouldn't the logical thing to do be to fight back when your opponent is hurting you?"

—HICKAM DUNEHEART, LAYTHIAN CITIZEN

Wall Construction Site, Laythia
09:57 hrs, 24/07/2258 (3 months A.F.)

Joax was on watch, looking over the Kotang workers as he stood atop one of the buildings to get a good view of the workers along the wall. The Kotang had spread across the entire wall, working both outside and inside the city to accomplish the job faster. The Saint was working elsewhere, so Joax was in charge of making sure things didn't get out of hand today. *Easier said than done.* Joax could tell there was still tension between the Kotang and Laythians. Even his own people hadn't looked at him the same since he'd supported freeing the prisoners a few weeks ago. It was something that would take time to heal, but then again, they had nothing but time. There were no massive wars to worry about or demand for survival. The world had gotten smaller since The Fall and time was an ever-present resource.

Joax eyed the four young Laythians who'd attacked the Saint, making sure they weren't causing any ruckus. Fortunately, the four seemed to have learned their lesson and were humbled as they worked in the heat. *Nothing a little hard manual labor won't sweat out of you.* Joax chuckled at their struggle. He didn't mean to be cruel, but it was ironic. The very men who'd tried to make life hard for the people building the walls were now the people building it. It was almost laughable, like that joke the Saint had cracked when they'd attacked him.

Joax looked over and saw a crowd developing. Some of the Laythian people were throwing stuff at the young guards who'd attacked the Saint. Joax struggled to remember the name of the group's ringleader, and thought it was Jack.

Jack and his three buddies were working on shaving down the tree trunks so there wouldn't be any branches sticking out, but they were being harassed by the townspeople because the Laythians believed the rumor that Jack and his buddies were willingly helping the Kotang. It was also because the people were bored and needed something to do. It was almost laughable. They were their city guard and the people were still treating them like dirt.

To his surprise, Joax saw a young Kotang step out from working on the wall and stand between the angry crowd and the guards. The young Kotang, Noah, was trembling but standing firm. He called out to the crowd, "LEAVE 'EM ALONE!" Noah gestured toward Jack and his buddies. "They are your city guard. They fought for you and protect you, so why are you trashing them?"

One of the men in the crowd, dressed as a farmer, asked, "Why do yous care? We hate yous just as much since yous and your ravenous band of thieves tried to kill us. If these lot are associating themselves with yous then they are no different."

Noah was young but he also was brave; Joax had to admit the kid had guts. Noah called back, "Treat me as I deserve. For I am paying for my sins, just like the Saint. But these are your guards, so treat them kindly as such."

Both Joax and Jack's mouths dropped in response to the young Kotang standing up for them. It was unprecedented. Some people in the crowd began to throw horse manure toward Noah, who took a slam to the face but didn't fight back. He merely turned his cheek away and allowed the crowd to torment him. The sight was impressive. Then three more Kotang stepped forward, shielding Jack and his buddies with their bodies. Here were four

Kotang protecting four Laythians, two groups that horrendously hated each other, now protecting the other. Joax saw Jack's eyes and how surprised he was to receive such kindness.

The crowd continued to throw their trash toward the Kotang until they got bored. The four Kotang stood drenched in manure and spit. Some were bruised, and others were trying not to vomit. Then one Kotang heaved. Then two more Kotang upheaved as well, but Noah remained standing, looking stoic despite being covered in manure. Joax could smell the stench from ten meters away and he already wanted to gag. How Noah didn't was beyond him.

Then Jack stood up and walked as close as he could to the stinky Kotang and asked, "Why did yous do that?"

Noah turned, trying to look cool despite his appearance. "Because that's what the Saint taught me. And if the Saint says that God wants me to love on my enemies, then I will."

Jack replied, dumbfounded, "That doesn't make sense."

"I don't get it much either," Noah replied, shrugging his shoulders. "I just do what the Saint says."

Jack and his fellow buddies lowered their heads in shame. "Well, thanks . . . for standing up for us."

Noah gave a kind smile. Jack seemed touched. He clenched his nose with his hand and waved off the stench. "Now yous get a shower. Yous stink."

Noah turned and put his hands on his hips. "You stink too," he said sarcastically, as both of them were covered in manure.

Jack lifted one corner of his mouth in a smile, leaning forward to retort, "But I don't stink as much as yous do."

Noah paused, searching for something comical to say, then replied, "You've got a point there." The two boys laughed. Joax couldn't believe the sight. Two boys from opposite cultures, previously enemies, drenched in manure, were jesting with each other like they had been best friends for years.

Joax found it was time to step in. He raised his hands in the air. "Now

now. That's enough for today, boys. Y'all get yourselves a nice bath and rinse that dirty manure off you. That's not a request, that's an order. Understand?"

Both the Kotang and Laythians stood up straight and saluted. "Yessir!"

Joax smiled, feeling a sense of pride coming from both groups. He liked the respect they showed him. Joax waved them off. "Alright, now get."

They all ran off, taking the stench of manure with them. Joax waved away the scent of the manure left on the ground and went to find some shade. "What a weird day."

CHAPTER TWENTY-NINE

COMING TOGETHER

*"There's something in the air. Something that's
changing people from within. I can feel it."*

—JOAX

Wall Construction Site, Laythia

14:27 hrs, 26/08/2258 (4 months A.F.)

"Push!" Marcus pushed with all his might despite his injuries. His knee still hurt but he was able to walk on it more and more.

He pushed the log with all his strength but it was not enough. Luckily, he was not alone. Jack, Noah, and other Kotang were pushing with him to lift the final log into place around the broken walls of the city, while Mak, Joax, and even Faal were on the outside wielding a rope, pulling the log up from the opposite side.

"Push!" Marcus called again. The men from both sides pushed and pulled with all their strength as the massive thirty-foot log lifted and was planted into the ground alongside the others. Once the log was in place, cheers erupted from both groups. Men hugged and shouted with each other at their accomplishment, while Gobbie and his Laythian guards stood on watch with no emotion.

Marcus's men hugged him, and he could smell sweat off every man around him but didn't mind. He had spent most of his life around soldiers, so the smell of stink and armpits was common. Marcus didn't show much cheer in his expression but he was happy with the accomplishment and with the work they had done together. They had completed the new walls in roughly a month and even reinforced the structure. He even felt happy about both the young Laythians and the Kotang working together.

Marcus turned his attention to the hundreds of broken homes that remained inside Laythia. He could tell from the shattered windows, burned rooftops, destroyed haystacks, and the splatter of blood across the buildings that the physical effects of war were still prevalent inside the city. They may have fixed the walls to prevent invaders from outside, but they still needed to address the problems within.

Marcus stood atop a small boulder to try and grab everyone's attention. He waited for all the workers to gather before he called out, "Gobbie."

Gobbie didn't look happy about being called for. "Yeah?"

"I have an idea."

"What?"

Marcus turned to the men in front of him, the dozens of Kotang workers, and the few Laythian guards looking at him with awaiting eyes. Marcus addressed them. "In light of our success, I think we should spend the late afternoon at Goldberry Lake."

Marcus didn't need to shout for the words to echo. The Kotang looked up in excitement, throwing their arms up in cheer while Jack and his crew looked around in confusion. Marcus saw Noah whisper to Jack, and Jack slowly nodded in understanding.

Marcus waited for the cheers to die down before asking Gobbie, "What say you, Gobbie?"

There was a slight pause before Gobbie replied with a hint of reluctance in his voice, "Sure. Why not?"

"Meet us at Goldberry Lake. We'll head over there now."

"Understood, Saint."

Marcus looked back at the men, and said, "Let's move out."

As Marcus and his group marched out of the city and into the Bog, Joax,

Jack, and Noah paused to look toward the new and improved Main Gate, while Gobbie and his Laythian guards followed behind at a distance. But before they could go, Jack looked up at Marcus with his blue eyes and asked, "Saint?"

"Yes?" Marcus replied.

"Can I go and invite some of mi buddies to come along?"

Marcus put his hands on his hips. His armpits were sweating beneath his black undershirt. He contemplated the request and nodded, saying, "That'll be fine."

Jack quickly called for Noah and the two ran into the city of Laythia like the young boys they were. They both had to be no older than sixteen, but they acted like they were ten years old. Marcus would have smiled if he could but he let the emotion slide. "Meet us at the lake," he called out to them. They gave him a thumbs-up as they disappeared into the city.

Marcus turned back to the group of men still waiting, feeling the heat cooking their skin. "Move out," he said, not having to raise his voice.

The men turned and walked alongside each other in two long lines. Marcus extended the invitation to the other Kotang before they left but they declined, while Noah, Jack, and his Laythian buddies caught up to them on their hike.

The Laythian guards accompanied them, watching from a distance. Marcus understood Gobbie's orders; since every Kotang worker was under complete watch, nothing was done in secret. Marcus didn't mind that. He knew the Laythian guards were harmless. Besides the early attack from Jack and his group, they hadn't done anything to stop or impede their work on the wall. It was their city being rebuilt, anyway.

The six guards following the Kotang into the Arghast Forest were armed with their AX5M rifles. Marcus could tell the Laythians carried their weapons with more competence than they had when he first came here. Marcus had even offered the Laythian guards some training on firing and maintaining their weapons. Gobbie had found the gesture helpful, even if he didn't show it much. As a show of good faith, Gobbie had even permitted Marcus to carry his .44 and kukri on him when working on the walls outside the city. So, Marcus was glad to have something on him in case things got hot.

Marcus looked over towards Gobbie as they walked together in silence. He noticed Gobbie's heart was still cold toward the Kotang, as he didn't seem to have forgiven them yet and wasn't as happy these days. The wound on his shoulder had been healing well, but not as quickly as Marcus's wounds. Marcus could tell the fire of rage inside Gobbie's heart had died ever since he heard of the king's betrayal in killing Bo, but that didn't mean his hatred for the Kotang had diminished.

Marcus looked over towards Mak as well. Despite not being in command of the Kotang when the first battle started, Mak had grown in character and honor among his men, becoming a stoic and respectable leader. Even some of the Laythians admitted that he was an honorable man, or at least was trying to be.

Marcus shifted his eyes back to the forest. He knew the Kotang were unarmed and were not permitted to have weapons inside the city, but it hadn't crossed the men's minds to bring weapons as they ventured out into the Arghast Forest. This left only the six Laythian guards and himself with their limited supply of ammunition to protect them.

Marcus focused on the surrounding forest, now encompassing their view, shielding the men from the bleeding sun. He heard sighs of relief among the workers, who were grateful to be in the shade. It was about 95 degrees outside plus humidity, so a nice dip in the lake would soothe them nicely. The leaves in the forest had changed color, signaling the approach of autumn, creating a canopy of beautiful orange, red, and yellow above, while forming a carpet of beauty on the ground.

Marcus and the men hiked for a couple of miles before they reached Goldberry Lake. The Laythian guards lowered their weapons and marveled at the crisp blue beauty before them. It was not a massive lake but it was nothing short of beautiful to their eyes.

All the Kotang and Laythians looked at Marcus like they were a bunch of kids. Marcus realized just how much of an age difference there was between him and these young men. A majority of them were in their late teens to early twenties, while Marcus could easily be construed to be in his thirties or even his early forties, which was considered an "old man" to these young men. They all looked at him with eager eyes, even the Laythians from Jack's crew.

Marcus nodded and waved them along, saying, "Go on."

They all looked at each other and began charging toward Goldberry Lake, taking their sweaty clothes off and running into the cool refreshing water. Marcus, Mak, Faal, and Joax stood watching the group of fifty-four men play in the water, while Gobbie and the other Laythian guards stood aside in the shade. Marcus looked from side to side at the men standing next to him and said, "Go on, guys. You know you want to."

"Alright," Joax said, and then he turned and grinned slightly at Marcus. "But you gotta come with us."

"No, no, I'm fine." Marcus waved them off. But Joax, Mak, and Faal had already surrounded him, grabbing his arms and leading him toward the water.

"Come on," Mak said.

"You're coming too," Faal added.

Marcus pretended to fight, allowing the men to drag him closer to the water. He didn't feel comfortable being held by three men, but he fought to keep himself under control.

Marcus waved his arms around, gently breaking their grasp on him. "Alright, alright. I'll come in." He took off all his weapons and kept his black undershirt on. The three men hooked his arms and hoisted him up by his legs. Marcus could hear their grunts as they struggled to heft him into the air.

"Geeze Saint, how much do you weigh?" Joax groaned.

"Around one hundred kilograms."[15]

---

15. 220 lbs

"Indeed," Faal grunted.

Mak laughed. "You're all a bunch of sissies!"

Joax jested behind his shoulder. "Well, sorry if I ain't as strong as you!"

Mak grinned. "You just need to eat more."

"Oh, I'll get you for that!" Joax jibed.

"Can't wait."

The four men approached the side of the lake, the drop-off very distinct. The lake was notoriously deep despite being small, but that's why it was called Goldberry; because at the bottom, there was suspected gold.

The fifty-four members of the work party were all swimming, jumping around, and enjoying the nice water. They looked up at their leaders as they hoisted the Saint up into the air. Mak called out, "We got ourselves a live one here!"

Joax added, "Give him a warm welcome!" All the Kotang and young Laythians cheered as the three men hoisted Marcus by the limbs and prepared to throw him like a swing.

Mak called out, "Ready? One, two, three!" They threw Marcus as far as they could, which wasn't far, and he splashed into the cold refreshing water, soaking away all the heat and sweat from his body. Marcus came out of the water to be greeted by fifty-four men splashing him. Cheers went out and spirits were high. Marcus blinked to cover his eyes from all the splashing as the members of the work party erupted and started having fun. Guys were picking each other up and throwing each other around, tackling others, or pretending to be tackled. Marcus took in the whole scene and thought, *It's funny how such a simple lake could turn out to be so much fun to these kids.* Marcus allowed a brief glimmer of happiness to slide into his heart at the sight. It wasn't healthy for him to bottle up all his emotions, but it was dangerous for him to experience too many emotions as well. So, Marcus kept his joy in check, allowing himself to feel only a small sense of happiness with the men.

The fun lasted more than an hour as the men in the work party never got tired of the refreshing water. Fish swam in the freshwater lake and some of the men tried to grab them. Marcus, Mak, Joax, and Faal all laughed at the sight until one of the men came bursting out of the water with a fish in his hands. "Look what we're having tonight!" Then the fish flopped out of the man's hands, smacking him in the face as he tumbled into the water. The others erupted in laughter.

Marcus couldn't help but smile, even if it only lasted a second. He had missed the comradery of brotherhood, and this reminded him of all the good times he'd had in the military with his brothers in arms. He supposed that these men were his brothers in arms now too, given that Marcus had fought both for and against them. But that was all in the past now. Now they could focus on fixing what had been broken and regaining what had been lost.

Marcus glanced toward Gobbie and the Laythian guards standing by the tree line. None of them looked very happy, and Marcus could tell they wanted to hop in the cold refreshing water.

Marcus called out, "Hey Jack." The young blonde teenager stood up at the sound of his name and approached Marcus. Marcus gestured over toward the Laythian guards. "Why don't you invite them to join us?"

Jack nodded, got out from the lake, and approached Gobbie and the six Laythian guards. The guards looked at him first with skepticism, but then they shifted their attention to the water. Slowly but surely, the Laythian guards nodded and put their weapons down. All six of them undressed to their undershirts and pants and came walking with Jack into the refreshing water of Goldberry Lake, all except Gobbie. Marcus watched the six of them sigh with relief in the cold water. The Kotang members did not look at the Laythian guards with any contempt or anger. Instead, they welcomed them as brothers into the lake. The Laythian guards were semi-pleased to be in the water but were still unsure if what they were doing was the right thing or not.

Marcus had been there before, but he knew that downtime was an important part of keeping morale high. A simple game between two parties could unify a group and improve their fighting ability for the next day.

Marcus had learned many games spending time with his men in the military over the years.

The new Laythians blended in well with the other Kotang. Most of them were around the same age, which caused them to bond easier than Marcus had expected. It was the sad reality that Marcus remembered. War was a young man's game.

Together, they continued having fun for hours. Playing like friends at a summer camp, like no war had ever happened. The sun was slowly setting as the red-orange sky dimmed over the horizon. Mak looked at the others and asked, "You think we should set up dinner or something?"

Marcus said, "I'll come up with something." Faal, Joax, and Mak all looked at Marcus with curious eyes, wondering what he had in mind to feed sixty-five men.

Goldberry Lake, Arghast Forest
18:21 hrs, 26/08/2258 (4 months A.F.)

Mak stood in the growing darkness as he heard two gunshots in the distance from Marcus's .44 magnum. That weapon was so powerful it could blow a man's head clean off. Marcus emerged from the woods with two massive boars in both his hands. Marcus looked out at the platoon of men and threw the dead boars in their direction. "Dinner."

The men already had a couple of small fires going but realized they were going to need a bigger one. They ran together to set up a larger pit while Marcus took out his kukri and began to skin the boars, removing the organs and hides. He and the men heaved the pigs on sticks over the fire and slowly cooked the carcasses until they were ready. Marcus continually turned the pigs and used his kukri to slice off chunks for each man. They all lined up and received their portion, eating with pure delight. Even Gobbie lined up for food, finally joining the party.

He took a bite and with the food still in his mouth, said, "This is delicious." He looked at the other men. "It's so tender and juicy. It's perfect."

Marcus allowed for a tiny smile; he had been doing that a lot lately. He bowed his head in appreciation and continued to serve all the men, even those coming back for seconds.

The daylight faded, being replaced in the forest with only the light from the fires. Marcus looked to his right after hearing something in the woods. He drew his .44. Everyone silenced and all attention drew to the new figures arriving, but it was only twelve Laythian guards coming from the city with their hands up. The first Laythian was a man in his twenties with brown hair and hazel eyes. "We don't want any trouble," he said. "We were just wondering if we could join yous?"

Gobbie stood up and asked them, "What are yous doing here?"

The leader responded politely, "We heard about the outing when Jack invited us earlier. First, we said no, but after thinking about it we decided to come along." Gobbie looked to Jack, who nodded.

Marcus lowered the weapon, gesturing for them to get in line. The twelve new Laythians bowed in thanks, got in line, and received their portion. Marcus spotted no ill intent and gave them their food as the scene quickly turned into a massive barbeque with chuckles and stories mulling about. The Kotang and the first group of Laythians were suspicious of the newcomers but didn't question it.

Some of the men wished they'd brought ale but the trek back for some was too far in the night. Every man sat around the handful of firepits in circles, trading stories and laughing. There were no boundaries between the groups as men shifted about. Kotang members were sitting with Laythians and Laythians were sitting with Kotang. The sight was unbelievable. A couple of months ago these groups were at each other's throats. Now they were best buds. The only people who weren't interacting were Gobbie and some of his Laythian buddies, as they kept to their own firepit on the edge of the party.

Marcus and the officers sat together, reveling in the sight.

"Quite something, isn't it?" Mak asked Marcus. Marcus didn't answer; instead, Faal spoke in his place.

"Indeed, my friend," he said.

"Yeah," Joax added. "It's truly a sight, mi friend."

Marcus shifted his attention to study the body language of the officers. He could tell they were all thinking the same strange thought: how two groups of people who once hated each other were now eating together like nothing ever happened. It was odd for things to change so quickly, but such is life. Marcus wasn't surprised by it because it had happened to him so many times before. Enemies suddenly becoming allies and allies suddenly becoming enemies. Marcus had fought and killed so many, both on his side and the other, that it was hard to not get lost or to question what it was all for. Marcus didn't dive into that thought. He had to keep his mind focused on the present.

And the present wasn't that bad. At least things were getting better between the two groups and there was a hopeful future ahead. The days of fighting were done, but there would still be social strife between the two groups. Marcus wasn't surprised by that. There had been social strife between humans since the beginning of time. The simple fact that people were different from each other was enough reason to start a war. But at least right now these two groups were starting to like each other and the wounds from before could finally heal, or at least begin to heal.

Marcus realized he was becoming attached to these men. They were men he had fought, killed, and bled with. He could feel his heart reaching out toward them and tried to stop it, but he couldn't help it. It was part of being human. Still, Marcus stifled the connection as best he could and brought his emotions down until he was blank again. He knew it was unhealthy but after losing so many comrades he didn't want to experience the pain of losing someone close to him again, yet he knew he had to should the time come.

Joax shook his shoulder with a lukewarm greeting. "You alright?"

Marcus turned to Joax. "I'm fine."

Joax's face expressed concern but he didn't want to start something. "Whatever you say," he said, taking a bite out of his food.

Mak turned and looked at Marcus knowingly. "So, Saint," he said, as all eyes focused on him. "Where are you from?"

Immediately the conversation went cold. The entire group could see the question hit Marcus's blank expression like a brick wall. He remained silent and didn't answer.

Mak tried to reinvigorate the discussion. "I was just asking."

Marcus deflated a little. "Forgive me, but . . . I'm not comfortable answering that."

"Why is that?" Joax asked, but Marcus was silent again.

Faal stared at Marcus, who noticed and raised his defenses in response. Faal studied him for a minute but finally shook his head. "I can't get a read on you, my friend," he told him.

Mak asked, "Why do you not want us to know where you're from?"

"Are you a spy?" Joax asked.

Marcus shook his head slightly. "No."

"Then why aren't you being honest with us?" Joax asked.

Marcus met his question with more silence. The men frowned. The question died and Marcus could tell his actions were pushing them away.

Marcus said, "Forgive me . . . There's a reason why I'm not so open with many people." He took a breath, finding it hard to say the words. "I've been betrayed more times than I can count, so it's dangerous for me to reveal details about myself."

Joax asked, "So, have you been lying to us?"

Marcus shook his head. "No. I may be silent, but I won't lie to you."

"Sounds like omitting the truth," Joax said.

Marcus looked at Joax. "While I may not tell you everything, I will never lie to you." He looked at each of their faces. "I promise." Their gazes were all curious and slightly hurt. Marcus saw his mistake and wished to rectify it, but he didn't know how.

"Well, what can you tell us?" Joax asked.

"Ask me another question," Marcus offered.

Joax leaned back, frustrated. "Okay, uh . . . Where'd you get your fighting abilities?"

Marcus met him with silence again. Joax tried a different question.

"Were you a soldier?" Marcus said nothing. " 'Cause I can tell by the way you walk that you were a soldier."

"From what nation?" Faal asked.

"Gideon?" Mak asked. Silence. "Norwalk? Esthceptum?" Mak eyed Marcus, trying to peer deeper into his being, but the man was as difficult to read as a statue.

Joax asked, "How old are you?"

For once, Marcus replied. "How old do you think I am?" he asked, raising his eyes to Joax.

"Forty," Mak guessed.

"Thirty-five," Joax added.

"Thirty," Faal said.

Marcus gave none of them an answer. They all looked at him, disappointed.

"How old I am doesn't matter," Marcus said. "What does matter is that I'm old enough."

Joax leaned forward. He eyed Marcus for a long while before asking, "Which of the wars did you partake in?"

"All of them," Marcus answered. The answer sent a silent shock through them all. The men exchanged glances with each other.

"That's a lot of combat," Joax said nervously.

"Too much," Marcus agreed, staring down into the fire.

"Did you lose friends?" Joax asked. Marcus nodded.

This time, Faal asked a question. "Do you have a family?" Marcus looked at him and shook his head. Faal was surprised. "No family? No wife or children?" Marcus shook his head again. Faal stroked his goatee. "Peculiar."

Joax added, "What about parents? Siblings, even?"

"All dead," Marcus answered. He looked down at the dirt beneath his feet. Joax and the others thought the conversation would end there but Marcus spoke up again. "I do . . . or I did . . . have an adopted family. They took me in. Raised me."

"Are they alive?" Joax asked, but Marcus said nothing. It was starting to get on Joax's nerves.

"What about a love?" Mak asked.

Marcus stared into the fire. "I did—" he started, but he cut himself off.

Joax leaned forward, interested to hear about this. "Well, what happened?"

Marcus looked at Joax, his dark black eyes were not accusing but sadly admissive. "I went to war."

Joax cocked his head aside. "Yeah, but you can still have a love in war." Then Joax tilted his head more, the idea forming in his mind. "Are . . . are you a virgin?"

Marcus looked up and said, "Yes, I am." They all reared back, stunned.

Joax blinked and lowered his brow. "How?" He looked at Marcus, who was a stunning figure. He was a perfect stud in shape and muscle, big enough to tackle a football player, but stone cut like a statue from the Renaissance. Even the man's rugged face and beard were attractive. Joax could not understand how this man did not have a woman. He bet the Saint could have any woman he wanted. Just throw them at him and they'll come knocking.

Marcus tried to find the right words. "Umm, it's . . . complicated."

"Oh, come on!" Joax said. "You gotta give us something, Saint!"

Marcus looked aside for a second and then said, "Carmen."

Joax shook his head to make sure he heard correctly. "Hmm?" His interest was shooting up. Everyone around the firepit leaned closer. Marcus almost lightened a bit at their sudden interest. "Did I just hear you say a woman's name?" Marcus looked at Joax with hardened sadness as the young man asked, "Who's Carmen?"

"My sister." All the guys were repulsed with groans of disgust. Marcus rolled his eyes. "Not my actual sister. My *adopted* sister." They all breathed a sigh of relief.

Joax put his hand to his chest. "For a second there, Saint, I thought you had a weird quirk about you. Something to explain why you're single and whatnot." Marcus retreated into his gloomy staring, and Joax saw he was losing him. "Okay, okay! So, Carmen . . . tell us about her?" Joax shook his head nervously. "What does she look like?"

Marcus thought about it for a moment. "She has sleek long blonde hair and beautiful blue eyes. A dimple of a nose." Based on his description, it almost appeared as if Marcus was happy describing her. His words began to falter. "And a kind heart . . ." Marcus just stared blankly. Joax didn't see any emotion but he could tell it was hard for the big man to open up about this. His expression solidified but the emotion remained weak in his voice. "Such a kind and loving person." He nodded. His voice trailed to a whisper. "I miss her so much."

Joax could tell the big man was trying his hardest not to lose composure. Whoever this Carmen was, she had an impact on the stone-cold brute. Faal put a hand to Marcus's shoulder. Marcus regained some of his composure, and once again Joax barely saw any emotion in the man. Yet he could still hear the emotion struggling to cry out in Marcus's voice. Whoever this Carmen was, she was very meaningful to Marcus. And yet he'd lost her.

Marcus reached into his jacket and pulled out a small wallet. Inside was a picture of a much younger Marcus standing next to a beautiful blonde girl. Joax's face went red and his body flushed with heat. She was gorgeous. Her skin was silky smooth and her smile wide. The girl was easily a ten out of ten.

"That's Carmen?!" Joax looked up at Marcus as he showed the picture to Mak and Faal. They gave him warm compliments until Joax said, "Man, I'd like to ride her all day."

Then he saw Marcus glaring at him with a look of pure hatred. It wasn't much of a change in expression but the eyes captured the hateful emotion. It was a look Joax had never seen before. Those black eyes were ready to kill him, actually kill him. Joax went pale. Marcus stared at him hard. It was a warning and Joax heeded it. If he broke it again, he legitimately believed that Marcus would kill him.

Joax quickly apologized. "I'm sorry. I'm sorry."

Marcus's anger vanished and he looked aside. "It's fine."

Joax tried to relax, still fearing for his life after that death stare from Marcus. The man clearly took his family very seriously. Whatever relationship he had with this woman was special to him, and he didn't want anyone to interfere. Joax took it down as a rule. Never insult this guy's family or loved ones.

Mak was holding the wallet now, scrolling through more photos Marcus kept in there. "Who are these three men here?" He showed the picture to everybody, which featured three men all in special forces uniforms that Joax didn't recognize. Both Mak and Faal recognized the uniforms, but they didn't say where they were from. They all wore black, brown, and green camo face paint and were holding up their weapons for a photo that was decades old. They looked to be in their mid-twenties, nearly the same age that Joax was now.

Marcus looked up. "Those are my brothers."

"Your adopted brothers?" Joax asked.

Marcus nodded. "Yes."

"But you still call them your brothers?"

Marcus looked aside. "I, personally, use those terms loosely to refer to anyone close to me as family. While I may be adopted, I still consider them my family."

"Are there any other family members we should know about?" Joax asked. But he was met again with Marcus's silence. Perhaps that was too much for one night. Joax wondered what Marcus would say if he were drunk. Maybe they could get more info out of him.

"And where are they?" Faal asked. "The brothers, I mean."

Marcus was silent as if reliving an old memory. After a long pause, he said, "They're dead." Joax thought Marcus was going to stop there but he added one last comment that he wasn't sure he should have said. "Died right in front of me." They all raised their heads slightly in surprise.

"I'm sorry," Joax whispered.

"It's okay," Marcus said.

The conversation went quiet again until Joax threw it out there. "So, you're a virgin, that's what you're saying." Their moods lifted again as the guys all laughed.

Once the laughter died down Faal looked into the fire and said, "I miss my wife and children."

"You're married?" Mak said.

"I am, my friend."

"Where are they?" Joax inquired.

"I don't know."

Joax tilted his head. "What do you mean?"

Faal stared back into the past but remained half-present in the moment. The hurt was still too fresh. "When the bombs fell and the Fall began, entire cities were wiped out in an instant. My wife and two children were on the outskirts of Mithra."

"Is that where you're from?" Joax asked.

Faal shook his head. "No. My wife is, but I am from the neighboring country of Falaysha."

"Do you think they are still alive?" Mak asked.

Faal raised his head hopefully. "I like to think they are. Millions of people went missing once the bombs fell but that doesn't mean they're dead."

"Maybe they're still alive."

Faal seemed to warm to Joax's comment. "Perhaps you're right, my friend."

" 'Course I'm right!" Joax said sarcastically. "I know everything!"

The whole group chuckled except for Marcus. The rest of them shared about their pasts. Loved ones lost, new people come and gone, all of them experiencing loss. Marcus didn't want to listen to their stories. He knew it would cause him to become attached to them, but he couldn't bear to shut his ears. It pained him but he had to listen.

Mak once had a wife but lost her early in the first wars. Joax used to be part of a rogue gang and roamed the countryside trying to make a living until he joined the Laythian military. And Faal was part of the Falaytian special forces for ten years until the bombs fell and he became separated from his wife and children. They were a bag of misfits from every random place you could think of. And here they were, rebuilding a city and helping a people reconcile with a rogue group of bandits, or former bandits, that is.

The conversation went long into the night, and eventually, Marcus pulled out his kukri and began whittling down a piece of wood until it was a sharpened stake. The rest of the group didn't mind but knew he was excluding himself for some unknown reason. Marcus didn't say anything on the matter and kept whittling.

The night went on until the fires were embers and the men began to fall asleep from overeating. Marcus remained awake while everyone was asleep. The dark night shrouded all movement. The moonlight was barely able to break through the covering of the trees. He continued to whittle down the wood until it was nothing but shavings. Then he picked up another stick and began whittling again.

The night dragged on and only the sound of Marcus's whittling, aside from the occasional snore from the sleeping men, filled the cool air. Marcus remained awake, knowing the nightmares would claim him at some point. He looked at Joax, Mak, and Faal. Good men he could be comrades with. New faces to lose in his inventory of growing casualties. He didn't want to get close to them but he had to. It wouldn't be very godly to merely keep people at a distance. And a good leader had to know his men well. So, Marcus watched them sleep while remaining their protector in the night. Even the new Laythian guards had fallen asleep, while Marcus sat there, whittling into the night. Trying to fight against the encroaching darkness of sleep.

Do you think that someone like you deserves happiness? Marcus opened his eyes, not realizing he had closed them, and saw a man shrouded in darkness standing before him. Marcus was still in his seat with the kukri and stake in his hands, but none of the other men were around him. He saw the darkness around the figure dissipate, revealing black hair and a handsome face. Marcus wasn't surprised to recognize his own face, only this version had red eyes, gazing at him with judgment.

What makes you think that after all you've done, you deserve to be happy? The words were vicious and tart, coming from his own voice. Marcus merely looked at the figure of himself, not surprised at all by the matter.

Don't you think it's hypocritical of you to get to know these people without letting them know anything about you? You're just a killer. A worthless killer with nothing to live for. Your family is gone. Your brothers are gone. Your country is gone. You have nothing.

Marcus merely said, "Back away from me, Satan." The black figure recoiled in surprise, his previous competence waning. His red eyes narrowed and his handsome face looked at him with contempt. Marcus paid no attention and went back to whittling his stick of wood.

You're not changing anything. Just think of all the blood you've spilled.

Marcus ignored the figure. None of this was new to him.

The shrouded figure watching him lifted his chin, grinning. *I'll see you soon,* he promised as he faded away into the night.

Marcus opened his eyes to find himself in exactly the same spot as earlier, only everyone else was there, back beside Goldberry Lake. Marcus chuckled, laughing silently to himself. Marcus let his guard down for a few seconds as he lowered his head and whispered, "Thank you." Then he went into his rucksack and pulled out his book of Scripture.

The moonlight broke through the leaves, providing Marcus with just enough light to read. He turned to Isaiah and started reading chapter 41:10. *"Don't be afraid, for I am with you. Don't be discouraged, for I am your God. I will strengthen you and help you. I will hold you up with my victorious right hand."*

The white light shone down over all the sleeping figures. Marcus smiled and felt happy to see everyone sleeping so soundly as he read in the night.

CHAPTER THIRTY

A New Assignment

"To prevent future wars you need to take the first step forward and forgive."

—THE SAINT

Laythia

07:47 hrs, 27/08/2258 (4 months A.F.)

Marcus held a clipboard, standing on the main road atop a rock so they could all see and hear him. They stood at the mouth of the Main Gate as he addressed all the Kotang workers present. "Now that we've completed the outer wall, we will begin working on every home in the entire city." All the Kotang and even some of the Laythian guards dropped their mouths. Marcus saw their reactions and almost wanted to laugh but hid his expression and addressed them promptly. "You will each be assigned a group, and each group will be assigned a certain section of houses to work on. Your main priority is to fix any problems that you find inside each home."

The Kotang looked around in confusion. Marcus didn't address it and carried on.

Faal stepped forward next to Marcus, saying, "We have allotted you each your own set of tools to work on the homes, and food will also be prepped before the day starts so you may bring it with you." That seemed to brighten their moods. The breeze shot through the front gate, cooling their sweat. "Any questions?" Faal asked. No one made a move. "Good." Faal took the clipboard from Marcus and announced, "Here are the groups and their assigned housing . . ."

Once organized, the groups all left to their assigned sections. "You think they'll do a good job?" Faal asked, walking alongside Marcus.

Marcus said, "I am curious to see how they do. This is mostly a test for the Kotang to see how they interact with the locals after what happened. I want to see their reactions, both the locals and the Kotang."

Faal wanted to shrug his shoulders but held back. "You certainly have a way of testing things, Saint."

"That I do."

«——»

Mak felt naked walking into the city without any weapons. He looked out at the hundreds of houses all decimated from the two recent battles, with bloodstains still marked on the streets. The city had clearly not forgotten its previous wounds and maybe it never would.

Four companions joined Mak, hoisting tools over their backs. The Laythians had been hesitant to allow the Kotang the use of tools inside their city, which was fair given how the Kotang had attacked before, but if they didn't then it would inhibit their progress and the work would take longer. Mak still hadn't forgotten how the Laythians were willing to kill all of the prisoners without a second thought a couple of months ago. There was still bad blood in the city and it needed to be addressed.

Mak brought his men up to their first house and looked over the damage. There were bullet holes sprayed throughout half the building, the roof had been burned off, and the scent of charcoal filled the air. Yet, someone was still living in it. That stung Mak's heart, knowing how people have had to endure wars for centuries, with everything being literally reduced to rubble, and having to live in those kinds of conditions. Mak thought back to the bonfire last night and how much joy he'd felt while spending time with his fellow Kotang as well as with the Laythians that had joined them. It taught him something. It taught him that even though they may hate each other, they could still live together as human beings. There would always be some conflict but that was guaranteed to happen between groups of people. That bad blood doesn't go away overnight. He had stolen and deprived too many lives to think that people would simply forget his past deeds. He could still see the looks of distaste on the Laythian guards who watched them 24/7.

Mak hefted his tools and piles of wood and approached the first home. He knocked on the broken door, watching the hinges come loose as the door hung halfway open. A woman dressed in a black burqa opened the door the rest of the way and looked at them, her eyes quickly scanning their bodies up and down. Mak knew she was searching all of them for weapons or even some malicious intent. By orders of Gobbie and Faal, the citizens had the right to deny the Kotang from fixing their homes if they wanted. This woman clearly did not want them here, but she also did not want to be living in poverty either, so she opened the door, revealing only her eye slits through her burqa.

She held open the door for the Kotang to enter. Mak and his four companions found that the home was only ten feet long and ten feet wide. The charcoal burns littered the floor with dirt and grime. There was a small blanket laid off to the side and some cooking utensils over what used to be a tiny fire. Mak wondered where the woman's family was. Every woman in this city had a family, even those who weren't married. The family was the basic foundation of the society in Laythia, and to find a woman living on her own was strange.

"Where would you like us to begin?" Mak asked the woman.

She said nothing and pointed to the opposite side of the house. Mak and his men saw the destruction, finding that most of the walls were destroyed with gaping holes in several portions. Mak wondered what caused these massive holes. He looked down and saw there were two massive bloodstains on the stone floor. He grimaced. *More than one person died in this home.* He didn't want to picture who it was or how it happened but he had a feeling he would learn soon enough.

Mak remembered the command the Saint had given them. To help with any problems within the home. It was a vague instruction because that left it up to the Kotang to decide how they fixed the home. Mak paused, considering the command, but he pushed it aside and focused on the task at hand. "This wall," he said, putting his hand against the broken stone, "needs to go."

He turned to the woman, who looked at them blankly with her hazel green eyes. Despite not seeing any of her other features, Mak felt a warm sense rush through his being. He stifled his emotions and focused on the task at hand. "Alright men, we need to take down these walls first, then start taking the measurements, adding the wooden structure, and overlaying the foundation with wood, brick, and stone."

They all nodded and got to work. It didn't take much time for them to figure out how to destroy the remaining wall. They took out their tiny hammers and began breaking away at the broken stone. Mak looked at the woman, who had her arms crossed, but her eyes showed both sadness and hatred paralleled at them. That look was more than enough for Mak to realize the shame of what he and his men did when they attacked this city. He looked back at the bloodstains on the ground and wondered if it was her family who had died inside this very building. He wanted to ask her but now wasn't the time. So, Mak took out his tools and began doing what he did best. Break things.

CHAPTER THIRTY-ONE

RESENTMENT

*"Not everyone agrees that the Kotang should be here. I don't. But we
need them in order to rebuild. So I will let them stay for now."*

—GOBBIE

Laythia

12:46 hrs, 29/08/2258 (4 months A.F.)

"This ain't a good idea," Jack said.

"Nah, it's the perfect idea!" Noah and a few of his Kotang members, as
well as Jack and some of his Laythian buddies, walked together through the
Townsquare at midday. Noah walked like he owned the place. The teenage
boys puffed out their chests, trying to appear more like men, while Jack, for
once, was hesitant.

Jack shook his head and repeated, "This ain't a good idea."

"Come on, you know the food those guys out in the Bog make ain't the
greatest. So, let's get some nice food here in the Townsquare."

Jack looked at Noah with concern. Even Jack was aware that the Kotang
weren't exactly welcome in the city, and he got a creeping feeling that something bad was about to happen. But Noah skipped along like a busy bee
with no worries. That concerned Jack, who was surprised that he was the
cautious one for once.

Jack and the others found the Townsquare bustling with activity. The
midday lunch rush was bolstering and the city appeared to be on the rise
from the recent events. Shops were open and people were selling all kinds of

foods and knickknacks. Jack eyed the sticks of frogs, his stomach growling. Noah and the others were wowed by the sight of the market and were eager to check out all the shops.

Jack eyed Noah and asked, "Ain't yous ever seen a marketplace before?"

Noah didn't take his attention off the raging market. "No, I grew up at Tettenhall. All we had there were weapons and fighting. This ain't exactly what we're used to." Noah put his hand to his head, realizing he was beginning to talk like the Laythians now. He guessed that's what happened when your best friend was a Laythian.

Jack's cautious expression didn't go away. "I'm going to warn yous. Yous ain't exactly welcome here." He was talking to all the Kotang members in their group. "We should probably get back and have lunch out with the rest of the Kotang where it's safe."

"Nah man, let's go. I wanna try some of that fried frog yous been telling me about."

Jack hid his expression, although he leaked another cautious glance to his Laythian buddies, who all shared the same look. Together the group of ten teenagers tried to go up to one of the shops to purchase some food, passing a few taverns along the way. Jack even spotted some of his fellow guards sitting around the taverns, drinking and enjoying the prostitutes. He spotted their weapons as well. Always present, all the time. Jack had to forsake carrying his weapon since he was still being punished for his actions, and so he could not carry any arms until all the homes were rebuilt. Right now, he really wished he had one.

Jack had money stored up from his work on the Guards Watch, so he was eager to spend some of it with his buddies. They approached a nearby stand that was selling an assortment of fried little critters. Jack spotted roasted squirrels, rabbits, and even the exotic frogs the Laythians were known for. The region's famous frogs inhabited Goldberry Lake. They were delicious when cooked correctly and had a nice tangy flavor to them that made them nice to nibble on for hours.

Jack ordered one of the frogs from the stand's owner, an older man, and by old he meant in his late thirties. Older than thirty was practically the new eighty. The lifespan of people had dropped so dramatically since the Fall that living a long life in retirement just wasn't possible. Everyone died at some point, whether they got kicked in the head by a donkey or bitten by a rattlesnake.

Jack ordered a few frog sticks from the owner and at first, the man didn't hesitate to hold the sticks out to them, but then he realized who he was offering the sticks to. Jack saw the man's expression turn from happiness to grimaced rage. His face boiling red at the sight of the Kotang. The man's gaze shifted to Jack and his fellow Laythians and looked at them with contempt. He retracted the frog sticks despite having been holding them mere inches from their hands.

The man said, "We don't serve your kind here."

Noah responded, "But I'm hungry, man. Don't you want our money?"

Jack furrowed his brow. *Our money? I'm the one paying for it.* Noah saw the look on Jack's face and laughed. Jack couldn't help but laugh also.

Their laughter died when the man said, "I'm not giving yous a single piece of food. Go and take your business elsewhere or I'll call the guards."

Jack furrowed his brow again. *We are the guards.* He brushed it off and tried to leave but Noah was persistent. Jack put his hand on Noah's shoulder and tried to pull him away before anything bad happened. "Come on, let's go, Noah. We don't wanna cause no trouble," he whispered.

Noah let go and allowed himself to be pulled back. He lowered his head and sighed. "Yeah, you're right. I'm sorry. Let's go before we get into any—" Noah turned and there stood twenty Laythian guards, all with rifles in their hands. "—trouble."

Jack raised his hands calmly in defense. "Look, we're just gonna leave. We don't want no trouble."

The leader, a man with long brown hair, looked at them with determined eyes. "But we do."

Thankfully, Noah and the group said nothing, allowing Jack to do the talking to his fellow guards. He recognized this guard, who went by the name of Lylack. Quite a character too. How he'd survived the two battles was beyond Jack's understanding.

Jack kept his hands up, saying, "Look, please let us go and we'll be on our way."

Lylack looked down at the ground, his long brown hair covering part of his face. "Yous see, that's the thing." He gave Jack a devious look, one that signaled trouble, and played coy. "As fellow guards of Laythia, we can't stand by while a couple of Kotang trash on our city and cause problems."

This time, Noah spoke up. "We weren't causing any trouble."

Lylack grinned and shook his head. "Now, that's not what I see." His grin lowered and he became serious. "Take 'em, boys."

The ten teenagers, five Kotang and five Laythians, were quickly surrounded by twenty guards all armed with AX5M rifles. The Laythian guards smacked them with the butts of their weapons and began beating and kicking all the workers. Jack took a smack to the face from Lylack, his face turning red with blood from the blunt force.

Jack fell backward as the rest of the guards began beating them all in broad daylight while the market went on as normal. The Laythians beat the group to a bloody pulp and then dragged them out of the Townsquare and rolled them all the way down the hill. They smacked into the Main Gate in a bloody heap. Some in the crowd cheered at the sight of their fellow Laythian soldiers kicking out the oppressors.

"And don't come back!" Lylack yelled, gaining more approval from the crowd before he and the other guards returned to their usual duties of drinking on the job and enjoying the prostitutes. The city went on as usual, like nothing ever happened.

Laythia

13:33 hrs, 29/08/2258 (4 months A.F.)

Gobbie stood over the group of boys. All of them were beaten purple, lying on patches of hay they'd laid out in the officers' lounge where Gobbie and his buddies would drink. He looked down at Jack, and asked, "Jack, who did this?"

Jack could only whisper, unable to see anything, his face wrapped in bloody bandages. "It was Lylack."

Gobbie nodded in understanding and stood. "I'll handle this. Yous rest."

"Thank yous, Captain," Jack whispered.

Gobbie looked over to his right to find Mak staring at Noah. The two had become extremely close since Noah's father died. He could see the shock on Mak's face to see Noah so beaten. The boy was still sixteen yet Gobbie could tell Mak felt responsible for him.

Despite his reluctance, Gobbie put a hand on Mak's shoulder, telling him, "This ain't your fault."

Mak deflated. Gobbie's words reassured him. It was what he needed to hear, even if he didn't believe it himself.

The two men faced each other. "I knows who did it," Gobbie said, answering Mak's unspoken question.

Mak nodded. "Do what you must. Just be careful about the social ramifications."

Gobbie was all too aware. Ever since the second battle of Laythia had ended, the city had been teetering on a knife's edge. People were still angry and frightened by the prospect of the Kotang attacking, and the Kotang were equally frustrated about being nearly executed when the Laythians broke their promise of using them as indentured servants. The people of Laythia had proved fickle and easy to manipulate. Their emotions steered them too easily in whatever direction evil drew them toward. Gobbie knew that himself after he'd led a crowd of two hundred people to try and kill the Saint, forcing the man to kill every single one of them in self-defense.

Gobbie raised his head and looked through the open window toward the city. *What an irony. To have the title Saint and yet be hated and loved at the same time. It's quite the conundrum.* Gobbie was curious where he'd even heard the word 'conundrum' before but he brushed that out of his mind. He had to discipline those guards or else things would get out of hand. But if he did discipline them then the people would possibly revolt against him.

The Saint entered the room and asked them, "What happened?"

Mak answered, "They were attacked by Laythian guards in the marketplace. They didn't want to cause any trouble but the guards attacked them anyway."

"I'll discipline those men appropriately," Gobbie added, looking to the Saint for confirmation of his actions.

"Do what you must," he said, saying the same thing Mak had.

Gobbie nodded and left the room to Mak and the Saint. Outside, he was greeted by none other than Lylack and his men. They stood before him arrogant and cocky. Lylack had a stupid grin on his face that Gobbie wanted to smack. He knew Lylack wanted to be in charge but that was never going to happen. He was too idiotic to lead.

"Eager to show your face so suddenly," Gobbie said contemptuously.

"Well Captain, we's were just out for a nice stroll is all. Now ain't that right, boys?" His men all nodded behind him.

Gobbie was tired of this. "Leave all your weapons and armor at the barracks and get ready to walk," he said.

Lylack's grin disappeared. "What are yous talking about?"

Gobbie continued, "Head to the Main Gate and be prepared to walk."

Lylack stepped closer to Gobbie. "If yous say anything or do anything to us, then I'll make sure the people don't care about yous as their commander one bit." Lylack tapped Gobbie's chest hard. "Yous hear me . . . *sir?*"

Gobbie wanted to throw a punch at this weak man but Lylack was just a young guy like he was. He knew that Lylack would cry wolf and moan about his oppression for what he was about to do. Gobbie debated the consequences but he knew that this kind of behavior could not be tolerated.

Gobbie constrained himself with all his self-control and said, "Report to the Main Gate for marching drills."

Lylack and his men exchanged looks. "Marching drills? What's that?"

Main Gate Catwalk, Laythia

18:55 hrs, 29/08/2258 (4 months A.F.)

Joax stood with his arms crossed, looking over the city walls at the group of marching guards. Lylack and his men had to walk for miles with no shoes out of the city and back for the rest of the day. Joax chuckled to himself, it had been a hot day, making it an absolute pleasure watching Lylack and his buddies walk in the sun till dusk. He turned to Gobbie who just stood there with a stoic expression. "You sure had fun with them, eh Captain?"

"This will cause problems," Gobbie said solemnly, "but it had to be done."

Joax sighed. He missed the old Gobbie, the Gobbie who was light-hearted and arrogant and fun. This new Gobbie was so serious all the time since the battles ended. But that's what happens in war. You're never the same again.

"The people will look at them as martyrs when they see 'em," Gobbie continued.

Joax looked out toward the horizon, watching the fading sun over the trees. "Eh, don't worry about it. The people fluctuate between emotions like the wind. They'll come around."

"I hope so," Gobbie said, still staring out at the moaning prisoners. He found a little satisfaction in the punishment of the group, but his main concern was more about how the people would feel when they found their Laythian commander punishing his own soldiers for attacking Kotang workers, despite the fact that there were Laythian guards among the group attacked. People wouldn't care about that detail. They'll only see the Laythian commander protecting Kotang workers and that would cause him to lose popularity.

Gobbie rolled his shoulders to try and relieve his newfound stress. Joax put a hand on his shoulder and said, "Relax, Gob, we'll get through it. The problems won't last forever."

Gobbie found relief in that and was glad. He turned and focused on the repairs in the city, watching the Kotang work on the houses. "Maybe you're right," he said.

Joax threw his whole arm over the back of Gobbie's neck. " 'Course I am! Have I ever been wrong?"

Gobbie narrowed his eyes. "Yeah. What about the time with the boulder?"

"Okay, one time."

"And the event with the cat and wolves?"

"Okay, two times." Joax grinned, feeling no shame.

Gobbie looked at his friend and started laughing, this time throwing his arm over Joax's shoulders. "We'll get through it, like yous said."

Joax smiled. "Like I said. Now, could you let go of me?"

Gobbie smiled back. "Only if yous can get out."

Joax chuckled. "Let's find out."

CHAPTER THIRTY-TWO

LOVING YOUR ENEMIES

"It is easy to hate. It is harder to forgive."

—THE SAINT

Laythia

12:05 hrs, 01/09/2258 (5 months A.F.)

Mak had returned to the same broken home with the single woman inside. It was strange; Mak and his men had worked on this home for the past five days and the woman hadn't said a word. It's not like she was fearful these men would rob her, as there was nothing left to steal. All this woman had was a blanket to sleep on. Mak remembered the recent nights, the cold dragging in. Autumn was coming and with that came the cold winds at night and hot temperature during the day, making living outside utterly miserable.

Mak and his men sat inside the house, eating their food as he leaned against one of the walls and nibbled on his bread, observing the woman in the burqa kneading dough. Mak wondered why this woman had never spoken to them. Working in this home and trying to rebuild the house she had lost only tore at Mak's already guilty conscious. He was beginning to become attached to this city and its people from simply working in it.

Mak imagined if someone tore down his house after he had done all this work on it, and how it would be infuriating; maybe that was what the Laythians were feeling. Now they were getting a pity work party to try and make things better by fixing up their homes.

Mak saw the bloodstains on the stone floor and then looked at the woman kneading dough. He put his bread down and stood up, cracking his rusty knees. He walked over, his buddies eyeing him the whole time. Mak stepped in front of the woman. She ignored him and continued kneading dough. "Do you need help with that?" he asked.

The woman said nothing. Mak knelt down to her eye level, looking around for things he could do to help out. The Saint's command to help in the homes was still ringing in his mind. His gaze was drawn toward the two bloodstains again. The woman's gaze followed and they both stared at them.

Mak looked toward the woman and her eyes met his. He felt another flush in his chest as his heart warmed looking into her eyes. It was like her eyes were a galaxy to be explored, filled with thousands of stars, unknown to the world. Mak was captivated by the sight and stared for a little too long. The woman broke her gaze and looked aside. Mak tilted his head after seeing the emotion in her body language. *Was she . . . embarrassed?*

The thought made Mak's heart jump. He wondered if this woman had a husband, then dismissed the thought. *Of course she does! How could a woman living by herself not have a husband?*

The woman went back to kneading the dough and remained silent, but Mak couldn't help but feel some connection had developed between them. He thought of the Saint and what he would do in this situation. His gaze drifted back to the two bloodstains and then back to the woman. He stood up and walked over to his work buddies, all stretched out and sweaty from the heat. Mak held out his hand to one of them and said, "Rudon, give me your handkerchief."

Rudon had the white cloth held on his face, the water dripping from the material onto his forehead. He relinquished the handkerchief, curious as to what Mak was going to do with it. But instead of walking back to the woman, Mak knelt, dipped the rag in some water, and began wiping away some of the blood from the floor. The noise drew all the attention in the household, even the woman's.

Her hazel eyes marveled at the sight of Mak cleaning the bloodstains. Mak's rag quickly turned red, doing a poor job of removing the blood from the floor. He had only removed a small percentage of the bloodstains before the handkerchief was all dirty. The stains remained mostly intact. But the woman couldn't help but stare at him in disbelief.

Mak just knelt, tired and sweaty, leaning over in exhaustion. The work and the heat were getting to him. He craned his head back and looked in the woman's direction. This time he saw her staring at him like he was a ghost. That made Mak uncomfortable. He wasn't sure what emotion this woman was experiencing right now.

Mak got up, his knees killing him from squatting so much, and turned back to his men. "Alright, get off your rumps, and let's get back to work," he ordered.

The men groaned and stood up, resuming their work. The only difference this time was that the woman continued to stare at Mak, forgetting the dough between her fingers.

Laythia

21:01 hrs, 01/09/2258 (5 months A.F.)

Mak sat in the Kotang's camp out in the Bog. The night was young and the fires were rolling, but it was relatively quiet. There was not as much activity or joking around as he had expected. He looked around and could tell the other Kotang were sullen like he was. *Could they be feeling the same as I do?* It was hard to fully tell when it was dark out, but Mak could catch a glimpse of some of his men as they stared into the fires, hanging their heads in shame. *They're dealing with their sins, but what about mine?*

Mak was alone outside his tent, glad to not have any company. He needed time to think and contemplate everything. With all that had changed, he couldn't help but wonder if he should change too.

He sat atop a wooden log, a small fire in front of him, his boots touching the dirt beneath. He hung his head forward, thinking about that woman and her home. The two bloodstains on her floor haunted him. *Those were people before, those two bloodstains. I don't know who they were, but they were people.* Mak remembered the destruction of the city. He saw it every day when he went to work. It was beginning to haunt him. The sight of the burned homes and bullet holes, the slashes of blood spread across the entire city, all of it sent his mind into a whirlwind.

He kept coming back to the sight of those two bloodstains on the floor of that woman's house. *That could have been me.* He thought. *I could be the one who killed them.* But even if he wasn't directly responsible for the death of that woman's family, he was still responsible for attacking this city and bringing all this destruction.

Mak could feel the weight upon his chest. The guilt coated his mind and caused confusion and lack of clarity. All he could think about were those two bloodstains. He had tried to remove them but they wouldn't come off.

He looked at both his hands and saw blood on them, blood he could never wash off. His hands trembled and his breathing became irregular. He blinked and suddenly the blood was no longer visible, but he knew it was still there.

Mak lowered his hands and whispered, "What have I done?"

He looked over toward the city of Laythia. The number of homes lit up in the night had decreased due to the recent battles. He remembered the day he attacked this city, and for what? Riches? Revenge? Mak had lost more in that battle than he could have possibly imagined, and all it did was leave him with this tremendous guilt.

He looked around and realized other Kotang members were experiencing the same thing. They shared a sense of guilt for their past actions. Mak's expression shifted to terror and desperate horror. "I need to pay for my sins. I need forgiveness." He lowered his head in submission. "But I don't deserve forgiveness."

Then he thought of the Saint. How did he forgive Mak and the rest of the Kotang, as well as the Laythians? Mak thought, *Can I be forgiven? Can God truly forgive me for the wrong I've done?*

A thought dropped into Mak's mind as he remembered a prayer the Saint had once said over them. *"Father, I know we have done evil. We have broken your laws, but Jesus please forgive us for our sins."*

Mak lifted his hands in surrender and said, "God if you're real, then please . . . please give me a sign."

CHAPTER THIRTY-THREE

UNDESERVED MERCY

*"I don't deserve forgiveness. For what I've done, I
deserve to be sent to hell if there is one."*

—MAK, COMMANDER OF THE KOTANG

Laythia

09:02 hrs, 02/09/2258 (5 months A.F.)

Mak and his men approached the same home the next day. The house was looking more and more complete, with a skeletal structure of wood properly settled as well as an outer layer of brick for the base and a wooden roof. They were almost finished repairing the building but Mak got the feeling that wasn't the point.

Mak knocked on the door and it opened quicker than he'd expected. The woman still wore her burqa and didn't speak as she allowed them in, but this time, Mak and his men had brought small buckets of water and more rags. They all knelt next to the bloodstains, but before they could start, Mak gestured to the stains and looked at the woman for consent. Mak and the woman's eyes met and she considered it for a moment, then nodded.

Mak and his men got to work, dousing the rags with water and rubbing them along the stone flooring. The rags were able to get some of the stains off but they weren't doing the job well. They had to scrape hard on the stone to remove even just a little bit of the blood. It was true; blood really did stain.

Mak and the others worked tirelessly for hours but made little progress. Hours went by, lunch, and then a few more hours and they had not made much of a difference.

Evening came and the men stood up, stretching their aching knees. Mak remained knelt over, continually rubbing against the stone flooring.

His buddy Rudon looked to him and said, "Mak, come on, the day's over."

"I'll catch up," Mak said.

Rudon and the others wanted to argue but they were all exhausted, having worked on nothing but the bloodstains the whole day. Mak remained inside the woman's home, continuing to scrub the floor with his dirtied rag, now stained red. Out of the two stains of blood on the ground, they had only removed 15% of the first stain.

The woman returned home with a basket of produce after she'd left to get some groceries and nearly dropped it at the sight of Mak continually scrubbing. She put the basket aside and watched Mak in silence as he continued to work, scrubbing tirelessly against the bloodstain until his hands were blistered. She could see the desperation in Mak's movements, the guilt driving him to remove the blood on his hands.

The woman looked at him with growing concern. Mak paid no attention to her and focused on removing the bloodstain, achieving little progress. He was exhausted but his body refused to stop. He knew he had to do this. To repay somehow for what he did. But he also knew he never could. He could never bring back the lives he had taken. So, this was all he *could* do.

Mak continued to scrub and wash the stain over and over again until the woman finally knelt next to him.

"Stop," she whispered.

But Mak didn't stop. She looked at Mak's guilt-ridden face as he continued to scrub. She could see the weight he was carrying, could see the horrors he'd had to endure as well as the horrors he'd caused. Mak refused to look away from the bloodstain until the woman gently cupped both sides of his face and pulled him to look at her. Mak's deep oak-brown eyes stared back at the woman's hazel irises. They were so beautiful, like a galaxy to be explored.

"Stop," she whispered again.

Mak finally took in a breath. The woman still resting her hands on both sides of his face. Mak lowered his head and whispered, "I'm sorry." He started to tremble. "I'm so sorry for all that we've done to your people."

She paused for a moment and then pulled Mak into a hug, allowing his head to rest on her shoulder. Mak was surprised. He'd expected judgment but received none. She was remarkably warm and her touch was soothing.

She held him there until his body calmed completely and his breathing steadied. Mak pulled away, his attention drifting toward the bloodstains underneath him. The woman followed his gaze. Mak didn't want to, but he had to ask the unspoken question.

"Who were they?"

"My husband and son," she replied.

Mak wasn't surprised. A woman didn't live on her own unless she was widowed. Women in the Laythian society weren't permitted to have many economic opportunities, so finding a man and having sons was the way they survived.

"They were killed during the first battle of Laythia," she explained. "My husband and son were guards and sought to defend our home."

Mak remembered the battle. Remembered charging through the Laythian gates. Using the charge tactic to rampage through the city. Killing whoever they could. It was then that Mak felt the weight of his guilt reach its apex. It crushed him like a boulder atop his soul, removing from him any sense of joy and hope. He had no idea if he had killed this woman's family; it had been so chaotic that most of that day was a blur. God only knows who killed them.

Then Mak thought of the Saint and how he interacted with the Laythians and the Kotang after fighting them. It hurt when you got to know who you were fighting, learning they had families too. And it was all for . . . what? What had those battles accomplished? What was gained through it all other than death and loss? Mak was slowly losing himself in his whirl-wind of guilt.

The woman's hands slowly found their way to his face again and she said, "It's okay."

Mak closed his eyes and lowered his head. "No, it's not. I'm the leader of the Kotang. We attacked your city. All for self-profit and revenge." He raised his head. "I don't deserve your forgiveness."

"That's up to me to decide." The woman cupped her hands around Mak's chin, feeling how soft her hands were. Her mere touch disarmed him completely. Then Mak realized something. He looked at the woman with new eyes, "Are you . . ."

"Yes," the woman answered. "And I forgive you." Mak broke down, unable to stop the tears from flowing down his face.

"How? How could you forgive me?" he asked with weeping eyes.

The woman didn't show a single sign of anger or regret. She was as competent as the Saint. "Because Jesus forgave me when I didn't deserve it."

Mak stared at the woman, unblinking through the tears. His mind focused on that one name, *Jesus*.

He asked, "Do you think I could be forgiven? After all I've done?"

The woman said, "You've already been forgiven. You just need to accept it."

"How?"

The woman cupped her hands around Mak's hands and lowered her head. "Like this," she whispered. Mak closed his eyes and followed along with her, repeating after her, "Father, I know I am a sinner. Please forgive me for the people I've killed and for all the things I've stolen. I don't deserve your mercy. I believe Jesus is my Lord and Savior and I will follow you for the rest of my life. In Jesus' name, amen."

"Amen," Mak whispered. He opened his eyes and instantly felt a Presence enter his soul and wipe away all sense of shame and guilt. He immediately felt whole as he looked down at his hands, realizing the blood was gone. He looked up and was greeted with the sight of the woman smiling under her burqa with tears in her eyes. It was the happiest sight he'd seen in a while. One he would never forget.

He hugged her and the two held each other there for a while. Mak lifted his head from her shoulder as the two knelt together on their knees. "Thank you," he whispered. His gratitude knew no bounds. Then he looked at her again. "What's your name?" he asked.

"Mara."

Mak gestured to himself. "I'm Mak."

Mara bowed her head. Mak wanted to reach over and pull the mask from Mara's face but he held back, knowing it would be inappropriate. Yet he still wanted to.

Holding his hand up to her, he asked, "May I?" Mara paused, then after a moment of consideration, she allowed him to pull off her burqa. Mak removed the black cloth, revealing a beautiful woman with olive-colored skin and a sweet face. She was dressed in typical black wool and dark clothes. Her eyes had a mixture of green and hazel in them. Mak could stare into them for an eternity if she let him.

Without thinking, Mak raised his hand slowly and cupped Mara's cheek, feeling her warmth match his. Mak pulled her in slowly and kissed her on the lips as the two embraced each other amidst their pain, forgetting about all the horrors around and enjoying the benefits of life God had given them.

They slowly came apart and rested their foreheads against each other. "Thank you, Mara," he whispered. "For showing me the way."

"It was a sign from God," she said.

Mak was stunned for a moment, then replied happily, "Yes. It was a sign from God."

CHAPTER THIRTY-FOUR

FIRST STEPS FORWARD

"We can never move forward until we forgive. And we can never forgive, until we realize how much we ourselves need to be forgiven."

—THE SAINT

Laythia

18:47 hrs, 03/09/2258 (5 months A.F.)

Gobbie sat with his mug in his hand, chatting with his good friends Dante, Chris, and Evans. They were in the Laythian officers' lounge where Gobbie and his buddies could enjoy some ale while finishing the work for the week. The four of them all sat around a small fire pit in the middle, enjoying ale and trading stories. It had been a busy week and the heat had been blistering, but now the chill was setting in as autumn was approaching, causing cold winds in the night. The firepit cast warmth throughout the room. The evening sky filled the windows of the lounge.

After the incident with Lylack, things had calmed down a bit inside Laythia. Gobbie was more than relieved the people hadn't started a riot over the whole affair. Of course, there was still bad blood between the two groups and Gobbie was still wondering how to rectify that. He was staring at the fire, sipping a little more ale than he should have, when he heard footsteps coming from across the way. Gobbie turned and saw it was Mak, Noah, and the other leaders of the Kotang. For a moment there was tension between the groups. Not all the Laythians had come to trust the Kotang and the Kotang did not completely trust the Laythians, as both groups stared for a brief moment.

Gobbie saw they were dressed in nice leather jackets, wool shirts, and clean trousers. They carried no weapons and had depressed looks on their faces. Gobbie almost wanted to reach for his weapon, but he held back to see what Mak would do.

Mak looked down at the floor, not meeting Gobbie's gaze yet. He spoke, "We are sorry to disturb your evening, Captain."

Gobbie was curious; why wasn't the man looking up? Mak was still older than Gobbie but somehow Mak respected Gobbie's authority as an equal to his own. Gobbie responded, "It's fine. What can I do for yous?"

Mak lifted his head slowly and met Gobbie's gaze. Gobbie could see his brown eyes looking at him with remembered sadness and shame. His eyes dropped again and Gobbie waited. Mak lowered his voice but still kept it loud enough for all to hear. "We never officially apologized for what we did to you and your people."

Gobbie was taken aback, his focus centered on Mak as he gave him his full attention. Mak bowed his head, as did the other Kotang leaders. "As the leader of the Kotang, I take full responsibility for my actions against your city and its people. And we as members of the Kotang apologize for attacking your city and threatening its people."

For a moment, Gobbie didn't know what to do. That rage inside him was still there; it had been doused to a couple of embers but it was still alive, directed at the Kotang for attacking his city and killing Bo. But now he was watching those very killers apologize for what they'd done, and mean it! Gobbie felt ashamed for harboring anger in his heart. He knew it was wrong to keep this rage within yet didn't know how to ignore it. He thought he would always hate the Kotang, even if they had been getting along recently. But now it was different.

The other Kotang leaders kept their heads bowed until Gobbie stood up, pushed his chair aside, and approached Mak. "Yous can raise your heads now," he said. Mak lifted his head and looked Gobbie in the eye. Gobbie straightened up and extended his hand, hiding his reluctance. "As Captain of the Laythian Guard, I accept your apology."

Gobbie witnessed a flicker of hope in Mak's eyes. The expression of relief coming from Mak's face actually made Gobbie feel jealous, as he could see the man was finally making peace with his actions. Gobbie wanted that, but he didn't know how to get it. He didn't know *how* to forgive.

Mak took Gobbie's hand and shook it. Gobbie may have shaken the man's hand but that didn't mean he still didn't harbor anger inside him. He wanted to let go of his anger but couldn't. It was attached to him like a parasite.

Then Mak and his leaders tore their clothing, ripping the seams down the middle. Gobbie's eyes lit up in horror at the sight of the clothing ruined before them. Their nice wool undershirts were torn in two with a massive V going down the middle. Gobbie looked at them with so many questions. Mak answered him. "We Kotang tear our clothing to signate our apology."

Gobbie understood but he still felt it was weird. "Um, okay," he said awkwardly.

Mak and his men only bowed and whispered, "Thank you." Then turned and left, leaving only the sound of crackling wood from the fire.

Dante stood up and asked, "What was that?"

Gobbie stared as Mak and his comrades faded into the night. "That was the official apology of the Kotang for attacking our city."

Chris remained seated but asked, "Yous mean they feel sorry for what they did?"

Evans joined in. "And they're paying for it too, with rebuilding the city. This whole project was something to curb their guilt as well as clear their plate."

Gobbie just stood there in his typical brown leather clothing and stared at nothing. Some of the men were skeptical but Gobbie could tell that Mak's apology was genuine. He could see the shame in the man's eyes as well as the peace. Mak may have been the bad guy initially, but he was also the first one to find redemption. Gobbie wondered what it was that was causing Mak to change so dramatically. They had been enemies before and the Kotang were a ravenous band of thieves and bandits, but now they were . . . what? Different? Could people like them even change?

Gobbie didn't want to admit it but he could see the Kotang changing day by day. After watching them, he could tell they were just as broken as he was. Yet they were finding peace despite their mistakes. How? It made Gobbie both jealous and eager to have what they had.

Gobbie turned to his men, looking for any signs of advice. They all looked at him with equal puzzlement, shaking their heads or shrugging their shoulders. Gobbie looked back into the direction Mak and his men took and wondered, *How did they . . . find peace?*

Main Gate Catwalk, Laythia
22:08 hrs, 03/09/2258 (5 months A.F.)

Gobbie stood atop the new and improved walls of Laythia. He stared down into the Bog, where only the light of torches illuminated the details. The moon hung bright in the night sky, the stars flickering in the distance. Gobbie could almost see the red star they called Mars as he hung his arms over the railing, pondering.

The cold wind flickered against his leather clothing, making him wish he had a jacket. The glow of the city behind him sought his attention, but Gobbie didn't give in and kept his focus on the horizon with the Kotang in his peripherals. He didn't have anything to say. For once, he was too tired to be angry at something. Somehow, it came as a relief. To be so angry for so long, and to find a brief buffer from it all was nice.

Gobbie leaned against the wooden railing, staring at the stars and the black forest in the night. His mind was calm. He had no thoughts. It seemed healthy somehow just to stand here and ponder, letting his mind go blank after all that had happened.

Gobbie thought about how in the span of a few short months his whole life had been turned upside down. He'd started as a lowly guard at the Main Gate, and now he was the Captain of the Laythian Guard. He'd survived two devastating battles and the loss of a lot of friends. Gobbie leaned forward, not even attempting to cover himself as the cold wind blew against his face. It sharpened him, allowing him to focus on the present matter.

He finally looked down at the Kotang and could see Mak and his fellow compatriots and murderers laughing and sharing ale like they didn't have a care in the world. Gobbie's envy returned and it burned his heart like a candle to a cloth. His expression was saddened. This was getting old. And it's not like he was without fault either.

Gobbie's thoughts dragged to when he lost Bo, and the anger he felt toward the Saint because of it. He knew it was misplaced anger. That didn't matter. He just needed someone to blame. Technically, it was the Kotang's fault, and Gobbie had nearly gotten his revenge on them in the second battle. But Gobbie was responsible for some ills in the conflict as well. He'd deliberately stirred up the crowd out of his own lack of control of his emotions, and as a result, two hundred people died for nothing. They had been his friends and neighbors, people who wouldn't have attacked the Saint if it hadn't been for Gobbie and his misplaced anger.

Gobbie lowered his head, closing his eyes. "There's so much wrong here. Wrong that I've done and harm I've caused." He felt a sense of resonance with the Kotang now, understanding that he was wrong in some cases too. He desired forgiveness. But how could you forgive when subconsciously you didn't want to? How could you let go of someone murdering one of your close friends? One could simply say 'I forgive you,' but did they really mean it? A part of Gobbie did want to forgive the Kotang, but he knew down to his core that he hated them. He remembered that bitter memory of holding Bo in his bloody arms as he bled to death. It was like an iron ball of hatred in the center of his soul, spreading bitterness throughout his body, and he despised it. He didn't want to hold it but couldn't let it go.

Gobbie opened his eyes and looked down toward Mak, seeing the smile on his face. There was laughter and joy. All of it was real. He could tell when someone was faking it and when someone was not, and Mak was not faking it. *He managed to let go. He somehow found forgiveness.*

Gobbie's view shifted toward the rest of the Kotang spread throughout the Bog in front of him. All of them shared the same expression as Mak. They were murderers before, but now they were something else. Something had changed inside all of them that made them different. Gobbie shifted and looked back at Laythia for the first time. *Yet we live stuck in the past. We can't move on and accept. We can only hate. It's part of our nature.*

Gobbie turned his attention back to the Kotang. He envied them. He couldn't help but compare himself to them. *It feels like I've fallen behind, while they have gotten ahead. Those murderers and rapists are somehow godlier and more righteous than mi and mi people. And I don't know what to do about that.* Gobbie may be twenty-five but he still felt young and naïve. He had to come to terms with the fact that his arrogance and pride had prevented him from growing, from becoming a better person. Now murderers looked more righteous than he and his people. He hated that. And he hated them.

Gobbie stared at the Kotang, forcing himself to swallow the bitter pill. "They're better people than mi." The wind blew hard around him. "They've come to terms with their guilt and with what they've done, and are repenting because of it. While mi . . . I'm just sitting here's moping about it, feeling bitter that some people are doing better than I am."

Gobbie thought back to the outing to Goldberry Lake and how he hadn't joined in the swimming because of his bitterness toward the Kotang. Another instance of regret came into play.

Gobbie sighed. "I'm no different than they are. While they are rapists and murderers, I still tried to murder the Saint by spreading lies and fueling mi people to hate him. And because of that two hundred people died." Gobbie lowered his head, covering his face with his arms. "I guess I'm the same as them."

He humbled himself, and by doing so Gobbie felt the regret he hadn't realized he'd stored up. "I've got a lot of regrets that I ain't dealt with. So, maybe I need to take a play from their playbook."

Gobbie sighed. It was time for action. Sitting around feeling sorry for himself wouldn't do anything. "It's time . . . to make amends."

Kotang camp, Laythia

00:36 hrs, 04/09/2258 (5 months A.F.)

It was late in the evening when Gobbie and his men approached the Kotang camp in the Bog. He knew this was going to be uncomfortable but he had to do it anyway. Gobbie led the way as Dante, Evans, and Chris followed behind him with a cart full of supplies and tarps.

With reluctance, Gobbie entered the camp, already receiving looks from the Kotang around. He asked the nearest Kotang, "Where's Mak?"

"Who's asking?" Mak stood up from the crowd, facing them.

Gobbie turned and faced Mak. "Um . . ." He straightened up to appear more formal. "On behalf of the Laythian people, we wanted to apologize for our actions as well."

More Kotang members shifted their attention toward them until a small crowd surrounded Gobbie and his men. If they decided to get violent then they could tear them apart. Gobbie had no intentions of violence himself and kept his head cool. He looked at Mak, this time showing weakness in his expression.

"We're sorry that we tried to execute yous," he said, looking around at the growing crowd of Kotang workers. "All of yous." Gobbie returned his gaze to Mak, "On behalf of the Laythian people, we offer yous these supplies." All heads turned toward the wagon Gobbie and his men had brought, revealing large piles of tarps and tents. Gobbie said, "We spoke to the blacksmith and to some women who were willing to contribute and they pitched together to create better tents for yous since yous are living so close to the city. Besides, the cold winds are coming and we don't want yous getting sick."

Mak walked over, touched one of the tent materials, and saw that it was valuable goods they had just been given. Mak turned to Gobbie with wonder. Gobbie looked aside and gripped his undershirt. "And I know I'm going to look uncomfortable doing this, but . . ." Gobbie and his men tore their clothing, creating deep Vs down the center of their shirts.

Gobbie and his men stood there, uncomfortable, feeling the cold wind break through their now torn clothing. He would have to get this stitched up, and fast. Gobbie looked around, expecting the crowd of Kotang to look at him with surprise. But they slowly started laughing. Gobbie felt offended and wanted to know why.

The crowd died down as Gobbie's gaze fixed on Mak, who was laughing too. Mak calmed down as Gobbie asked, "What?" sternly.

Mak stopped laughing and wiped a tear from his eye. "Sorry, it's just . . ." Mak gestured to his men and back. "We didn't think you would do that back to us, so we made that part up."

Gobbie frowned in disbelief. "What?" He looked at all the chuckling Kotang. "Does that mean your apology was a lie?"

Mak shook his head and held his hands up in defense. "No, no, it was genuine. It's just . . . that last part we made up to make it look more . . . official."

Official? Gobbie glared at Mak with disbelieving eyes. He looked down at his torn shirt and back up to Mak, who started laughing again. "We didn't think you would do it too," he said.

The rest of the Kotang started laughing again as well. Gobbie couldn't help but be infected by their glee. It defused his anger and he rolled his eyes. The whole tearing of their clothing had been a joke that Gobbie had accidentally repeated.

"You gotta admit, Captain," Dante said. "They got us good."

Gobbie forgot all his anger and gave in to the laughter. He put his hand on his buddy's shoulder and laughed with the rest of the men hilariously into the night.

❰—•—❱

Marcus watched from atop the catwalk as the crowd of men reconciled before his very eyes. He allowed himself a half-smile at the sight before him. "That's all you, God. Not me." As he enjoyed the sight of humans loving and forgiving one another.

CHAPTER THIRTY-FIVE

THE AUTUMN FESTIVAL

*"I wonder how things will move forward from here. What does
the future look like for the Kotang and the Laythians?"*

—MAK, COMMANDER OF THE KOTANG

Mara's House, Laythia

12:44 hrs, 07/09/2258 (5 months A.F.)

Mak and his men had finished working on Mara's house. The new roof, over-
laid with strong wood, and the surrounding walls, embedded with fresh
brick and stone, gave the house a whole new look. With the brick, it was
less likely to burn if a fire caught, and they had even installed a chimney to
allow Mara to cook food properly in her home. Some Laythian stonemasons
had helped teach the Saint and the Kotang brickwork, while the Saint also
taught them carpentry to improve their skills.

Mak and his men finished up the remaining work, hammering the final
nail into the rooftop. Mak slammed it into the plank. He looked over the
rooftop and called out, "We're done up here."

Mara looked up from below as Mak and his men relished in their work.
They looked over the new home and felt a growing sense of pride. The
work had been hard but they were able to build Mara a new house, one that
looked better than before. They knew it wouldn't be the same and that the
memories would remain, but at least there were no bullet holes or burnt
doors remaining.

Mak and his men looked at each other and he said, "Only one thing left to do."

His men nodded and said in unison, "The bloodstains." They all got their rags together and went into Mara's new home. They knelt on the stone where the bloodstains were and worked tirelessly to try and remove them, this time making more progress than they had before. Mara watched as they worked for hours until the sun went down, watching the men who'd previously attacked her city now try to fix it. She brought them fresh snacks and water to help them as they worked, and all of them thanked her for her assistance. Mara gave a warm smile as the men worked, who were now witnessing the beautiful woman before them without her burqa.

Rudon whispered to Mak, "Mak, how long has she looked that beautiful?"

Mak didn't raise his head but smirked. "For a long time, sonny."

"Do you think I could—"

"Sorry, she's taken," Mak interrupted.

Rudon's head lowered in defeat. "Whoever that guy is, he is one lucky guy."

Mak and the others returned to the bloodstains. There were now only a few marks left. The five of them scrubbed tirelessly until the final remnants were gone. They all straightened up, gripping their forearms from how sore they were, groaning but grateful to be done.

Mak turned and saw Mara beaming at this wonder with surprise. She could not believe the bloodstains were finally gone. Mak knew it would do nothing to remove the memories of the family she lost but it would at least help her move on.

Mak said, "Mara." Mara looked at him after a long moment. "Would you like us to put new wooden floors into your house?" he asked.

Mara nodded timidly and happily.

Mak turned to his men. "One last thing, fellas." They all craned their heads back and groaned. Mak only chuckled. "Come on, you sour bunch. All of you."

They waved him off and got to work loading the house with new planks of wood the Saint had crafted for them. Hammering them into a new floor, they covered the old one with dark oak planks, completely concealing the spot where the old bloodstains had been. When they were finished, Mak, Mara, and his men stood at the door looking inwards toward the new home. They were all amazed at the woodworking and how well it turned out. Mak himself could not believe how good the flooring looked as well as the ceiling and brickwork. It was as if the home had gone through a complete transformation. What was once a burnt and broken building, was a new and refurbished household, ready for people to live in it. Mak stared in awe at a job well done. It had been hard and grueling, but he had never felt this alive before. He was filled with a sense of satisfaction in his heart from completing this task. Never before had he felt this fulfilled in doing something. In all his years of thieving and killing, Mak had never felt this . . . purposeful before. It was like he had found a new purpose in living and was doing it.

Surprisingly, the Saint was walking down the street with a massive log over his shoulder and Mak and the other Kotang called out to him. "Saint! Saint come here!"

The Saint put down the massive log and came over to inspect their work. They welcomed the Saint into the home and showed him around. At first, Mak was worried the Saint would critique them, given how blank his expression was. But the Saint lowered his guard and admired the craftsmanship.

He put his hands on his hips and nodded. "This is some nice work." The Saint turned to Mak and his men. "Excellent work, gentlemen. A job well done."

Mak and the others cringed with pride at hearing that. Their hearts beamed with hope as if receiving the satisfaction of a father telling his son how proud he was.

The Saint turned to Mara and bowed his head. "Thank you, for allowing them into your home."

Mara put a hand to her heart. "It was God's plan to have them here."

The Saint smiled. "Amen," he said. Then he walked out the doors and departed.

A small crowd had developed outside as the neighbors looked at Mara's new house. What were once angry glares were now filled with awe and curious admiration. The Laythian neighbors looked at the Kotang as a man in blue overalls pointed to Mara's house. "Wow. Yous did this?" he asked.

Mak and his men nodded happily. "That was us."

The neighbor nodded with his hands on his hips. "Fine work. I mean it." He turned to them. "Do yous think yous could improve mi house too?"

Mak and the others stared, dumbfounded. Slowly, they nodded, and Mak said, "Yeah."

"Great," the man said. "How much do I pay yous?"

Some of Mak's men began whispering, curious about the possibility of making money, but Mak cut them off and said, "Nothing. We'll do it for free."

The man's eyes lit up. "Really?"

Mak nodded, taking command of the group's decision. "That's what we're here for, to fix up Laythia after we destroyed it."

The man tilted his head, curious. Then he shrugged his shoulders. "Alright, feller. Yous get your men up on mi house tomorrow and get started."

"Yes sir," Mak said.

He turned back to his men. They complained quietly to him but Mak brushed it off. He looked up at the sun lowering in the sky and realized they still had an hour and a half of daylight. While the sun dipped and the sky darkened, the city slowly lit up as lanterns and candles filled every household.

Mak saw movement in the city streets as people gathered and headed toward the Townsquare. He turned to Mara and asked, "What's going on?"

Mara said, "It's our annual Autumn Festival. We celebrate it once a year with a feast. She looked at Mak and his men. "I'm going with some friends of mine . . . would you like to join us?"

Mak and his men were a little uneasy but excited at the same time. They were excited to go to a festival but they were uneasy because the last time a group of Kotang went into the Townsquare, they got beaten. It was risky to go in.

Mak said, "Well, we're not entirely sure if it's okay for us to go there. Not everyone has forgiven us for what we've done."

But Mara's soothing words won him over. "I don't think it'll be like that this time. People will want to have fun tonight."

Mak knew it was a bad idea, but if he dressed differently then maybe nobody would recognize him.

Yeah, right, he thought. *I'll stick out like a sore thumb.* But against his better judgment, Mak nodded and said, "Okay, we'll go, but at the first sign of trouble we'll leave. We don't want to ruin your festival."

Mara brightened. "Great! But first . . ." She pointed to Mak and his men's dirty clothes and sweating bodies. "You boys need a bath. You can't go to the festival like that."

‹‹—•—››

Mak tried to find the best clothes he had in preparation for the festival. He shaved some of his stubble, forming his goatee into a perfect upside-down U to compliment his bald head. He had washed as best and as quickly as he could; the night was waiting for no one. His sharp black overcoat outlined the white undershirt he wore and was accompanied by nice dark trousers. He looked like a mixture of a fancy pirate and a young nobleman.

Mak felt the cool air brush against his sweating neck. He quickly joined Rudon and his men as they dressed in new suits as well. His buddies tried to loosen their clothing while still staying formal as they regrouped at the Main Gate.

Mak broke off and said, "I'll meet you guys there. I need to pick up Mara."

Rudon and the gang glanced at each other with puzzled looks, whispering, "When did that happen?"

Mak was now walking through the Laythian streets in the early evening. The sun had fallen behind the forest and colored the sky indigo-blue over the horizon. The nighttime air was calm and partially humid, with a slight breeze blowing through the city, cooling Mak in his formal attire. For some reason, he felt safer now walking through the streets of Laythia. He had been working in Mara's neighborhood for so long that he had gotten used to being in the city. Candles and lanterns lit the streets, leaving a dim orange glow throughout the town. It was somewhat comforting. It felt like all the activity in the world had gone somewhere else.

As he approached Mara's new house, he admired the work they'd done on it again. He paused outside the door, realizing he didn't have any flowers. Mak panicked and looked around for something to bring Mara. To his amazement, there were some yellow daffodils right next to his feet. Mak grabbed a handful, leaving some to continue growing, straightened his clothing, and knocked on the door.

A few moments passed before Mara slowly opened the door. She wore a silk black dress embroidered with small lines that draped around her body. She stepped out wearing red lipstick and her long black hair shined in the moonlight. Mak was lost for words as he stared at the Laythian woman. He had never seen someone look so beautiful before.

Mara glanced aside in embarrassment and blushed. "Do I . . . look nice?" she asked.

"You look wonderful." The words came out before he could think them through.

Mara blushed with a kind smile. "Shall we?" she asked.

"Yes," Mak said, still captivated by her beauty.

Mara wrapped her arm through his, causing Mak to blush as they walked together through the streets toward the festival. They walked up the hill toward the main entrance of the Townsquare, finding Mak's Kotang buddies there waiting for him. All of his buddies stared in disbelief at Mak and Mara walking together like they'd been dating for years. Mak looked at Mara, then gestured to each of the four men standing before him. "I'm sorry, we haven't done proper introductions," he said. He pointed to his Kotang compatriots. "Mara, this is Rudon, Grant, Alf, and Ty."

Mara addressed them courteously. "It's a pleasure to meet all of you." They had met before since all of them had worked in Mara's home for a while but it somehow felt like they were meeting each other for the first time.

Rudon and the others looked at the festival, finding it was roaring with activity and laughter. The din was of a jovial mood as stringed instruments played in the background and a band filled the festival with laughter and joy. There were stores lined up, decorated in flowers and all kinds of colors and banners. A majority of the coloring was black, orange, maroon, and red, symbolizing autumn. Stands around were frying all kinds of food. Mak saw the different stores and shops, laid out with their amazing festivities, and felt a deep hunger in his stomach. He wanted to try it all. It had been a while since they had a party like this, aside from their recent trip to Goldberry Lake. All of them look inwards towards the festival, waiting at the front entrance.

Grant, one of the shorter Kotang, said, "Uh, guys?" They all exchanged looks with him and then looked back at the festival. "Is it just me or are there a lot of women here."

Rudon, the tallest Kotang, leaned over to whisper into Grant's ear. "That's because we killed most of the men," he said flatly.

"Oh . . ." Grant said. They all lowered their heads, realizing what they had truly done to this town. They hadn't just attacked it. They had robbed it of its population. Families needing fathers were now in high demand. Hundreds of women who were once wives were now widows.

Grant lowered his brow in caution. "Is it, alright for us to be here? After what we've done?"

Mara stood in front of them. "Hey," she said. They all looked at her. "I invited you here because I want you here." Mara returned her gaze to the festival. "Not *everyone* wants you dead."

Surprisingly, Mak retorted, "But not all of them will forgive us either.

But I don't think we can do much about that. People can hold grudges for the rest of their lives. But it's up to us to ask for forgiveness and move on."

"I think it'll be alright," Mara said.

Once again, her defusing words infected them all. Mak exhaled and took in a breath. "Alright. Let's try it then."

Mara held him back. "Before we go in, I'm waiting for my friends to arrive." Mak's men turned to her in puzzlement.

"Your friends?" Rudon said.

Mara nodded. "Yes." She looked down the hill and saw a group of people approaching. She pointed, saying, "Here they are now."

Four gorgeous women in different colored dresses approached the group. The Kotang men stood in disbelief at the Laythian women before them.

Mara broke from Mak and gestured to each of her friends. "This is Myra, Annie, Carna, and Elise."

They all waved courteously at the Kotang men. If Mak had an idea of what his men were thinking, he could imagine all of them falling backwards comically like a cartoon. The Kotang men greeted the Laythian women and each of them got acquainted with their date. They all took each other's arms and walked in together to the festival.

Mak could not believe what was happening. The Laythian women were treating his fellow Kotang members so kindly. He looked at each of his men's faces and saw they were having a blast chatting with these women. Mara was especially having fun, watching how cute the other couples looked. She led Mak and the others into the festival where they endeavored to buy food from the shops and play small games with their dates. Mak was relieved, feeling a sense of normalcy settle over him. He hadn't felt like life was normal since The Fall, and even before that life wasn't calm. The whole world had been wracked with war for decades to the point where people forgot what it was like to be normal. Mak had felt that way too, and perhaps that's how the Saint felt.

Mak thought, *Wait a minute? Where is the Saint?* He looked around but couldn't spot him anywhere. Mak frowned, wondering why the Saint wasn't here. He would ask about that later.

His attention was brought elsewhere when Mak recognized more Kotang were hanging out in the Townsquare with another group of women. Mak was skeptical of the sight and thought it was a joke, but then he saw another group of Kotang, and then another, until he realized practically everyone from the Kotang workforce was here at this event. The ratio of women to men was perfect as the Kotang had all found dates and the women were all ready to meet them. It was as if over time the city had come to accept the Kotang as their own.

Mak asked Mara, holding her with his left arm, "Why are there so many Kotang here?"

Mara didn't skip a beat. "Because they were all invited." She gestured widely toward the whole festival, at the nighttime lights, the fires, the shops, the music. She said, "Every one of the Kotang workgroups was assigned a certain district to work in and repair. These are the Kotang workers helping in those districts."

Mak paused in contemplation. *So, we haven't been the only group connecting with the Laythians. Every group in the Kotang workforce has been doing acts of kindness throughout the city, and now the city has come to accept us.* Mak was surprised by his own reasoning. He started to realize what the Saint had asked them to do.

He didn't just ask us to fix houses. He asked us to fix relationships. He could not deny the effects laid out before his very eyes. Dozens upon dozens of Kotang men were courting Laythian women. What Rudon had said was true. The recent battles had drained Laythia of its male workforce, which meant there was little the women could do to rebuild their homes. But now the Kotang, after receiving guidance from the Saint, were changed men. And Mak could see the effects right in front of him.

Mak was seeing the Kotang, a previous group of gangs and bandits, now treating women with kindness and love. They were caring and courteous towards them. He wasn't entirely sure how much of it was fake, but after the Saint had saved the Kotang from the Laythians, Mak could tell there was a definite change of heart in all of the Kotang members. It was eye-opening because Mak was starting to see not just the city but all the Kotang find healing and come together. Despite their struggles and their past hatred, the Kotang and Laythians were actually merging into a new people. One Mak never thought possible.

Mak looked at Mara and realized the same had happened to him. He'd fallen for Mara despite all the horrible things he'd done to their city, and she forgave him despite the darkness of his past actions. It was amazing to see two people coming together after hating each other so much. The sight of it made Mak want to cry, as he had never truly belonged anywhere in his life.

"Are you okay?" Mara asked, gripping his arm with concern.

Mak held his composure but allowed some weakness to ebb into his expression. He took a sharp breath and nodded. "I'm alright." He nudged Mara forward. "Come on, there's more of the festival to explore."

⟨⟨—•—•—⟩⟩

Gobbie, Joax, and Faal watched from the catwalk as the Kotang mingled through the Autumn Festival. Gobbie and Joax could not believe what they were seeing, while Faal just watched with a happy smile.

"Wow. I ain't never seen that before," Gobbie said.

"You stole the words right outta mi mouth," Joax said.

Gobbie chuckled but still watched the festival. He was unable to comprehend the Laythian people accepting the Kotang. But after all the homes the Kotang had fixed, it turned out the people rather enjoyed their company and the work they'd done. Most of the homes were finished and the city was already improving in quality because of it. The lack of father figures in the families seemed to have been replaced by the new Kotang in town, as all the young widows enjoyed mingling with their Kotang counterparts.

Joax said, "Well, it looks like things are getting better."

"Yeah," Gobbie said, puzzled. He could not wrap his head around how the Kotang were able to accomplish this. They might as well have brainwashed everyone. But Gobbie knew no one here was brainwashed. After the recent battles, people were free-minded for sure. It was just surprising how the Kotang had changed so much. They were originally the people attacking his city, trying to murder them all, and now they were welcomed into the Laythians' very homes. Gobbie himself had recognized the new kindness and honor the Kotang had developed. He knew the Saint was behind it. Those rogue bandits would have stabbed their own mother if it wasn't for him guiding and teaching them. Gobbie himself couldn't help but admire the man.

Gobbie looked around in curiosity. *Wait a minute. Where is the Saint?* Gobbie didn't see him anywhere and wondered why he wasn't at the festival. After a minute of searching Gobbie gave up and returned his gaze to the crowds.

Gobbie said, "Quite a sight, ain't it?"

"Indeed," Faal agreed.

"Darn right!" Joax said. "Never thought I'd see that."

"Mi too," Gobbie said. "Mi too."

〈〈—•—〉〉

Marcus watched the festival from a distance. Overlooking the city lights from the darkness of the Arghast Forest, he smiled. What warmed his cold heart was the sight of the two peoples coming together. Marcus saw that his work was not for nothing and that true change was actually happening. The city had been at war and filled with hatred, but now it was healing. Not just the Laythians, but the Kotang as well.

Marcus leaned one arm against a strong Kaisk tree, watching the festival happily. "Thank you, Father, for restoring this city and its people, as well as for changing the Kotang and the Laythians."

CHAPTER THIRTY-SIX

REDEMPTION

"Everyone needs redemption. For we have all messed up at some point."

—MAK, COMMANDER OF THE KOTANG

Laythia

13:19 hrs, 20/09/2258 (5 months A.F.)

Gobbie felt more curious today than he'd felt in a long time. He approached Mak, the man who recently had always piqued his curiosity. The man was sitting alone at a table in a tavern. Mak greeted him with a smile and stood up to shake his hand. Gobbie returned and took a seat.

"You asked me to meet you out here?" Mak asked.

Gobbie nodded. "I wanted to ask yous something. Something personal."

"Ask."

Gobbie felt fear well up in his chest. "I wanted to ask how yous were able to forgive me's. How did yous do it?"

Mak softened his demeanor. A manner of humility flowed over him. "After we attacked this city, when we were taken prisoner, the Saint treated us kindly. He told me that I was valued and loved by God. That I am a child of God. That made me curious. Because I had never heard those words before. I couldn't bear with the guilt from what I'd done. Then, when we were tasked with rebuilding the homes, Mara told me about Jesus and forgave me. I couldn't understand it, but she told me how to accept Christ, and I did. And from that moment on, everything changed. I felt the change in my heart and I felt mercy pour over me." He nodded. "That's when I knew it was real." He looked at Gobbie. "That's how."

Gobbie, rested his elbow on the table, his mind trying to grasp this concept. "So that's it?"

Mak nodded once, "Yup." Gobbie was silent a long moment. So Mak enquired, "Do you want this forgiveness?"

Gobbie felt his heart harden, but he was dead on the money. He nodded. Mak then reached out and put his hand on Gobbie's shoulder. "Then pray this with me."

"Jesus, I am a sinner. I have done wrong. Please forgive me for my sins. I believe you died on the cross for me. I promise to repent and change my ways and follow You. In Jesus' name, amen."

"Amen." Gobbie opened his eyes and immediately felt something fill his heart. The bitterness inside his soul melted away, replaced with overwhelming love. A single tear fell from Gobbie's eye.

Gobbie took it in and felt fulfilled. But more than that, he felt forgiven. The two of them stared at each other. Former enemies, now brothers.

It was over. The conflict between them was finally over.

CHAPTER THIRTY-SEVEN

WHAT THE FUTURE HOLDS

"I'm glad things are improving. Mi only question is, what happens next?"

—JOAX

Laythia

11:15 hrs, 27/09/2258 (5 months A.F.)

Mak and the Saint hoisted up the final plank to be placed atop the roof. The Saint held it in place while Mak hammered the final nails into it. He hammered the last nail into place and the sound of hammering suddenly stopped.

The whole city lay quiet as Mak and the Saint stared at the final plank and then looked at each other. They stood on the roof of the two-story building that overlooked the entire city. Every rooftop in Laythia was lined with fresh wood planks and every home was improved. The wind blew, soothing them as the weather turned south. Both Mak and the Saint put their hands to their mouths to warm them.

"Oh my goodness," Mak said. "It's finished."

The Saint looked at the city from the two-story building with a proud smile. Mak saw the look on the Saint's face and was surprised to see such a strong emotion.

The Saint turned to Mak and said, "Good job."

Mak felt a massive swelling in his chest in response to that compliment. Tears were rising to his eyes but Mak blinked them away. He faltered in his stance as he stood on the side of the roof. He suddenly started shaking and was lost for a moment.

The Saint grabbed him and prevented Mak from falling over. Mak looked up at the Saint and found comfort in the man's stature. The Saint's stoicism and calm manner brought Mak comfort and stability when he had none. It was like the man was a rock he could lean on.

The Saint put an assuring hand on Mak's shoulder, leaving him to stand on his own as he looked out among the city. "We did it," he told him.

Mak looked out at the marvelous city and could not comprehend the work they had done. They had completed hundreds of homes and practically rebuilt the entire city in the span of a couple of months. But what amazed Mak the most was the difference in the world they had made. Mak looked down at the Laythian people walking by, along with some of the Kotang members joining them as they waved each other on. Mak felt his heart warm at the sight of a peaceful city, one that he had helped rebuild.

At first, when this whole project started, he and the Kotang were prisoners, forced to reconcile and pay for their sins by fixing the city, but after gaining their freedom, they came back and paid fully for their past mistakes. Now things were better and the city looked healthier than it was before. Of course, there had been a lot of bloodshed and resulting wounds that Mak wasn't sure would entirely go away, but at least he could say that things were better now.

He looked at the Saint, wondering about the pain he'd had to go through to create this outcome. The Saint could have left the city after he defeated the Kotang or after he defeated the Laythians, but instead, he stayed and was determined to rebuild the city despite its hatred towards him. Mak marveled at the Saint's character and perseverance. A man loved by few, hated by many, yet loved on all. He was truly a one-in-a-billion type of person.

Mak returned his gaze to Laythia and stared out amongst the city. The blue sky was peppered with clusters of thick clouds, revealing a large gap of blue in between. The cold winds brushed against Mak's face, the icy chill drying his skin. The weather growing colder.

Then, for the first time, Mak asked the question, "What now?" The thought stymied him. He had no idea. He had never thought about it before. His mind automatically drew towards Tettenhall, the fortress miles away and his days spent there, and Mak couldn't help but feel sad thinking about it. It wasn't like he could stay here in Laythia, though. There might be too much bad blood between the Laythians and the Kotang for a long time. But then he thought of abandoning Mara, and that thought was more painful than a knife to the heart.

What if we can stay? Mak wasn't sure. It would have to be up to the Laythians.

The Saint said, "We should get going. Regroup with the rest of the workers at the Main Gate." Mak nodded and followed the Saint down the ladder.

They approached the Main Gate where the Kotang workers stood outside clustered together. Mak saw they were waiting around for something to happen, as curious as he was about what would happen now that the construction was done.

The Saint stood before the group, allowing Mak to join them, and said, "Well done, men." He nodded with pride, smiling. "You all did excellent work here. I am honored to have worked with you."

The Saint straightened his posture and saluted. In response, the Kotang straightened and saluted back. The Saint felt a surge of pride that he hadn't experienced in a while, the pride of leading men into success. It was a rare feeling, one not to be taken for granted. "You are all free to go," he said. "The work here is done. You may do as you like."

But the men, Mak included, just glanced at each other in confusion.

One Kotang with a red bandana said, "Sir, we're not really sure what to do now."

Mak saw the opening. He didn't want to say it, but he was the leader of the Kotang and he needed to take responsibility. "I guess . . ." All eyes shifted toward him. "I guess we go back to Tettenhall."

Heads lowered, Mak's included. The idea pained him. He didn't want to go back to Tettenhall. After all that work in Laythia, Mak couldn't help but feel attached to this city and its people. He thought of Mara again and what would happen. Would she come and live with them? The thought brightened him a little but he knew it was childish to ask her to abandon her home for a fort.

Just then a large group of Laythians approached from the Main Gate. The Saint turned and Mak saw the crowd of men, women, and children, all of them standing at the front gate. Gobbie, Joax, and Faal were nowhere to be found, and Mak found that curious. He read the expressions of all the people there and the majority of them had no malice in their eyes. Although he could spot a select few who still hated them, he understood that was their choice. The rest of them, the majority, looked at the Kotang members with concern and worry.

The same man who had asked Mak and his men to work on his house stepped forward and said, "So, what now?"

Mak stepped forward, straightened his posture like the Saint, and said, "Our work is done here. We will return to Tettenhall as before and leave you to your devices."

The Laythians lowered their heads in gloom. Mak was surprised by their reaction. He spotted Mara in the crowd and could see the tearful reflection in her beautiful eyes. It killed Mak inside to be saying this but he could not force anything on the Laythians. They had to leave.

The Laythian man said, "Well, I guess I'll be the one to admits it first but . . ." He raised his head and looked at Mak. "We really enjoyed your company." He nodded. "Yous did some fine work on these walls and our homes. You're welcome back anytime."

Mak was stunned. He scanned across the couple hundred Laythians standing before him and saw they all felt the same. Could they really have come to enjoy their company while they were here? Mak could feel the distance between himself and the Laythian people in front of him and wanted to close that space. To come closer and speak with them more.

Mak stepped forward and approached the man. "What's your name, sir?"

"Dustin. Dustin Hooper."

"Mr. Hooper." Mak held out his hand. Hooper took the hand and gave it a strong shake. "It really has been a pleasure working with your people." They exchanged smiles and ended the handshake.

Regrettably, Mak turned his back to the Laythians and returned to his men. He rejoined them and turned to see all the Laythians were bowing their heads in respect. Mak and his fellow Kotang saluted the Laythian people. *Here comes the hard part*, Mak thought. Standing on the gravel road leading away from the city of Laythia, Mak pivoted on his foot to turn his back to the Laythian people.

"Wait!"

Mak turned and saw it was Mara. She came pushing through the crowd and ran out towards him. "Mak!" she shouted.

Mak went out to meet her. They stood in the middle ground between the two groups with all eyes on them. Mara spoke loud enough for all to hear. "I don't . . . I don't want you to leave." Silence stilled the air. "I want you to stay. I enjoy your company and your friends."

Mak's heart flipped inside his chest. He didn't know what to say.

Mara turned to her people and called out to them, "I know in the past these men have done horrible things to us. I know that some of us will never forget." She gestured a hand out to the Kotang, putting her other hand over her heart. "But look at what they accomplished in trying to repay for what they've done!" Mara lifted her hand toward the city of Laythia. "Look how beautiful our city has become with their presence. I don't know about you, but I have come to enjoy them and find they are decent men."

Mak tilted his head and said, "Decent?" pretending to take offense.

Mara turned and faced him, smiling. "Admirable. Is that better?"

Mak returned the smile. "Better."

Mara turned back to her people. "If any of you feel the same then come forward! Show us that you don't want them to leave."

There was a pause for a moment, and then slowly, starting with the women, one by one, more and more people began filing to the front. They stood just before Mara, closing the gap between the two groups until every person was standing with her.

A young man called from the Laythian crowd, "We like yous. Yous did a good job on our homes and such. We'd like to show yous the same, if that's alright?"

Mara looked at Mak, and Mak saw it was his turn to speak. He turned to face his Kotang brothers. "Men." He lifted his hands. "If you feel the same then come forward now."

The same result occurred with the Kotang as every member slowly stepped forward until they were face to face with the Laythians. Mak and Mara stood in the center and looked at each other over their shoulders with mild surprise.

Then a young Kotang boy stepped out, approaching a blonde girl wearing a blue dress, and pulled out a piece of paper. The boy said, "I wanted to give you a drawing I made. I made it 'cause I was thinking of you."

The girl took the paper and cupped her hand to her mouth. The paper revealed a highly detailed penciled drawing of her. The girl clutched the drawing as she looked at him with blue eyes. "I love it!"

The boy slowly took the girl's hand. Pretty soon other Kotang members and Laythians were stepping forward, initiating conversations with each other.

Mak and Mara were soon enveloped by the crowd but kept their focus on one another. Mak stood before Mara, his handsome figure looking down at her, and Mara looked up at Mak with her beautiful womanly features. The two felt a strong connection as they kissed each other, not caring who was watching. But they weren't the only ones. Other Kotang and Laythians started mingling as well, as a result of the Autumn Festival. Oh, how the drama begins.

The Saint stood leaning against the Main Gate watching it all unfold. His cold heart gladdened at the sight of the two peoples coming together. He was glad that all the conflict had been for something. Something good had come out of this horrible mess. Now the Kotang and Laythian people were one.

Gobbie, Joax, and Faal stepped out from behind the Main Gate and greeted the Saint. Gobbie was the first to speak. "Even after all this, I'm still surprised by what's happened."

"Join the club," Joax said.

Faal stayed quiet but smiled alongside the Saint. The four men looked at the two merging peoples, glad that things had worked out. The Saint watched the scene unfold, happy that things were getting better for the world.

Joax frowned. "But one question." They all looked at him. "Where are the Kotang going to live now?"

All their eyes shifted toward the city, then down to the Bog where the Kotang's supplies and tents were set up. The realization struck Joax with horror, and then he sighed. "Oh, you gotta be kidding me." He looked at the Saint. "We're going to build new homes *here* in the Bog?" The Saint smirked at him, knowing there was more. Joax looked out then back at the walls, and the idea clicked. "No . . ." He looked at the Saint. "We're going to have to rebuild the walls *again*!"

❮—❯

After the Laythians and Kotang communities merged, the Kotang presented themselves to build new homes where their current tents and supplies were stationed in the Bog. Regrettably or laughably, the Kotang, the Laythians, and the Saint had to build *another* wall now surrounding the Bog, creating a new district within the city of Laythia.

A majority of the Kotang members married the Laythian widows and fathered new families. But, they were not the same men they once were. The Kotang had shown a surprising change in character from their time in Laythia. Most of the men had become kind and honorable towards the people of Laythia. There was still some hate between both groups but that would never go away entirely.

The king had vanished after the second battle and Faal, Gobbie, Mak, and Joax became the elected leaders of the new Republic of Laythia. The Kotang and the Laythians merged into one army, improving the size of the military, and began using Fort Tettenhall as a base of operations.

Three months passed before the new wall was completed and winter came.

CHAPTER THIRTY-EIGHT

PREPARATION

"The winter settled as did the people of Laythia with their new Kotang neighbors. I sense this is a good sign. A sign that the hostilities are over and we can begin anew."

—FAAL

Laythia

12:37 hrs, 18/12/2258 (8 months A.F.)

Faal sat down at his desk scribbling desperately on the paperwork. His hands were shivering from the cold even inside the Barracks HQ. All the guards wore thick coats now, created from wild boar skin and whatever animals they could find in the Arghast Forest.

He'd had enough of writing reports and got to his feet. He had to stretch his legs but regretted his decision when he stepped outside. The cold wind struck his olive-brown skin and sucked away any warmth he'd had. Faal went to the top of the catwalk along the Main Gate and overlooked the new district in front of him.

It had been a couple of months since they had blended the two communities, and Faal was still getting used to how things had changed. He looked down at the freshly built homes for the new Kotang families. There were some children scurrying about, but they weren't the next generation of Kotang yet. They were the children the new Kotang fathers had adopted when they married into their homes. Faal looked up and saw the sky was opaque white, the clouds not allowing a single ray of sunshine. *Winter is here,* Faal thought.

For some odd reason, Faal thought of his family. He brought his attention back to the Kotang homes and felt nothing. He felt neither sad nor happy as he watched the families. Some of the Kotang had created their new homes in the Bog while others moved into the city with their Laythian wives. It was definitely a blending of two peoples. Faal exhaled and watched his sharp breath leave his lungs in white clouds.

He heard footsteps as the Saint said, "I heard you'd be out here."

Faal glanced at him and saw the man was not wearing much different from his usual attire. The Saint still wore his black jacket, along with his black military pants and boots. The Saint didn't wear most of his usual weaponry but Faal could see he always kept at least some throwing knives, his kukri, and his .44 on him at all times. The man never truly relaxed.

"I needed to stretch my legs, my friend." Faal returned to his study of the Kotang families.

An awkward silence fell between them.

"When do you leave?"

"Once winter is over."

Fall nodded. "I see," he said, then faced him as they clasped forearms. "Good luck, my friend."

The Saint nodded. "And you too. God bless you, brother."

"God bless you too, my brother."

He watched as the Saint disappeared from the catwalk. Faal would miss him. But he had a feeling he would return, just in different circumstances.

CHAPTER THIRTY-NINE

A New Beginning

*"A man without purpose is nothing, but a man following
the purposes of God has everything."*

—THE SAINT

Arghast Forest

07:30 hrs, 21/03/2259 (11 months A.F.)

Marcus stood at the tree line of the Arghast Forest, looking back at the city of Laythia. Six months had passed since the two peoples had merged and the city boundaries were extended. With spring here, the homes were filled again and the city was prospering.

In the time between, Marcus had contemplated the actions he'd taken and the results that followed. He looked up at the sky and said, "Father, I often think about what would have happened if I had never come here." He lowered his gaze back to the city, his dark eyes watching the people scurry about like ants.

"I often wonder if my actions were just. Whether it would have been better for me to never show up at all." He was met with silence. The wind brushed against him as he leaned against an oak tree. "But the more I think about it, the more I realize the better outcome that has occurred, not because of my actions, but because of your intervention."

Marcus looked up at the clouds and said, "Only you could have brought these two peoples together. You worked through Mak and Mara to unite them. You worked through Gobbie as a leader of the Laythian army. You worked through Faal and his wisdom, making him the new church leader of Laythia. Through all the bloodshed, you were able to unite two people and get them to love each other and find Christ. And now, hundreds of people will be in your Kingdom forever. Only you could do that, God, not me."

Marcus finally realized that his actions were the result of something greater, that although terrible things had occurred, God could use them to bring good out of bad. Marcus finally saw a new purpose forming for him. A new life, a new adventure. It would be different than his previous life but just as fulfilling. Marcus saw that he would travel the world and repair cities, building churches in the process and fight any evil that lurked there. He was both a builder and a destroyer. A lover and a fighter. A warrior and a Saint. He saw that his actions were worthwhile and that there had been meaning in what he did. That he had a purpose outside the military. He wasn't meant for just one job; he was more than that.

While Marcus was overjoyed to see the city improving, he also felt sadness in his heart. It was time to move on, to wherever God called him next. His time here had been brief, but he'd been here long enough. Marcus lifted his eyes to the east, where the road followed past the Hillsong Mountains overlooking Laythia and into the hills and valleys beyond. The work was not yet finished. He had more stories to write and lives to save. By taking the Gospel and living it out, he would share the Good News wherever he traveled. No matter where it led him, no matter what battles he would fight, he would not be defeated. He would accomplish his goal and fulfill his duty to the very end.

Marcus took his hand off the tree, his weapons and gear all packed up. His ammo was slightly restored, and he felt equal amounts of joy and sadness at leaving. Marcus turned and put his hands together in prayer, looking toward Laythia. He gave a blessing to the city and hoped to return one day. Then Marcus looked toward the rising sun over the mountain and took his first step into his next adventure. If only he knew what was coming . . .

FINAL REMARKS

I hope you enjoyed my story. I know it can be a bit controversial putting a religious man in certain scenarios where he has to make tough moral decisions but that was the point. I wanted this character to make you question things and see whether his actions were morally just or not. While the character isn't perfect, there are some things that we can still learn from him.

Regardless, I hope you enjoyed my story and I look forward to showing you more stories in the future.

Acknowledgments

Thank you Dad for all your encouragement and giving me the opportunity to pursue my dream of writing books of hope and faith to the world. I'm so glad you get to be part of this wonderful journey and for all the wisdom you have imparted onto me. For God blesses those who endure and are faithful to the very end.

Thank you Mom for your equal support and your love in all my work. I couldn't have gotten this far without you and Dad in my life.

To my awesome brothers. I hope you enjoyed this awesome story of action and thriller! It was truly fun to make and I can't wait to get more of this stuff out to you guys.

About the Author

Jake Lynch is an author specializing in contemporary religious fiction and action-adventure novels. Having grown up under the teachings of Rick Warren, he has a strong devotion to God and actively seeks to love on others.

While writing stories is entertaining, his main mission is to help spread the Gospel of Jesus Christ and to bring hope and healing into the world.

But when he is not writing, some of his favorite hobbies to do are watching anime and going surfing. Some of his favorite anime are Naruto, Rise of the Shield Hero, and 86. As a local of Southern California the call of the ocean is never far as his love for surfing constantly brings him back to the water.

 www.AuthorJakeLynch.com

 @authorjakelynch

 AuthorJakeLynch

 @authorjakelynch

BOOK REVIEW

Please leave me a review on Amazon or Barnes & Nobles
to let me know what you thought of the book!